P9-DNR-108

PUBLISHED BY:

Kenni York via Kindle

Copyright © 2012 by Kenni York

All rights reserved. No part of this book may be reproduced, stored in a retrieval system, or transmitted in any form or by any means without the prior written permission of the publisher.

The characters in this book are fictitious, and any resemblance to real persons, living or dead, is coincidental.

Miranda

"This marriage is a sham," Alex whispered loudly. The woman in front of her turned around slightly and quickly took note of who had just made the rude comment. Ever the polite, nice-nasty princess, Alex simply smiled and reiterated her belief.

"This is a joke."

Jada nudged Alex's left arm in an attempt to shut her up just as Stephanie sucked her teeth and nudged her right arm in agreement.

"You're right," she said. "That negro don't make enough money for her. Soon as she finds somebody else with fatter pockets and a bigger dick she'll be ghost."

Alex and Stephanie chuckled at their not so private joke and Jada tried hard not to laugh.

"You two are incorrigible," Jada stated, shaking her head and staring straight ahead.

Miranda was silent, staring at the altar as one of her best friends was staring into the eyes of a chocolate teddy bear and pledging her life to him forever. Miranda Wilson-Cox was jealous. She envied Candace for having such an elaborate, beautiful wedding. The Rose Garden venue was the perfect choice for the spring-time, outdoor wedding. Candace's wedding colors of white and silver were a beautiful contrast to the white and pink roses that adorned the area. She was gorgeous in her A-lined gown with the plunging neckline and back. A very sexy selection that Miranda was sure Candace's parents were not too fond of.

Together Alex, Stephanie, Jada, and Miranda watched amongst Candace and Quincy's friends and family as the couple commenced their oneness with the ceremonial kiss. After the couple strolled down the aisle as husband and wife, the crowd dispersed, and headed toward the banquet hall nearby for the reception. The girls sauntered over to a nearby gazebo, the designated meeting place for after Candace was done with taking pictures. As they chatted about the beauty of the gardens and the simplicity and elegance of the wedding, Miranda's phone began to chime the familiar Nokia ring. She rejected the call and checked the time.

"Who keeps blowing you up girl?" Alex asked.

Miranda stuffed her cellphone into her purse, trying to appear nonchalant.

"Norris," she answered. "Trying to check up on me."

"You not gon' call him back?"

Miranda pursed her lips and shook her head no.

"Well shit, tell him to stop calling," Jada said, gazing over towards the ceremony area where Candace and Quincy were posing for their wedding photos. "If he wanted to talk to you so bad, he shoulda came with you."

"Girl, you know men don't like going to weddings," Stephanie interjected.

"He'll be alright," Miranda replied, silently planning to make a break for home as soon as Candace was done with her pictures. Norris had called her four times since she'd left home for the wedding. He'd been adamant about not wanting to accompany her. However, he'd been just as adamant about her returning home in time for him to meet up with his boys to play poker. Not wanting to risk pissing him off, Miranda thought it best to just wrap up her visit with the girls and head home immediately.

As if sensing her thoughts, the girls watched as the photographers moved their equipment to the banquet hall and Candace kissed Quincy on his lips before quickly sashaying her short, brown frame towards her awaiting friends. She approached the gazebo and instantly the girlfriends found themselves huddled together in a heart-felt embrace. Candace ravished in the spotlight, loving the attention.

"I did it ya'll," she boasted, kicking off her stiletto, diamond studded heels. "I finally did it."

"Finally?" Alex questioned. "Are you kidding me? You've known this man for all of two months and you've married him.

You quickly did it is what you should be saying."

"Shut up," Candace giggled. "Don't hate."

She flashed them with her modest 1.3 carat wedding band, smiling proudly. Miranda forced a smile, fighting back the green monster in her that was reminding her that she no longer possessed a wedding band.

"So when are we getting drunk?" Stephanie asked, glad to be free from her child and mother.

"The real party goes down after my parents and our older family members leave," Candace assured them. "They won't be around long."

The Nokia tune sounded again. All eyes went to Miranda as she fumbled to silence the small phone.

"Sorry," she offered.

"I know you do not have your cell on at my wedding, girlie," Candace pouted. "Today is all about me. Tell that negro you'll see him later."

The girls laughed and Miranda shyly shook her head as she began to say her goodbyes.

"Do you have to leave now?" Jada asked suspiciously.

"Yeah, Norris needs the car," she explained.

As the others began to protest, Candace stood firm, supporting Miranda.

"It's alright," she said. "Hubby comes first."

Alex rolled her eyes, already not feeling Candace's fake happily married attitude.

"I'm just glad all my girls could be here with me. Ya'll do understand why I didn't have you as bridesmaids, right?"

Alex, Stephanie, Miranda, and Jada all nodded and waved off Candace's apology.

"We just wanted to keep it simple," she stated.

"It's alright girl," Jada replied. "We understand."

"I love ya'll!"

The group embraced again, giggling at each other and feeling blissful in each other's company. Regretfully, the others wished Miranda a safe ride home and parted ways with the short, light skinned woman. Moving swiftly, Miranda trotted to her Nissan Maxima and began the journey home to her awaiting husband.

** **

She dreaded going home to him, never knowing what type of mood he would be in when she arrived. They had been married for a year now, yet Miranda felt like she didn't really know Norris at all. Perhaps they didn't know each other well enough when they first wedded. Miranda had been so swept up in the courting process, that she had been blind to Norris' shortcomings.

Fresh out of high school, Miranda had decided to visit

her brother Malachi who was stationed in Virginia. While on her summer vacation there, she'd met Norris on the Navy base. He'd approached her all mannish, telling her how fine she was and filling her head up. Having lived a somewhat sheltered life in Atlanta with her parents, Miranda wasn't used to such advances. She rarely dated in high school and had never been in a serious relationship. She had never even come close to any type of physical encounters. She'd been surprised at herself when she had allowed Norris to kiss her on the very first day that they met, let alone take her virginity that very same night. At the time she thought it was romantic. He had taken her on a tour of the city and then back to his place where they drank Belvedere mixed with cranberry juice. He proceeded to seduce her with his probing fingers and talented tongue. Never mind that she didn't even know his last name on that first night, she was sexually free and decidedly in love.

Nose wide open and heart filled with a school-girl notion of love, Miranda moved to Virginia soon after attaching herself to Norris. She would cook and clean his off-base apartment during the day and allow him to ravish her body ruthlessly at night. It felt liberating to be away from her parents and doing whatever pleased her, or mostly whatever pleased Norris. It didn't take long for her to convince Norris that they should get married. He never proposed to her directly. He simply shrugged and agreed when she approached him with the idea.

Their big day was the polar opposite of Candace's ceremony. There were no fragrant roses, no lavish gown, no smiling friends and family to wish them well, and no lively reception to celebrate their union. The couple elected to exchange vows at their county court house, in the small, impersonal space of a judge's chamber. It was a hasty decision for they had not even purchased rings. Miranda was simply excited about the addition of the title Mrs. to her name. The honeymoon period was short lived and just several weeks following their commitment, Miranda began to see Norris in a different light.

He was a difficult man, manic at best. When he was happy, times were good. He'd joke around, make her laugh, and make love to her. When he was down, he made sure Miranda was down as well. He belittled her around company, ignored her when she tried to communicate, and was unpleasantly rough when he decided to have sex with her. There were even times when he would leave and not return home for days. Miranda never complained about this to her friends back home or her parents because she never wanted to hear them say that she should have never married so young anyway.

It was Norris' antics that had caused the couple to have to relocate to Atlanta. Shortly before he was due to ship out on tour, Norris found himself in a dangerous bar fight. Drunk, high, and belligerent, he'd pulled a knife on a senior officer, a move which ultimately led to his being discharged from the U.S. Navy. Disheartened and desperate, Miranda had pleaded with her parents to allow her and her husband to stay with them until the couple was able to get back on their feet. In Virginia, Miranda hadn't worked. In Atlanta, she knew that it would take two incomes for them to repair their lives and become self-sufficient. But, instead of them both obtaining employment, Miranda ended up working two jobs while Norris sat home drinking, smoking, and hanging out with his buddies, not exactly the life she had imagined for herself.

Whenever Miranda complained about his lack of ambition and their dire need for money, Norris would scold her. He accused her of doubting him as a man and being an unsupportive wife. When he was really mad he would throw things around or hit the furniture or walls with his fist. Not wanting to feel the impact of his ferociousness, Miranda would never continue on with the argument, electing instead to walk away and leave him to deal with is own raging emotions.

No one really liked Norris. Not her parents, not her friends. But, despite their blatant disapproval of the man, he was still her husband. Miranda always tried to focus on the good in their relationship. She'd felt a small ray of hope when Norris had finally gotten employment at a body shop. Not only had they been able to move into their own apartment, but they'd also been able to purchase the Maxima. For that, Miranda was grateful. Riding Marta for two hours just to get somewhere that was really fifteen minutes away was not fun. Sure they shared the car, which was purchased in her name, but it was better than relying on the public transit.

However, with more money in his possession, Norris developed a new bad habit, gambling   He was an avid poker player and would bet on a sports game in a minute. He lost more than he won, but that was not enough to discourage him. Rather than complain, Miranda tried to overlook this additional shortcoming. She kept a private bank account, in which her paychecks were direct deposited into in order to assure that Norris didn't smoke or gamble away their rent money.

Pulling into her usual spot in front of their Shoals Crossing apartment building, Miranda sighed. She wished she was back in the beautiful atmosphere of the rose garden with her girls instead of the stifled environment of her unhappy home. Not looking forward to seeing Norris, who was sure to be in a foul mood, Miranda drug herself up the stairs to her second-floor apartment. Entering the door she could smell the aroma of marijuana lingering in the air. She'd asked him a million times not smoke in the house, as if he ever listened.

"Bout time," she heard his voice boom from the back of the apartment. Placing her keys on the coffee table, Miranda plopped down on the ash gray couch and watched as Norris emerged from the bedroom.

She took in his appearance. Jeans, sagging like he was a high school kid, black tee with matching plain black baseball cap, and the requisite black air force ones. He was short for a man, 5'7, and thin. His dark skin was a perfect contrast to her lighter skin. It was his beautiful white teeth that made the man's face light up. But tonight he wasn't smiling.

"What took yo' ass so long?" he snapped, grabbing up the car keys. "Told you I had somewhere to go."

"That's why I'm back, Norris," she responded, leaning back and shutting her eyes, willing him to just leave.

"Yo' girl all good and married?" he asked.

Miranda nodded.

She heard him walk into the kitchen. The sound of the cabinet door opening and closing resounded throughout the otherwise quiet house. Norris poured himself a drink of something and then threw his cup carelessly into the sink.

"Still don't know who the hell would marry her gold digging ass. She looks like an ant."

Miranda peeped with one eye open, catching only his back as he moved to exit the apartment. She was astonished by his gall. If only he knew the names the girls used to describe him. Miranda smirked to herself and glanced over at the clock on the VCR. Seven P.M. In fifteen more hours she would have to rise to get ready for her part time job at Rainbow. She only worked every other weekend and had been reluctant to give up this Saturday for the wedding. Realizing that he hadn't told her when he'd be back, Miranda hopped from the sofa and ran to the door. As she swung it open the house phone began to ring.

Leaning over the railing, she called down to her husband in the parking lot.

"Norris! Norris when will you be back?"

She watched as he slammed the car door shut and revved the engine.

"Norris!"

Unfazed, Norris backed out of the parking spot and tore through the maze of the complex to hit the street. Miranda sucked her teeth and scurried back into her home. The phone was still ringing. Absentmindedly, she answered without checking the caller id.

"Hello?"

Instantly the line went dead. Stunned, Miranda plopped down onto the couch again and pressed the end button on the cordless. As an afterthought, she clicked the caller id button to see who the rude caller was. The number was foreign to her. The name read Tamara Williams. *What the fuck?* An uneasy feeling crept into her heart. Something just didn't feel right.

Stephanie

"How was the wedding?"

Stephanie entered her mother's home and was greeted by Ms. Johnson who was peddling breathlessly on the exercise bike she kept in the living room. Stephanie kicked her shoes off and walked past her mom into the kitchen.

"It was nice," she offered in response.

Stephanie didn't want to hear her mom rant and rave about how accomplished Candace or any of her girlfriends were. Ms. Johnson had been so elated to hear that Candace was marrying someone and not just sleeping with him or shacking up. Whenever possible, she constantly reminded Stephanie of how disappointed she was in her for being an unwed mother. She'd never heard the end of it when she had to confess to her mother that she was pregnant during her very first and only semester at Morris Brown.

Even though the incident was nearly four years in the past, Stephanie remembered it as if it were just yesterday. Ms. Johnson had informed her that she had ruined her life and asked her if it was her desire to be a welfare mother. Stephanie had been forced to quit college in November of 2001, after she'd found out that she was expecting. Her mother had made it perfectly clear that the baby would be Stephanie's responsibility and that she was not about to support her and her unborn child. With no other alternative, Stephanie was forced to get a job. Luckily, she had an aunt that managed to pull some strings and got her hired as a librarian assistant at a Dekalb County library. The pay was decent and the hours were good. To her surprise and much to her benefit, Stephanie's mother never kicked her out of the house. But, she was adamant that the young woman would pull her own weight.

Ms. Johnson got over the fact that her only child had gotten pregnant at a young age and at the start of her collegiate career. In fact, when Damien was born she was right beside Stephanie, ever the proud grandmother. What really infuriated Ms. Johnson was Stephanie's relationship with Damien's father. Corey Polk was every mother's nightmare. He was five years older than Stephanie and was a thug, in Ms. Johnson's opinion. Corey lived in their neighborhood and was known as one of the neighborhood hustlers. Four years ago he would have been found on any corner near or around Line Street in Decatur. Like all the other misguided brothers of his generation, he made his money in the streets.

It was Corey's persistence that drew Stephanie to him. She'd seen him around the way for years and he had frequently made advances toward her. No matter how many times she'd said no, he never backed down. It was an ego-booster having him give her so much attention. In high school, none of the guys really paid much attention to her. Stephanie was not a conventionally pretty girl, definitely no cheerleader or dance team hottie. She was generally meek and quiet. That is, of course, until she got around her girls where she felt confident. Sure, she'd dated some guys and even had sex with a few before Corey. But, it was something about this man that made her throw all caution aside. She loved him for reasons even she couldn't understand. She knew he was the neighborhood weed man. But she also knew that no one else ever made her feel beautiful and wanted the way he did.

Stephanie couldn't understand how someone she loved so much could hurt her so badly. When she had told Corey she was pregnant his initial reaction was typical.

"That can't be my kid," he told her. "How I know you ain't been fucking around?"

She'd gone to his mother's house where he was living at the time. She thought telling him face to face would be more personable than telling him over the phone. They were alone in his room, she was greasing his scalp with him sitting between her legs. At the mention of being pregnant he quickly jumped up from the floor and glared down at her small frame. The argument resulted in them calling each other all types of four letter words and ultimately he'd told her to leave. They didn't speak for several weeks. Ms. Johnson never missed an opportunity to say I told you so. Not being able to deal with the silence or Corey's absence in her life, Stephanie ventured over to his mother's house one day after work. It was then that she'd learned that he was no longer living there. Feeling hopeless with regards to reconciliation, Stephanie simply left a message with his mom for him to call her.

Two more weeks passed and he finally called from an unknown number. He spoke to her as if nothing had happened, as if they'd just spoken the day before. When she told him that she had to quit school and didn't know if she'd be able to return, he seemed disinterested. He was too excited about his own news of having his own place over in Midtown. It was a one bedroom, luxury apartment in a Gables community.

Stephanie didn't question how he was able to afford such lavish accommodations. She was simply hurt that he had not asked her to move in with him.

Their relationship sparked back up. He succumbed and given her his new cell number. Every so often, he stopped by her house to hang out. Ms. Johnson was never pleased by his visits, so Stephanie began to visit Corey at his place after work most evenings during the week. On the weekends she would spend the night.

"That boy is never going to marry you," her mother warned her one Sunday night as she strolled in late from her weekend visit. By this time her belly was swollen and she was beginning to tire from the weight of the pregnancy. She'd ignored her mother's comment, feeling that things between she and Corey were going great. Secretly, she prayed that he would hurry up and move her in so that she could escape her mother's disapproving glares and hurtful comments. Stephanie reasoned with herself that he just didn't want their family to be cramped into the one bedroom unit and was waiting until he could afford a bigger place. But, just when she was feeling good about their relationship, Corey withdrew again. He would go days, sometimes weeks, without calling. He cut their visits down to the point where she rarely got to see him, let alone have sex. He advised her to never just show up to his place without his permission and she respected that.

Stephanie realized that any other chick would have just left him alone, but she just couldn't bring herself to give up on him. Not when he missed the birth of their son, not when he failed to put in an appearance at the hospital when she'd experienced complications following Damien's birth, and not even when he neglected to pitch in with caring for the infant.

Corey came around when he was ready, never mind what Stephanie or Damien needed. He often told her that he loved her and she wanted more than anything to believe him. Their relationship continued on in this same manner. She never really knew when she would see or hear from him, but was always pathetically eager to receive him when she did.

Today it had been two days since his last call. He'd told her that he wanted to go to the movies tonight and that he would call her back to confirm. Stephanie poured herself a glass of juice and wondered if she should change into something cute or into her pajamas. Walking back into the living room she saw her mother abandon the exercise bike, mopping her face.

"Was it pretty?" she asked panting.

Stephanie didn't want to talk about the wedding. She shrugged her mother off and headed towards her room.

"It was alright."

"Mmm-hmm," Ms. Johnson responded. "And don't be going back there messing with that child. He's already had his bath and is sleeping like a log."

Stephanie tiptoed into her bedroom and quickly shut her door behind her in an attempt to ward off further conversation with her mother. Damien lay sprawled across her queen sized bed, arms and legs everywhere. In his SpongeBob pajamas, he was precious. Stephanie eased onto the bed, struggled to straighten his body, and covered him with his favorite Elmo blanket. She kissed his forehead and the child didn't budge. She marveled over how much he favored Corey with his fair brown skin and partially slanted eyes. Damien was a beautiful child and

Stephanie couldn't imagine what her life would be like without him.

The phone rang, interrupting her thoughts. She grabbed it quickly, not wanting her mom to complain about the late night call. Besides, she was sure it was Corey calling to see if she wanted to catch the last show of the night at the AMC.

"Hello," she answered, putting on her sexy voice to entice him in the event that he was calling to cancel.

"This is the Fulton County police department with a collect call from..."

"Corey."

Stephanie's heart plummeted.

"Will you accept the charges?"

"Yes," she answered without thinking. "Hello?"

"What's up, baby?"

She hated how he was acting like there was nothing unusual about this situation.

"You tell me," she countered.

"I got a problem..."

"Clearly."

"Look I need you to come get me. You got some money?"

"Not much…how much are we talking?"

"Two hundred."

Stephanie looked over at her sleeping son and caressed his head.

"I don't have that, Corey," she said softly. "Don't you have it somewhere?"

"Yeah, but that ain't helping me cuz you can't get to it," he replied with attitude. "Look, get up what you can. I'll get it back to you ASAP."

He wasn't asking, he was ordering her and Stephanie knew she would do whatever he said. Getting up to change into some jeans, she sighed.

"Ok. I'll be down there."

"Don't take forever, man," he complained. "Ok?"

"Ok. But what happened Corey?"

"It ain't nothing."

"It ain't nothing?" she questioned, her voice a little muffled as she pulled her dress over her head.

"Just come on."

He disconnected the line and Stephanie simply pressed flash and dialed the first number that came to mind."

"Hello?"

"Hey girl, it's Steph. I need a favor."

CANDACE

A relaxing vacation on a beautiful beach on a tropical island with fruity drinks and half naked waiters attending to her every need would have been nice. Instead, it was business as usual as Candace sat at her desk in the downtown Decatur law firm. Would these phones ever stop ringing? Everyone had been surprised that she was returning to work after just having gotten married this past Saturday. Ideally, a honeymoon would have been nice. Realistically, she knew that she had to show up to work because the bills weren't going to pay themselves.

Lost in her thoughts, Candace ignored the ringing phone. As she stared into space, she thought of the splendor of her wedding ceremony and reception. She was sure that her girls were envious of her on Saturday. She was finally married and had done it in style while on a budget. Her parents, on the other hand, were probably still livid with her for running off with Quincy in the first place. *At least we got married,* she thought. They had to give her some credit for that. Candace's relationship with her parents was strained at best. Just a couple of years ago she'd been living in their house and struggling to abide by their rules. Mr. and Mrs. Lewis were strict parents.

They were also very disciplined Jehovah's Witnesses. They expected their children to walk in the same faith as them and to practice Jehovah's teachings and commandments in all aspects of their lives. Additionally, Mr. Walter Lewis, a high school assistant principal, was big on education. His hope for his girls was that they would excel academically throughout high school and go on to strive for magna cum laude in college.

Candace could never meet their expectations. By her senior year of high school, she simply just stopped trying. She stopped studying constantly, causing her grade point average to slide downward. To her, a C was just fine since she was never able to surpass a B+ when she did try harder. Feeling like she was missing out on fun, Candace started hanging out more with her girlfriends. At times she would sneak out to meet a guy for a date. Her parents were against dating, even though she was eighteen. They claimed that they wanted her and her younger sister, Amelia, to stay focused on that which was most important. Candace loved her parents, but was feeling as if she was out-growing their old-school frame of mind.

She met Quincy just one year after graduation. She'd been working at the law firm for half a year. Quincy Lawson was a simple mail clerk. Candace met him at a convenience store near his job when she was out with her girlfriends one Saturday. She'd accepted his number only because she never knew if she'd need him one day. It was superficial, but she'd taken note of his clean, black 2003 Impala. Candace had assumed that the man had money. Physically, she was not completely attracted to him. He was a little thick for her taste, but he could definitely dress. At twenty-five, Quincy also owned his own home. Candace was impressed by this.

For several months she dated Quincy, sneaking

out and lying to her parents about where she was going. Eventually they caught on and decided to teach her a lesson. She'd gone over to Quincy's one night, just to hang out. Of course they'd had sex and Candace accidently fell asleep afterwards. When she finally awoke, it was two in the morning. She shook Quincy awake and he took her home, only for her to discover that the door was locked. Sure, she had a key, but it didn't seem to work. Candace was confused. She walked around to the back of the house and tapped on Amelia's window to no avail. It had been her mother, Barbara Lewis, who finally opened the front door. Candace simply lowered her head and attempted to pass over the threshold into her home. She was surprised when her mother blocked her way and shook her head.

"No," she'd said. "No floozies live here. Only floozies and whores stay out until the early hours of the morning. You want to be out in the streets, you can stay out in the streets."

Mrs. Lewis then shut the door in her eldest daughter's face. She'd been stunned, but Candace's first reaction was to call Quincy who had eagerly returned to get her. Candace knew her mom would eventually let up and allow her back home. However, she didn't want to go back. She also knew that they would only become more infuriated with her had she simply moved in with Quincy without being married. It went against their beliefs, both religious and personal. So, she devised a plan. Quincy wanted her to live with him, but she told him that she would only stay until she could get her own place unless he married her. Once the seed was planted in his head, Quincy was on board with the idea. It was the perfect plan to Candace. Quincy already had a home and money. She figured that all she would have to do was buy her own car with her income and splurge on herself with the rest. The added plus was that her relationship with her parents would be repaired once she told them that she was getting married. She thought they would be proud of her for doing the right, wholesome thing. Sure, they'd paid for the wedding, but the relationship between Candace and her parents still needed work. *In time*, she thought to herself.

The intercom was buzzing and Mr. Japlan was calling her, interrupting her thoughts.

"Candace, the phone lines were all lit up. What's going on out there?"

Snapping back to reality and thinking quickly on her feet, Candace put on her polite, professional voice.

"Sorry, Bob. I was with the delivery man. That package you were expecting has arrived."

She glanced down at the box behind her desk. UPS had delivered it an hour prior, but he didn't know that. At the time she'd been too busy to advise him that it was there. Looking up, she saw a familiar face wave to her through the glass door to the firm. She smiled, reached for her purse, and buzzed Bob back.

"Going to lunch," she informed.

"Enjoy."

Candace picked up her office phone and pressed the series of buttons to forward all calls to the voice mail during her lunch break. Slipping back into her tan stilettos, she sashayed out of the office suite and out to the elevators. She knew that her friend wouldn't be waiting there. It was customary for them to meet across the street at one of the local eateries. Today it would be Crescent Moon. Feeling confidently sexy, Candace descended in the elevator, walked quickly across the street and down the walk before sauntering into the already crowded restaurant. Without breaking her stride, Candace made a right and headed over to their usual corner booth. There she was greeted by her tall, ebony companion.

Khalil stood to hug her, briefly brushing his lips past her cheek. He waited until she was seated, then slid back into the booth across from her.

"Good afternoon, you beautiful goddess," he said seductively.

Candace blushed. "Hey yourself."

"I took the liberty of ordering for you. Hope you don't mind."

She did. "No. Thanks."

She stared at the man across from her, taking in his long, neatly kept dreads, his beautiful dark skin, and his nicely trimmed mustache and goatee. Her eyes met his hazel ones, which she knew were really contacts. He smiled at her, bringing attention to the fine wrinkles that kissed the corners of his eyes. Khalil Bradley was nearly twice her age. At nineteen, twenty in two more months, Candace was surprised at herself for being the interest of this older gentleman. Khalil was forty-three with three children, one of which was two years older than Candace. He never seemed to mind her age, for it was he who had pursued her.

Candace met Khalil in passing just two short

months ago, around the time she'd been put out of her parents' place. He worked for the firm across the hall from hers and they had shared an elevator up to their floor one morning. By the time the doors opened on the fifth floor, they arranged to meet for lunch. Ever since that day, lunch was on Khalil. . She had been honest, telling him about Quincy and their abrupt engagement. He'd been honest, telling her about Sheila, the woman he lived with currently. Neither had cared when they'd skipped food one day, devouring each other instead on their lunch break. The sex was good, but had only happened once. Candace didn't expect a repeat performance.

"So you did it huh?" he asked, nodding toward her left hand.

She looked down at her wedding ring and quickly removed her hand from the table.

"Yeah," she said. "I did."

"So, how do you feel?"

"No different right now I suppose. Why you ask that?"

Their waitress brought over two glasses of iced tea and advised that their orders would be up shortly.

Khalil sipped through his straw and shook his head.

"I don't know why you married that man in the first place."

"Why not?"

"Why so?"

She sucked her teeth. "This is juvenile."

He chuckled. "Says the woman who married some out of touch dude just to escape her parents."

She was offended. "I resent that."

"Why? It's the truth. When you talk about him I don't get the impression that you are in love with him. It was a calculated move of survival for you. Either marry dumb ass or go back to living with mommy and daddy."

"Don't call him dumb ass."

Khalil laughed again. "That's right, gorgeous. Defend your husband. But I'd like to point out that you didn't disagree with what I said."

Their food arrived and Candace concentrated on dowsing her fries with ketchup. Khalil had this *I'm always right* attitude that she couldn't quite get with. But, she never complained. After all, he wasn't her man. They were just friends.

Khalil took the ketchup bottle from her and covered his home-style meatloaf with it. Taking a bite of it, he nodded his head, moaning and pointing his fork at the red lump.

"Mmmm. That's it right there. That's good stuff."

Candace giggled. "Ok…"

"Can you cook?"

She sucked her teeth. "Yeah. I can cook," she said. "I got skills."

"Uh-huh. I'm a real man. I likes to eat me some good ole fashion home cooking."

She cut her club sandwich into fourths and smirked at him.

"Well you better tell Sheila to get on it."

"Ha, ha," he said between chews. "Sheila can't boil water."

"Better get her some lessons then."

"That's like teaching a blind man to read."

"Ah! But blind people do read," Candace retorted. "In Braille."

"Touché. But there's only one method of cooking and that's simply to get in the kitchen and do it."

Candace bit into her sandwich and immediately regretted letting Khalil choose her meal. The sandwich was dry. She needed more mayo. Not wanting to complain, she continued to chew all the while willing the waitress to return. They sat in silence for a moment, each eating and entertaining their own thoughts. By the way Khalil kept looking at her cleavage, which was nicely accented by her V-neck shirt, Candace knew that he was having erotic thoughts. She smiled at him and licked her lips seductively. He winked at her between bites of mashed potatoes.

She wondered why he hadn't made any advances toward her since their one encounter. Not that she was disappointed. She simply wondered what his thoughts on the matter were. They'd never really discussed the little tryst and at times she asked herself if maybe she just didn't do it for him.

"You look like you're deep in thought about something," he commented. "Care to share?"

She picked at a fry and instantly felt shy. She didn't want to say what she had been thinking, especially if he hadn't been pleased by their love-making.

"Not really thinkin' 'bout anything worth mentioning," she answered, not looking at his face.

"You're lying," he said bluntly. "Come on, be real with me. We can talk about anything."

She looked at him as he gave her his serious look. Candace was turned on by the way he focused on her so intently. He was nothing if not attentive.

"Well," she hesitated, wondering how real she should keep it. "I was just thinking about that time."

"What time?"

He was actually playing dumb with her. *What is he, like 16,* she thought. *He's gonna make me spell it out for him?*

As if hearing her thoughts, he stated, "Just say it, Candace. Say what you're thinking, don't beat around the bush. Straightforwardness is sexy."

She hated the way he spoke to her like she was a naïve idiot.

"I was thinking about when we slept together," she said, staring square into his eyes without blinking.

"Oh?" he said, picking up his cup and taking a long gulp. "What about it?"

She felt deflated. His nonchalant response was all the assurance she needed to know that he definitely had not been feeling her. It didn't matter, she was married now anyway. It wasn't as if she was losing anything.

She shrugged. "I was just remembering it. Nothing in particular about it...Just the fact that it happened."

He nodded. "It pops up in my mind like that sometimes too..."

"Does it?" she tried to sound disinterested as she polished off the last of her fries.

"Yes. Particularly the image of you moaning in my ear with your eyes shut tightly and your fingers caressing my dreads...Very sensual image. No memory could be sweeter, so I figured I'd hold on to it versus trying to recapture the moment...Especially since you are a married woman now."

Slurppp. Khalil drained his iced tea and placed his glass on the table. Taking his napkin from his lap, he thoroughly wiped his hands and mouth before smiling at her devilishly.

"What man wouldn't remember experiencing the essence which is you, pretty lady?"

Candace was stunned. Her assumption had been wrong. Obviously he had enjoyed their episode. Listening to him speak was almost like reading erotica. He knew exactly the right words to say to excite her. She looked down at her half-eaten sandwich and immediately forgave him for ordering her a crappy lunch. Any man that could be so smooth and have so much game could order her whatever he liked. Feeling sexy and desirable, Candace lightly touched Khalil's hand and smiled. This man was definitely good for her ego.

JADA

"No she didn't."

"Yes the hell she did!" Jada shouted into her cellphone.

Holding the cell with her left hand she guided her little Focus with her right, trying to focus on the highway signs as not to miss her exit. It had been a long, tedious day at the office and the last thing she wanted to be doing was traveling 285 South at six thirty in the evening. But here she was, heading to I-75 to rescue the damsel in distress. Somehow in her circle of friends, Jada had become the rescuer, the one everyone turned to. Maybe it made sense. After all, she was the most reliable one in the group. Jada Presley was twenty-two and was an administrative assistant for an adoption agency. Just a few short months ago she'd worked with Candace at the small downtown Decatur law firm. Having recently graduated from Agnes Scott College, Jada was working toward building up her career as a social service worker. Her girls had always envied her for being so driven and goal-oriented. Once Jada decided to do something, she carried it out one hundred percent. Her personal life was no different. As a junior, Jada met and fell in love with the man she knew she'd spend her life with. Jordan Presley was a communications major when the two met. Now, he'd excelled at becoming a popular DJ on one of the hottest radio stations in Atlanta.

"In the middle of the night, she called asking me for money to bail that asshole out of jail."

"That's some bullshit," Candace remarked in her ear. "For real...So...Did you give it to her?"

Jada sucked her teeth, exiting to Tara Boulevard.

"Are you kidding me? I told her that I didn't have the cash cuz I don't."

"So what did she do?"

"Hell if I know," Jada answered. "But I'll tell you this...I'm tired of her asking me for money to help that boy out."

Jada made a right into the Value City parking lot and scanned the crowd for her stranded friend. Thinking about Stephanie's antics was upsetting her and she already wasn't happy about riding around Riverdale in search of her other troubled girl.

"Well, she knew to call you," Candace said. "Cuz had she called me I would've had to tell her what's up."

"She wouldn't have called you on your wedding night," Jada reasoned.

"I'm just saying."

Jada shook her head. "Yeah." *You probably would have given it to her,* she thought.

Jada's eyes fell on the tall, dark chick posted at the entrance to Value City. Her cell phone to her ear, lip gloss shining, sporting sparkly hip huggers and a colorful shirt depicting a woman with a large afro accented with rhinestones. She looked like a model. The problem was that she behaved like one too.

"Let me call you back, girl," Jada said to Candace, leaning over to unlock the passenger door. The pretty girl slid into the seat, clicked her phone shut, and closed the door.

"Thank you, friend," she said in her sugary sweet, innocent little girl voice.

Jada pulled off and headed towards home.

"Thank you nothing," she responded. "You wanna tell me how your ass ended up stuck out here?"

Alex took a deep breath and stared out of the window.

"That lame dude left me."

"Who?"

"Ronnie."

"Where do you know him from?"

"The club. He said he was gon' take me to dinner, then he brings me to some bootleg Chinese food place," Alex said. "I assumed we'd go to Outback or Red Lobster, somewhere like that. Then the punk was late picking me up, talking ' bout he was at the studio with his boys."

"Ok, so how did you end up here?" Jada interjected.

"He got mad cuz I was complaining about him being cheap, so he said I was a spoiled little princess and that I should find my ass a way home. So, I got out the car and he left."

Jada laughed so hard tears welled up in her eyes. The thought that some dude had called Alex on her attitude was hilarious. Yes, it was messed up that he would leave her in an unfamiliar place, but Jada was sure that this would be a lesson learned. She loved her girl, but ole boy was right. Alex was a spoiled little princess. She often complained about not being able to find a nice, decent guy. The reality was that Alex's attitude was often the cause of her boyfriends mistreating her.

"Don't laugh at me!" Alex squeaked, making a pouty face.

Jada laughed harder.

"Did you give him that same look as he pulled off?" she asked.

"Ok. You got jokes."

Recovering from her hysteria, Jada shook her head and adopted a more solemn look.

"Why are you out with no money?" she asked her friend. "I'm assuming you don't have any money or else you would've caught a cab home."

Alex fidgeted with her little pink cell phone, avoiding eye contact with Jada.

"I'm broke right now. That's why I agreed to go out to eat with that fool. I was hungry."

"You wouldn't be broke if you got a job," Jada advised.

"I'm trying cuz I know mommy and daddy aren't gonna pay my bills forever."

Mommy and daddy? Jada drove in silence, thinking to herself how privileged her friend really was. As long as she'd known the girl, Alex had never worked. Her parents basically took care of all her financial needs from her rent to her personal spending expenses. Jada was not jealous of the girl, but it irked her that she had to work hard throughout college while Alex partied hard. Kudos to the Masons for being able to afford to support their only child. However, with school over and her parents still fronting the bill, Jada felt that they were hurting Alex more than helping. Alex had no sense of responsibility or independence. Her being stranded in Riverdale after going out with a dude she barely knew only confirmed this.

Jada was officially annoyed. When would her girls ever learn? She was tired of being the one everybody turned to for help. It was exhausting. And now, because she was rescuing Alex, she would be late getting home and late starting dinner. Jordan would understand, but personally she just wanted to be home with her husband. The thought of Jordan made a smile creep upon her lips. Alex noticed immediately.

"What are you thinking about?"

Jada shook her head. "Nothing."

The rest of their ride back to Decatur was quiet. When Jada dropped Alex off at the front gate of her apartment complex the two said cordial goodbyes and Jada sped off. Jordan hadn't called to check on her and she had not called to check in. She wondered if he was even home yet.

She arrived home in record time, letting herself into their beautiful apartment with a great feeling of relief. Relief was replaced with surprise as she kicked her heels off and noticed the flicker of light cascading on the wall of their dining room. Quickly she entered and saw the candles and roses adorning their cherry oak dining table. Two place settings had been arranged. Her right brow rose in anticipation as the aroma from the kitchen filled her nose. Taking one last look at the ambience of the dining room, Jada turned and entered the kitchen just in time to see Jordan pop open a bottle of wine.

"Welcome home, beautiful," he said without looking up.

He poured her a glass of Riesling and walked over to her, placing the glass in her hand and a long, lingering kiss on her lips. He pulled away and watched as she sipped the chilled wine.

"To what do I owe this pleasure?" she asked

He chuckled. "What? A man can't pamper his woman?"

"Trust me, I am not complaining."

Jordan walked away to grab two awaiting plates from the counter. He walked past her and into the dining room. She tailed behind him.

"What's for dinner?" she asked.

"Cube steaks, creamed potatoes, and sweet peas."

He sat the plates down and turned to his wife, taking her glass and placing it on the table. Jada smiled and allowed herself to be pulled into his embrace. She inhaled the wonderful scent that was him, a mixture of Right Guard deodorant, Curve for men, and sweat. She felt the tension in her body ease up as he massaged her back. Jordan kissed her forehead.

"I love you woman."

Jada sighed. It felt good to be with a man she knew

would never leave her stranded.

ALEX

Alexandria Mason was exhausted. Upon entering her apartment, she discarded her cute maroon sandals by the front door and trotted over to the couch. Kacey, her roommate, would be furious with her for leaving the shoes in the middle of the floor like that. But Alex didn't care. She was tired, hot, and humiliated. Throwing her head back against the sofa, she sucked her teeth. The nerve of that punk for leaving her! *Why is it so hard to find a good man?*

Alex knew she was smart and beautiful. Perhaps this intimidated the brothers. Ever since she moved to Atlanta for school it seemed as if all the jerks literally flocked to her. She had not experienced one serious relationship. Being single was starting to suck. All of the girls were getting married, leaving her alone, feeling pathetic and lonely. Sure, she was young and should be simply enjoying life, but life seemed empty when she came home to a quiet apartment with no one there to care for her.

Alex laughed aloud at her thoughts. *Even Candace's vain ass has a husband!* She was happy for her girl despite her belief that the union was destined to be broken. But, at least the girl had someone to spend her nights with. Alex reached for her remote and tuned into her usual prime-time shows. *I only have Kim, Nikki, and the Professor to chill with,* she thought, as her favorite show, The Parkers, started its theme music. At the first commercial, she sauntered to the kitchen and peered into the refrigerator. There was nothing, aside from some orange juice, a container of old Chinese take-out that Kacey had three days prior, and some cheese. She contemplated making a grilled cheese sandwich, but that idea was canceled out when she realized that they were out of bread. Feeling herself about to have a serious break down, Alex pulled her cell out of its holster and dialed her favorite number.

"What's up pimpin?"

She was used to this greeting.

"Hey friend," she replied, being sure to put on her innocent voice.

Laughter filled her ear.

"What's wrong with you, girl?"

Alex hopped up on the kitchen counter and swung her legs back and forth.

"I'm hungry."

"Thought you had a date with your new boo."

"Yeah well, he's a punk and I'm hungry. So..."

"Say no more." She could hear the jingle of keys through the receiver. "Chicken or beef?"

"Beef," she answered.

"Aight. Be there in twenty."

"K."

She flipped the phone closed and jumped down from the counter. Ignoring the laughter from the living room television, she headed to her bedroom and quickly changed into purple lounging pants and lavender tank-top. Brushing her wrapped hair into a ponytail, she toyed with the idea of applying her MAC Lusterglass to her full lips. On second thought, she abandoned the idea, wondering why she should go an extra mile to be cute for her homeboy. Twenty minutes later there was a tap at the front door and Alex went to greet her friend.

Standing outside her door was Clayton Paul, an old friend. She and Clayton, better known as Clay to others and Precious to Alex, had gone to high school together in Beaumont. When Alex decided to go to Agnes Scott, Clay had decided upon Morehouse. They figured at least they would have each other in Atlanta. Clay was a thin, average looking guy. He was no athlete or stud, but there was a certain cuteness to him that never left him without a date. His sense of fashion was unique, preppy boy style if you will. Only Clay could wear a soft pink polo and not emit a gay vibe. Alex liked that about him. Clay dared to be different and didn't care what anyone thought about him.

Alex stepped to the side and allowed her best friend to enter her apartment. He carried a Wendy's bag along with what Alex knew was a chocolate Frosty for her. Alex loved chocolate and Clay, being the ever attentive, good friend that he was, knew exactly what she liked. The two set up their meal on the floor, resting their backs against the front of the couch.

Delighted and relieved, Alex bit into her Junior Bacon Cheeseburger Deluxe.

"Mmmmm."

Clay laughed at her, shoving fries into his own mouth. His eyes crinkled up when he laughed, giving him an almost Asian look. Alex had noticed it many times, never realizing how cute it was.

"What are you laughing at?" she asked him.

"You," he simply replied.

"You think I'm a joke?" she retorted playfully.

Clay shook his head solemnly. "Never that, pretty lady."

Alex ignored the compliment, beginning to savor her Frosty.

"No date tonight, playboy?" she asked between slurps.

Clay shrugged. "Naw."

Alex clutched her chest with her right hand.

"What?" she asked in mock belief. "You with no date? The world must be coming to an end."

Clay gave a half smile and shook his head, not really amused by Alex's humor. He reached for a fry and Alex quickly took it from him.

"What's up with that?" she asked, popping the fry into her mouth.

Clay looked at her and was hesitant to speak. It was as if he was lost in his glare. Alex raised her right eyebrow and as if snapping back to reality, Clay quickly looked away.

"Nothing," he finally replied, reaching for another fry. "Just tired of hanging out with all these apple-head ass chicks...It's just not what's up for me anymore."

Alex nodded knowingly. Using her straw, she stirred up her rapidly melting Frosty while listening to her friend speak the words that mirrored her own emotions.

"I just wanna go out with one girl," Clay said. "I just want one girl with some business about herself that likes me for me, just the way I am. I want someone that I can chill with, someone I can joke with, someone that's hella fine cuz she just has mad confidence like that...someone I can spoil..."

Alex giggled. "And I want to be all that to someone who is worth my time and won't treat me like shit."

Clay looked up at his homegirl. Alex missed the hopeful glint in his eyes.

"Yeah," Clay said. "Guess we're both looking for the same thing, huh?"

Alex discarded of her burger wrapper and sat her half-finished Frosty on the coffee table. As she'd often done before, Alex leaned over and rested her head on Clay's lap. Instinctively, he began to caress her hair, removing her ponytail holder. Alex closed her eyes, allowing herself to be comforted by her friend's gentle strokes.

"Are we ever gonna find it, Precious?" she asked softly.

Clay lightly touched her face. "Yeah, Alex. I think we will

STEPHANIE

A week had passed since Stephanie had bailed Corey out of jail. It had not been easy to get up the money. She'd had no luck with Jada so she'd asked the old man up the street for a loan. Mr. Carter had a thing for her, always had. Stephanie knew that he would be more than willing to loan her the money. The issue was how the man would want to be repaid. Stephanie's plan was to get the money back quickly from Corey so that she could return it to Carter with no problems. The flaw in her plan was that Corey was pulling one of his disappearing acts. She hadn't heard from him and he was not answering or returning any of her calls.

It hurt her feelings that he would show such disregard for her after she had helped him out. The night of the incident, he hadn't even bothered to fill her in on what had happened. Once he was released, he simply told her to go home. Without so much as a thank you, a kiss, or a hug, he just turned and walked away. Stephanie didn't know where he was going on foot and wondered how he would get home. But, like the obedient girlfriend that she was, she got into her Sentra and drove home.

Now, completely pissed that the whole weekend had come and gone without a peep from him, Stephanie was determined to have it out with Corey. It was a Monday and she was tired from working. However, as soon as six o'clock hit, Stephanie hopped into her car and headed straight to Corey's Midtown apartment. She hated that he lived in a gated community. But, even that obstacle wasn't going to stop her as she tailed a resident inside the iron gates. Driving through the maze of the complex, Stephanie started to become apprehensive about her decision to just show up. *What if there's a girl in there? How will I react?* Parking in front of his building, she shrugged off her misgivings and decided that whatever happened was just gonna happen.

She noticed his car parked in its usual spot and was confident that the jerk was home. Slowly ascending the stairs, she pulled out her cell and dialed Corey's number. As she reached the top floor she also reached his voicemail. Disgusted and further infuriated, Stephanie walked up to his door and began to bang loudly. For several minutes she stood there knocking and banging like a mad woman possessed. Her inhibitions began to leave her as she found herself shouting out obscenities to the heavy door.

Bang, bang, bang. "Open the damn door you fuckin' bastard! I know you're fuckin' in there, you ass!" *Boom, boom,boom.*

In mid-knock, the door flew open and Stephanie barely had time to blink before she was grabbed inside and tossed to the floor. Corey was on top of her, pinning her to the ground, a look of hot fury upon his face.

"Are you fuckin' crazy?" he asked repeatedly. "Are you fuckin' crazy, girl? Are you stupid? What the fuck is wrong with you?"

Stephanie was scared speechless. She was not sure what his intentions were and feared that he was about to brutally kick her ass.

Corey shook her. "How many times have I told your ass

not to just show up at my spot? You think I'm fuckin' playin' wit you girl? You think this shit is a fuckin' joke?"

He glared down at her small, tensed up body and shook his head. Finally, he released his grip and climbed off of her. He turned away, heading for his kitchen.

"Stupid ass," he muttered.

Stephanie rose from the floor and watched him retreat. Anger replaced fear and she followed him into the kitchen. Coming up behind him, she tried to push the man up against the refrigerator.

"Fuck you, Corey," she spat out.

Corey quickly spun around and grabbed her left arm.

"What the fuck is wrong with you, girl? You don't put yo' hands on me."

Stephanie shook her arm free from his hold.

"Don't put yo' damn hands on me then," she retorted.

Corey shook his head and turned back toward the fridge. He opened it and reached inside for a beer.

"You need to take yo' crazy ass on somewhere wit all dat shit, Steph."

He turned back to face her.

"You out here making a fool of yo' self. What the fuck's wrong with you, man?"

Stephanie's eyes widen and she put her hands on her hips and glared back at Corey.

"What the fuck's wrong with me?" she repeated. "What the fuck's wrong with you? You're the fuckin' trifling one. Ignoring my calls. Haven't called me or come to see your son. Didn't even bother to say thank you for bailing yo' sorry ass out of jail."

"So what? You doing all this shit for me to say thank you? You trippin..."

Corey tried to step away, but Stephanie moved in front of him.

"Stop playing, man. Take yo' ass home."

Stephanie stepped up to him and poked him in the chest, realizing for the first time that he was shirtless.

"I didn't come for a thank you, I came to see why you acting like you don't care about me and Damien. But yeah, a thank you would be nice."

"I don't need this shit, Steph," Corey said, slapping her hand away. "I ain't down with all this drama and shit."

"You cause the drama," Stephanie shouted, trying again to push him. "This is all you, Corey."

They struggled for a minute, Stephanie trying to punch at Corey and Corey pushing her away. Tired of the commotion, Corey picked the petite woman up, carried her to his leather sofa, and threw her down. Stephanie was breathless as he towered over her, pulling her arms over her head and pinning them down.

"You want me to say thank you?" he asked. "You want me to thank yo' ass? Well, here you go. Here goes your fuckin' thank you."

He leaned down and began to suck on her neck. Stephanie was powerless underneath him and struggled without success to move. Moving away from her neck, Corey tried to kiss Stephanie. Still infuriated, she turned her head to the right while trying to move her legs.

"Get the fuck off of me," she ordered.

Corey ignored her and turned her face towards his with his right hand. His left hand still held both of her small wrists above her head.

"This is what you came for right? Over here all heated up and shit...Ain't this what you came for?"

He crushed his lips against hers and forced his tongue into her mouth. She tried once more to free herself, but was disappointed in her own lack of endurance as she felt herself succumb to the effect he was having on her body. Corey could feel her relax and begin to thrust her tongue against his. At that point he released her arms and began groping her breasts through her shirt. Becoming more and more turned on, Stephanie could feel the moisture seeping between her legs. As if he could sense her growing arousal, Corey unzipped her slacks and disposed of them and her bikini briefs. Stephanie's heart rate increased as Corey entered her with two fingers, then three. The slight penetration teased her, driving her into a sexual fit. Spreading her legs for him, Stephanie began to rotate her hips to better feel the pleasure of his fingers.

"Mmmm. This is what you came for, huh?" Corey whispered, watching as she moved around and around.

She felt helpless to his advances and did not protest as he entered her bare and began to thrust ferociously. His grunts filled her ear as he moved in and out of her. Stephanie tried to caress his head, but he shook away. She tried to grab his face and engage him in a kiss, but Corey turned his head to the side, avoiding the romantic exchange. His pumping became fiercer and Stephanie's arousal began to diminish. Arms lying flat by her sides, she found herself staring at the ceiling, waiting for the encounter to be over. She didn't have the nerve to tell him to stop. She didn't want to start another argument just as they were making up. Oblivious to her growing dryness, Corey mannishly pushed her legs over, forcing her to turn around.

"Lift your ass up more," he ordered her, pushing her back torso into the sticky wetness of the couch.

He re-entered her in the doggy-style position. Stephanie buried her face into the sofa, wiling herself not to cry. His roughness was beginning to hurt, but Corey seemed more turned on by her discomfort. As he slapped her ass and squeezed her cheeks, Stephanie grimaced, trying to remain silent. They'd never had rough sex like this and she wasn't sure what it meant.

Corey tried to spread her cheeks wider and pushed her legs open more causing her left leg to dangle off the sofa. He pushed himself deeper inside, grabbing her hips as he climaxed inside of her. Stephanie was gripping the arm of the sofa. As Corey came, she breathed an inaudible sigh of relief. Without hesitation, Corey quickly jumped up and headed to his bathroom. As she lay there, Stephanie heard the water running in the shower. Sitting up, she looked around for her clothes thinking it best for her to just dress and leave. In mid-thought she decided that it was unfair for Corey to be the only satisfied one. With renewed confidence, she strolled into the bathroom and pulled back the shower curtain. Corey was stunned by her presence and gave her a questioning look.

"What's up?" he asked. "What you doing?"

"I can't join you?" she asked, stepping one foot over into the tub.

Corey held his soapy hand out in protest.

"Naw, hold up. I'm almost done. Plus I gotta bounce real quick. I got business to take care of. Aight? Just give me a minute."

Feeling rejected, Stephanie just nodded and retreated from the bathroom. The whole visit had not gone according to her plan and she was disappointed in herself. She quickly dressed and grabbed her purse, but was not out of the door before Corey entered the living room wrapped in a towel.

"Aye man, you can wash up if you want to, but I'm leaving in like ten minutes."

Stephanie walked past him to the door, half expecting him to stop her, half knowing that he wouldn't.

"You out?" he asked her.

She turned to look at the man she undoubtedly loved,

but hated.

"Yeah, why? You wanna kiss me goodbye?"

He surprised her by walking over to her. However, he simply pecked her forehead and patted her ass.

"I'll call you," he said, opening the door to usher her out.

"Yeah," she replied, leaving. "Sure."

Stephanie descended the stairs back to her little Sentra, mission unaccomplished.

MIRANDA

It was 11pm and he still wasn't home. Miranda glanced up again at the clock on the VCR. It wasn't unlike him to not call, but it was becoming an annoying habit as of late. For the past two weeks Norris had been coming and going with no regards to her. Ever since the infamous hang up after Candace's wedding, he'd been behaving more and more suspicious. Her eyes were getting heavy as she grew inpatient watching the Golden Girls i on Lifetime. Miranda had half a mind to go out and search for the car. The thought was desperate, but Miranda was becoming increasingly angry wondering where the hell her husband was. Between working two jobs, Miranda rarely had time alone with Norris, the nerve of him to not be home to spend quality time.

Just as she was about to give up for the night and silence Rose in the middle of a St. Olaf antidote, Miranda heard the lock turn on the front door. In strolled Norris as if it were five in the afternoon. Tossing his red and white A cap onto the coffee table, he began to walk right past her. Miranda was astonished by his gall.

"So you just ain't gon' say nothing?" she questioned him.

Norris walked into their bedroom. Not backing down and ready to confront his late night creeping, Miranda followed behind him. He emitted his usual marijuana scent, but tonight Miranda's nose was picking up on a hint of something else.

"Where have you been, Norris?" she asked, standing in the doorway, hands on hips.

Norris unbuttoned his jersey, beginning to undress himself. His back was turned to his hot-tempered wife. Miranda was not appreciative of his silence. As he shrugged off the jersey, Miranda quickly stepped forward and snatched the shirt.

"What the fuck!" Norris shouted, turning to face Miranda. "Man, stop playing."

Norris reached to grab the jersey from her, but Miranda turned and took a quick sniff of the material. The scent of Victoria's Secret Pear fragrance was unmistakable. She allowed Norris to snatch the jersey from her hands as she looked at him, anger reflecting in her glare.

"Look at me," she demanded.

He ignored the command, tossing the shirt into the nearby clothes hamper. He busied himself with removing the rest of his clothing as if Miranda was not even in the room.

"Look at me!" she screamed at him.

He looked over at her as he stood in his boxers, ready to head to the shower.

"For what?" he asked, his voice laced with attitude.

Miranda stepped up to him, fists clinched as if she was going to hit the man. She fought back tears as she looked into the eyes of the man she'd tried so hard to be good to.

"I have been a good wife to you," she said. "And this is

the best you can do for me?"

"What are you talking about? Ain't nobody done shit to you."

"Norris! You're cheating on me!" her voice shrieked. "You think I'm too stupid to notice that something's going on?"

He sucked his teeth. "Whatever."

Norris pushed past her and walked into their bathroom. He turned on the water in the shower, then turned to open the linen close situated behind the bathroom door. Miranda approached the bathroom, pushed and held the door ajar, hampering Norris from accessing the closet.

"Man, watch out," he told her.

"I worked two jobs to support us, Norris. Begged my parents to let us live with them when you fucked up and got discharged."

"Get out of my way, Miranda," he said warningly.

"I stuck by you when you didn't have shit. I should've left your sorry ass. But, I stayed with you and this...this is how you repay me?"

"I'm not gon tell yo' ass to move no more," he warned again, balling up his fist.

"How you gonna have the nerve to be cheating on me? Who in the hell is even messing with your sorry ass? All you do is smoke all day and you barely keeping ya' lil piece of a job."

Without warning or hesitation, Norris slapped Miranda with such force that the blow made her tumble backwards. Capitalizing on her moment of vulnerability, Norris shoved her over and over until she'd fumbled to the floor.

"You wanna talk shit?" he asked her, kicking the woman's legs with his bare foot. "Go head, talk shit now. Go head."

Miranda's cries for help resounded throughout the otherwise silent apartment. She pleaded with him for some mercy, swatting at his leg and trying to get him to stop kicking her. She turned her body away from him, curling up against the wall. There she found no solace. Norris turned his concentration from her legs to her side, giving her two swift kicks in her ribcage. As she winced from the contact, Miranda felt one of her contacts slip. Doubled over in pain from Norris' blows, she frantically tried to find it. Realizing what she was doing, Norris quickly surveyed the floor. They spotted it at the same time. Norris was quicker, stomping the tiny lens with his right foot while pushing her away with his left hand.

"Get the fuck up!!!" he ordered, laughing at her helplessness. "Let me see you get up now."

"Stop," she pleaded desperately. "Please leave me alone."

"Naw. You wanted a confrontation, right? Walking up on me like you're ready to go at it. Come on, get up."

He reached down and pulled her up by her arms. Miranda struggled with him, trying with all her might to shake herself loose from his grip.

"You wanna hit me?" he spat out at her, using his right hand to enclose her throat as he pinned her up against the wall. "I don't hear you talking no more. You ain't saying shit."

Tears streamed from Miranda's eyes as she tried to pry Norris' fingers from her throat. Her vision was slightly skewed, but she could see that he was looking at her with the most devious smirk. Miranda was scared for her life. Norris tightened his grip and gritted his teeth.

"Shut the fuck up whimpering," he ordered.

She closed her eyes in prayer, hoping that he would not kill her.

"Understand this. If you ever call me sorry again, if you ever step to me like you want to scrap again, I will fuckin' kill you. You understand?"

Miranda was quiet, eyes still shut, breath escaping her. Norris shoved her forehead causing Miranda's head to bang against the wall.

"Answer me damn it. Do you fuckin' understand?"

Miranda's eyes blinked rapidly as she shrugged to give him a slight nod. He stared at her briefly, and then released his hold on her. Unsure of what to do next, Miranda stood awkwardly in the hall, waiting to see what Norris would do. Her husband simply shook his head at her.

"I don't want to go through this shit again," he told her.

Miranda just stood there, trying to regulate her breathing. She watched as he turned and went into the bathroom, slamming the door behind him. She could feel herself beginning to hyperventilate. Walking to the bedroom, she felt immense pain in her side. Her senses were leaving her as she was beginning to panic all over again. Standing at the dresser, she picked up her hair brush and frantically brushed at her mane, her sobs coming more quickly and loudly. She caught her reflection in the mirror and dropped the brush to the ground in mid-stroke. Her eyes were swollen with tears, bottom lip busted and bleeding, and a bruise was becoming discernible beneath her right eye and on her neck. She barely recognized herself.

Afraid of the image staring back at her, Miranda turned from the mirror, turned out the light, and crawled into her bed. Common sense told her to pack a bag and get out. Fear of others ridiculing her along with fear of failure and pure shock kept her from moving. She balled up at one corner of the bed, hysteria overcoming her. Lost in her struggle for breath and her inability to block the memory of Norris' blows, she slowly began to slip into unconsciousness until she was enveloped in peaceful darkness.

CANDACE

"What are you doing here?"

Candace was just making it home from a long, exhausting day. Her plan had been to come home, throw some chicken wings in the oven, pour herself a glass of Hypnotic, and enjoy a hot bubble bath in peace while Quincy was still in commute towards home. Her dream was deflated when she had pulled into the driveway and found his car sitting there. He never beat her home. She was genuinely surprised and equally suspicious. As she carried her purse and lunch bag towards the door to the kitchen, she reached out to touch Quincy's car. It was cool to the touch.

Inside Quincy was chilling, feet up, shirtless, watching 106 and Park with a gobbler full of the Hypnotic she'd been craving all day.

"What's up?" she asked him, sitting her bags down on the breakfast nook and walking over to the sofa.

Quincy simply nodded his head in acknowledgement and took a hearty gulp of the Hypnotic.

Candace sat next to him on the couch, waiting for some form of explanation for his unexpected presence. Seeing that none was forthcoming, she kicked off her pumps and shrugged her shoulders.

"I'm guessing that you don't want to tell me why you're home so early."

Quincy sucked his teeth.

"I gotta give you a reason for me being in my own house?"

Candace rolled her eyes and ran her fingers through her wrapped hair.

"I'm just wondering because you never get home before me. Is everything okay?"

Quincy nodded.

"How long have you been home?"

"Dang man, why you asking all these questions?"

She sucked her teeth. "I'm just making conversation."

Quincy changed the channel to Sports Center and took

another swig of the blue liquor.

"I don't feel like conversating."

Candace rose from the couch and eye-balled Quincy.

"Conversate isn't a word," she stated.

"Whatever."

"Yeah. Whatever."

Candace turned and climbed the steps to their bedroom. She wasn't surprised to see Quincy's clothes strewn all over their bed. Reluctantly, she began to rummage through the clothes, sorting the laundry. Quincy never put his things away no matter how many times she complained about his sloppiness. He was also notorious for leaving money and paper, usually receipts, in his pants pockets. Candace had banned him from doing the laundry because he never checked his pockets.

Tired and not wanting to pick up after her grown husband, Candace picked up Quincy's work pants and hurriedly inspected the pockets. Her search yielded two dollars in change, a five dollar bill, and a folded up sheet of paper. Tossing the pants into the clothes hamper, she stuck the money in her own sock drawer and moved toward the trashcan to discard of the folded piece of paper. Mindlessly she unfolded it just to ascertain that it wasn't anything of importance. The big bold print at the top of the page made her gasp. Understanding hit her instantly as to why Quincy was laid out in their living room as if on vacation. Quickly, she exited the room, descended the stairs, and approached her husband snatching the remote from his hand.

"Aye man, what the fuck?" he protested as she snapped off the television.

She threw the remote down on the coffee table and glared at the big man.

"Yeah, what the fuck?" she repeated, waving the paper in his face. "What the fuck is this?"

Quincy squinted to see what she was waving around. He snatched the paper from her and took a quick glance at it, then threw it on the sofa beside him.

"You going through my stuff now?" he asked her, trying to change the subject.

"Nobody's going through your stinking stuff. I was sorting the laundry and…" she caught herself. "No, hell no. Don't flip this. What the fuck is up, Q?"

He shrugged.

She shoved him.

"What the fuck? You're not going to say anything?"

"Don't touch me like that, man," he replied.

"You owe me an explanation. This is serious, Quincy."

"It ain't nothing."

"It ain't nothing?" she repeated him. "It's a separation notice, dude. That's a whole lot of something. You want to tell me what happened and how we're going to manage these bills without your income?"

"Man, that ole trick ass supervisor never liked me...he been trying to get me fired for the longest."

"Uh-huh..."

Quincy reached for the remote and Candace quickly knocked it off the table. He looked at her and rolled his eyes.

"Don't worry about it, aight?"

"Don't worry about it?" Candace couldn't believe her ears.

"Yeah, man. I got an interview somewhere else tomorrow. It'll be alright."

She stared at him in total disbelief. Why wouldn't he tell her something as important as this? His unemployment could be a major setback for them and he was acting as if nothing had happened. The sight of his chunky, chocolate body clad in nothing but his boxers, some sweatpants, and dingy socks was making her sick. There was nothing worse than a broke slob to her. Annoyed with his presence and nonchalant attitude, Candace hurriedly stepped into her shoes, retrieved her purse and keys, and headed for the door.

"Where you going?" Quincy had the nerve to ask her.

"Non-ya," she replied, slamming the kitchen door behind her.

Hopping into her car she realized that she truly had no destination in mind. All she knew was that she had to get away from Quincy immediately. Backing out of the garage, she took her cell out of her bag and scrolled through to the first name that came to mind. He answered on the third ring.

"Pleasant surprise," he greeted her.

Candace zipped through a four-way stop without stopping, mind set on hastily getting away.

"Can you meet me somewhere?" she asked.

Khalil caught the urgency in her tone. "Something wrong, beautiful?"

"I just need to talk."

"Hmm. Have you had dinner?"

"No," she answered, making a quick right onto Stone Mountain – Lithonia Road, clueless as to where she was headed.

"Come to my house. I'm making Jambalaya. You like spicy foods?"

Candace thought for a second. "Where's Sheila?"

"Out of town for a week. You coming over or what?"

She was hesitant, but needed somewhere to seek solace and was not yet ready to inform any of her girls of Quincy's recent antics.

"Yeah," she said. "I'm coming. Give me directions."

Twenty-five minutes later she found herself parked outside of a ranch-style home off of Columbia Drive. Taking a deep breath, she silently prayed that this man's woman would not return home early to find Candace in her home. A confrontation did not sound appeasing to her at this time. Reaching the front door, she rang the bell and patiently waited to be let in. Khalil opened the door looking sexier than ever. His long, gorgeous locks hung loosely. He wore a cream colored lounging suit with the top completely unbuttoned, exposing his firm and nicely sculpted chest and abs. In his left hand he held a glass of white wine. He stepped back, opening the door wider to allow her to enter. As she crossed the threshold, he closed the door and promptly handed her the glass.

"For you," he stated.

She took the glass and before she could say thank you he leaned in and kissed her so softly and quickly she barely remembered if it had just happened or not. He ushered her into the living room where he had Sade playing softly and candles burning on the mantel.

"Sit down," he ordered.

She did as instructed, allowing herself to melt into the velvety plushness of the cream colored couch. Khalil pushed an ottoman over to her and she instinctively lifted her legs to rest her feet upon it.

"Let me check on the food and I'll be right back," he informed her.

Candace simply nodded and savored her wine. Looking around the room, she took in the ambience, trying to discern between which items of décor reflected Khalil's style and which reflected Sheila's. Over the mantel hung an ethnic painting in a bronze frame of a man and woman, scantily dressed, their bodies intertwined as they engaged in a passionate kiss. Many

African replicas and statues adorned the end tables and the base of the fireplace. Pictures of smiling children filled several shelves of the entertainment center. Candace noticed that there were no pictures of Khalil and Sheila together. The room smelled of fresh jasmine. On the coffee-table Khalil had a new stick of incense burning from its respective stand, the ashes falling onto an ashtray centered strategically underneath it. The ceiling to floor bookshelves held various genres of authors from classic works by Thoreau to the urban favorite Jerome Dickey to the trashy delights of Jackie Collins. *Those must be Sheila's*, Candace assumed.

The wine was starting to take its effect as Candace felt herself beginning to mellow out. She let the sound of Sade's sultry voice, the light fragrance of the incense with the hint of spices wavering in the air from the kitchen take her away from her earlier emotions. Khalil sauntered back into the room carrying the bottle of Riesling. He tipped off her glass and sat the bottle on the table. Looking into her eyes, he began to stroke her soft hair. His fingers combed through her relaxed locks, massaging her scalp and giving her comfort.

"What's going on, pretty lady?" he asked in a delicate whisper.

Candace closed her eyes, not wanting to remember Quincy's situation.

"Quincy lost his job," she answered. "His dumb ass wasn't even going to tell me."

"So how did you find out?"

"I found his separation notice when I was sorting

through his laundry."

"Hmmm."

They sat in silence, Candace's eyebrows knitted up in concern and Khalil continuously stroking her mane.

"Turn around," he ordered her.

Candace opened her eyes and turned her back to him. Khalil placed both hands firmly on her shoulders and began to massage her. He could feel the tension in her neck, she was sure. His firm probes into her skin helped her relax. She lifted her glass to her lips and swallowed its sweetness.

"I don't know what we're going to do about these bills now, especially the mortgage," she stated.

Khalil kissed her neck gently.

"Don't worry about it tonight" he told her. "He's your man. It's his job to provide for you no matter what. Let him figure out how to fix his own mess."

He kissed her neck again and then kissed the other side.

"Don't worry about it tonight," he repeated. "Tonight, just relax and let me pamper you."

She felt his tongue trace the ridges of her right ear. The sensation sent a tingle down her spine. He commenced to sucking on her lobe delicately, now massaging her back. Perhaps sensing that she'd reached a pivotal point of relaxation, Khalil took her wine glass from her, sat it on the table and turned her towards him. Before she could speak or protest, his lips conquered hers in a kiss that began gently and ended up wild with passion. She didn't stop him, giving in to the pleasure of his tongue instead. Her hands grabbed at his dreads as she eagerly received and matched each thrust of his tongue. She felt his hand slip under her blouse and cup her right breast. She moaned, wanting to encourage him to dispose of the top and her bra. Without warning, he withdrew from her, and Candace struggled to catch her breath wondering what was going on.

Slowly, he rose and reached over to lift up her black skirt. Underneath he edged her thongs downward, his eyes focused on hers seductively. She lifted her hips slightly to aid him. Still looking into her eyes, he kneeled down in front of her and grabbed her legs with his big, strong hands. He pulled her, causing her to slide towards the end of the sofa. Softly he trailed kisses down her right leg until he reached her foot. Once there, he slipped off her pump and took her pedicured toes into his moist mouth. Candace could barely contain herself. He sucked until her head fell back onto the couch and she released a pleasurable sigh. He repeated the routine with her left leg, giving it and her toes the same great pleasure and attention. Candace could feel herself dripping onto his sofa.

As if becoming aware of her raging pheromones and the moisture seeping from her kitty, Khalil spread her legs, draping each over his muscular shoulders. With his tongue, he expertly traced the walls of her labia minora, flicking his tongue up and down, up and down. He licked around her pleasure point, driving her insane and forcing her to grab onto his glistening locks. He hardened his tongue and drove it inside of her, an act she'd never before experienced. He darted his tongue in and out as her hips rose from the couch, her pelvis moving in a circular motion. She heard him moan from giving her pleasure. This increased her wetness.

Khalil withdrew his tongue and used it to flick across her clit rapidly. The sensation was sending her into sheer ecstasy. Picking up on her increased excitement, Khalil took her clit into his mouth and sucked with such might and intent, showing Candace no mercy. She pleaded with him to wait, to slow down, to stop. She was overcome by the intense sensation but, he forced her to handle it. He wanted her to relinquish all control. As if to drive his point home, Khalil inserted two fingers into her slippery entrance and instantly found her g-spot as if he had a long-term familiarity with her body.

She lost control, her body bucking ferociously against his fingers, nestled deep inside of her, and his lips which held her clit hostage. His sped increased to match the passion-driven fervor of hers. Within seconds Candace felt herself reach the point of no return, experiencing a g-spot orgasm more powerful than any clitoral orgasm she'd ever had. As her cum slid out of her, Khalil's tongue moved to catch and savor it. He licked her until she was dry and her body ceased in its convulsions.

She was spent. Khalil lowered her weakening legs, leaned upward to kiss her gently on the forehead, and then rose from the floor. He left her without a word and Candace curled up on the sofa. He was gone long enough for her to drift off into an ecstasy induced sleep. She was startled awake by Khalil lifting her from the sofa. He carried her down the hall to the master bedroom and then into the adjourned bathroom. A lavender scented bubble bath awaited her. Candles lined the four steps to the exquisite garden tub. He put her down and slowly unbuttoned her blouse. Candace remained speechless as he removed the top and unhooked her bra. As the material slipped down her arms and fell to the floor, he caressed each breast softly. He helped her out of her skirt and ushered her towards the tub. Once she was settled, he turned on the spa jets to increase her pleasure.

"Relax," he told her, placing tiny kisses upon her face. "Tonight is all about you. We'll have dinner after your bath."

He left the room to retrieve her wine glass, which he promptly tipped off once more, and then he left again. Candace relished in the moment, enjoying the delight of being pampered by such a sexy and enticing man. Remembering the way he took her with his mouth made her hot all over again. Penetration was needed. She drained her glass and quickly bathed in the heavenly lavender water. Upon exiting the tub and drying off with a nearby towel, she found one of Khalil's white t-shirts lying across the chaise lounge in his bedroom. With nothing else to put on, Candace pulled the shirt over her head and got a whiff of Khalil's unique scent. It made her smile.

She momentarily forgot that this was another woman's home and man as she comfortably maneuvered her way through the house and to the kitchen. Khalil was just lighting a candle on the table. He smiled at her as she entered the room and sat at the table.

"Refreshed?" he asked, dimming the overhead light.

"Mmm-hmm. And relaxed."

Khalil sat a bowl of steaming hot jambalaya before her. The spices accosted her nose immediately. Beside the bowl set another glass of wine. Picking up her spoon, Candace sampled the well-seasoned blend of rice, cheese, peppers, sausage, and shrimp. The hint of Cajun flavoring pleased her taste buds, providing just enough spice without going overboard.

"Mmmm." She was delighted. *A man that knows how to*

please in many ways, she thought.

Khalil lifted his glass to her in mock cheers.

"I take that to mean you like it," he stated, sipping from his glass.

"It's so good," Candace answered between bites. "You have a little bit of skills, I see."

Khalil laughed. "You haven't seen anything yet."

He winked at her seductively and Candace could feel her temperature rising. This man evoked such erotic thoughts and emotions within her that Candace was not sure she would make it through the meal. But, make it she did. Upon emptying their bowls, Khalil cleared the table, retrieved a new bottle of Riesling and reached for Candace's hand. Obliged to follow, she placed her hand in his and allowed him to lead her back to his bedroom.

The second they crossed the threshold, Khalil sat the wine on the floor near the foot of the bed and embraced Candace from behind. He kissed her neck on both sides and slid his large hands up and down her body. He followed the curves of her hips, cupping her ass as he licked and nibbled on her earlobe. Candace felt her legs grow weak with desire. Sliding his left hand up his t-shirt that she'd thrown on, Khalil grabbed her left breast and squeezed it gently, while firmly pushing her back with his right hand, forcing her to bend over the foot of the bed. Candace kneeled over and waited only seconds as he discarded his lounging pants. Her breath escaped her as he slowly entered her from behind. The thickness of him filled her walls completely and Candace's wetness became intensified.

He slid his hands over her ass, spreading the cheeks apart in order to plunge deeper inside of her. She could hear him grunting with each forceful, pleasurable thrust. Sensing that she could no longer stay on her feet, Khalil guided her onto the bed and turned her over. He lifted the shirt over her head and took both breasts, one in each hand as he effortlessly slid back into her. Candace wrapped her legs around his perfectly toned waist. His girth was incredible. She'd never had anyone so well endowed. Each thrust caught her by surprise. Wanting to dive deeper, Khalil spread her legs apart and pounded into the depths of her plushness.

"Damn, you feel so good, baby," he said in a raspy, seductive voice causing Candace to moan.

"You're so wet."

His speed increased and Candace reached out to touch his long, thin locks. She fingered them, and then ran her hand over his cheeks, his nose, and his lips. He took her fingers into his mouth and sucked them gently as he lifted her right leg over his shoulder.

"Yes," she cried out as he rhythmically stroked her insides with his manhood. The bed squeaked and rocked in unison to the sounds of their lovemaking. Khalil's eyes were closed as he pumped in and out of her. Candace tried to keep her focus on the look of satisfaction that showed on Khalil's face, but her own pleasure caused her lids to flutter as she continuously cried out.

"Yes, yes, yes."

Releasing her leg and leaning into her, Khalil expertly

suckled her right breast while riveting in a circular motion inside of her. Candace wrapped her arms around him and Khalil reciprocated. They clung to each other's misted bodies and created a rhythm all their own. They kissed with a hunger that could not be satisfied. Khalil was the first to approach release.

"Come with me, baby," he urged, trying to postpone his pleasure for the sake of hers.

He sucked on her bottom lip. Her moans filled his ear.

"Come with me," he whispered once more.

Before either of them could utter another exclaim of ecstasy, Khalil reached orgasm, causing him to ferociously pump into her once more. The intensity of the friction his movement created brought Candace right over the edge behind him. In the aftermath of their climax, the couple lie stuck to one another, still tight in their embrace, waiting for their breathing to become regulated.

Khalil kissed her forehead then the bridge of her nose before pulling himself from their embrace. With no more energy to spare, Candace simply rolled over and curled up into a ball. Khalil cuddled up behind her. Together they fell into a comfortable sleep that only good sex could create.

Jada

The grills were fired up. The balloons were blown up and adorned all the walls. The coolers were loaded with ice cold sodas and beer galore. DJ Johnny Dynamite was getting the growing crowd crunk as he played the popular hits of the season. The party was definitely on. It was Jordan's birthday and Jada had gone all out to make it a memorable celebration. To accommodate the large guest list and have room for the DJ, Jada's brother Antwan had been kind enough to offer the use of his four-bedroom home in Lithonia. Jada had spent half of the previous night and all morning cooking the side dishes. There were meatballs, macaroni and cheese, potato salad, spinach dip, baked beans, and collard greens. All prepared by Jada herself. She was thankful that 'Twan and Jordan's brother, Sean had volunteered to cook the meat. Ribs, chicken thighs and wings, hot dogs, hamburgers, and sausages filled the grills. The aroma of barbecue lingered in the air, tantalizing everybody's taste buds.

Jada was in the kitchen stirring up a fresh pitcher of lemonade. Jordan approached her from behind, wrapped his arms around her, and kissed her on her right cheek. Jada smiled and swatted his head with a nearby dish towel.

"Thank you for my party, baby," he said to her, stealing another kiss.

"Yeah, yeah," she joked, wiggling free from his embrace. "Go play with your company."

Jordan swatted her playfully on the ass and sauntered out of the kitchen. As he exited, Miranda and Alex entered.

"Hey, friend," Alex shrilled.

Jada smiled. "Ya'll having fun?"

"You got enough people up in here?" Miranda asked, glancing out the patio door to the backyard.

DJ Dynamite was bumping Outkast's Hey Ya and Alex was moving her body to the beat. Jada surveyed the backyard and the living room area. She laughed aloud.

"Shit. It is a lot of people."

Miranda opened a nearby cooler and retrieved a Zima.

"Where's Norris?" Jada asked her, putting the lemonade in the refrigerator.

Miranda shrugged and put the bottle up to her lips.

"Don't know," she answered.

"You don't know," Alex repeated. "How do you not know where your husband is?"

Miranda gulped the alcohol, draining the bottle, and rolled her eyes at the tall, dark beauty.

"He's my husband, not my child," she retorted. "It's not my place to keep up with him. You would know that if you had a husband."

"Whoa," Jada piped in, walking over to the two women, prepared to run interference.

"Dang, girl," Alex said, seemingly unfazed. "I was just

asking."

Miranda discarded her empty bottle and reached into the cooler for another. Without a word she opened the beverage and turned to leave the kitchen. Alex and Jada watched her retreat then looked at each other and shrugged.

"She's acting weird," Alex stated. "Maybe she's on her period."

Jada proceeded to wipe down the counter with a dish towel. She shook her head in response to Alex's assumption.

"Nah," she said. "She's obviously pissed the hell off with Norris and you struck a nerve."

Alex shrugged. "So, that ain't my fault. She shouldn't take it out on me."

"Now you know she didn't mean nothing by that," Jada advised her friend. "She's just venting...acting out. You know?"

"Uh-huh," Alex muttered. "Well, I hope that Stephanie doesn't act out on her."

"What?" Jada looked up and followed Alex's focused glare into the living room. In a corner by themselves, Stephanie's man Corey was whispering something into Miranda's ear as she blushed and continued to nurse her malt beverage. Jada bit her bottom lip lightly and her left eyebrow rose. *What the hell*, she thought.

"What do you think he's saying to her?" Alex asked.

Jada quickly glanced around, trying to spot Stephanie

through the thicket of guests. She finally saw her outside on the patio sharing a laugh with one of their former classmates. Jada threw the dish towel down on the counter and grabbed a fuzzy navel out of the cooler.

"Don't know," she answered Alex, who was quick on her heels. "But I'm 'bout to put a stop to it real quick."

Jada approached the couple who was oblivious to her heading their way. Corey was sucking on a piece of ice and Miranda was watching him intently.

"I'm dead serious," Corey was stating, slurping at the ice in his mouth.

"What's up ya'll?" Jada interrupted their private moment. Her eyes searched Miranda's face for some clue as to what the hell was going on. Miranda refused to give her eye contact.

"Sup, J," Corey replied nonchalantly. "Crunk party. Jordan enjoying his birthday?"

Jada gave him a heartless half-smile. "Of course. Corey, can you do me a favor and take this drink out to Steph?"

She handed him the bottle before he had time to protest.

"Thanks."

Corey lifted his head up at her, understanding that he was being dismissed. He looked over to the shorter girl.

"Aight then, Miranda," he stated before moving to leave

the group.

Miranda stepped forward to follow him.

"I think I'ma get another drink myself," she said.

"Naw, I think you've had enough drinks," Jada replied, lightly grabbing her friend's arm.

The women were silent as Corey walked out of earshot. Alex stood observing the scene from beside Jada with her arms crossed, shaking her head accusingly.

"What's wrong with ya'll?" Miranda questioned them. She looked down at Jada's hand resting upon her forearm. Jada quickly removed her hand and eyed her friend.

"It looked like Corey was over here macking you," Jada offered.

"And you looked like you were enjoying being macked," Alex added.

Miranda sucked her teeth and rolled her eyes at her girls.

"Puh-lease," she spat out. "He was over here ragging on Norris. Trust, there is nothing going on over here. Ain't nobody trying to get at Stephanie's lil' dope boy."

The girls turned to watch the interaction with Corey and Stephanie outside. His arm was around her and she was beaming up at him like he was a prince. Jada shook her head.

"I don't like him," she stated. "I don't like him at all."

"Well, Stephanie is obviously crazy in love with him so he must be doing something right," Alex reasoned.

Jada crossed her arms and shook her head.

"Uh-huh," she said. "He's full of shit. Something ain't right."

Miranda remained silent, not voicing any opinion on the matter. Alex simply shrugged. Jada had an uneasy feeling in her stomach, something that told her that the presence of Corey in their lives could mean trouble for the girls. *Could it be his street hustle?* Jada thought. They all knew that Corey was the neighborhood weed man. The girls didn't condone Corey's hustle and many times warned Stephanie against having a relationship with him. But, once Steph became pregnant with Damien, all of their warnings flew out of the window. Steph was too far gone into her emotions and obsession with the minor league thug. No one wanted to waste their breath. Jada just frequently prayed that her friend would find a better man, someone worthy of her time and love.

"Stop it."

Jordan was behind her, tweeking her butt. She turned around to face him with a questioning look. She couldn't feign innocence with Jordan. She knew from his look that he'd seen her surveying the interaction between Steph and Corey with her usual look of disdain.

"It's a party," Jordan reminded her. "Have fun."

Jada kissed him dead on the lips and plucked at this wide nose.

"Happy birthday, baby," she said to him.

Jordan grinned. "Thanks to you it is."

Miranda

The Nokia ring sounded. Miranda scrambled to find her cell nestled inside of the bedcovers. Finding it near the pillows, she raised her eyebrow upon seeing the name and number on the caller id. She quickly glanced at the clock. 1:30 a.m. Was he serious? She pressed the green talk button.

"Hello?"

"What up? You still want to fall through?"

"It's late..."

"I told you it would be," he cut her off. "I can get at you some other time. I know you don't want ya' man to be tripping."

Miranda sucked her teeth and descended from her bed, ready to throw on some decent clothes.

"Norris isn't home so don't be worrying about him."

"Yeah so, call me when you're in your ride and I'll give you directions."

"Okay."

"And Miranda, don't be telling everything you know to ya' girls and shit. Some shit you keep to yourself."

"Do you think I'm stupid or something?" she asked him, grabbing a nearby pair of jeans.

"Just saying, boo."

"Uh-huh...I'll call you back in ten minutes."

"Bet."

The call was disconnected. As she quickly dressed herself, Miranda tried not to think of the potential damage she was about to cause herself. She only knew that she desperately needed something to help her escape mentally and emotionally from Norris and the hurt he inflicted upon her. Thinking about it she chuckled at the irony. How funny was it that the one thing that started all of their troubles was the one outlet Miranda decided to turn to as a way of avoiding their issues.

Alex

Things were starting to look up. Alex had secured a sales position at a downtown Decatur boutique and was awaiting the start of classes at AIU where she would be taking up fashion design. Being on the track to her dream career, Alex was feeling pretty good. It also helped that she'd met a pretty decent guy. Mario Johnson was a 26 year old admissions representative at Dekalb Area Technical College. When she'd first met him, he was an admissions rep for AIU. Mario had his own apartment in Clarkston, drove a clean cream-colored PT Cruiser, and was as fine as they come. Alex had been drawn to his sense of style. Mario was GQ all the way, donning a blue button down dress shirt with a white collar and white cuffs with blue slacks and blue Stacy Adams dress shoes. His hair was cut low with waves so neat and well groomed that Alex couldn't imagine him any other way. His face was devoid of any facial hair and the chocolatiness of his skin itself turned her on. The man was very well put together and always smelled so manly with his mixture of Sean John cologne and Right Guard deodorant.

Mario had enrolled Alex into AIU. Shortly thereafter, he quit AIU and took his current position at Dekalb Area Tech. It had surprised Alex to hear from him after he quit AIU. She was flattered that he had been so attracted to her that he made a point to take down her number before leaving the college. For their first date he took her to the movies and dinner. Not once during the course of the evening did he try to so much as kiss her. At first she wasn't sure if he was interested in her, but those misgivings quickly vanished one they'd had a second, a third, and a fourth date.

Tonight would make date five. Alex wanted to do something special for him given how sweet Mario had been to her within the last few weeks. With Kacey spending the weekend with her boyfriend, Alex had the apartment to herself. She planned to have a simple, candle-lit dinner alone with Mario. Never mind the fact that Alex couldn't cook. This obstacle was easily overcome by purchasing take-out from the neighborhood soul food restaurant, This Is It. Ever the good friend, Clay willingly drove her to the restaurant and back home. Then he hung around as Alex cleaned her bedroom and prepared for her date.

"You expecting to get laid?" he said, rather than asked, tossing a pink teddy bear into the air repetitiously.

Alex was stunned by his inquiry and threw him a quizzical look as she tied a scarf around her roller-filled head. Clay caught her look and laughed.

"I'm just saying. You cleaning up your room like you're expecting someone to see it. You never clean it when I come over."

"Shut up," Alex retorted.

"It's true."

"So...You ain't nobody. Plus you already know how junky I can get so why I gotta try to impress you?"

Alex missed the hurt expression that crossed his face yet quickly vanished. He threw the teddy bear at her, hitting the back of her head.

"Hey!"

"So the answer to my original question is yes," he said, leaning back against Alex's headboard.

"I didn't say that," Alex responded, tossing the bear back at him.

"Yeah…Ok."

Alex walked over to her friend and poked his nose.

"Why do you care so much anyway?"

Clay smiled at her. "I don't."

Alex rolled her eyes and retrieved some underwear from her dresser drawer.

"Why are you still here?"

"You want me to leave?" he asked sitting up.

"If you're going to be rude, meanie."

Clay laughed at her and leaned back once more.

"That wasn't mean, cry baby. If you fuck him, you fuck him."

"Agh!! Is that all you're thinking about?"

"That's all he's going to be thinking about. Trust me."

Alex headed towards the door shaking her head.

"It's so not going down," she told her friend as she made her exit.

She headed to the bathroom and started up the shower. Only pushing the door up slightly, she discarded her clothes and stepped into the warmth of the water. Her nostrils filled with the scent of grapefruit as she began to lather herself with Dove body wash. *Clay is tripping,* Alex thought to herself. Mario had been a perfect gentleman and she had no reason to expect him to behave any differently tonight. Sure, she was setting a very intimate mood. Sure, she was planning on wearing a very revealing slip dress. Sure, she secretly wished he would hold her tighter and longer whenever he hugged her. But all of that was irrelevant. *Right?*

Alex closed her eyes and let the water cascade down her back. Her sexual experiences were very limited and she was a little nervous of the prospect of going there with Mario. Mainly, she feared disappointing him. As fine as he was, Alex knew that he must be getting offers from women left and right. How could she compare to the older, more experienced women he'd sexed?

"You gonna stay in here forever?"

Alex blinked profusely and turned her head to the sound of his voice. Stunned, she stuck her head out of the shower curtain. Clay sat smiling back at her, perched atop the toilet seat, his figure enveloped by the steam from the shower.

"That's a little rude, you know," she told him, ducking back into the shower.

"You left the door open. Sheesh. What? Are you afraid I'll see your goodies?"

Alex snickered behind the curtain.

"Anyway, I'm about to bounce and let you get ready for ole' boy."

Alex quickly rinsed off, turned off the water, and reached for her towel, which she thought she'd hung over the shower rod. She sucked her teeth and looked up to see his hand holding the pink terry cloth towel. She grabbed it, wrapped it around her body, and pulled back the curtain. There he stood, Clayton Paul, her long-time friend turned hottie, staring her dead in the eyes at such a vulnerable moment.

"Thank you," she said softly, barely able to utter the words.

Alex was unsure of what she was feeling. Why did looking at Clay give her stomach butterflies? He just stood there almost as if he was expecting her to do or say something. And when the expected failed to occur, he lowered his eyes and stepped backwards.

"I'll get at you tomorrow," he said as she stepped out of the tub.

Alex nodded. "Okay, friend...Thanks for coming over."

"Yep."

He quickly turned from her and left the bathroom. Alex listened as he made his way through the apartment and let himself out the front door. She hadn't realized that she'd been holding her breath. The awkwardness of the moment lingered with her. She was unsure of what the encounter meant. Perhaps Clay wanted to tell her something, but just couldn't find the words. That would explain his stares and lost expression. Hurriedly, Alex focused on getting herself dressed and ready for her night with Mario.

Candace

For the next few weeks, Candace and Khalil's relationship became hot and heavy. At any and every opportune moment the two of them were together. Candace never questioned Khalil as to where Sheila was and Khalil never expressed an interest in Quincy's existence. Khalil sent her flowers at work for no apparent reason, continued to buy her lunch on a daily basis, and escorted her to various upscale restaurants in Midtown on the weekends. Khalil made her feel so happy and special that Candace almost lost sense of the fact that she was only borrowing this man and his affection.

She was becoming so involved that she barely had time to chill with the girls. Her absence was obviously noticed given the many messages and texts she'd been receiving. So, when Stephanie asked her to go to lunch on a Saturday, she felt obligated to attend. It wouldn't do any good to piss off the girls any more than she already had.

The duo met at the O'Charley's on Northlake Parkway. Stephanie had requested Chilli's but Candace was not in the mood for the baby back ribs. Settled in a corner booth and munching on spinach dip, Candace was trying to focus on their cordial conversation. In the back of her mind she was really awaiting the text she knew would soon come. She told Khalil to get at her during the early afternoon so they could hook up for a movie. She was anxious to see him again, especially after the way he'd put it on her the night before.

"There's something I have to tell you," Stephanie was saying.

Candace shook her head free of her sensual memories

and focused on her friend.

"Huh?"

"There's something I gotta tell you...And I haven't told Jada or Alex because both of them would just be disappointed."

"What's wrong?" Candace became concerned. Stephanie's eyes were starting to well up and she began to assume the worse.

Candace reached out and touched her hand softly.

"What is it, Steph? Whatever it is, we can work through it together."

"I'm pregnant," Stephanie whispered. "I'm pregnant again."

"By Corey?"

Stephanie shot Candace a hurt look.

"Of course by Corey," she snapped. "What the hell kind of question is that?"

"I was just asking. So how far along are you?"

"Six weeks. Six fuckin' weeks."

"Does he know?"

Stephanie shook her head and looked away.

"He's barely helping with Damien...what's he going to say or do if I tell him I'm expecting another kid? You're the first person I've told."

Candace picked up a chip and nibbled at it in contemplation.

"Why do you think that Jada and Alex would be disappointed?"

"You know them. Alex is the last adult virgin and Jada is just 'Ms. Goodie-goodie'...they wouldn't understand."

"Shit happens," Candace stated bluntly. "And while I don't necessarily condone your relationship with Corey's ass either, I don't think you should feel like any of us would shun you for this."

Candace leaned forward and touched Stephanie's hand once more.

"We love you girlie and the girls will always have your back."

Stephanie gave her a weak smile and nodded.

"I know. I just needed an empathic ear right now. I know I can count on all of my girls."

They shared a smile and focused their attention on the entrees being placed before them. Neither spoke for several moments, each caught up in their own thoughts and their meals. Stephanie was busy wondering how she was going to tell her mother she was knocked up again. Candace was becoming irritated because her phone had yet to vibrate.

"So, what are you going to do?" Candace asked

Stephanie.

Stephanie shrugged. "I'm going to leave my mom's house for one thing. She loves Damien, but she was not pleased with me when I first told her about him."

"Can you afford your own place?"

"Maybe somewhere, but nowhere decent, you know what I mean?"

Candace nodded.

"I'll figure something out," Stephanie said with feigned confidence.

"That which doesn't kill us makes us stronger," Candace offered.

Stephanie simply nodded and polished off her pasta. Candace silently said a quick prayer for her girl and was guiltily thankful that she wasn't in Steph's shoes. It had never been a goal of Candace's to have children. She didn't feel like she possessed any maternal instincts. She saw her life filled with traveling, a glamorous legal career, and shopping. Crying babies, soiled diapers, and childhood illnesses just didn't fit into her plan.

After lunch, the girls hugged, said their goodbyes, and rode off in their respective cars. As Candace headed towards 285, she pulled out her cell and dialed a familiar number. She was surprised when her call was sent straight to voicemail. Too pissed to leave a message, she simply clicked the phone shut and drove home to her husband.

Quincy was sitting on the couch in his favorite spot with his cordless Play Station controller playing Madden when she walked in. Her eyes fell upon the dishes resting in the sink as she walked through the kitchen and into the living room. It was so typical of him to ignore the necessary housework and sit around playing all afternoon. Candace held her tongue though, not wanting to spark an argument. She was grateful that he'd finally gotten a new job. His position with UPS didn't pay exactly as much as his Bell South gig, but income was income.

"What's up?" he asked her as she sat beside him on the sofa.

"Nothing."

"Where you been?"

"Since when have you taken an interest in where I go and what I do?"

Quincy shot her a look and sucked his teeth. Candace sat silent for a moment, watching the football game on the screen.

"I had lunch with Stephanie," she finally said.

"You didn't invite me."

"Didn't know you wanted to go."

Quincy playfully pushed her leg and Candace giggled. He paused the game and put his arm around her. Licking her left ear, he whispered to her.

"I'm gon tell you where I wanna go."

Candace raised an eyebrow.

"Where's that?"

"Trapeze."

Candace crinkled her nose and cocked her head to the side, trying to understand where the conversation was going. She'd heard of the popular adult club, but knew of no one that had actually gone. She looked at her husband in askance.

"Don't be looking like you not interested," he teased her. "You know you wanna go."

"Why you want to go there?" she questioned.

"To spice shit up," he said earnestly. "Ain't nothing wrong with that is it?"

Candace considered it. She'd be lying if she said she wasn't at least curious as to what went on in the private club. Since the loss of his Bell South job, there had been a lack of romance and affection between herself and Quincy. She looked at her husband. He was no Khalil and there was little sexual attraction there. Deep down, Candace wanted to make her marriage work, if for no other reason than to save face with her parents. Perhaps this adventure would add a little spice to their relationship.

"Man, imagine all the butt-naked chicks walking around that place" Quincy thought aloud, throwing his head back on the sofa in bewilderment.

He nudged her. "You might see something you like."

Candace rolled her eyes and dismissed the idea. Quincy's real intentions were becoming evident to her.

"Ain't nobody trying to have no threesome," she said, shooting down his hopes and dreams.

Quincy laughed and grabbed her playfully, trying to nibble at the side of her neck. He knew that was her spot.

"Aww, come on. Don't act like that," he urged her. "It ain't about that."

Candace tried to free herself from his embrace but Quincy's hold was firm. She maneuvered her neck, trying to avoid contact with his tongue. She was in no mood for his sexual advances.

"Stop, Q," she pleaded, elbowing him in his gut. "Quit it."

Quincy started tickling her until she erupted in fits of laughter. Trying to squirm away from him, Candace ended up toppled onto the floor. Quincy towered over her, tickling away and showing no mercy.

"O...k..." she relented breathlessly. "O...k...k..k..We can go..."

Quincy ceased in his torture and smiled wickedly at his wife.

"When?"

Candace sat upright on the floor and struggled to even out her breathing.

"Let's look it up online first to see how much it costs to get in."

Quincy jumped up from the floor and moved towards the stairs.

"Where you going?" she called after him.

"To check it out now."

Candace rose from the floor and followed her eager spouse up the stairs and to their guestroom where the computer was sat up. Quincy was already clicking on the big E.

"Damn, you act like you want to go right this minute," Candace stated, sitting on the bed next to the desk.

Quincy winked at her. "No time like the present."

Candace sucked her teeth as she watched Quincy do a Yahoo search for the club. Finding it listed, Quincy clicked on the link and bypassed the intro page. Taking a look at the admission prices, Quincy sucked in his breath.

"What?" Candace asked, leaning in closer to take a look at the screen.

"Daaammmn….This shit costs a grip for a dude," Quincy stated. "Couples and single men cost the most. Single chicks have it made."

Quincy was shaking his head and Candace understood his meaning. Their finances were tight these days due to their recent setback. Lavish spending was not feasible and judging by Quincy's face and the price list waving on the screen to them,

Candace knew that they would not be making a trip to Trapeze any time soon. Candace stood up and placed her arms around Quincy's neck.

"Well, we can do something else," she said sweetly.

"What's that?"

"We can join a website and meet other couples that might wanna hook up or something."

Quincy turned around and looked at his wife. "A swinger's website?"

Candace smiled devilishly. "It's like bringing Trapeze to us."

Quincy began clicking the keyboard once more.

"You ain't said nothing but a word, boo," he said. "Nothing but a word."

Stephanie

She wasn't sure what she was going to say. She hadn't even alerted him that anything was going on when she'd previously called to say that she was coming over. Grateful that he hadn't acted like an ass when she called, Stephanie was feeling a little confident that there wouldn't be a big scene between the two of them. Taking a deep breath, Stephanie took the familiar path to Corey's apartment and raised her fist to knock on the door. In mid-knock, she paused her fist in the air, opened her palm and rested it against the heavy door. Her left hand grabbed at her stomach as a wave of nausea hit her. Or was it her nerves? Or perhaps it was both.

What am I doing? she asked herself. *What the hell am I doing having another baby with a man that acts like he can't even stand me half of the time?* She contemplated turning around and going home. But, determined to stand her ground and not be a punk, she raised her hand again and knocked on her boyfriend's door. She knocked twice before Corey answered.

"What up," he greeted her, opening the door and then quickly walking away towards the kitchen.

Stephanie entered the living room and closed the door behind her. She started to follow him into the kitchen but something began to nag at her senses. Stephanie just wasn't sure what it was. Looking around, surveying the room for any sign of something being amidst, Stephanie sat down on the comfortable sofa. Corey entered the room drinking a Heinken and sat next to her.

"What up?" he repeated.

Stephanie looked up at her longtime boyfriend and reached up to hug him. Corey put one arm around her and gave her a half hug in return. Snuggled up to him, Stephanie's senses began to flare up once more. She pulled her head back slightly, making her nose even with his neck. *Uh-huh,* she thought to herself, recognizing a familiar scent lingering on him that was certainly not a masculine cologne.

Stephanie pulled away from him and leaned back against the couch.

"What you been up to?" she asked him, knowing that he wouldn't admit anything.

Corey shrugged. "Nada. Handling business...making some money. What's good?"

"I'm pregnant."

She just blurted it out in an effort to get it over with. She stared at her hands, waiting for the vulgarities to pour from Corey's mouth. Instead all she got was laughter. Corey was cracking up as if she'd told a world class joke.

"Stop playing," he managed to say.

"I'm not playing," she said curtly. "And I wish you'd stop laughing at me."

Corey looked over at her and searched her face for the truth.

"Oh shit," he said. "For real?"

Stephanie wasn't sure if that was a smile she saw forming at the corner of his lips.

"For real." She stared at him. "What you thinking?"

Corey sat his beer on the carpet and rubbed his hands together.

"Shiittttt.....I hope it's a girl this time."

Stephanie leaned towards him and rubbed his head.

"You're not mad?"

He considered her question before pulling the petite woman towards him in a bear hug.

"Naw, I ain't mad. Shit, it takes two and I'm a man. Plus I needa start taking better care of my shorty and my girl....I'm on top of my game deez days baby so money ain't shit."

Stephanie knew better than to inquire about Corey's 'game'. Instead, she decided to push further to see if today was really her lucky day.

"I haven't told my mom yet. You know she's going to be pissed. I think she's gon' put us out."

Corey sighed. Stephanie felt his body tense up as her unasked question sunk into his mind.

"Tell you what," he said, kissing her forehead. "Let's gon' and try to do this family thing. You and D can move in here and we'll see 'bout getting a bigger place before the baby's born."

Stephanie pulled away from him and stared at the dark brother in disbelief. She had waited a long time for Corey to offer to move her in and the day had finally come. Ecstatic about this pending change in their relationship, Stephanie consciously decided to overlook her suspicion regarding Corey's activities prior to her arrival and that hint of perfume resting on his neck. Now that they would be living together Stephanie would no longer have to worry about Corey and his little indiscretions. In her mind, they were one step closer to getting married and being a real family.

"You sure about this?" she asked him for clarity.

"Yeah, ma. I'm sure."

Stephanie crawled up on top of him and began to kiss his lips, cheeks, nose, and forehead. Corey's hands found their way underneath her shirt.

"Thank you, baby. Thank you," she cooed in his ear as he began to ease her jeans down.

"You wanna thank me?" he asked.

"Mmmhmmm."

He released himself from his joggers, exposing his erection.

"Go 'head and thank me then."

Stephanie wasn't really in the mood for sexual activity. But, feeling it best to play it cool and keep him happy, Stephanie raised her hips to guide him into her all the while trying not to think of where his dick had been before she arrived.

Miranda

Norris strolled into the bedroom apparently oblivious to the stench in the room. Miranda ignored his presence, lying peacefully on their bed reading the new Star magazine. Her husband sat on the edge of the bed and looked at her as if he was waiting for her to acknowledge him. Miranda said nothing. As she turned a page of her magazine, Norris reached over and grabbed the periodical from her.

"What the fuck?" she questioned, finally addressing the man.

"Yeah, what the fuck," he repeated after her. "You act like you ain't even notice me sitting here."

Not interested in his fake need for attention, Miranda reached for her magazine. Norris snatched it back out of her reach.

"What do you want me to say, Norris?" she asked him. "Welcome home sweetie? I missed you? You want me to lie to you?"

Norris threw the magazine at her, the paper hitting her in the face. She grabbed it and tried to focus her attention back to the story about Brittany Spears.

"Any other nigga goes home to his wife, he gets a fuckin' hug and kiss and some dinner," Norris spat out. "I don't get shit from you."

"You don't give shit either," Miranda muttered, not realizing that she'd vocalized the thought.

"What did you say?" Norris asked her. He crawled up on the bed, snatched the paper away once more, and held Miranda's neck against the headboard with one hand.

"What the fuck did you say?"

Miranda shook her head, eyes staring blankly at Norris. She was a little numb to the pressure he was applying to her neck and simply sat there staring at him as his rage grew.

"Is it too much to ask for my *wife* to cook dinner for a change? To be affectionate?"

He shook her a little yet Miranda still failed to respond to his ranting. For a second, they sat staring into each other's eyes, each trying to figure out what the other was thinking. Bored with her being nonresponsive, Norris released his grip and walked out of the room. Miranda felt her neck and shook her head from side to side. She was so over him bullying her. Determined to talk to him in what she wanted to be a civilized manner, Miranda rose from the bed and followed Norris into the kitchen.

He was reaching for a can of salmon in the pantry when she entered. Thinking it would be a sign of peace, she retrieved an egg, onion, and bell pepper from the refrigerator. As she placed the items on the counter, Norris lightly shoved her out of the way.

"I don't need your help," he told her. "A nigga nearly gotta beg you to fix him some food. I don't need that shit. I can take care of myself. I don't need your sorry ass."

"My sorry ass?" she asked in disbelief, anger filling her. "Are you kidding me, Norris? I have always taken care of you and our home. How you gonna act like that's not true?"

"It hasn't been true lately, has it?" he countered, using the electric can opener to open the salmon.

Miranda let the hum of the machine calm her down. The noise gave her a chance to think of what she would say next. The objective was not to argue or fight. To achieve this, she knew she had to set the tone verses setting Norris off. She watched Norris pour the fish mush into a bowl. Grabbing a knife from the nearby cutting block and the cutting board, Miranda set up an area to dice the onion.

"I just want to help, Norris," she said, beginning to chop the vegetable into tiny pieces. "I'm sorry. I didn't mean to upset you. I just want to help you with dinner and try to see what we can do to make things better."

Norris chuckled. "You just want to help Norris, huh?"

Miranda ignored his sarcasm and kept on chopping and talking.

"Things aren't right between us, Norris...anybody can see that. We got married for a reason and I think that if we really tried to make it work...it could."

Norris loudly banged a pot down onto the stove top, the water in it sloshing over. Miranda jumped a little, but did not look up at her husband. Still chopping, she continued on with her speech.

"I think you love me, Norris...and I love you, you know...we just need to...I don't know. Maybe we can go to counseling or something to..."

"Shut up!" Norris demanded, cutting her off. "What the fuck is wrong with you? Have you been watching Oprah or something?"

Miranda shook her head and reached for the bell pepper.

"I'm just trying to preserve our marriage. That's all."

Norris poured white rice into the boiling pot, his eyes glued to his frantically chopping wife.

"Preserve our marriage, huh? What do you think is wrong with us, M? Let me guess... you think I'm a bad husband?"

"I didn't say that," she protested. "It's not just you. It's me too."

"Damn right it's you too," he agreed, walking up closely behind her. "It's you that always looks at me like I'm a fuckin' failure every time I have a setback. It's you that thinks you're better than me with your two fuckin' jobs like I can't manage to take care of my family."

Miranda stopped cutting. "Nobody called you a failure. I have only tried to be a good wife...to be helpful."

"You are helpful in making a nigga feel like he ain't shit," he whispered into her ear. "You think I don't know that you talk shit about me to your phony ass girls and to your parents? Your parents don't even respect me as a man because of YOU and your bright idea for us to move in with them like some lil' ass kids."

Knife firmly in hand and tired of listening to her husband talk down to her like she was the root of all their problems, Miranda spun around quickly, aiming at his dick.

"I am so fuckin' tired of you talking to me like I ain't shit," she told him.

Norris began backing up from her, but Miranda steadily approached, the sharp knife resting dangerously close to his member.

"Put that fuckin' shit down, man...Stop playing," Norris said weakly.

"Fuck you, Norris," she responded, having backed him up against the counter. "Fuck you, fuck you, fuck you. I am so tired of the way you walk around here acting like you are the only one suffering. You think I *wanted* to live with my parents? HELL NO! But I swallowed my own pride and asked them for the favor for *us*! For us, Norris....Just 'til we could do better."

"I didn't ask you to do that shit."

"You didn't have to! You see, that's the kind of shit you do when you love someone...when you're committed to your relationship. You do whatever you gotta do to keep that shit intact and that's what I did....or at least that's what I was trying to do."

"So what you trying to prove now by holding a fuckin' knife to my balls?

Miranda stared at him in disbelief that he had the audacity to still be talking shit to her as she stood before him, threatening his manhood. They stood silent, squaring off and willing the other to say something.

"I've been a good wife to you, Norris," Miranda stated. "I've been faithful, supportive, and caring...I am not your enemy, Norris. I'm your partner, your wife. I'm your fuckin' wife!"

Norris blinked at her and said nothing. Miranda lifted the knife to his neck and she saw him flinch slightly. It felt good to be in control for a change. Touching the knife lightly upon his skin, she stared directly into his eyes.

"I've been a good wife, Norris," she said slowly, for effect. "But if you ever put your hands on me again, I swear that I will fuckin' kill you. I will slice your shit from here to there..." dragging the knife across his neck. "..should you ever, ever, ever put your fuckin' hands on me again. Do you understand?"

Norris gave her a sinister half-smile.

"Fuck you, bitch," he said slowly before quickly shoving the woman backwards.

Norris tried to rush her and extract the knife from her hand, but Miranda's movements were so frantic and swift, that he was unsuccessful. In their struggle, Miranda managed to slice her husband across his left cheek. Surprised at the sting of the cut, Norris reached up to touch his face. Blood dripped from his fingers. Miranda watched his movements, shocked at herself for having actually wounded him. The anger in his eyes told her that she had better do something quickly. Turning to run from the room, Miranda was not quick enough. Norris was fast on her heels, pulling her left leg and causing her to hit the floor. She lost her grip on the knife and Norris kicked it away before she could reach for it.

He turned her over and Miranda struggled to free herself from his grasp. She was unsuccessful. He pulled her glasses off her face and she began to protest. Ignoring her, Norris threw the glass to the floor and stepped on them.

"Nooo....Norris, no!" she hollered, knowing that she could barely see without the glasses.

"You cut me!" he spat out at her. "You fuckin' cut me!"

He kicked her swiftly in her right side once, twice, three times. Miranda whimpered. Her hands flailed this way and that, trying to grab his leg to get him to stop. But he wouldn't. Norris kept kicking and kicking in the same tender spot over and over. Miranda kept trying to scramble from his blows and raise herself from the floor. Each time, Norris simply knocked her right back down.

"Stupid bitch," he yelled at her. "Trying to preserve our marriage? Preserve this shit!"

Norris kicked her extremely hard to let his last blow have a lasting effect. Miranda screamed out in pain. Not only was her side aching from the abuse, but a horrid cramping was beginning to overcome her abdomen. She was doubled over in pain. She held her left hand up in surrender, pleading with Norris to leave her alone.

"I hope you lay there and bleed to death," he told her, touching his face again, once more astonished by the fact that she cut him.

Bleed to death. Miranda concentrated on his last words. Was she bleeding? She was unaware if she was. Only the cramping and aching of her side could she focus on. Through her blurred vision she watched the figure of Norris exit the kitchen. She could hear him let himself out of the apartment. Sore, bruised, and in excruciating pain, she struggled to lean over to feel around underneath her. Sure enough, her lounging pants were damp. Apparently she was bleeding. As the realization hit her, so did a forceful tear through her abdomen down to her lower stomach. Miranda experienced a pulling feeling in her lower abdomen.

"Agggghhhh," she screamed out, overcome by the pain. "Help me!!!! Pleaseeeee. Somebody...."

She laid her head back on the linoleum floor, feeling defeated. No one was going to hear her. Norris had literally left her there to bleed to death. Just as she was beginning to lose consciousness, Miranda heard a voice.

"Hello? Ma'am?"

Was she hallucinating? The voice was an unfamiliar female voice. *Where's it coming from?* she wondered. Miranda continued to lay on the floor cradling her bruised side and trying not to pass out before she could see who it was that was calling out to her.

"Hello...oh my god!"

A woman was beside her, touching her face and sounding completely taken aback.

"Why did you let him do this to you?" she was asking. "Oh my god. Howard!!!! Howard!!!!"

The woman was calling out to an accomplice. Miranda was couldn't make out who they were, standing over her and calling 911. The woman asked her a series of questions that she couldn't answer because she was gradually fading away. Just as sirens could be heard in the distance, Miranda heard the woman speak to her male partner.

"What kind of man does shit like this?"

This was the last thing she heard before slipping into the darkness

Jada

Jada stood in a state of shock. She knew that things weren't good between them, but she had no idea that things were this bad. The room was cold and sterile, the sounds of the many machines beeping and clicking. Miranda was lying still on the bed, cords hanging from her all over. They'd just wheeled her in from surgery, repairing the broken ribs that her husband had caused her. Miranda was still sleep from the anesthesia. Watching the frail woman, all bandaged up and laid out, Jada had to fight back her tears. *Why the hell did you stay with him*, Jada wondered of her friend. Anyone would be a fool to believe that this was the first time Norris had abused her. Jada was just grateful that he hadn't succeeded in killing her. Her thoughts were interrupted by the creak of the room door. A tall, slender woman and a muscular man she'd never met entered the room.

"Hi," the woman said softly. "I'm Tasha and this is my boyfriend Howard. We're her neighbors."

Jada sighed and reached out to shake the pretty woman's hand. The man also held his out and Jada obligingly shook it too.

"I'm Jada, one of her best friends," Jada said. "She has me listed as her emergency contact on something in her purse."

"It's good to know that she has some friends that love her," Tasha said solemnly. "Because her husband obviously doesn't."

"Tasha," Howard said warningly.

"I'm just saying…"

"It's okay," Jada offered. "You can be candid with me. The girls knew that she was having marital problems, but this…."

Jada drifted off and looked at her battered friend. It was all so unbelievable.

"This was totally unexpected."

Tasha and Howard shared a look that Jada didn't miss. The man grabbed the woman's hand as she looked Jada squarely in the eyes.

"Or perhaps not?" Jada asked, more so than said.

"Look, Jada," Tasha started. "Since you are one of her best friends, I want to encourage you to um…well, encourage her to leave that asshole. This isn't their first altercation. We hear them arguing all the time…"

"Everybody argues," Jada interjected.

"Yeah, but everybody doesn't get their ass kicked on a regular basis. There's arguing and then there's abuse. And your girl is constantly being abused."

"If you thought he was hurting her, why didn't you ever call the police?"

"We like to mind our own business," Howard answered.

"Mind your own business?" Jada was becoming upset with the couple. "You don't think that if you'd done something before that maybe all of this could have been avoided?"

"With all due respect, ma'am, this incident isn't because of our negligence. Remember that your girl decided to stick around and put up with this shit. At any time she could've said enough was enough, but she didn't."

"We went over to her place this time because we could hear her calling for help," Tasha stated. "I was scared that he'd nearly killed her this time....I guess I was right."

Jada nodded her head, coming to terms with all they had just told her. They were right. It wasn't their fault that Miranda was in this predicament. But, still Jada wished that the good neighbors had had the insight to call the police during prior incidents. Maybe Norris could have been arrested and Miranda wouldn't be lying in this hospital all broken up.

"Thank you," Jada said softly. "Thank you for helping her."

Tasha nodded. "I just hope that she is smart enough to go ahead and leave him. She was bleeding so profusely, I was afraid that she really would die."

Jada took a deep breath, tears trailing from her eyes despite her fight to hold them in.

"He caused her to have a miscarriage," she whispered. "Apparently she was six weeks pregnant."

Tasha gasped and quickly moved to hug Jada. The two embraced in silence before Tasha pulled away and extended her apologies for Miranda's loss. Shortly after, the couple left Jada to cry over Miranda in silence and private. Sitting in the chair next to her friend's bed, she said a silent prayer for the girl mirroring the hopes of Tasha, that Miranda would have the right mind to leave Norris' trifling ass.

Alex

The relationship was going smoothly. Alex and Mario were getting closer and enjoying each other's company more frequently. Unfortunately, Alex hadn't gotten up the nerve to seal the deal. But, she was glad to see that he was still interested in her nonetheless. Mario would call several times a day just to say hi and send text messages to let her know that he was thinking about her. Alex never felt more special. Between school, work, and her budding relationship, Alex's time was consumed. She hadn't spent much time hanging out with the girls or chilling with Clay. Clay was beginning to notice her absence.

Catching her just as she was on her way home from school, Clay called Alex's cell with attitude lacing his voice.

"Oh shit, she's alive," he commented upon her

answering the phone.

Alex, crossing the street on East College Ave, sucked her teeth and rolled her eyes.

"Whatever. What's up?"

"What's up is that I haven't heard from you in a minute. Ya' boy got you going like that?"

"Don't be jealous," Alex joked.

Clay didn't respond.

"What are you doing?"

"Getting dressed."

"Where you going?"

"To the movies."

Alex smiled. "Want me to come with?"

Clay laughed at her self-given invitation. "Not unless you mind being the odd ball."

"What's that 'pose to mean?"

"I have a date."

Alex made a right into her apartment complex and ascended the sidewalk to her apartment. She was surprised to hear the Clay had plans.

"Who you going out with?"

"Nobody you know. But aye, I just wanted to try and get at you since you don't know how to return calls."

"K. You can come over when you get done with your date if you want to. I'll be here."

Clay made a funny sound before responding. "Yeah, I'll keep that in mind. Lata."

The call was disconnected. Alex let herself into her apartment, throwing her book bag on the floor, and slamming the door behind her. Mario was hanging out with his boys for the night and Alex wasn't sure what was up with her girls. Her Friday night was starting to look a little bit bleak.

Alex sauntered into the kitchen and surveyed the contents of the refrigerator. Settling on left over spaghetti, she fixed herself a plate, placed it in the microwave, and went off to her room to get comfortable. As she sat on the bed to remove her shoes, Alex pulled out her cell and dialed a familiar number. There were three rings before she answered.

"What's up stranger?" Jada's voice boomed.

Alex removed her jeans and smiled. "Hey girl. What's poppin?"

"Nothing honeychild. I'm waiting on Jordan."

"Ya'll going out?" Alex asked with a twinge of disappointment in her voice.

"Nope. We're gonna make it a blockbuster night. I'm tired girl. It's been a long week."

"Oh yeah?"

"What you doing at home? I'm surprised you don't have a date."

Alex pulled on a pair of shorts from a nearby drawer and laid back on her bed, missing the ding of the microwave.

"Mario's having boys' night. Kacey ain't here…"

"Kacey ain't ever there. You sure you even have a roommate?"

Alex laughed. "I'm sure she's paying her half of the rent. But girl, get this…Clay has a date."

"Your boy? What? Is that unusual?"

Alex turned over on her side and considered Jada's question.

"I mean…I'm just use to being able to hang out with him when I want to."

Jada made a tsk sound through the phone. "That sounds a lil' bit selfish, girl."

"Nuh-uh…I'm a princess and…"

"Oh, girl please. I gotta go, with all that princess shit. Look, all us girls needa get together real soon. So much has been going on. I'll organize something. K?"

Alex sat up on the bed, ready to end the call.

"Alright. Bye girl."

Clicking the phone shut, Alex got up and headed to the kitchen. She checked the temperature of the food and decided it was fine for her. Sitting at the kitchen counter eating, she thought about Clay. She wondered what movie he'd gone to see and what the chick was like that he was with. Alex reconsidered Jada's statement that she was selfish for wanting Clay at her disposal.

That's just the nature of our relationship, she reasoned with herself. *Clay is always there when I need him.* Having resolved that in her mind, she polished off her dinner and returned to her room. Settling into bed, she turned on her television, prepared to watch TV Land reruns until she fell asleep. In the back of her mind, she was sure that Clay would show up later in the night.

At some point, she drifted off and was startled by the ringing of her phone. Regaining consciousness, she fumbled around in the bedcovers looking for the hot pink phone. Not wanting to miss the call, she hurriedly flipped it open and gave a sheepish hello.

"You sleeping?" It was Clay.

Alex rubbed her eyes and yawned. "I was. What's up?"

"I'm down the street. Thought I'd see if you were still up. I got Krispy Kremes."

Alex smiled. "Come on boy."

Within minutes, Clay was sauntering through her front door with the doughnut box in tow. He sat the box on the kitchen counter and flipped open the top.

"Whatever you want I got it," he told her.

Alex peeked into the box and did a giddy school girl dance as she reached for a cream filled doughnut.

"Mmmm. This is so good. You are the best."

Clay smiled. "I know."

He kicked off his shoes and plopped down on the sofa, getting comfortable. Alex stretched out over the armchair and devoured her pastry.

"How'd your little date go?"

Clay threw his head back on a throw pillow and smiled.

"It was good. I think she's digging me."

"It must wasn't too good cuz you're over here now."

"Trust me," he said with a confidence that would have seemed arrogant on anyone else. "If I wanted to stay over, I could have."

"Uh-huh," Alex teased him. "So why didn't you then?"

Clay looked over at the ebony beauty.

"Because I respect her and I want to see where this is going to go."

Sensing that Clay was serious about this, Alex

looked at her friend intently. She wasn't sure what to say next. Clay had such an earnest look on his face.

"You're serious about her?" Alex asked him.

Clay shrugged. "I mean, it could get there. I don't wanna ruin it before I get the chance to see. I wanna be like you."

Alex raised her eyebrow. "Like me?"

"Yeah...Boo'd up."

Alex cut her eyes at him. "Whatever."

"So where's your boy? Why weren't you with him tonight?"

Alex sat up straight in the chair and wiped her hands against each other, ridding them of the sugary crumbs of the doughnut.

"He had boys' night with his friends." She shrugged noncommittally. "I'll probably see him some time tomorrow."

"So did you?"

"Did I what?"

Clay gave her the evil eye. "Don't act. Did you give him some ass or what?"

Alex's eyes grew big in shock at Clay's bluntness. She pouted her lips and crossed her arms, giving him a hurt expression.

"You don't have to say it like that."

"Like what? It is what it is."

She sucked her teeth. "Well it *isn't* anything then."

"So you didn't do it?"

Alex shook her head. "No...I don't know...I just couldn't."

Clay made a noise that sounded like a sigh to Alex. She didn't give him eye contact and hoped that he wouldn't press the issue further.

"Good. You should wait. Get to know him a little better and see where his head's at. See if he can put up with you for longer than three months."

"So what, you're playing my daddy now?"

Clay cocked his head to the side. "You'd like that huh? Calling me daddy?"

Alex reached over and slapped Clay's leg playfully.

"Shut up! Ain't nobody calling you daddy...unless you get your little girlfriend pregnant."

Clay grabbed Alex's hand and pulled her over to the couch. He began to tickle her mercilessly and Alex broke into a fit of hysterical laughter.

"You jealous of my lil' girlfriend or something?"

he asked her. "You don't like me going out with someone that isn't you?"

He stopped tickling her and just sat staring at her face, as if he was waiting for an answer. Alex tried to compose herself as the question he asked finally sunk into her head. She coughed off her laughter and sat up right on the sofa.

"You're crazy," she said, trying to play it off.

"Am I?" Clay's voice was soft and questioning.

When Alex didn't respond, Clay cleared his throat and moved to the edge of the sofa.

"Look, I think there's something that needs to be said," he stated. "For a long time I've felt like we've skirted around this issue, but I can't do that anymore."

Alex took a deep breath and leaned back against the sofa cushion, giving Clay her full attention.

"We're best friends," he started. "We've been friends for a long time. I know everything about you and you know everything about me. And uh...I think friendship is a very solid foundation. I don't know what you've been feeling over the years. But, I know what I've been feeling and ...well I think it's either now or never..."

Ring Ring Ring

Alex's cell interrupted Clay's speech. Alex reached to grab it and held a finger up to Clay, indicating that he give her just a moment.

"Hey, Mario...nothing...now...um..okay, yeah. That's fine. I'm here."

She ended the call and looked up at Clay.

"Um, I'm sorry..."

Clay reached for his shoes. "I guess it's never."

Alex was speechless. She watched as Clay put his shoes on and clean up their mess from the doughnuts. When he was ready to leave, she walked him over to the door.

"Clay, don't be mad. We can talk later."

He kissed her on the forehead. "It's cool. I think that was a sign for me to keep my thoughts to myself. It's all good."

Before she could respond he opened the door to leave. He started to pull the door up behind him, then stopped and looked back at her.

"By the way, you know this is a booty call for him right? It's late...you don't really think he's coming over here after drinking all night for some conversation do you?"

With that, he closed the door leaving Alex with her mixed up thoughts.

MIRANDA

Miranda was dressed and sitting on the hospital bed when Jada walked into the room. Her body looked frail as she sat slumped over. Trying to remain composed, she jutted her chin out and rose from the bed.

"Thanks for the ride," she said to Jada.

"No problem," Jada responded lightly. "Where am I taking you?"

"Home."

"No."

Miranda stood at the side of the bed staring at her plastic bag of belongings. She sighed.

"Don't do this, Jada. Please."

"You don't do this, Miranda. You cannot go back to that man. You can't go back to that house."

"It's where I live."

"Can't you go stay with your parents?"

"No...I...I don't want them to know.

Jada walked over to Miranda and turned her face towards her.

"You cannot go back to that man, Miranda. You just cannot. You're lucky it was only a couple of ribs this time, girl. But next time, next time that man *will* kill you."

Miranda shook her head. "No he won't. He's probably gone for good. I'm not worried about him and I'm not letting him run me away from the home I pay for."

Miranda moved away from Jada, grabbed her bag and headed for the door.

"And please don't say anything to the other girls about this…if you haven't already."

"Miranda," Jada called out to her friend's retreating figure.

Miranda turned around and looked at her.

"You don't want anyone to know what's up with you, you keep letting this dude pound on you, and you expect me to take you back to him? I'm not doing it, girl. I don't want any part of this."

Jada moved to walk past Miranda.

"What? You're not going to take me home? You told me you'd give me a lift."

"That was before I knew your intention was to go back to him. If you want me to take you there just to get your stuff, that's cool. Otherwise, you're on your own, boo."

There was a brief silence. Miranda looked at Jada in disbelief and Jada returned the stare with a challenging expression of her own.

"That's what I thought," Jada said, breaking their silence. "I'm not going to sit around and watch that man kill you, girl. I'm going to be praying for you."

Jada brushed past her friend and left the hospital room. Miranda watched as she descended the hall and disappeared around the corner. Seconds passed before Miranda realized that Jada truly was not coming back. Dropping her bag onto the hospital bed, Miranda walked over to the hospital room phone and called a cab.

~ ~ ~

The apartment was still and quiet as she entered. Dropping her bag by the door, Miranda eased into her home and slowly walked through the space she shared with her husband. In her bedroom, an uneasy feeling came over her. Something wasn't right. Standing and looking around her room, she searched for the source of her discomfort. She found it laying on the floor on her side of the bed, a cheap pair of gold heels that weren't hers. Miranda kicked the shoes. Sighing, she went into her bathroom and gasped as she turned on the light and saw that someone had totally redecorated.

"What the hell."

The words barely had time to escape her lips before she heard the lock turn on the front door. Bracing herself and totally prepared to have it out with Norris, she quickly headed to the living room. He was startled to see her walk in, but not more than the chick by his side was.

"Excuse you?" the woman blurted out. "Who the hell gave you permission to be coming all up and through here?"

"Tammy, I got this," Norris interjected, holding his hand up at the younger woman.

He approached Miranda with his head tilted back and his nose flaring.

"What's good, Miranda? What are you doing here?"

"What am I doing here? This is my home....The real question is what is that bitch doing in my house, Norris?"

"Un-uh, no this trick ain't calling me no bitch," Tammy piped up, stepping up beside Norris. "I got your bitch, bitch. Don't be coming at me all sideways just cuz you can't handle yours, boo. Cuz trust, I'm handling him very well."

Miranda bit her lip, rolled her eyes at Tammy, and then addressed Norris.

"Get this woman out of my house or..."

"Or what?" Norris challenged.

"Oh you've forgotten? My name is on this lease...not yours. Technically, you're both trespassing. "

"I ain't got time for this shit, Miranda. I didn't even expect your ass to come back."

"Why? You thought you killed me? I'm your wife, Norris. Your WIFE! You didn't so much as check to see if I was okay...you just try to move some lil' girl into my home like you're just going to forget that I exist? Who does that?"

"Shut that whiny ass shit up," Tammy smirked. "Sorry ass."

Fed up, Miranda ran off to the bathroom, ripping down towels and knick knacks. She hurried back into the living room where Norris and Tammy were arguing.

"I said let me handle this, aight," Norris insisted.

"Hell, she's the one starting with me..."

"Fuck you!" Miranda screamed, throwing the bathroom items at the two of them.

"Fuck you, fuck this bitch, and fuck this situation....Take y'alls pathetic asses the hell on out of my house before I call the police."

She ran back into the bedroom and snatched up the stripper shoes off the floor. Back in the living room, she tossed the left shoe barely missing Norris' head.

"You want to lay up with trash, do it! But you will not do it in my house. I'm not fuckin' scared of you anymore! Get out!"

She tossed the right shoe which connected with Tammy's face, the heel grazing her cheek and leaving a bloody scratch.

"Bitch!" Tammy exclaimed.

"You're lucky that I haven't kicked your ass, bitch. But you have all of ten seconds before that changes."

Norris ushered Tammy towards the door.

"Fuck you, Miranda. I'm done with your ass. I wish I'd never married your ass."

The couple exited the apartment and Miranda quickly ran to put the night latch on. She touched her side gingerly, just becoming aware of the immense pain she was feeling. She picked up her bag and fumbled for her phone. Finding it, she scrolled through the phonebook, and then dialed the desired number.

"Hey...can you come though? I can't make it over there....No, he's not here. He's not coming back, so don't worry about that...Okay, that's fine. Thanks."

Disconnecting the call, she sunk onto her couch, willing the pains in her side and her heart to go away.

Dressed in a short, thin, black dress, Candace walked slowly through the crowd holding on to a cheesing Quincy. Couples were dancing, drinking, and laughing just as at any normal club. The only difference was that some people were naked and others were practically making out right there in the open. Quincy led her over to the bar.

"If you grip my hand any tighter you're going to pull it off, woman," Quincy complained.

He signaled the bartender and ordered a martini for her and a long island iced tea for him.

"So, you see anybody you like?" he asked her.

"Like who? Dang, you're ready to jump somebody's bones already? What's wrong with just observing?"

Quincy sucked his teeth. "We coulda *observed* a flick at home if it's like that."

"Shut up...don''t start with me please."

He turned his attention to his drink and Candace continued checking out the scenery in awe of the freeness of it all. She would have never noticed the woman next to her if she hadn't lightly touched her arm. Candace jumped and stared at the slender, light-skinned woman with curly hair.

"I'm sorry," the woman offered. "I didn't mean to startle

you...You just look so tense."

"Oh..yeah...it's our first time here." She motioned to Quincy. "This is my husband, Quincy and I'm Candace."

Quincy said a quick hello.

"I'm Lydia. Listen, I'm a massage therapist...licensed. I'd love to give you a full body massage...you really do seem to have a lot of tension built up..."

Candace was at a loss for words as she toyed with the stem of her glass.

"Well...I..."

Quincy cut in. "Can we make it a massage for two?"

Lydia gave a polite smile and reached inside her clutch bag. She handed Candace a business card.

"I'm sorry," Lydia said. "I didn't intend the offer as a come-on."

A man approached Lydia and Candace threw a dirty look at Quincy.

"Babes, I want you to meet someone," the man said to Lydia, reaching for her hand.

Lydia smiled at Candace. "This is my husband, Michael."

Michael nodded.

"Nothing wrong with a foursome," Quincy blurted.

Candace elbowed her husband. "Excuse him."

"It's alright, dear," Lydia said lightly. "Try to relax...both of you. You'll find what you're looking for. Consider the massage, okay?"

"Okay. Thank you."

"Enjoy your evening," Michael said politely, ushering is wife away and not waiting for a response.

Candace put the card in her bag and looked at Quincy in disgust as he ordered another drink.

"Unbelievable," she muttered.

'What?" Quincy responded.

"You have no class, dear."

"You married me, so I must have something."

"Grow up."

"What's your problem? I thought we came here to have fun...why you acting like a crab?"

Candace sighed. "You know what...this was a mistake. We should have never come here."

"So what you saying?"

"I'm saying that I want to go home...now."

"All the money we paid to get up in here and now you want to go?" he asked a little loudly.

"You're embarrassing me…Please….let's just go."

Quincy sucked his teeth and drowned his glass. Reaching into his pocket he grabbed the keys and threw them at her.

"Fine…Designated driver…be a punk…let's go."

She snatched the keys up and began to walk off.

"Whatever."

~ ~ ~

Candace took a deep breath as she checked her reflection in the rearview mirror. Satisfied with her appearance she exited her car and slowly strolled up the walk to the all brick mini mansion. Anxiety filled her with each step she took past the beautifully arranged flowers decorating the lawn. It was apparent to her that these people had money. Before she could reach out for the doorbell, the door flew open.

"Hey Ms. Ma'am," Lydia greeted her. "Come on in."

Candace smiled and walked into the foyer. The scent of lavender quickly filled her nose. She took note of the crystal chandelier overhead and the black art adorning the walls. Lydia led her to a room just past the formal living room. She looked very comfortable in her blue sarong tied tightly at the top of her bosom.

"You look so tense," Lydia commented. "You must have a lot going on in your life…either that or you're nervous about being here. Which is it? You're safe here. I won't bite."

Lydia chuckled and Candace cracked a smile.

"No, I just have a lot going on...a lot on my mind."

"Well, you definitely need to relax and that's what I'm here for. A massage could really do you some good."

Lydia gestured toward the middle of the room at her massage table and display of oils.

"This is the sanctuary of peace. Get completely undressed and cover yourself with the sheet that's on the table. "

Candace was a little hesitant.

"Is your husband here?"

"No. He's playing golf. But relax, hun. This is my business. He has respect enough not to barge in on a session. Get undressed. I'm going to bring you a glass of wine. Back in ten minutes."

Lydia left her alone, pulling the door up behind her. Candace took a look around and shrugged. Quickly she disrobed, placing her clothes on a nearby chair then wrapped the soft white sheet around herself.

"What am I tripping about?" she asked herself.

There was a tap on the door then Lydia poked her head inside.

"You ready?"

Candace smiled. "Yes."

Lydia entered and kicked the door shut behind her. In hand she carried a bottle of wine and two glasses. Candace watched as she poured up the drink.

"What is that?"

"Moscato. You've never had it before?"

Candace shook her head no. Lydia handed her a glass.

"Tell me what you think."

Candace took a sip of the drink and raised an eyebrow.

"Mmm. Its sweet and smooth. I likes."

The ladies giggled. Lydia took a swig from her own glass. "That's why I like it, girl. Sweet and smooth just like me."

They shared another laugh and finished off their drinks.

"How long have you been doing this?" Candace asked.

"Just a couple of years now...I was into real estate, well Michael and I both did real estate, but after a while I decided that I wanted to do something different...So, I went to school, got licensed, and here I am."

"That's cool."

"What do you do?"

"I'm a legal assistant...but, I'm trying to figure out what

my passion is."

Lydia sat her glass down and turned on some soft jazz music.

"Believe me, once you figure it out you'll feel so good inside. At peace with yourself, kinda."

Lydia took Candace's glass and sat it down.

"Okay, dear. Lie on your tummy for me."

Candace got into position, closed her eyes, and let the music lure her into relaxation. Lydia lit a few candles and sorted through some oils. Finally, Candace felt her soft hands firmly gripping her shoulders as she began to work her magic.

"Wowww," Candace murmured.

"Just relax, girl," Lydia instructed. "You are so tense in this area."

She continued to knead for a while, engrossed in her craft. Candace became increasingly relaxed. Just as Lydia moved down her back, she spoke again.

"So, how often do you and Michael go to the club?"

"Every once in a while. Just something to do to spice things up a little bit every now and then. You plan on going back?"

"Probably not."

"It's not for everyone, that's for sure."

"Have you guys ever met someone? You know…"

"Have we ever had a ménage trios? We have once. We've never actually had sex at the club…I have….well…"

"What?"

"I've had like foreplay at the club…even some personal encounters in private."

"You mean without Michael? Does he know?"

"Of course he knows." She moved down to Candace's lower back. "They were with other women."

There was silence as she continued to massage the small of her back deeply. Each woman engaged in their own private thoughts. Lydia moved down Candace's legs and shivers rose up her spine. In a matter of time, the session was over, the music was still going, and Candace was completely relaxed.

"Okay girl. You're done," Lydia informed.

Candace sat up slowly, pulling the sheet around her, and stretching.

"Wow. That was so amazing. Thank you."

Lydia refilled her wine glass and handed it to her before refilling her own.

"Not a problem. You just make sure that you tell a friend. Gotta make that money."

They clinked their glasses in agreement.

"How much do I owe you?"

"This session is free. Hopefully you'll be back."

Lydia sat her glass down then approached Candace. She placed her hands in the crook of Candace's neck.

"This is your problem area, where all your tension goes, girl. We may want to continuously work out this area."

Lydia's scent was so sweet and inviting. Perhaps it was the alcohol or the serenity of the room that prompted Candace to reach out and touch Lydia's curly mane.

"Your hair is so beautiful."

Lydia smiled. "Thank you."

Her hands lingered on Candace's shoulders. She began to caress her skin.

"Your skin is so soft. Smooth like a baby's."

Before Candace could find the words to respond, Lydia ran her hands gently up and down her arms. Looking into her eyes as if for a hint of permission, Lydia took Candace's glass and sat it down. Candace sat still on the massage table not sure of what to do next or what would happen next. Lydia slowly pulled the sheet from Candace's body. Candace did not protest. She sat openly as Lydia massaged her breasts gently with both hands. Watching Candace's response, she massaged a little more intensely as a soft moan escaped Candace's lips. Lydia smiled sinfully and took Candace's right breast into her mouth. Her tongue was so warm on Candace's skin. She flicked her nipple playfully over and over, until Candace reached for her head as if to signal for more pressure. Lydia licked circles around her areola before taking the whole breast in her mouth once more, sucking with a hungry passion.

Candace could feel the pressure building between her legs and the moisture began to seep involuntarily. Lydia must have sensed it because she moved her hand slowly up Candace's thighs, one then the other, teasing her. Candace spread her legs a little to encourage her to enter. Slowly, Lydia's index finger toyed with her clit. Candace moaned impatiently, her heat rising by the second. She began to gyrate against Lydia's flickers while stroking the woman's mass of curls. Without warning, Lydia stopped and looked up at her. Candace's breathing was heavy and she didn't realize that her eyes had been shut until she opened them to look back at Lydia.

"There's no going back," Lydia said softly. "Do you want this?"

"Yes," Candace answered, nearly inaudibly.

Lydia kept her eyes on Candace as she slowly inserted her finger into Candace's hot and throbbing pussy. She stroked in and out slowly at first and then more forcefully with two fingers as Candace began to thrust back.

"Oohh shit," Candace exclaimed as she grabbed her own breasts and began to squeeze.

Candace's juices flowed down Lydia's hand as she pounded her with her fingers. To intensify the sensation, she lowered her head and took Candace's clit into her mouth. Perfectly in sync, she sucked her clit relentlessly and fingered her deeper and rougher. Candace spread her legs wider, giving complete access to her womanhood.

"Cum for me," Lydia encouraged seductively. "I want to taste you. Cum for me."

Candace bucked ferociously against her hot tongue and probing fingers. It felt so good, she wanted to feel her deeper inside. Lifting her hips a little, she lost control and climaxed in shutters against Lydia's face.

Spent from the experience, Candace fell over on the massage table. Lydia stood up and ran her fingers cross her stomach.

"It's not nap time yet," she told her. Candace sat up, unsure of what to do or say at that moment.

She didn't have to say anything. Lydia slowly untied her sarong and let it fall to the floor, exposing her beautiful, fit body. She reached out and grabbed Candace's hand, guiding it across her silky skin. Candace didn't need much direction. She found pleasure in toying with her breast just as Lydia had done her. Surprised by her second wind as well as her moxie, Candace kneeled on her knees and buried her face in Lydia's woman hood. Lydia slightly raised her leg and leaned on the massage table, getting into the groove of the moment. Candace sucked and licked with vigor and passion she didn't know she had. And when she began to feel as if she couldn't breathe, she came up for air and inserted her perfectly manicured fingers inside Lydia's gush.

Lydia moved with her, but soon hungered for a different sensation. She reached down and caressed her clit with a sensual back and forth motion. The harder she rubbed, the louder her moans got. The louder her moans, the wetter she became. The wetter she got, the harder Candace dove her fingers into her insides. In moments, Lydia was bucking madly on Candace's fingers, still assaulting her clit passionately until her climatic wave had passed. Candace, turned on by the feeling of Lydia's pussy muscles contracting her fingers, laid down on the plush carpet and opened her legs wide. Watching Lydia, she began to ferociously play with herself just as Lydia had. Lydia joined her on the floor, licking around her lips as Candace pleasured herself. She caressed her breast, becoming aroused once more herself. Candace reached over to feel Lydia's wetness. An idea occurred to Lydia. She mounted Candace backwards and initiated a sixty-nine. They sucked, licked, and probed, daring the other to cum first. Lydia lost, her pleasure juice dripping down onto Candace's face. Seconds later, Candace finished with a startling shudder. By far, the strongest orgasm she'd ever achieved. The two collapsed against one another, too tired and worn out for words. Surprised at herself, Candace merely turned over and let the sound of smooth jazz lure her into a lust-induced slumber.

ALEX

Ah-choo. Ah-choo.

"I think your germs are creeping through the phone."

Alex blew her nose and coughed.

"Shut up...you turd."

"Whatever. You want me to bring you over some soup? Some medicine? Some disinfectant spray?"

Alex started to laugh then choked on mucus.

"You suck," she spat out. "Don't bring me nothing."

Clay laughed. "I was just joking cry-baby."

"Ha, ha. Anyway...ugh," *Ah-choo, ah-choo.* "Mario is coming over in a minute."

"Oh yeah? Your knight in shining armor, huh?"

"Why does it seem like you don't like him when you've never even met him? Why you hating?"

Clay chuckled. " Yeah right. I'm the last to be hating...game recognize game."

"You ain't got no game."

"Let you tell it."

"I gotta go get ready for Mario."

"What you getting ready for exactly? Isn't he coming over to nurse you back to good health? What? You still gon' primp ya' self so you can give that lame some ass even though you're burning up with a fever?"

"Clay, shut up. You don't know what you're talking about."

"We'll see. Hope you feel better pitiful princess."

"Bye, Clay."

"Later."

~ ~ ~

The sound of the doorbell scared her out of her sleep. Alex looked at the clock. It was just past eleven. She struggled out of bed and out to the living room to open the door.

"Seriously? Eleven?"

Mario raised an eyebrow and gave her a shrug.

"I got caught up. My bad. You gon' let me in?"

Alex moved to the side as he entered with a grocery bag. He took the bag to the kitchen and Alex followed him.

"You could have called."

"I could have not come at all. Would you have preferred that?"

Alex looked hurt. She pulled a piece of tissue from the pocket of her robe and blew her nose, trying to ward off her tears.

"I'm sick, Mario...if you were going to be nasty to me, you could have stayed home...or wherever you were...for real."

Mario sighed, walked over to her, and gave her a hug.

"Sorry, baby. I'm just tired. I came to see about you, okay? Let's just chill, okay? I brought you some soup."

Alex buried her face in his shirt. With her cold, her senses were a bit altered, but Alex could have sworn that she smelled the faint scent of Victoria' Secret Pure Seduction. *What the hell,* she thought, moving away from his embrace.

"I don't want any soup. I just want to go back to bed."

"Ok, but you have to drink this first."

Mario went back to the bag and pulled out a fifth of E & J.

"Ew, no. You know I don't drink," Alex protested.

"It'll make you feel better. I promise."

Alex watched as he pulled out a Theraflu box and began to mix his medicinal concoction. With a huge smile as if he'd really done something great, he retrieved the cup from the one minute warm-up in the microwave and handed it to Alex. The smell of the liquor opened up her nose.

"This smells."

"Drink it. Trust me. You are going to feel so much better."

Alex took a sip and frowned in disgust.

"Mario, I can't drink this…"

"Don't be a punk."

He retrieved a glass and poured himself a shot of the E &J, never once turning to face her as she stood there cringing at the smell of her drink.

"But baby…"
"If you're going to whine and moan I can always leave," he snapped.

He downed his liquor then poured up another.

"I'm trying to help you. Just drink the stuff and get in the bed. Why do you have to make such a big deal about it?"

Alex pouted, opened her mouth to speak, and then closed her mouth. Taking a deep breath she sat down at the kitchen table and nursed her drink.

"You sure you don't want the soup?"

"I'm sure."

Mario busied himself with putting away the groceries he'd brought and straightening up the kitchen.

"So what were you doing tonight?" Alex asked, taking a hearty gulp of her drink.

"Hanging."

Alex sighed, feeling the conversation going nowhere. She inhaled then knocked back the remainder of her drink. Plopping the cup down on the table, she stood up and looked over at Mario who was now on this third drink.

"I'm going to get in my bed. Are you staying?"

"You want me to stay?"

"Mario, I wanted you to be here all evening...nevermind."

She moved to walk away and felt herself sway.

"Whoa..."

Mario was by her side.

"You better be careful. That E&J is the truth. Come on. Let's go watch a movie."

He led her to her bedroom and helped her into bed. She laid there watching him as he popped in a DVD, turned off the lights, kicked off his shoes, and crawled onto the bed beside her.

"You okay?" he asked.

She shrugged.

"I'm floating...and I feel all warm inside."

He got under the covers and hugged her.

"That's the point. To get you all warm and make you

sweat it out."

The opening credits for the movie began to play and Alex was lured off into a cinema, virus and alcohol induced sleep. At some point she felt herself slipping in and out of consciousness as warm kisses covered her face and neck. Mario's hand was caressing the inside of her thighs, tickling her awake. Alex wasn't sure if she was dreaming or not. Her answer came when she felt a very real finger probing inside her vaginal walls.

"Mario," she whispered barely audibly. Her mouth felt like cotton. She opened her eyes to the darkness and reached for his hand. He shook her off and planted a loud wet kiss over her ear. His breath was hot on her skin as he whispered in her ear.

"I love you, Alexandria."

Confused and sedated, Alex tried to sit up, but Mario's body was already towering over. He moved his kisses to her abdomen, having lifted her night gown and easing her legs apart.

"I can't...I can't," she protested, grabbing his shoulders.

He rose up to mount her and kissed her lips to silence her.

Her moans of pain were lost in the murmur of his kisses. When the sensation felt unbearable, she grabbed his arms, shaking her head.

"I can't...it hhhhurts....I cccan't.."

"Yes you can," he encouraged, still penetrating. "Yes you

can. You can. I got you…Come on, baby."

He continued to thrust until her lining gave way to his advances and let him in. Alex lay beneath him, eyes shut tightly holding on to his arms as he moved in and out of her. She didn't return his thrusts or his kisses. She had no energy to participate or protest. Her thoughts got lost in the sound of his body meshing with hers and the fever that was overcoming her. She was not sure when he'd stopped or how it had ended. Hours later, in the stillness of the night she turned over to find him hanging off of the opposite side of her bed. Her womanhood was sore and her night gown was drenched with sweat.

Quietly, she slid from the bed and pulled a clean night gown from her dresser. In the bathroom, she turned on the light to find that the moisture on her gown was not just sweat, but blood as well.

"Great," she muttered, getting a wash cloth to clean herself up. Once cleaned and changed, she pulled down a towel and returned to bed. She laid the towel down on her side, then laid on top of it. Sighing, she looked over at the snoring figure of Mario. A beeping sound was coming from his side of the bed. Mario did not move. Alex reached over him slowly and picked his cellphone up off the floor. The phone beeped again, indicating he had a text. The screen read 'Erica'. Lying back against her pillows, Alex debated on whether or not to read the text. Before long, the phone beeped again. She looked over at Mario. He was still sound asleep.

She pressed view on the phone.

Are you coming back over tonight?

She clicked back to the previous message.

I'm ready for round three.

She clicked to the first message.

You missing me yet?

Disgusted and disappointed she threw the phone onto the bed and turned her back to Mario. The tears were uncontrollable and her sobs were loud. Mario never budged.

THE GIRLS

Jada sat the pizza boxes on the coffee table next to the paper plates. Stephanie, now three months pregnant, sat on the sofa directly in front of the boxes with her plate in hand. Sitting next to her, Alex gave her a sideways glance.

"Is it like that?" Alex asked.

"Girl, I stay hungry," Stephanie answered flipping open

the top of the meat lover's pizza.

She bit into a slice and cheese dripped down her chin.

"Mmmmm," she taunted Alex, chewing slowly and savoring the taste. "Divine."

Alex threw a napkin at her.

"You're a pig."

The girls were meeting at Candace's house for girls' night. The group hadn't been together since Candace's wedding. As Alex and Stephanie began to feast on the pizza, Candace entered the room with a piping hot bowl of her infamous dip.

"Watch out ladies," she instructed, sitting the bowl on the table beside the pizza. "This is very hot."

Jada opened the bag of tortilla chips and scooped one through the cheesy concoction. She took a bite and smiled.

"Just right, girl," she complimented her friend.

Candace plopped down into the nearby arm chair with a bottle of Smirnoff in hand.

"You know how I do."

Jada laughed. "I know that you usually don't, so it's amazing when you actually do."

The others laughed.

"Whatever," Candace protested. "I can cook girl. Everyone loves my food."

"Uh-huh. I hope you cook Quincy something other than cheese dip," Stephanie piped in.

"He's the main one that loves my culinary skills. Why you think he married me?"

Alex laughed. "That's a good question. Why DID he marry you?"

Candace reached for a slice of pizza, rolling her eyes at Alex.

"Ha, ha."

"I'm just saying…he doesn't even seem like your type."

"Alex," Jada intervened.

"What? I'm just saying. We've known you for a long time, girl, and he just don't seem like your kinda guy."

"Please get off it. We're married. We're in love. End of discussion…God, if I didn't know any better I'd say that you were jealous."

"That must be your alcohol talking," Alex snapped.

"Ladies, really," Jada jumped in. "We're supposed to be having fun."

"And we are," Candace retorted, rising from her chair. "I just don't get why some people can't be happy for me and leave it at that. I'm going to make some margaritas."

Candace left the room and Jada stared at Alex who was munching nonchalantly on chips and dip. She caught Jada's glare and shrugged.

"What?"

"Don't what me. That was mean, girl."

"I was just being honest. I wasn't trying to hurt her little feelings or anything. But come on, you know good and well this marriage is ridiculous."

"Who are we to judge?"

"We're her friends."

"If the woman says she's happy then believe her and shut the hell up about it."

"If she was happy why did she get all pissed by what I said?"

Jada sighed. "Steph, can I get a little help here?"

Stephanie chugged her soda and shook her head.

"Nuh-uh, girl. I'm with Alex on this. Seeing Candace and Quincy together does not make me think that they are in love."

"And what are you comparing them to? You and ya' baby's daddy?"

Stephanie sucked her teeth. "Well, we can't all be perfect like you and Jordan, can we?"

The doorbell sounded then in walked Miranda before anyone could move to answer the door.

"Hey chicks," she greeted the group, unusually upbeat. She went around the room and hugged the others just as Candace entered with a pitcher of Margaritas.

"Well, look who decided to finally show up," Candace commented.

Miranda hugged her. "I love you too, bitch."

"Yea, yea."

Miranda made herself comfortable on the floor by the sofa and reached for a slice of pizza.

"So what have I missed?"

Candace poured her a glass of the margarita mix and handed it to her.

"Just Alex trying to persuade me to get divorced."

"Stop exaggerating," Alex said.

"Ignore them," Jada interceded, changing the subject. "How are you doing?"

Miranda covered her mouth with a napkin. "I'm good."

The other girls simply looked at her gingerly, waiting for her to say more. Miranda began to feel uncomfortable with their stares. She sighed and looked at her friends sternly.

"Stop it, guys. I'm fine. Really."

"We're girls, right?" Candace asked her, sipping her drink.

Miranda nodded.

"Well, why didn't you call us? Either of us? Why didn't you tell us what was going on with you? That you were in trouble?"

"Because I didn't want you looking at me the way you are now…feeling sorry for me."

"Why did you stay?" Stephanie asked. "I mean, I'm assuming this wasn't the first time. So why would you stay with a man that hits you?"

"Why do you stay with Corey?"

"Corey doesn't hit me."

"No, but he blows you off. He treats you like a toy. Takes you out when he wants to play with you then abandons you when he's bored with you."

"Wait a minute now, that's not fair, Miranda. We're concerned about you. Where do you get off attacking me and being judgmental?"

"I'm sorry…but it's the truth." Miranda stared down at her napkin. "Maybe we all just have some fucked up relationships."

The girls sat in silence, munching and considering their own thoughts. Alex broke the silence.

"Mario is cheating on me."

A series of awwws filled the room as the others tried to console her.

"How do you know?" Stephanie asked.

"I saw messages in his phone one night after he came to my place smelling like a girl. And ever since then, I've barely heard from him or seen him."

"I'm sorry, girl," Jada offered. "I know you really liked him."

"Maybe it's for the best," Candace said.

"What?" Alex questioned. "What is this? Payback?"

"No, I'm not studying you like that, girl. I'm just saying that perhaps that's not who Jehovah intended for you to be with."

Alex considered it. "I guess not."

Candace threw a pillow at her friend.

"You are sooooo slow."

'What?"

"Clay…that's what."

"What about him?"

"She's asking what's up with him," Stephanie answered. "Why aren't you hooking up with him?"

Alex helped herself to some more dip. "Ya'll are crazy. Clay and I are just friends. That's it."

Jada's attention wandered off to Miranda, who was sitting quietly on the floor nursing her drink. She looked so frail and simply different. Before she could say anything, Jada was pulled into the current conversation by Stephanie.

"Jada, please tell Ms. Princess over here that she needs to stop messing with these crazy dudes and get with that fine ass Clay."

"Umm…I don't know…has he ever said anything to you? Given you a sign that he's interested?"

"I don't know," Alex answered unsurely.

"Yeah right."

"All I know is that if I had a fine ass friend like Clay always hanging around, Corey would shoul' nuff beat my ass thinking we were messing around."

The girls started to laugh then realized what had just been said. The laughter ceased as all eyes went over to Miranda. Sensing their stares Miranda looked up and once again felt uncomfortable.

"Oh damn. I'm sorry, girl," Stephanie said.

"Sorry for what?" Miranda asked.

"I didn't mean to make light of….I mean, I was just kidding…"

"It's okay. I'm not offended. I'm more offended that ya'll keep treating me like I'm broken or something."

Candace sat her cup down and kneeled down beside Miranda.

"You had a broken rib, girl. You *were* broken. And we are concerned about you."

"Don't be," she said softly. "It's over now."

"Is it? Have you filed for divorce? Have you pressed charges against his sorry ass?'

Miranda shook her head no. Stephanie leaned forward.

"Please don't tell me that you are still holed up over at the apartment with his trifling ass."

Miranda shook her head again.

"He moved in with some chick."

Candace leaned against her chair. "You're a stronger person than I could ever be, girl. I would have whooped his ass."

Miranda shrugged. "I'm dealing with it. I've been going to my battered wives meeting and…"

Jada cut her off. "Battered wives meeting? Do you hear yourself? That doesn't even sound right. You are 22 years old and you're sitting up in some group for battered women? What the hell?"

"You need to file those papers, girl," Stephanie added. "Get rid of that man for good. What are you waiting on?"

"Divorces cost money."

Candace patted her on the leg. "The attorney I work for handles divorces. I got you."

Alex sat her plate on the table and moaned a little.

"What is wrong with all of us?" she asked, rising from her seat. "We sound like a pitiful Lifetime movie….Excuse me."

Alex hurried from the living room in the direction of the

bathroom. Jada chuckled a little.

"Alex is right. We have got to get it together, ladies."

"We?" Candace countered. "What kind of problems do you have little Ms. Perfect Princess?"

"Don't start with me, Candace. Everybody has issues."

"Uh-huh…so I'm asking you what are your issues? I never hear you utter a word about your relationship. Nada. So, either you're holding on to the secret of how to make shit work or you're holding out on us."

Jada rolled her eyes and took a sip of her drink.

"I just don't have these types of issues."

"That's some sadity shit to say."

"But it's some real shit."

Candace left the room and the others looked at Jada in awe. Jada shrugged her shoulders and grabbed a slice of pizza.

"What was that about?" Stephanie asked Jada.

"Hell if I know. As often as I go to bat for her…I don't know why she felt the need to come at me like that."

"It's funny," Miranda said softly. "It's funny how you want something so badly…Then when you get it you realize it ain't what you really wanted at all. But, instead of admitting that you made a mistake you just stick it out…You try to mask it but in the process every bit of who you are gets destroyed. The way you think, your outlook on life, your relationships with others in your life…you start lashing out, at others…or at yourself."

Tears rolled down her cheeks as she spoke, staring at the carpet. Taking a deep breath she looked up at her two friends who were too stunned to respond to her unexpected revelation. Jada sat down her pizza and moved to the floor beside her, wrapping her arms around the frail frame of her body. Stephanie moved beside her as well, grabbing her hand.

"It's funny," Miranda whispered between sobs. "It's funny how we get to this place and don't even know how we got here…all because we want to be loved."

"Love doesn't hurt, though, Miranda," Jada said softly. "Not like he's hurt you. That's not love."

Miranda looked into Jada's eyes innocently.

"Sometimes, we take what we can get, even if it is a lie."

~ ~ ~

In the bathroom, Alex leaned over the toilet, gripping the seat, eyes shut tightly. She tried to take a deep breath before her body convulsed once more, involuntarily freeing her of her lunch. With her right hand she held her stomach, trying to will it to settle down. In moments, it was over and she flushed the toilet and rested her head against the cold porcelain. Her face was wet with tears and sweat.

"Get it together," she ordered her body. "Get it together."

She rose from the floor, went to the sink and splashed water on her face. Catching a glimpse of herself in the mirror, she almost didn't recognize the woman looking back at her. How long could she ignore the weakness of her stomach, violent hurls, or the fatigue that was evident in her eyes? No one else noticed, but she did. No one else knew and she didn't want to be certain. Quickly, she patted her face dry, washed her hands, and left the bathroom before anyone decided to come looking for her.

~ ~ ~

Candace was in the kitchen preparing another batch of margaritas. She found herself literally throwing the ingredients into the blender and ferociously pressing the blend button. She sighed, not sure if she was frustrated at the others for pulling her card regarding her marriage or with herself for being jealous of Jada. Sure, they were girls, but it was hard to follow in someone else's shadow. Everything seemed to come with such ease for Jada. Why couldn't her marriage be like Jada's?

Her phone buzzed, interrupting her thoughts. She pulled it out her pocket and looked to see who the text was from. It was Khalil. A smile crossed her lips.

"Want to see you tonight."

She quickly texted back. "Call you when I'm done with the girls."

Alex sauntered into the kitchen and poured herself a cup of cranberry juice. She looked at Candace as she put her phone back into her pocket.

"Look," Alex said. "I wasn't trying to be rude or piss you off in there."

Candace shrugged. "I know. And between you and me, I know my marriage isn't perfect...but it's mine."

Alex leaned over the counter and smiled slyly at her

friend.

"Do you really love him? I mean...really?"

Candace bopped her on the nose.

"He's my husband. Of course I love him."

Alex turned up her lips and cocked her head to the side.

"I guess," she said and giggled.

Candace poured herself a drink.

"I guess too," she said and laughed.

Candace

Candace agreed to meet Khalil at a coffee shop on his side of town. When she entered he was sitting at a cozy table tucked away in the corner of the shop. She glided over to him, his eyes dancing as he watched her approach. He gave her that sexy killer smile of his and she could feel her panties moisten at the thought of where his lips had once been. He stood up to greet her with a soft kiss on her cheek and a firm hug as he lightly and quickly grazed her ass. She sat in the vacant seat across from him.

"How are you?" he asked, sipping from his latte.

"I'm good. Thanks. How are you, dear?"

"Doing much better now that you're here. I've missed you."

She blushed. "Have you? You haven't called."

"I've been busy. You know how it is."

Her eyebrow rose. He reached over and grabbed her hand.

"You look very beautiful today. Can I get you anything?"

She shook her head. "No, thank you. So tell me, what have you been so busy doing?"

Khalil leaned back and took another swig of his drink.

"Dealing with this crazy woman and her nonsense."

"Oh? What's up with Sheila?"

"This nut had the audacity to give me an ultimatum. She wants to get married. Talking about she's tired of shacking up and wants me to make a commitment to her."

"So why won't you. Marriage can be a beautiful thing."

"Could be, but I've been married before and it wasn't beautiful. Marriage doesn't fix a situation that's already jacked up. It just complicates things. I don't want to mess up my life or her's anymore than I have to by promising her forever and then failing her when it ultimately doesn't work out. That's just foolish."

"Do you love her?"

He chuckled. "I stopped loving her a long time ago. It's just a relationship of convenience now."

"Then why won't you break up with her? Move on and

find someone you actually love?"

"Because you're married."

Candace was shocked by his insinuation. "Is that right?"

"And love is over-rated."

"Is it? You don't believe you can be in love with someone, Khalil?"

"I don't know. All I know is that I am definitely not marrying Sheila. I'm not doing that again."

"What made her bring up marriage?"

He stared down into his cup as if to debate whether or not he was going to answer her. He toyed with the rim and relentlessly answered.

"She's pregnant."

There was silence. Candace didn't know what to say to him.

"Are you happy?"

"What am I going to do with another kid? She knows I don't want any children."

"Well you impregnated her."

"Mistake...I'm tired of arguing with her, damn shoul' ain't about to marry her and then she up and tells me she's knocked up..."

"Wow," was all she could think of to say, relieved that

she wasn't the woman carrying this man's baby.

"Enough about my problems though. What's up with you?"

She smiled slyly. "Nothing much...trying some new things."

"Like what?"

"Trying to spice up our love-life...let's see, we've been to a swingers club...um...i've been done by a girl...and..."

"Hold up...you turning lesbian on me?"

Candace was slightly offended. "A little experimentation doesn't make me a lesbian."

"Really? Let a man do another man and he would quickly be labeled a fag."

"Okay...don't act like the thought of me with another woman doesn't get you all hard and horny."

He laughed. "It doesn't. It makes me think that you need a real man dicking you down so that you don't feel the need to chase after another woman's pussy."

"Fuck you, Khalil," she said with angrily, grabbing her purse. "What happened to 'we can talk about anything'?"

"Nothing happened to it. We're talking...but I'm not going to mask my opinions just to make you happy, young lady. I'm being real with you."

"Hmmm," she looked at her watch. "Well, as much as I'd like to stay here and get berated by you, I really gotta go. My husband's expecting me. Tell Sheila I said hello."

She rose from the table and moved to walk away.

"Stop acting childish. Sit down," Khalil said. "Come on. You know you want to stay."

She gave a fake smile. "Some other time."

She quickly left the shop, pissed with herself for even showing up. The nerve of his ass talking down to her when he wasn't even man enough to tell his live-in girlfriend that he no longer wanted her. She trotted off to her car and hurried home to the other trifling man in her life.

Stephanie

Over the next few weekends, Stephanie finally moved into Corey's apartment with their son. Already five months pregnant, she was tired from the hustle and bustle of getting everything moved in. Her mom had been reluctant to accept the fact that she was moving in with her baby's daddy.

"I don't know what you see in that thug," her mom had told her. "He's nothing but trouble. Your nose is too wide open for you to see it."

She hadn't wanted to argue. She just went along packing her boxes and ignoring her mother's negativity, not heeding the warning she was being given.

"It's not a stable environment for Damien. Let something happen, DFCS will shol' nuff come and snatch that child clean away from you. You'd be better off to leave that child right here with me. You want to mess your life up, fine. But you shouldn't be taking that child into that house of ill-repute."

That was where Stephanie drew the line. Damien was her son, not her mother's.

"Corey is his dad. A child should be with both their parents. Anywhere I go, my child goes."

"And what are you going to do the next time his *daddy* gets arrested? What you gonna do if he gets arrested while Damien is with him?"

"Why can't you be happy for me? This is my family. Don't worry about us."

That had settled the conversation. Ms. Johnson was out of words and fight. She simply turned and left the room, leaving Stephanie with her own thoughts as she continued packing. Now she sat in the living room of the place she now called home as Damien napped in his new bedroom. Corey wasn't home. He told her that he had a run to make. Looking around at the unopened boxes left to put away, Stephanie rubbed her stomach and smiled to herself.

Finally, she thought. *All that's left is to get married.* She was sure it would come. Moving in together was a big step on Corey's part. Marriage was seemingly inevitable. Wanting to be the best wifey possible, Stephanie pushed herself up from the couch and wobbled into the kitchen. Already the weight of her baby bump was affecting her movement. She rummaged through the refrigerator trying to find something to throw together a decent lunch for her family. Settling on some ground beef in the freezer, she decided to make hamburgers. She placed the meat in the microwave to defrost, grabbed a knife out of the drawer, and retrieved an onion from the fridge. As she meticulously chopped up the onion, the house phone began to ring. She had never answered Corey's phone before, but since she now lived with him it only felt natural that she would.

She grabbed it on the third ring.

"Hello?"

"Who is this?" a female voice ordered.

"Who were you calling?"

"Where's Corey?"

"He's not in. May I ask whose calling?"

The line went dead. She held the cordless phone in her hand staring into space as the dial tone returned to the line and began to buzz. She clicked off the phone and quickly pressed the button to view the caller id. The screen read PRIVATE NUMBER. Her intuition told her that something wasn't right, but her heart didn't want to listen to any hints of doubt. She returned the phone to its cradle and continued with preparing the family's lunch.

Lunch time came and went, still no Corey. Dinner time came and went, still no word from Corey. She'd called his cell phone twice and each time she was sent straight to voicemail. This was their first official night at home together and he had the audacity to not come home. To keep from worrying or crying, Stephanie occupied herself with playing with Damien. Together they played with his train set, had dinner, and she assisted him with his bubble bath. Now, they lie together reading his favorite Thomas the Train book for the umpteenth time. By now, Damien knew the plot by heart. As he told the story to her, Stephanie felt herself falling asleep. Damien noticed it too.

"Wake up mommy," he told her in his precious voice.

"I'm not sleep," she lied, forcing a smile. "I'm listening."

"Nuh-huh…mommy, when's daddy coming home?"

Stephanie sat up and put her arm around her toddler.

"I don't know baby. Daddy had to work."

"Where does daddy work?"

"He works with people…"

She didn't know how to explain to her son that his father was the neighborhood dope man. You spend your whole life teaching your kids to just say no. How do you then tell your child that their father is the man you're supposed to be saying no to? Damien rested his head on her chest.

"I like staying at Daddy's house," he told her. "Are we

going to stay?"

She kissed his forehead.

"We sure are."

"When are we going back to grandma's house?"

"We're not going to live there anymore," she told him.
"We'll only go to visit."

They both heard the front door close and keys hit the
table.

"Daddy, daddy!" Damien exclaimed hopping from the
bed and peeling through the apartment to the living room.

He ran right into Corey's open arms and Corey lifted him
up into the air and spun him around making the child giggle with
delight. Stephanie entered the room and was instantly pleased at
the sight of her son and his father. It was a touching moment.

"What's up big man?" Corey asked him playfully. "What
you doing up? It's late."

"I was waiting on you," Damien answered, poking his
dad in the chest.

Corey sat the young boy down and patted him on the
head.

"Well, I'm here now. Go on and get in your bed."

Damien wrapped his arms around Corey's leg and
squeezed.

"Mommy made dinner and you didn't come home to eat

it. Mommy was looking sad, daddy. I think she wanted you to come home. I wanted you to come home too."

Corey pulled the little boy away from him and patted his head once more.

"Okay son. Go on to bed now."

"Dadddddyyy. I wanna stay up with you…"

Stephanie intervened. "Go to bed, Damien. You can play with daddy in the morning."

"Awww man."

The little boy reluctantly and slowly removed himself from the living room. Corey went into the kitchen and Stephanie followed him. She waited for him to offer an explanation and when it was apparent that one was not forthcoming, she spoke up.

"I called you twice tonight," she said softly.

"I was busy."

"You couldn't have called to let me know you weren't coming home anytime soon or something?"

Corey opened the refrigerator and rummaged through it in search of his dinner. He ignored Stephanie's concerns. Unable to find anything to eat, he closed the refrigerator door with only a beer in hand.

"I thought you cooked dinner," he challenged her.

She sighed. "Your plate is in the microwave."

Corey went over to the kitchen table and took a seat, swigging his beer. As if on cue, Stephanie walked over to the microwave and pressed the reheat button. Two minutes passed and the microwave beeped. She took the plate of cubed steak and potatoes out and sat it in front of Corey.

"Smells good," he said. "Lemme get a fork."

She retrieved a fork for him and sat at the table beside him as he began to eat his dinner. He ravished the food as if he hadn't eaten all day.

"So, where were you?" she asked him.

His left eyebrow rose and his nose flared up and Stephanie quickly sat up straight in her seat.

"I mean, I was worried is all," she tried to clean it up. "And Damien was asking for you. Like I said, I called you twice…it went to voicemail. You didn't call so I wasn't sure when to expect you."

"To expect me?" he repeated. "This is my house. I'm supposed to check in now? Let you know when I'm leaving and when I'm coming back?"

He chuckled. "That's some family type-shit, huh? Lemme get some steak sauce."

Stephanie rose from the table and gathered his A1 sauce from the cabinet. Sitting it in front of him, she slid back into her seat.

"I'm just saying…it's the polite thing to do so that I won't be worried about you…"

"Aight. Check it, you know when I gotta go to work, I

gotta go to work. I don't exactly punch in and out of no clock, you know what I mean?"

"I know…"

"Tell you what, I'll do better. I'll hit you up to let you know when I'm coming home from now on, aight? Just to give you some peace of mind."

Stephanie gave a weak smile.

"Don't be worried about me, boo. I'm on my grind out here. I got niggas watching my back, front, and sides. So don't be worried about nothing."

His cellphone chimed and Corey quickly pulled it from the holster.

"Yo…yep. Bet, come on."

He replaced the phone and gobbled down the last of his steak and potatoes.

Stephanie glanced at the clock on the microwave. 12:30 am. Who the hell could be calling him at that hour?

"The food was good, boo," he complimented, swigging the remainder of his beer. "I got my mans coming through for a minute, so go head and clean up and go to bed."

"Corey, it's the middle of the night. Who…"

There was a tap on the front door that was just audible enough for them to hear it in the kitchen. Corey patted her ass and headed toward the door.

"Clean up and go to bed," he called over his shoulder.

She sighed and hurriedly put the plate and fork into the dishwasher. She wiped off the table, threw his beer bottle in the trash, and entered the living room in route to their bedroom. Corey was sitting on the couch with another man Stephanie had never seen before. Their voices were hushed and the man fell silent when he saw Stephanie. Corey turned to face her.

"Good night, boo," he ordered, more than said. He made it clear and obvious that he wanted her out of the living room and he had no intentions of introducing her to his company.

She hurried from the room but lingered at the door of their bedroom, trying to hear what the hell was so important at midnight. She strained to hear bits and pieces of their conversation.

"Where's his bitch ass now?" Corey asked angrily.

"…the Dec…popping fly at the mouth."

"….into me for a key…run it."

"Bet."

She heard the shuffling of feet and the click of the front door. Quickly she hopped into bed and snuggled down into the covers. Just as she tried to regulate her breathing, Corey entered the room. He kicked his sneakers off and sat on the edge of the bed.

"I needa give you something," he told her.

Stephanie sat up, anxiety coming over her as she half expected her dreams to come true in the next moment.

"I can trust you, right?"

She nodded, speechless.

"This is some serious shit, Steph. I'm giving it to you cuz I trust that you'll ride or die with me. If I'm wrong about that shit, let me know now and I'll save myself the trouble later."

"Corey," she said intently, reaching out to touch his arm. "Baby, it's me. I've always been here for you and you know that."

He reached into his pocket and pulled out a set of keys. Taking her hand in his, he placed the keys in the palm of her hand and closed his hand over hers.

She looked at him in confusion.

"These are some important fucking keys. Put 'em somewhere where they aren't easy to find and you won't forget where you put them. Don't ever tell nobody where you put them, not even me unless I ask you. Don't show 'em to nobody."

"What do they go to?"

"Don't worry about that. Just know that they're important. I'm trusting you with my life, Steph. Don't fuck up."

She nodded and clutched the keys tightly. When Corey told her to shut up about something, she knew better than to press further. She just nodded her understanding and said nothing. Corey rose from the bed and went into the bathroom to shower. Listening to the sound of the water, Stephanie stared at the keys in her hand wondering what doors they were going to open in her future.

Jada

Jordan tickled her into a horrible fit of hysterical laughter. They were playing on the bed, enjoying their quiet time together. He wouldn't let up and Jada could barely breathe. They both could hear her phone singing and as she struggled to reach for the phone, Jordan kept pulling her back and attacking her armpits.

"Stop...stop," she panted and tried to protest.

Jordan laughed at her and finally decided to spare her some mercy. The phone continued to sing. Jordan grabbed it and threw it at her.

"Answer your punk ass phone," he teased her.

She pressed the talk button and could barely utter a salutation.

"Are you busy?" Alex's voice sounded a little frantic.

Jada tried to wave Jordan away and motion for him to be quiet. She sincerely hoped that her girl was not stranded on the side of the road in the SWATS or something.

"Not really. What's up?"

"Okay, you have to promise not to tell anybody."

Jada sat up in the middle of her bed and struggled to

compose her breathing.

"Okay."

"Definitely not the other girls."

"Okay, honey. What's up?"

"Not even Jordan, Jada."

"Oh my god, really? What is soooo secret that I can't tell Jordan?"

Jordan raised his hands up in the air as if to say 'what gives'. Jada simply shrugged her shoulders and watched as her husband turned on the television. White Chicks was playing on USA again. Jada loved that movie.

"I'm pregnant."

"Uh-huh," Jada commented, paying attention to Marlon Wayans as he pretended he was going to hang himself.

"Jada," Alex said crossly. "Did you hear me? I said I'm pregnant."

"Shut up, Alex. Seriously, what's going on?"

"That's it."

Jada sighed, so not in the mood for games tonight.

"Alex, you have to have sex to get pregnant."

"You don't think I know that? Why are you talking to me like I'm stupid?"

"I'm just saying…we *all* know that little Ms. Princess ain't giving up the drawers so, I'm just saying…"

There was a pause and Jada considered the possibility.

"Unless little Ms. Princess *has* given up the drawers…did you have sex with someone?"

"Yes, Jada. Ugh. Why did I call you? You're not taking me seriously."

Jada covered her mouth in disbelief.

"Are you serious? You're pregnant? For real, for real? Oh my god. Have you been to the doctor? How far along are you? What the hell is going on? You never told me that you did the do girl? And with who? That admissions rep guy?"

"Why are you sounding happy?" Alex asked pitifully. "This is *not* a happy occasion. I'm miserable. I can't have a baby. I can't even take care of myself let alone a baby."

"Well, boo... it's kind of late to be having that frame of mind now, isn't it?"

"This wasn't planned. I didn't even mean to have sex with that punk

"Wait a minute. Isn't he your boyfriend?"

Alex sighed. "At least I thought he was…I haven't heard or seen much of him lately."

"Have you told him?"

"He's coming over tonight…supposedly. Then I'm going to tell him. What am I going to do, Jada? My parents are going to kill me."

"You haven't told them yet?"

Alex began to sob into the phone. "I haven't told anybody. Just you. I'm so disappointed in myself…I don't want to have a baby. I pray to god I could just erase it."

"Did you say you've been to the doctor?"

"Yes. I went today…I'm six weeks. And sick to my stomach all the time. It sucks."

"You've got to tell your parents."

"I can't…I've already made an appointment for a consultation. I can't have a baby."

Jada rubbed her temples. It was all going too fast for her.

"Wait…you JUST found out. Are you sure you're ready to make that decision? Especially before you have the chance to even talk to Mario about it?"

"It's my body." A pause. "Don't judge me, Jada."

"I didn't say anything."

"Yeah… but I know you."

"You know me? Alex, I've had an abortion before. Take it from me, it's not an easy decision to live with. So whether you do or don't, it's your business…Just take some time to think about it."

Sniffle, sniffle. "Okay. I better go get cleaned up before the butthole shows up."

"Call me back if you need to, girl. I love you."

"I love you too."

Jada snapped her phone shut and looked over at Jordan who was engrossed in the movie. She hit him playfully on the leg.

"Did you catch all that?"

"I sure did."

She snuggled up to him and the laid in silence for a few seconds. Jada began to toy with his shirt and looked up at him.

"Why does it seem like all of my girls are getting pregnant but me? I'm the only one that's in a stable relationship. Well…minus Candace."

Jordan sighed and held his wife closely.

"Because it's not our time, baby. Come on. Don't start stressing about this. It'll happen when it's supposed to happen. I promise."

"It's not fair," she pouted.

"Life isn't fair, babes…" He shook her playfully. "Come on. We were having a good time. Don't stress okay?"

She nodded in agreement but the look in her eyes told him that she wasn't yet able to let the thought escape her mind. Jordan kissed her forehead.

"I love you, babes."

Jada smiled weakly. "I love you too."

MIRANDA

It had been a long day at work at the store. Miranda's

feet were throbbing from the overtime shift she'd just pulled. With Norris gone, she had to cover some extra shifts to come up with the small portion he contributed to their household expenses. She was planning to find a smaller apartment, somewhere more affordable. As she climbed the steps to her apartment, she saw the figure of a man with his back to her standing in front of her door. She adjusted her glasses and as she moved closer she recognized him immediately. Her defenses went up and she quickly scanned the area to see if anyone else was around. She considered running back down the stairs and high tailing it back to her car. Before she could make the decision he turned around and spotted her.

"What's up?" he asked as if they'd just seen each other yesterday.

She looked at him cautiously and grabbed her keys out of her purse.

"What are you doing here, Norris?"

"I needa holla at you."

Approaching her door, Miranda glanced down on the ground to next to the threshold. A bouquet of roses and a shopping bag were lying on the ground next to Norris' duffle bag. Miranda rolled her eyes and looked at her husband in confusion.

"Holla at me about what?"

"Why you all tense?" he moved towards her and she flinched.

He bit his lower lip as if to stop himself from saying what he was about say. He began using a lot of hand motions and speaking softly.

"Ok, check this. I know we've been through a lot of fucked up shit. I know I haven't been the best husband. But I am your husband. All I want to do is come in, sit down, and talk to you for a minute. Let's see if we can work this out?"

"I don't know…" her voice waivered.

"I'm not asking for a reconciliation…" A beat. "I just want to talk to you."

Miranda sighed. She walked past him, unlocked the door, and led the way inside. Norris, following suite, grabbed up his goodies and shut the door behind him. He handed the flowers to Miranda.

"Thought you'd like these," he said with a smile.

Her face was emotionless. "Thank you."

Norris walked over to the sofa and took a seat. He patted the space next to him, motioning for her to seat down beside him. She sat down, being sure to leave some distance between them.

"Where's your little girlfriend?" she asked him.

He waved her off. "Ah man, that chick ain't my girlfriend. She's just a girl I know."

"Right."

"For real. We worked together. I crashed at her place since I left here. That's it."

"Uh-huh…and while I was in the hospital you had her all up and through here like her name was on the lease."

"Just kicking it. Look, I don't want to argue about the past. I just want to move forward and see if we have a future."

Miranda crossed her arms.

"What? You don't believe me?"

"No," she spat out. "I don't."

"Ok, ok. I deserve that. So I guess I've just got to show you."

She shook her head. "What do you expect me to say Norris? Hhhmm? You want me to just forget that you broke my rib, Norris? That you left me laying in here for dead?"

"Baby, I'm sorry. I fucked up, I own that. I fucked up."

"Damn right. And then you bring another woman up in my house, treating me like I'm some trash in the street."

Norris got down on his knees in front of her and placed his hands on her lap. He looked into her eyes pleadingly.

"I can't take back everything that happened. I know that. I just want you to give me a chance to do the right thing. I want to try. I'm just a man, baby. I'm not perfect."

Tears welled up in his eyes. Miranda felt herself begin to loosen up. Norris noticed too and quickly grabbed the shopping bag off the coffee table.

"Here," he said, rummaging through the bag. "I bought you something I thought you'd like."

He pulled out a Coach purse with the tag still hanging from it. Miranda's eyes widened. She reached for the bag, turned it around to see if it was indeed real. It was. She looked at Norris in amazement. He'd never bought her anything just because and certainly not anything as lavish as a Coach bag.

"You like it, don't you?" he asked. "Look inside it."

She looked inside the purse and found a diamond tennis bracelet inside of a pocket. The bracelet was stunning and Miranda couldn't contain the gasp that left her mouth as she held it in her hand. This was definitely not the Norris she knew.

Silently, he took the bracelet from her and placed it on her arm. She turned her wrist this way and that way admiring the shine. Sighing, she looked at her husband who was still kneeling on the floor in front of her.

"I need you to go to counseling," she said softly. "By yourself and marriage counseling."

He nodded. "I can do that, I can do that."

"And you will never ever hit me again, Norris. Not so much as a slap on the ass."

"I won't, baby. I won't."

Her left eyebrow rose. "I mean it."

He reached up and touched her face gently.

"Baby, I promise I will never touch you like that again."

Miranda simply looked at him, trying to get a sense of whether or not he was being truthful and sincere with her.

"Can I kiss you?" he asked.

She was hesitant, but nodded her consent.

Norris rose to touch her lips softly and gently with his. It was the most delicate kiss he'd ever given her. Miranda felt tingles inside of her as their lips joined. Perhaps her husband really was ready to be the man she needed him to be. Needing to be loved, Miranda was ready to give it a try and see.

ALEX

You can do this, Alex told herself. *Just tell him. Open up your mouth and tell him the words…I'm pregnant. It's simple.* Alex and Mario were sitting in her kitchen eating a pepperoni pizza she had ordered just before he arrived. He had taken the liberty of helping himself to her dinner and Alex hadn't felt compelled to stop him. Watching him eat two slices on top of each other at once, Alex felt her stomach turn. Surveying him, she began to question why she'd even started going out with him in the first place. Feeling her stare, Mario glanced up.

"What's up? Why you stop eating?"

She shrugged. "I don't really want it anymore."

"What's up with you. Since you were sick last month your appetite has been like nonexistent. You don't want nothing."

Segue-way stupid!!! Tell him.

She shrugged again and decided to change the subject.

"Can we go to a movie?"

"I can't tonight. Already got plans to hit up this party."

"Oh, okay. I can just go with you."

He took a swig of his coke and shook his head.

"Naw, it's one of my boys. You wouldn't wanna go. You wouldn't even know anyone."

"I'd know you."

He reached for another slice. "We'll do something tomorrow."

"Yeah right," she mumbled.

"What's with you?"

"What's with me? You're the one that doesn't ever want to do anything with me. You barely come over. I'm wondering if we're even dating anymore."

"Okay, you're tripping."

She crossed her arms and pouted. "I'm not tripping. You act like you don't like me anymore."

He laughed at her.

"For real, Alex? Come on, please don't start this little girl shit. Quit with that whiny voice and pouting routine. I'm not in the mood for that."

"Whatever," she spat out and rose from the table. She moved to leave the kitchen. She heard him reply behind her.

"You must be on your period."

She spun around and walked over to him, slapping him on the back of the head. He dropped his slice of pizza and jumped up just as she retorted back to him.

"I would be on my period if I wasn't knocked up with yo' baby!"

He grabbed her arm and then froze as if processing what she'd just said. Quickly, he released her arm.

"What?"

She smacked her lips. "You heard me."

He looked her up and down and sat back down in his chair.

"Yeah I heard you, but you've got the wrong one."

She put her hands on her hips, still standing beside him.

"What's that supposed to mean?"

"That means, that ain't my baby."

She gasped in contempt and looked at Mario in disgust.

"That's some typical nigga shit to say."

"Watch your mouth."

"Watch yours. What you trying to call me a hoe now?

You know good and well you're the only one I've EVER been with."

He looked up at her.

"You better calm your tone. I'm the only one huh? We barely had sex, Alex. ONCE. And now I'm supposed to be your baby's daddy. Please. Try that high school shit on one of those young cats you're used to dealing with."

She pushed his head with her index finger.

"It only takes ONCE dummy."

He rose up once more and rose his voice.

"Don't keep putting your hands on me, Alex. For real, though."

He moved to walk past her and Alex stepped in his path.

"What? Are you seriously trying to leave? This conversation isn't over."

"What do you want me to say?"

The buzz of his phone vibrating caught their attention. He pulled the phone from its holster, looked at the caller id, and silenced the call.

"Is that your other little girlfriend?" Alex asked, reaching for his phone.

He moved away from her.

"Watch out," he said. "You talking crazy."

"I'm talking crazy? You're the one who just denied your kid. Let's be real, Mario. Clearly you don't care anything about me. So be honest. I know you're messing with someone else."

"Man, you're on some other shit today, Alex. I'm telling you, you better go on with all that."

"So you're going to deny that too?"

"Whatever."

He turned and walked into the living room and grabbed his jacket. Alex followed him and quickly grabbed the jacket out of his hands.

"You're not leaving!" she demanded, nearly in tears. "You do not get to impregnate me, cheat on me, and walk out on me."

"Yo, you're way too dramatic for me today."

The tears fell down her cheeks despite her attempts to control herself. She stared at her boyfriend defiantly.

"I know you're cheating on me, Mario. I've read your text messages several times. You're busted."

"So now you're going through my stuff? Didn't realize you were so crazy."

"And I didn't realize what an ass you were."

They faced off in silence. Mario ran his hand over his head and sat down on the sofa.

"Look," he said. "This isn't working out."

"I'm pregnant," she spat out, as if saying it for the first time. "And it's yours."

He sighed. "I'm going to need some proof of that."

She walked over to her purse on the chair and pulled out a piece of paper. She handed it to Mario. He glanced over it and shrugged his shoulders.

"Okay. You're pregnant. But this paper doesn't say it's mine."

She cocked her head to the side.

"Mario," she said softly, tears still falling. "You *know* it's your baby. You nearly forced me to have sex with you that night. If I wasn't ready to give it to my boyfriend what makes you think I'm really sexing anybody else."

Mario got angry. "You trying to say I raped you?"

"I'm trying to say we're pregnant…that's all."

Mario sighed and threw the paper down on the sofa. Ringing his hands together he looked up at Alex and shook his head.

"I'm going to need a minute, aight?"

He stood up and held his hand out to her beckoning for his jacket. She didn't budge.

"Come on now. I don't want to argue anymore. I'll call you later or I'll be back. I just need some time to think about this, okay?"

Reluctantly, she handed him back his jacket. She watched

him walk to the door and pause before he exited.

"I'll call you later, okay," he said, without turning around.

She watched him exit the apartment and felt herself fall to the floor in a fit of tears. Her breathing became uncontrollable and she forced herself to calm down. She reached for her phone and dialed a familiar number.

"Yo!"

She sniffled and tried to fight back her tears so that she could respond. But she couldn't. All she could do was cry hysterically into the phone.

"Alex? What's wrong?"

She couldn't answer. The tears kept coming."

"Hey, I'm coming over okay? Just stay on the phone til I get there...I'm coming."

~ ~ ~

It took a little over twenty minutes, but true to form her friend came right over. Alex was disheveled, eyes all red and puffy by the time the knock sounded at the door. Sluggishly, she opened the door and fell into Clay's embrace.

"What happened to you, girl?" he asked jokingly. "You sounded like your best friend died. I'm alive and kicking so it can't be that bad."

He ushered her into the living room and they sat on the

couch with Alex lying in Clay's lap.

"I hate my life," she said softly.

Clay stroked her hair.

"Please. Your parents pay your rent. Everybody loves you…what about your life is so bad?"

She was quiet, her tears falling slower now landing on Clay's pant legs.

"Okay…this is the part where you confess your sins."

She sighed. "I have to tell you something. And please don't make a joke about it."

"I won't."

"I'm pregnant."

Clay said nothing. Alex noticed he stopped stroking her hair.

"I am like six weeks pregnant, Clay. And when I told that jerk he tells me it's not his…insinuating that I'm sleeping with everybody and their brother. Then he denies the fact that he's cheating on me…"

Clay remained silent. She hit his leg.

"Say something."

Still nothing. Alex sat up and looked at her friend with her pitiful eyes. His look was hard and uninviting at first. But as he took in the sight of her, sensing her turmoil, he softened.

"I knew you were sleeping with him."

"It isn't like you think. It only happened once and it was horrible….I barely remember it. I was sick out of my mind and he more or less forced himself on me."

"Come on, Alex…"

"You don't believe me?" she whined.

Clay grabbed her hand.

"No, I believe you…but look at the dude you're talking about, Alex. Look at all the dudes you mess with. What did you expect from him? For him to ask you to marry him? You thought he was going to be happy? You already knew he was cheating on you."

"You're supposed to be making me feel better."

"Yeah, I'm here for you. But, as your friend I also have to be real with you. This isn't cool. Now you have another person to be concerned about. Forget that dude. Just make sure when the time comes that you get what you need out of him financially. Other than that, this is all on you, Alex."

Alex fell back into Clay's lap.

"I can't do this," she said. "I can't be anybody's mama."

"Yes you can."

"No, I can't. I can barely take care of myself. And I can't tell my parents about this. My dad would be so disappointed in me."

"You've got to tell them at some point."

"Ugh. I can't believe this is happening to me. This wasn't supposed to be me."

"Well, you know I'm here for you. Just call me Uncle Clay."

She slapped his leg. "Shut up, Uncle Clay."

She sat up and gave him a weak smile.

"I'm so glad you're my friend."

Clay nodded his head slowly.

"Yep. That's me. Your good ol' friend."

They were silent for a moment.

"So," Clay said, kicking his feet up on the coffee table. "Where's your baby daddy now?"

"Ugh, don't call him that. To me he's just a sperm donor now. I don't want him anywhere near me or my baby."

"Okay, then. Where's your sperm donor?"

"He left talking about he needs time to think this whole thing over. I mean, you'd think *he* was the one with a baby in his body. Jerk. I should have stabbed him in the eye or something."

Clay laughed heartily. "You're nuts. That was your boo though."

"Shut up. Speaking of boos, where's yours? You don't have some hot date to run off to?"

He shook his head. "Naw. I'm chilling. The chick I was

seeing…well, it wasn't meant to be. Besides, I'm holding out for someone else."

"Oh yeah? You just move from one to the next, huh? You sure you don't have some babies out there somewhere?"

"Ha, ha.. It's not even like that. I'm telling you Alex…this girl is the one. It's just gon' take a minute to get her."

"What? She's not falling over herself trying to get with Mr. Clayton Paul? What's wrong with her?"

Clay laughed. "I know right? She's a little slow. But it's all good, pimpin'. I'll wait. I'm a patient man."

"Don't you want to get me some ice cream, Precious?" Alex asked in her sugary voice.

Clay bopped her on the nose.

"Oh, you not concerned with listening to my saga, huh?" he joked.

"I'm sorry. I have a taste for it."

Clay rubbed her stomach.

"It's all good," he said. "I'll make a run for the munchkin. Ain't nobody worried about you. Uncle Clay to the rescue."

Alex laughed. "You're killing me with that."

~ ~ ~

Later that night after she had taken a nice long bath, Alex surveyed her body in the mirror. She noticed a slight bulge in her tummy that no one else would have caught. She viewed herself from all angles, trying to imagine her body with a more protruding figure. She couldn't see it. More to the point, she wasn't sure that she wanted to see it. Wrapping herself in a towel she sat on her bed and dialed her parents' number. She hadn't spoken to them in a few days and was trying to muster up the courage to get it all over with.

"Hey baby girl," her dad answered the call.

"Hi, dad."

"What's going on? Haven't heard from you in a few days. Everything okay?"

"Yes. Just been a little busy that's all. How's mommy?"

"She's good. She's in there talking to your brother. He came over for a minute."

"Oh okay."

"Mom wants to do a family vacation for Christmas instead of the usual festivities…like a cruise or something."

"Oh yeah?"

"Yep. We're going to pay for it if you want to go."

Alex sighed. "That sounds fun."

"Your aunt Polly called yesterday. She was asking about you. Mom told her you were doing well in school. Mom's real proud of you, baby girl. Me too. Real proud of you."

Alex sighed again, her nerve totally gone.

"Thank you, daddy."

"Mmhhmm. You wanna talk to Mom? I'll get her for you."

"No, I have to go study now, daddy. Can you tell her I said hello and I'll call her tomorrow?"

"Okay, baby girl. You have a good night."

"Thanks, daddy. Talk to you later."

She clicked the phone shut and lowered her head, ashamed at herself. As she replayed the conversation in her mind, her phone rung in her hand. She looked at the caller id and cringed.

"Hello," she said gingerly, preparing herself for more of his insulting behavior.

"What's up?"

"Nothing much. Getting ready for bed. So, you done thinking it over?"

"I didn't call to argue with you, Alex," he said, catching her tone. "I'm done arguing. It's not productive and neither one of us is getting anything out of it."

"Okay…"

"So, when's your next doctor's appointment?"

"In two weeks. They're going to do an ultrasound." She paused. "You want to come?"

"Let me check my schedule. I might be able to. What day?"

"Thursday."

"Yeah, I'll let you know by next week. Do you have insurance? I could add you to mine but you know…we're not married."

"I have insurance through my parents. It's okay."

They sat on the phone in silence, each considering their own thoughts.

"You hurt my feelings, Mario. All that stuff you were talking about me and other dudes and denying the fact that you're cheating on me…"

"I just don't think we're on the same page. I mean, I'm sorry if I hurt your feelings, but a brother gotta be careful, you know? Girls pull this mess all the time, trying to get dudes caught up…trapped. Plus, I'm not ready for no kid."

"Neither am I. I'm still in school trying to get my career going. How do you think I feel? I'm the one whose life is going to change. I'm the one that has to carry the baby to term."

"And I can respect that. But this affects me too. I have to look out for my best interests, you know?"

"Uh-huh." Alex touched her belly and quickly moved her hand.

"I have to look out for mine too," she retorted.

"For sho'."

"So, I don't really think it's in my best interest to have a baby right now."

Mario hesitated. "So what are you saying?"

"I'm saying that when I go back to the doctor I'm going to inquire about all of my options. I can't do this. I don't think I'm prepared to do this by myself like this."

"By yourself? You act like I just said to hell with you, Alex."

"You may as well have," Alex piped up. "I'm not trying to be somebody's baby mama. When I have children, I want it to be in a stable, family environment. Not some mistake with somebody who doesn't respect me."

"Oh my god…I was really trying to keep this drama free, Alex. For real, so you can stop with all the dramatics. We're not together anymore. So what? People have babies everyday out of wedlock. It's not the end of the world. You're not going to kill my kid just because we broke up. That's some selfish shit."

"First of all, didn't realize that we'd officially broken up."

"Stop playing…"

"Second of all, who you calling selfish when you're the one messing around with god knows how many chicks? I guess I should be thankful that you gave me a baby and not an STD with your trifling self. Third off, now you wanna claim the baby? I'm gonna need you to make up your mind. This is the exact reason right here why we *don't* need to have a baby together. You can't be the baby's daddy one day when it fits you then disown the baby the next day just cuz you feel like it, Mario. Now *that's* some selfish mess. Babies need stability. We don't have that…well, you definitely don't."

"Lower your voice when you talking to me. You're getting a little bit beside yourself. If you think I'm going to let you just kill the baby, *IF* it's my baby, and I'm not going to do anything you can forget it."

"Really? Last time I checked, this was my body. Tell you what Mario. When April 26 comes I'll call you and let you know if the baby came or if I aborted it. Don't bother calling back."

She clicked the phone closed, ending the call and fell back on her bed. Instantly the phone began to ring again. She sent the call to voice mail. Two minutes passed and the phone rang again. Once more, she sent the call to voicemail. On his third call, Alex answered without speaking then hung the phone up again. Before the phone could ring a fourth time, she powered off her cell and closed her eyes.

This is my body, she thought. *My body, my decision. Period.*

CANDACE

Candace took a deep breath as she entered her home. From the doorway she could hear the video game blaring. Walking through the kitchen she surveyed the dirty dishes in the sink and the half empty pitcher of lemonade on the counter. She sat her purse and cellphone down next to it and clutched an envelope in her hand. She stared at the back of Quincy's head, watching the round man as he whooted and hollered at his team winning the stupid football game. Candace raised her eyes to the heavens.

"Jehovah, give me strength," she whispered.

She walked into the living room and over to the big screen television. Quincy barely noticed her. Without warning she pulled the plug out of the wall and the screen went blank.

"What the fuck!" Quincy yelled at her. "Do you know what you just did?"

She tossed the envelope at him.

"What the hell is this and why the hell did you come in here fucking up my game in the middle of the damn season woman?"

"Read the letter, Quincy."

He threw down his wireless controller looked at the envelope addressed to him.

"It's already opened. You read it already. What you want me to read it for?"

She put her hands on her hips praying for inner strength. He pulled the letter out and she watched as his eyes went over the words she'd already memorized. *Your home is scheduled to be foreclosed.* Quincy sighed deeply and leaned back on the couch.

"Uh-huh," Candace said, looking at him with contempt.

"We are about to lose our house, Quincy. You care to explain that?"

"Don't worry about it," he waved her off.

"Don't worry about it?" she repeated. "Are you serious? That's all you can come with? I've been busting my bootie working and you won't so much as lift a finger around here. And now you've lost our house."

"My house…and we ain't lost nothing. I said don't worry about it. I'll take care of it."

"Your house? Oh you getting technical now? What's wrong with you? Have you lost your mind? What have you been doing with your money since you haven't being paying the damn mortgage?"

"Look, don't start trying to get in my shit. You ain't never been concerned about how the bills got paid before, so…"

"Hold up. Don't flip this on me! You are supposed to be the head of your household. Financially and spiritually so don't be acting like you've been burdened with responsibility."

"Whatever."

"In two weeks they are going to put us out, Quincy. So you haven't been paying the mortgage for a minute. And you didn't think that was something you're obligated to tell your wife?"

He didn't respond. He simply tossed the letter onto the coffee table and walked over to the wall to plug the television back in. She reached out to grab his arm and he violently yanked away from her.

"Get off me!" he exclaimed.

"You're just going to ignore me? Ignore our problem?"

He restarted his game.

"Quincy!"

He chose his team again.

"Quincy!"

She flailed her arms about, trying to get his attention. He continued to ignore her.

"You know what? You're a sorry excuse for a man. You can't keep a job. You have no sense of responsibility. Can't even handle your own business. That's not attractive and that's not the kind of husband I want."

"Shut up sometimes," he answered her. "Told you I'd take care of it so leave it alone."

"How are you going to take care of it? Do you have all the money you owe them?"

He went on to ignore her.

"I didn't think so. Why did I ever marry your sorry butt? What kind of man can't provide for his wife? You make me sick."

She turned from him and hurried upstairs. In the heat of her anger, she grabbed a suitcase and began packing some of her belongings. Quincy had the television blaring so loudly that she didn't hear her cell ringing in the kitchen. As he sat there playing his game, Quincy could hear the phone chiming. He ignored it. Then he heard the continued beeping of her text indicator. Intrigued, he went into the kitchen and grabbed her phone. He saw the missed call from Khalil.

Who the hell is that?

He clicked on the view message button to read the texts sent from Khalil.

Baby, are you still mad at me? If you can get away, text me so I can show you how sorry I am. I miss your sexy sleek body and I want to run my tongue down your legs the way you like. Come on, you know you want to.

Quincy bolted up the stairs and grabbed Candace as she was frantically packing.

"What…" the words could barely escape her lips as he pinned her up against the wall.

"You bring your ass in here talking about what kind of a husband I am…what the hell kind of wife are you?"

"You are hurting me," she winced from the pain of his tight grasp.

He threw her cell phone in her face hard, bruising her cheek.

"Who the fuck is Khalil?"

Her eyes grew wide and she opened her mouth to speak, but he cut her off.

"Save it you foul ass bitch."

He let her go and moved away from her.

"Walking around here talking about how spiritually superior you are. You're a hypocrite, a fuckin' joke. You think I'm supposed to bow down to your ass like you're some rare dime piece or something. How fuckin' rare are you if you're opening your legs to every dick that points in your direction? Oh my bad, let's not forget every pussy that drips your way too."

She rubbed her face and bent down to pick her cell up from the place it had fallen to on the floor. She looked up at Quincy in fright, having never seen him so enraged.

"Stupid bitch," he shouted, turning away from her.

He let out a piercing scream that scared her then he abruptly punched a hole into their bedroom wall. Candace was stunned. She slid to the floor and watched him, afraid of what his fury would lead him to do next. A thousand thoughts flew through her mind. An image of Miranda looking frail and hopeless included. She was scared that she was about to be the next one in her girlfriend circle to be abused by her husband. She clutched the cell in her hand and stared at Quincy as he paced back and forth punching the air and hurling obscenities. Once he tired of this, he turned his angry glare back to her. He eyed the bag she had been packing.

"What, you're leaving me? You think you hurting me by packing your sorry ass bag and leaving? Fuck you!"

He took her bag off of the bed and threw it at her.

"Fuck you and all the niggas you've been fucking and all the chicks you've been eating out. Fuck you."

She jumped.

"Get the fuck out of my house with your sorry ass. Think

you're God's gift to a man? I hope you lay down and get gonorrhea in your ass and Chlamydia in your mouth you sorry cunt."

He kicked her bag and Candace screamed, so sure that he was aiming for her body instead.

"Get the fuck up and get your fake ass out of my house."

She blinked, not sure if she should move or not. Thinking it best to go now, she grabbed her bag, tossed a few more items into it absentmindedly and hurried out of the room. She could hear Quincy throwing shit down the stairs behind her and cursing her as she scurried away.

"Don't bring your ass back here. I don't need you. Talking bout you need a real man. Tell Khalil's ass to buy you a house you second rate bitch. Think you got so much class. You ain't nothing but a hood rat with some typing skills. Flexing ass, you ain't even got a paralegal certificate, let alone a college degree. You ain't shit your damn self. You one step away from flipping some burgers. Fuck you!"

She ran out of the house, neglecting to close the front door behind her. Quickly she jumped into her car and sped off down the street. When she approached the first red light, she glanced at the text Khalil had sent. Damn his ass for texting her instead of just approaching her at work tomorrow. She could have kicked herself for having the lack of vision to leave her phone downstairs. Unsure of what to do next, she pressed the call button to hit him back up.

"I'm glad you called," Khalil answered. "Are you coming over?"

"Actually, I am."

"I'll cook you dinner."

"Where's Sheila?"

"Where's Quincy?"

"We're getting a divorce."

"She's kinda gone away for a while…let me go start dinner. I'll see you when you get here."

"Okay."

Candace wasn't sure if running to Khalil was a smart move to make. But she was determined not to return home to her parents and admit that her marriage was a mistake. They'd never let her live it down especially after she'd fought so hard to convince them that she truly loved Quincy. As she drove in silence, she thought about the girls questioning her true feelings about Quincy. They too would never let her forget how much of a front she put up about being married.

I tried to be a good wife, she reasoned with herself. *I admit that perhaps I lost my way…but Quincy was never a good man for me…and a home is only as strong as its spiritual head.*

She soon reached Khalil's place and was almost ashamed to look at him as he opened the door and allowed her entry. Stepping into the light of his foyer, Khalil could see the bruise forming on her face. He slammed the door shut.

"What did that nigga do to you?" he demanded.

"Calm down," she urged him. "It's not that bad. He didn't hit me or anything."

"It doesn't look like he didn't hit you."

"He threw my phone at me…he saw your text tonight."

Khalil grimaced. He reached for her hand and led her into the living room and on to the sofa. Slowly, he lifted her legs onto his lap and removed her shoes. He used his magical fingers to knead the soles of her feet. Candace lay back on the sofa and tried to relinquish the tension she'd been feeling throughout the evening.

"What did you say to him?" Khalil asked her.

She shook her head. "Nothing. He didn't really ask me any questions. He just yelled and cussed…and punched a hole in our wall."

"What made him look at your phone?"

"I don't know. We had just had an argument. His sorry ass has let our house go into foreclosure…and he's mad at me because of his stupidity."

Khalil shook his head.

"You need a real man, sexy. A man that knows how to take care of his woman and provide for her."

He slid his hand up her leg and under her skirt. She squirmed.

"Khalil," she protested weakly.

"Hmmm?"

His fingertips slightly caressed the fabric of her cotton bikini briefs which were already becoming soaked. It really didn't take much to excite her. She felt him slip inside of her undies and his thumb strategically brushed over her clit repeatedly. She relaxed her body and gave in to the intense sensation of his touch.

"You like it when a real man touches you, don't you?" Khalil whispered to her.

In seconds she was exploding in spasms against the back and forth motion of his finger. Her body shuddered and convulsed until the sensation passed her by. Satisfied with himself, Khalil removed his hand and licked his fingers seductively and with great production. Candace looked at him as he dragged his tongue back and forth, lapping up all of her juices.

"Great appetizer," he teased. "Now, let me go get your entrée, my dear."

Without another word, he left the room in pursuit of their dinner.

~ ~ ~

Later, as they lay in bed, limp, all intertwined and damp from their lovemaking, Khalil ran his hand up down the spine of her back. The smell of incense burning relaxed her mind in the aftermath of him relaxing her body.

"You can stay with me for as long as you need to," he said softly. "I'm here for you."

She sucked her teeth. "And what would Sheila say?"

"She's in jail for the time being."

Candace was stunned. "What? Why?"

"Domestic dispute."

She turned over to face him.

"Let me get this straight. You called the police on her and pressed charges against the woman?"

"She came at me with a knife. Threatened to cut my Johnson off."

Candace laughed. "Shut up."

"For real. She's crazy. I was breaking up with her and she went nuts. Rather than put my hands on the woman, I called the police."

"You couldn't just leave?"

"She wouldn't let me."

Candace laid back, looked up at the ceiling and laughed uncontrollably.

"Ridiculous. And how long is she going to be in there?"

"Until she makes bail. Or until her court date. I don't really care."

"You are something else." She sighed. "I can't stay here. As much as I need a place to stay for a minute, I don't think I should stay here with you, Khalil. If she comes home and finds me up in here…I don't want to hurt anybody if she clicks on stupid. And I damn sure don't want anyone running after me with a knife."

"She won't come back. She's not that crazy."

"Right."

Khalil kissed her cheek gently.

"Let's get some rest. You can figure it all out tomorrow. Tonight, just let me hold you."

He embraced her and she allowed herself to be cocooned in his arms.

JADA

They entered the building quickly. Jada headed towards the elevator and Alex followed her, dragging behind.

"Slow down, girl," Alex complained, leaning against the wall as they waited for the elevator to reach them.

Alex clutched at her left side and leaned over slightly.

"You okay?" Jada asked.

"Cramping. And you're killing me moving all fast. Geez."

They entered the elevator and Jada pressed the button for the lobby.

"You can use the exercise girl. Gotta get you ready for carrying that baby weight around."

"Well…you can cancel that because I'm not going to be carrying anything around."

Jada shot her friend a puzzled look.

"What are you talking about?"

The elevator buzzed as they reached their floor.

"I'm not having the baby."

They exited the elevator and Jada slapped Alex on the arm.

"What do you mean, you're not having the baby?"

Alex rolled her eyes. "What do you think I mean?"

Jada sighed. "Don't do this."

"No, you don't do this. Don't lecture me. I know you want to have a baby, Jada and you think the idea of being a mom is all grand. Good for you, you're married. You can do that. But I'm not, so I can't."

Jada stopped walking and turned to look at her prissy friend.

"No, you can do it alright. You were woman enough to lie there and sleep with ol' boy then you should be big girl enough to own up to the responsibility. You kill me."

"What?"

"You're so freakin' spoiled and clueless. So…selfish."

"Because I don't want to share my body with a little person I made with a man that doesn't even like me? Where do you get off judging me?"

Jada noticed that Alex was leaning to the side and kept cradling her left side.

"I'm not judging you…what's wrong with you?"

"I told you I'm cramping."

"You're pregnant. You shouldn't be cramping. Come on, let's take Jordan his lunch. You can sit down in his office for a minute."

Alex followed Jada through the corridor and into Jordan's office. The tall man was busy on a call when they entered. He waved at them and Jada waved back. She motioned for Alex to take a seat. Sitting next to her, she whispered to her friend.

"I think you should think about this before making a rash decision. Trust me, you don't want to wake up years from now regretting the decision you make."

Alex began to rock. "Let it go, Jada. Okay. It's my decision."

"I know that. Okay, okay…you're making me nervous, girl. You don't look too good. Is it painful?"

"A little worse than my menstrual cramps."

"You want me to take you to the hospital? It doesn't sound good girl."

"No. We can just stop and get some aspirin or something."

"Hey, babes," Jordan called to Jada.

She got up and walked over to her husband and they exchanged a quick embrace.

"You didn't have to come down here," he told her.

She shrugged. "We were in the area so I thought it would be nice to drop a little something off to you."

"That was nice of you."

Jordan looked over at Alex. At this point she was leaned over with her face in her hand. Jordan looked at Jada for an explanation.

"Call 911," she mouthed to him.

She walked over to Alex who was whimpering softly. She touched her friend lightly on the back.

"Alex," she said.

Alex looked up at her in tears. "Something's wrong," she cried. "I feel like I'm bleeding."

Jada looked over at Jordan who was already on the line calling for help.

"Stand up," she ordered Alex. "Stand up, just for a second. Let's check you out, okay?"

She assisted Alex to her feet and sure enough the young woman had blood staining her jeans. She eased her back into the chair and held her hand.

"Someone's coming to help us okay? Just stay calm for me."

Jada rubbed her friend's back and looked over at Jordan who was still on the phone directing the emergency team on how to get to the building. Time seemed to stand still as the trio waited for the paramedics to come to Alex's aid. They were all relieved to see the two men enter the office with a stretcher in tow. A short bald man approached the two women and looked down at Alex.

"Ma'am, can you tell us what's hurting you?"

"I have bad cramps in my left side," Alex cried. "And I'm bleeding."

The paramedic checked his computer device which he was carrying in hand. He peered over his notes.

"You're pregnant? How far along are you?"

"Two months."

"Okay, we're going to get you on the stretcher and take you to the hospital okay? Do you have a preference of which one you want to go to?"

Alex shook her head no.

"DeKalb Medical," Jada piped in.

"You're her friend or family?"

"Both."

The other paramedic unzipped a large bag he'd brought in with them.

"You don't wanna take her vitals first, Parker?" he asked his partner.

The short guy shook his head. "Don't want her to lose much more blood. We can do it in the truck."

"Are you allergic to any type of medications that you know of?" the second paramedic asked Alex.

She shook her head no.

"Latex?"

Another shake of her head.

"Does the cramping hurt worse when you move, hun?" the shorter guy asked.

Another shake of her head.

"Okay, we're going to help you up here and ease you onto the stretcher, okay. On the count of three."

He positioned his hand under her arm and proceeded to help her up.

"One..two…three."

Together the men eased Alex onto the bed, strapped here in securely, and covered her with sheets. Her blood had begun to stain the fabric of the chair she'd been sitting in. Jada looked over at Jordan.

"Sorry," she mouthed.

"How old are you ma'am?" the second paramedic asked Alex.

Alex didn't answer him.

"She's 21," Jada answered.

"Do you know her height and weight?"

"Um….about 5"8, 132 pounds."

"Come on, take her BP and temp in the truck," the shorter man ordered.

He looked at Jada. "Are you riding with us?"

Jada grabbed Alex's purse and moved towards the door.

"No. I'll meet you there."

She hurried out of her husband's office without so much as a kiss goodbye and sped down the stairs to the parking garage. She didn't want to take the elevator because she knew they would be bringing Alex down that way. Quickly she trotted to her car and began to exit the building. As she drove through downtown Decatur she could hear the sirens of the truck following behind her.

"They move quick," she said aloud.

As quickly as she could, she reached the hospital, parked in the deck and went inside the emergency room in search of her friend. Because of the severity of Alex's emergency she was soon ushered into an exam room and ordered to pee in a cup. After handing her an exam gown to change into, the nurse quickly left the room. Alex looked at Jada with saddened eyes.

"Can you help me please?" she asked softly.

Jada helped the tall beauty peel off her soiled jeans and underwear. She escorted her over to the toilet in the room. Alex leaned on Jada and began to sob heavily.

"I didn't mean it, Jada. I didn't mean to say I didn't want my baby…"

Her words were barely distinguishable through her loud sobs.

"God is punishing me," she cried. "Punishing me for being selfish."

Jada hugged her friend and tried to reassure her as best she could.

"That's not true. Things happen…and we really don't know what's happening now. Come on…pull yourself together sweetie."

Together they managed to help get Alex onto the toilet and she was able to leave her urine sample. Alex sat there as Jada removed her blouse and replaced it with the paper gown. By the time the nurse re-entered the room Alex was laying quietly on the exam table.

"Okay dear, my name is Brenda. Okay? I'll be your nurse. How long have you been bleeding?"

"Just today," Alex answered softly.

"And how pregnant are you?"

"Two months."

The nurse busied herself about with washing her hands.

"First pregnancy?"

"Yes ma'am."

The nurse turned to Alex and smiled.

"Awww, yes ma'am huh? Listen at you sounding all sweet as pie. How old are you child?"

"21."

The nurse felt around on her stomach.

"Tell me if it hurts worse in any particular spot."

She mashed and pressed along Alex's abdomen and Alex just lay still saying nothing.

"Anything?" the nurse asked.

"No. It just cramps badly on my left side."

The nurse pulled out a square package from the storage cabinet under the sink. She smiled at Alex.

"Okay, hun. The doctor is going to want to have an ultrasound and blood work done. I'm going to put this catheter in for you now and then draw your blood. Okay sugar?"

Jada cringed and Alex frowned at the nurse.

"What's that for?"

Nurse Brenda pulled a long tube out of the packaging and held it up for Alex to see.

"We put this part into your urethra so that your urine trickles out into this bag."

She held up the pouch for Alex to see.

"Why?" Alex asked.

"Need your bladder empty for the ultrasound, love. It's not that bad. Whenever you had sex for the first time…I promise you that *that* hurt worse."

Nurse Brenda laughed and patted Alex on the leg.

"Relax sugar." She turned to look at Jada. "Okay, baby. You can wait outside for just two minutes while we put the catheter in."

Jada moved to stand up and Alex held her hand out.

"No. Don't go." She looked at the nurse pitifully. "She can stay. It's okay."

The nurse shrugged and Jada sat back down.

"Scooch up, baby and bend your knees up."

Alex did as directed.

"Now move your legs apart for me."

The nurse went about putting in the tube and Alex winced from the discomfort. Nurse Brenda tried to take her mind off of it by keeping up idle conversation.

"You two must be good friends since you let her sit in here and see all your business like this."

Jada giggled a little.

"We're pretty close," Alex responded through clenched teeth.

"Mmmhmm. I wouldn't even let my sister be taking in all my business. Alright you can relax your legs now."

Alex put her legs down and sighed.

"That wasn't too bad now was it?" Nurse Brenda asked her.

"It was bad enough."

The nurse pulled her rubber gloves off and washed her hands again. She selected several tubes from a rack, a butterfly needle and what looked like a large rubber band.

"Okay, time to take your blood," she told Alex. "Which arm do they usually take your blood from, sugar?"

Alex held out her right arm. Jada watched as the nurse wiped her arm down with alcohol pads and proceeded to take her blood. In no time she was done. Tubes of blood in hand, she patted Alex on the leg and assured her that a tech would be in soon to transport her to radiology for her ultrasound.

Alex sat up on the hospital bed and looked at Jada.

"Thank you for coming with me," she said.

"You don't have to thank me."

"You're always there when I need you."

"That's what friends are for, girl. You'd do the same for me."

"Yeah, well…I'd probably panic and not be much help to anybody."

"Do you want to call Mario?"

Alex sucked her teeth and crossed her arms.

"For what? He can kick rocks."

"He should know what's going on."

"We don't even know what's going on…right?"

Touché chick , Jada thought to herself. Before she could respond, there was a knock at the door and in walked the tech with a wheelchair.

"Radiology?' he asked, rather than said.

Alex moved to get off of the bed and sensing her struggle, the tech assisted her into the wheelchair. He looked up at Jada and nodded.

"You can stay here. She'll be back in about thirty minutes or so."

She watched him wheel her out of the room, letting the door close behind him. Staring at the blood stains Alex had left on the white sheets of the exam bed, Jada sighed. She sat back in her chair and closed her eyes trying to relax her mind. A melody resounded interrupting her attempt. She could feel the phone vibrating in her lap as the melody got louder. Realizing that it was Alex's phone ringing, she quickly pulled the cell out of the girl's purse and uttered a rushed hello.

"What's up? I was trying to reach Alex..."

A man's voice sounded confused. Jada looked down at the caller id and saw that it was Clay on the line.

"Hey, Clay. This is Jada, Alex's friend."

"Oh what's up? Where your homegirl? In the bathroom?"

"Not exactly..." Jada was unsure of how Alex would feel about her disclosing her situation to Clay.

"She's in the hospital...the emergency room."

His tone was panicked. "Hospital? What happened? Is something wrong with the baby?"

Jada exhaled. "I wasn't sure if you knew she was pregnant or not...but she was cramping and bleeding..."

"The baby? What's the status on the baby?"

"They just took her down for an ultrasound so we don't know for sure yet, Clay." She sighed. "But...I think it's pretty safe to say that she's having a miscarriage."

"Which hospital?"

"DeKalb Medical."

"I'm on my way."

Clay didn't give her a chance to respond or protest. He clicked off of the line immediately. She was touched to sense how much the young man really cared for Alex. Too bad Alex wasn't able to see how he truly felt for her.

MIRANDA

"Something's different about you," Norris commented as she checked her attire in the mirror.

She tooted her nose up and straightened out her beautiful bracelet. Norris sat on the bed flipping through the cable stations and drawing on a blunt he'd just rolled.

"You seem more chill than normal. You're not even bugging about me smoking in the house."

She shrugged. "Just have decided not to beat a dead horse."

"Uh-huh." He held the blunt out in her direction. "Want a hit?"

She looked over at him and raised her eyebrow. Norris laughed and threw his head up at her.

"Go on," he urged her. "You know you want to."

She took one step towards him then stopped.

"Don't hesitate," he teased her. "Gon' and take it. You know you want to."

"Stop playing," she told him.

He chuckled. "You stop playing wit' yo' self."

"What is your problem?" she asked him.

He shrugged. "No problem. It's all gravy to me. I'm just saying, be real with ya' boy. I've been smoking for years, baby. *Years*. Trust me, I can smell the hint of the green from down the street. Especially if it's that good good."

Miranda sat on the bed and began to put her boots on.

"So what are you trying to say?"

Norris leaned forward and blew a puff of smoke into his wife's face. She barely flinched and didn't cough and choke as she usually did when he did that.

"I'm saying I'm not tripping that you've been hitting the blunt. Hell, that's alright with me. This shit here is good for you. It's all natural."

"Whatever, Norris."

"All I'm wondering is when did you pick up your new little pastime?"

She shook her head and rose from the bed

"Norris, I'm not entertaining this." She grabbed her Coach bag and headed for the bedroom door. "I'll be back later."

"Where you going? Off to blaze? That's something else that's different bout you. You're always running off somewhere. Ever since I came back home you stay gone. What's that about?"

"I'm just going to hang out with my girls," she said. "I'll be back in about an hour. Ok?"

"Yeah, alright. Least you could do is let a nigga hit whatever the hell you're sampling."

She waved him off and walked through the apartment to leave.

"Whatever, Norris," she called over her shoulder.

She exited the apartment and began to descend the stairs. Suddenly it dawned on her that she'd forgotten her cell phone in the house. She turned around and walked back to her unit. Hesitating before unlocking the door, she wondered if she should just tell Norris the truth. Sneaking off the nurture her new found bad habit was beginning to get on her nerves. Sighing, she turned the lock and reentered the apartment. She looked on the coffee table. The phone wasn't there. She looked on the kitchen counter and still no phone. She turned around and headed for her bedroom but suddenly stopped in her tracks as she heard Norris' voice.

"You know you miss me, girl…That's your own fault. All you had to do was act right and it woulda been all good…I might just stay gone until you learn how to treat your man…Watch your mouth now…How you gon' be mad because a nigga is with his wife? You knew what it was when we first started…Oh yeah? And what you gon' do for me if I do come over?"

Miranda couldn't listen to any more. She made the final steps into their bedroom and Norris quickly clicked off of his cell phone. She didn't say anything. Her eyes surveyed the room and spotted her cell laying on the night table. Slowly, she walked over to it, picked it up, and waved it at Norris.

"Guess it's a good thing that I left my phone, huh?"

Norris jumped up and walked over to Miranda.

"Baby, look…That shit wasn't nothing…"

She held her hand up to silence him. She moved to leave the room and he grabbed her arm. Instinctively she screamed and snatched and her arm away.

"Man, calm down," he begged her. "Nobody's going to hurt you, Miranda. I'm just trying to talk to you."

She shook her head and backed out of the room.

"No, I don't want to talk to you. I don't have anything to say to you. Tell it to Tammy."

Quickly she ran from the house and down the stairs to the safety of her car. Eyes filled with tears, she peeled out of the parking lot and down the road. Her cell began to ring and she ignored it, sure that it was Norris calling to plead his case. Four calls and many tears later, she was at her destination. It was a place she'd been visiting often. She walked the familiar path up the sidewalk and to the door of the luxury apartment. Knocking two times with no answer, she leaned against the doorframe unable to control her tears. She heard the lock on the door turn and stepped back just as the door swung open.

"Man, you're bugging," he said in a hushed voice.

Ignoring his reference to her dishelmed appearance Miranda walked past him and entered the apartment.

"I'm having a bad fucking day," she exclaimed as she entered.

"What's wrong, girl?"

Miranda looked to her left abruptly, completely taken aback to hear Stephanie's voice. There she sat, rubbing her belly on the couch with her feet propped up. Miranda's glance flew over to Corey who was standing by the front door shaking his head. Quickly she returned her confused look to her girlfriend who was looking at her with concern.

"Um..I...I don't know where to start," she babbled. "I'm

just so…in shock."

She felt herself begin to shake with nervousness. Trying to get herself together and remain composed, she drifted over to the couch and sat down. Corey walked over to the ladies and smiled.

"I'm going to leave ya'll to your little girl talk. I'm going outside to clean my car out."

"Ok, babe," Stephanie said cheerfully.

Corey left the apartment and Miranda leaned back against the couch. She placed her purse down beside her. Stephanie noticed it immediately.

"That's a nice bag, girl. Where'd you get it?"

"Norris," Miranda said without thinking.

She bit her lip right after saying it, knowing that this was going to lead to many more questions. She wasn't ready to tell any of her girls that she and Norris had reunited. Especially after what had just happened.

"Mmmhmm. What is he doing? Trying to buy back your affection?"

Miranda was silent.

"I hope you told him to dream on."

She rubbed her temples, so not wanting to have this discussion.

Stephanie leaned forward.

"Miranda? Please tell me that you did not take that sorry ass nigga back."

Miranda shook her head. "Don't judge me. He *is* my husband."

"Your husband is the same jerk that tried to kill you, honey."

She sighed. "He wants to try to make it work. He's truly sorry…He agreed to go to counseling."

"How long?"

"How long what?"

"How long have ya'll been back together?"

"I don't know. Two weeks."

Stephanie shifted her position.

"Are you kidding me? What are you thinking? You were just telling us about the desperation of some women…you know, just wanting to be loved. Are you that desperate for love that you'd go back to a man that beats you like some nigga in the street that's stole his money?"

Miranda grabbed her purse. "I really didn't come here to be berated."

Stephanie's brow frowned up as she looked at Miranda skeptically.

"Oh? And what exactly did you come over for? I don't even remember you calling my phone to say you were on the way. Since when do you just do a drive by?"

Miranda stood up and headed for the door with the very pregnant Stephanie following behind her in pursuit of an answer.

"Forget this. I just needed to talk. I didn't know that I needed to make an appointment with my girlfriend to have a heart to heart. Thanks for the memo. I'll know who not to run to next time."

Before Stephanie could respond, Miranda quickly exited her friend's apartment and slammed the door behind her. She felt guilty for her defensive outburst but was relieved to be out of the apartment as she hurried to her car.

"Aye," she heard Corey's voice calling out as she was about to get into the car.

She turned around and watched him walk over to her.

"What the hell is up with you?" he asked.

'I…I didn't know she was here…."

"I called you four times to tell you not to come through…And I sent you a text man. What? You don't use your phone anymore?"

"I heard the phone ring…I thought it was Norris."

"Whatever. Tell you what, you can't come back to the house no more. I don't make it a habit to do business at my house with my ol' lady and my kid here anyway."

"I'm sorry, okay. It was an honest mistake."

"That's cool. Just know that whenever you need to cop something you gon have to go to the trap."

She nodded her understanding.

"Can I get that though? This time I mean."

"Man, get outta here. I can't be doing that out here all willy nilly. Have my neighbors all suspicious and shit. And you know your girl is probably looking out the window at us. I'll text you the address later, aight?"

"Okay." She felt defeated. Nothing was going her way today.

ALEX

Waking from what felt like a long slumber, Alex turned over in her bed and grimaced. She felt so tired. She heard a knocking and sat straight up in bed. Slowly she slid from the bed and walked to the door. The sound of two male voices alarmed her. Then she remembered. Clay had been staying with her since she'd been in the hospital. Like a true friend, he never left her side without great reason. He fixed her meals, kept her company, even washed her clothes. Anything she needed, Clay was right there. She listened hard, trying to make out who the other voice belonged to. Then it occurred to her. It was Mario.

"Can you just wake her up and let her know that I'm here?" Mario asked Clay.

Clay popped his knuckles and hung his head.

"Naw, bruh. I can't do that."

"What's your problem, man? Why you blocking?"

"Gon' somewhere with that, man. Nobody's blocking. I'm telling you, straight up…Alex doesn't want to see you. It's my understanding that ya'lls business together is over."

"As long as she's carrying my seed, our business is very much still on and popping."

Clay pointed his finger at the other man.

"See, that right there shows just how out of touch you are. Alex isn't carrying your seed anymore."

"What the hell are you talking about?"

"It's been what? Two weeks. You haven't called her, haven't thought to come by. You've been ghost all this time. I don't even see why you're popping up now."

Mario rubbed his chin.

"So the bitch went and had an abortion anyway?"

Without thinking, Clay stepped to Mario bringing the two men face to face. Their noses were almost touching, he was so close.

"I'm gon' say this one time, and one time only so I hope you catch it so that you won't catch my foot up your ass. Don't you ever, *ever* call her a bitch again, my dude. The only bitch in here is you, you bitch ass nigga."

"Man, you don't want non' of this, so you can get the fuck out of my face with your lil' preppy boy ass. What? You fucking her now? All this time you're supposed to be her little BFF. I thought your punk ass was gay. I wouldn't be surprised if the baby was yours."

Clay shoved Mario causing him to fall back against the front door.

"Sorry ass excuse for a man," he spat out, walking up on Mario as he tried to regain his footing. "She loss the baby two weeks ago probably because of your bitch ass stressing her out. And for the record, you should consider your ass lucky that you're not in jail for raping her."

"Man fuck you. Nobody raped that girl. I'm a grown ass man. I got plenty of chicks willing to give it to me so why the hell would I want to take it from her young ass?"

"I'm giving you two seconds to raise up out of here, homeboy before I catch a case."

Mario shoved Clay.

"Get some then," he challenged.

Clay stood firm, fists clenched and expression hard.

"That's what I thought," Mario spat out. He turned to leave. "Tell Alex she doesn't have to worry about me anymore. I'm gone."

Alex heard the front door slam and returned to her bed. She considered what had just happened and was more thankful than ever to have a friend like Clay by her side. She thought he was going come to the room to check on her, but the sound of the television in the living room let her know that he was not coming back. Lying down on the bed, she stared at the ceiling deep in thought. Her cell phone rang from under her pillow. She retrieved it and answered the call.

"Hey, Jada."

"How are you girl?"

"I'm okay. Just over here resting."

"Clay still there?"

Alex smiled. "Yes, girl. And he just chomped Mario off not even five minutes ago."

"For real? That Clay is something else."

"Yes he is. My little knight in shining armor."

"So are you feeling any better?"

"Yes. I am…I'm just ready to get my life back to normal. This whole thing has been so depressing and difficult."

"Did you ever talk to your parents?"

"About what? There's nothing to tell now."

"Are you serious? You just had a traumatic experience and a surgical procedure girl. You don't think that's cause enough to let your family know what's going on with you?"

Alex sighed. "It would only upset them and I really don't see the point in upsetting them at this point. What they don't know want hurt them."

"But it'll hurt you. You need all the emotional support

you can get, girl."

Silence.

"Okay then. Think about this. When they get their little statement from United Healthcare showing them the services you recently had that their insurance covered…you know…those little statements that say 'this is not a bill'…what the hell are you going to say?"

Alex was speechless. The thought that the insurance company would send them anything hadn't crossed her mind. Now she was going to be forced to deal with the disappointment and hurt she thought she was going to avoid.

"Let me call you back," she said to her friend, anxious to end their conversation.

"Alright girl," Jada replied. "Just do me a favor and consider getting to your parents before they read about it in the mail. Okay?"

"Okay, friend. Talk to you later."

Alex disconnected the call and closed her eyes. If it wasn't one thing, it was another.

CANDACE

It was definitely time to move on. Candace had been back and forth between Khalil's house and an older cousin's house while trying to figure out what her next move was going to be. It was becoming increasingly difficult to hide her separation from her parents. Work was becoming a challenge as well because with all of her personal issues, Candace was becoming more and more moody. She used to love getting away from the office with Khalil during lunch breaks especially when there was tension in the office. But now that they'd been cohabitating, their afternoon trysts were no longer appealing to Candace. In fact, she tried to avoid him in the office building all together. She was grateful for a place to lay her head, but was getting sick and tired of his male chauvinist attitude and superiority complex.

Khalil liked to attribute everything he didn't agree with or like about her to the fact that she was so much younger than him. He treated her like she didn't know her ass from a hole in the wall. As if his purpose in life was to give her new direction. She was sick of him playing her daddy. His charm and charisma seemed to come and go, he was never consistent. He was either belittling her or bewildering her. Always from one extreme to the very next. It was exhausting. Nevermind the fact that he could never take it whenever she called him on his bullshit. Again, he considered her perspective to be juvenile and childish.

"Candace, can you bring me Sylvia Peterson's case file?"

She was being paged by Pat, one of the firm's junior

partners. Candace didn't care much for Pat and she certainly was in no mood to play anyone's errand girl today.

She buzzed Pat's office back. "I can't leave the front. Sorry."

Her matter-of-fact tone didn't sit well with Pat. She stormed out of her office, past the receptionist desk, and to the back of the suite where the files were stored. It took her maybe five minutes before she came back and stood in front of Candace with the case file in her hand. She waved it at the young woman.

"How difficult was that?"

Candace stared at her blankly.

"You're an assistant. Your job is to assist."

"No," Candace corrected her. "I'm the receptionist. My job is to receive your clients. I do that."

"It would behoove you to watch your tone. You should have a little more respect for authority."

Pat walked way and returned to her office. Candace rolled her eyes at the older woman's retreating figure.

"Dike," Candace murmured under her breath.

Her eyes reverted to her message pad lying on her desk. Rolling her eyes again, she realized that she hadn't given Pat her messages from earlier. Quickly, she ripped the message slips out of the book and walked to Pat's office. She didn't bother to knock.

"Here are your messages from lunch," she announced.

Pat was standing by her bookshelf near the door. She walked over to Candace and without a word plucked the papers from her hand.

"Okay, now that was rude," Candace said loudly.

"Excuse me?"

Just as the exchange was taking place, the senior partner's executive assistant Missy walked out of her office.

"What's the matter?"

Candace looked at Missy in disbelief.

"I think Pat has a problem with me. She just snatched that paper out of my hand all rude like."

"I'm not entertaining this nonsense," Pat replied. "Get away from my office."

"Who do you think you're talking to? You want me to exercise more respect for you but you get to talk to me like I'm some trash?"

Missy placed her hand on Candace's arm.

"Let's go back to the front," Missy insisted. "Come on."

"No. I want an apology."

Pat laughed. "Are you kidding me?"

"No, I'm serious. You need to apologize to me."

Pat stepped forward. "And you need to get out of my office."

Candace refused to move despite Missy's urging and begging. Fed up with the whole ordeal, Pat slightly pushed Candace away from her threshold. It was just enough to allow her to close her oak door.

"Rude ass bitch," Candace muttered, walking back to her desk in a furry.

Missy was right at her heels.

"You know Bob is not going to like this, right. She's going to tell him about it."

"So," Candace challenged. "You were right there. You saw her push me. Let her tell him cuz if she doesn't I am as soon as he comes back. I'm not working anywhere where people get to yell at me and talk to me like I'm not shit. Hell, if they didn't know, slavery is over."

Missy gave a nervous laugh.

"Well calm down. You know how Pat is. That's just her personality. She's really blunt and straightforward. You know?"

"Uh-huh. And I can be real hood when someone messes with me. I'm not intimidated by her rude ass."

Missy gave up on Candace, shrugged her shoulders and walked away. As if she needed any more aggravation, Khalil popped his head through the door of the suite.

"Hey pretty lady," he said. "You didn't come out for lunch. Wanna go across to the Starbucks for a minute?"

She shook her head and tried to make herself look busy.

"I can't," she said. "I'm swamped over here."

He looked disappointed. "Okay, I'll see you tonight then."

She was relieved to see him go and was in no mood to listen to his bullshit macking this afternoon. She tried to focus her attention on her work but was finding it difficult to do. Within the hour Bob returned to the office. Candace handed him his messages and was not about to let him walk off without addressing the incident with Pat.

"Bob, I need to talk to you about something," she said.

He gave her a curt smile.

"Pat called me already. We'll talk about it later."

He walked off before she could respond. Candace felt defeated and pissed. What part of the game was this?

~ ~ ~

The entire afternoon went by and there was no further mention of the situation between Candace and Pat. Candace closed down the firm and made her way back to Khalil's house reluctantly. He'd given her a key for her temporary use. When she arrived to the house his car wasn't in the driveway. She was pleased about that. She figured it would give her the opportunity to take the few things she had there and find somewhere else to stay for a while. Coming in the door she could hear rumbling in the kitchen. Puzzled, she began to walk in that direction and was surprised to be met at the door by a tall, slender woman with a short Halle Berry haircut.

"What the hell?" the woman asked.

She held a knife in her right hand and what looked to Candace to be the remnants of one of her blouses.

"Who are you?" Candace asked for lack of anything better say. Truly, she knew the answer to the question before it even left her lips.

"I'm the bitch that's about to cut your ass for lying up in *my* house with *my* man."

Sheila waved her knife in Candace's face and threw the fabric at her chest. Candace let it fall to the floor and slowly began to back up.

"You…you've got it all…all wrong," Candace stuttered.

"Do I?" Sheila asked.

Candace nodded, slowly moving backward into the living room.

"Cuz it seems to me like I've pretty much peeped game, sweetheart. You trying to tell me these aren't your clothes in my bedroom? That's not your deodorant laying on my bathroom counter next to your Summer's Eve like you live here?"

"I'm just a friend," she pleaded. "Please…Khalil was helping me out. My husband and I are having problems…He just let me stay here for a few days until I could get myself together. That's all."

"That's all?" Sheila challenged, smiling at her wickedly.

Candace nodded.

"You really think I'm that naïve? How old are you? 12? Your gullible ass."

Sheila laughed and put her hands on her hips.

"Tell me how you have the audacity to shack up in another woman's house and then lie to save the sorry nigga's life. What? You that in love with Khalil?"

Candace looked up at the ceiling and took a deep breath. It just wasn't her day. If this crazy bitch was going to kill her, she would have done so already. Candace decided to just let the chips fall where they may.

"I just came to get my stuff. I was leaving tonight. I swear."

"Let me ask you this…did you really think that the man's wife would never show up honey?"

"Wife?" Candace almost choked on the word as she spat it out in surprise.

Sheila's eyebrows knitted up.

"Oh lemme guess. He didn't tell you he was married. With all these pictures of me around here…and all my stuff…you really want me to believe that you didn't know he was fuckin' married?"

Candace was pissed now.

"He told me you *just* lived together…that you've been living together for a while. In fact, he told me that you were in jail for a domestic dispute."

Sheila laughed.

"And you believed that shit? I've been in Augusta visiting my mother for the last month and a half, honey. She was sick. But I told his sorry ass to pack his shit and get the hell out of my house while I was gone. And do you know why?"

Candace shook her head.

"Because I'm sick of him pulling bullshit like this. You think you're the first piece of ass he's fucked with in the six years we've been married? Naw baby, you're not that special. The last bitch had a baby by him and he still isn't claiming that child. I had him served with divorce papers last month. Sorry bastard changed my locks. I had to have a locksmith come out so that I could get into my own fuckin' house only to find your tramp ass prancing up in here with a fuckin' key."

No sooner than she uttered the last word the two of them heard the front door open. Candace spun around and the two of them watched Khalil take in the sight of them. Fear crossed his face and then he quickly began to save his ass.

"Baby, when did you get home?" he asked looking at Sheila, failing to make eye contact with Candace.

"Now I'm your baby?" Sheila asked him. "And who's this bitch? Your sugar?"

Khalil laughed and slowly walked over to the women.

"No, baby. What are you talking about? This is my good friend from the office. Candace."

"Yeah, me and your good friend have already met and had a nice little talk."

She pointed the knife at his chest.

"And your sorry ass is busted."

"Baby, I don't know what she told you. But, I swear I was only trying to help her out. She was desperate for a place to go. Her parents put her out and…"

"Fuck you," Candace spat out. "I'm not desperate for shit from your sorry, lying ass."

"Uh-oh," Sheila interjected. "Looks like your stories aren't matching up. Surprise, surprise."

"Candace," Khalil said slowly as if he were talking to an idiot. "You need to stop this."

Candace reached out and slapped his face.

"Fuck you," she said again. "You're the one that invited me to your house and then lied about your *wife* being in jail. Sorry bastard."

"His house?" Sheila asked. "No ma'am. This house is owned by me and only me. Always has been and always will be. And I'm just about tired of these shenanigans. So I'm giving both of your asses five seconds before I start slicing and dicing a motherfucker."

Candace looked from her to Khalil and quickly moved for the door.

"I'm outta here."

From behind her she could hear Khalil begging and pleading with Sheila to believe him. Sheila obviously wasn't playing because before Candace even reached her car she could hear Khalil scream. She looked up and saw him running out of the house holding his arm.

"You cut me!" he screamed. "You fuckin' cut me! Crazy bitch."

Sheila stood in the doorway flailing her arms every which way.

"You want crazy. I'll show your ass crazy. Bring your ass back on my property and I'll shoot you in the fuckin' foot. You and any of your tack-head ass baby mamas and your stank pussy ass girlfriends."

Khalil ran towards Candace.

"Call the police, call the police!" he screamed at her. "She cut me."

Candace tried to wave him off.

"I wouldn't spit on your ass if you were on fire."

Quickly she got into her car and hurried out of the driveway. In her rearview she caught her last glimpse of Khalil running down the driveway screaming and Sheila continuing to hurl insults at her wounded husband. What a fucking day!

JADA

"Are you kidding me?" Alex asked in disbelief.

She was sitting on the sofa in Jada's living room munching on popcorn, eyes wide open listening to Candace give them a play by play of the encounter she recently had with Khalil and his wife. Jada propped her feet up on the ottoman and shook her head.

"You better thank your lucky stars that woman didn't decide to play surgeon on your ass," Jada said. "What were you possibly thinking laying up in that woman's house with that man?"

Candace was sitting next to Alex, holding the bowl of popcorn.

"I didn't know they were married," was her defense.

"But you knew that they lived together. So that was reason enough for you to *not* be laying up in that woman's bed every night. You're lucky as hell. I would have killed you."

"Ya'll should have seen his sorry behind running around yelling about how she'd cut him."

"Too funny," Alex commented.

"That shit isn't funny," Jada countered. "It's crazy. I swear. All of ya'll get into the craziest situations. Ya'll got issues."

Candace moaned. "Okay, here goes Ms. Perfect."

"I'm not perfect. I'm not even trying to front like I am. But I have the common sense not to be all up in another woman's place playing house. That's just stupid."

"He told me she was in jail."

Alex laughed. "Wow."

Candace hit her. "Shut up."

"What about Quincy?" Jada asked her.

"What about him? We are so over. My dad is going with me to meet him this weekend to get my stuff out of storage."

"So they really foreclosed on the house?"

"Yep. At least the fat bastard had the decency to put all of our stuff in storage. He's just been giving me a hard time about getting my stuff out though."

"You've been going through it," Alex said.

"Speaking of going through it, has anyone heard from Miranda lately?" Jada asked.

The other two girls shook their heads.

"Then ya'll don't know."

"Know what?" Candace asked.

Jada hesitated. "She got back with Norris."

"What??" Alex asked.

"Are you for real?" Candace questioned. "You can't be for real."

Jada nodded her head.

"Yes ma'am. Steph told me that she came over her house one day out of the blue and told her that she was back with Norris. They fell out so Steph didn't really have much more to tell…but yep. That's the gist of it."

"After everything he did to her, why in the world would she take his sorry butt back?" Alex asked.

"I know I wouldn't have," Candace asserted. "Please, it doesn't matter what Quincy says or does, I'm never going back. Once it's over, it's over. You only have to mistreat me once."

Neither Alex nor Jada responded to this. Each woman just considered her own thoughts and they all sat in silence.

"So, let's get to planning this shower," Alex spoke up. "I know that Steph can't wait to not be pregnant anymore."

"I can imagine," Candace agreed. "I don't see how anyone ever *wants* to have a little parasite in their body to begin with."

"That's an endearing way to describe someone's child," Jada teased.

"I'm just saying…you'll never catch me destroying my body. My boobs are too perky for all that."

"You'll change your mind about that once you fall in love with the right man. You'll want to have his baby."

"I'm surprised you and Jordan haven't got pregnant by now. You're all in love and shit. Why aren't you pregnant?"

Jada smiled and toyed with her shirt.

"It's just not our time yet," she said. "We've been trying but…you know, sometimes it just takes time."

Alex remained silent, lost in her own thoughts.

"Well good luck to you on that," Candace said. "You and Steph can have all of that. I'll just continue to be the fabulous friend while ya'll chicks play mama."

"Whatever."

STEPHANIE

Stephanie and Jada sat on Steph's couch going through all the baby gifts from her shower. The room was filled with onesies, diapers, gift bags, and envelopes. The only noise in the apartment was the chatter between the girls. Damien was spending the night at a friend's house and Corey hadn't been home since the baby shower. She was concerned, but didn't want to let on in front of her friend.

"You got so much cute stuff, girl," Jada commented.

"Yep. It was a good turnout too. Thank you again for

everything. You know you always throw a mean party."

"I try," Jada beamed, folding up some long sleeve t-shirts.

"But what was up with Miranda?"

"What?"

"After blowing up at me a month or so ago she strolls up in my baby shower without so much as two words to say to me…like nothing happened. And did you see the way she was all cozied up to Corey?"

Jada smacked her lips. "Steph, stop it. They were not cozied up."

"Well, they were off to the side whispering about something and then she was ghost. Did she even bring me a gift?"

"Of course she did. And what is up with you? Why are you so fixated on Corey and Miranda? Nobody's trying to get with your boyfriend, girl. Especially not Miranda. She's too stuck on stupid with Norris."

Stephanie fidgeted on the couch, grunted a little and rubbed the side of her belly.

"I'm just saying…to me it looked like something was up…and the way she just popped up to my house that time without calling first. If I didn't know better, I could have sworn that she looked surprised to see me sitting in my own living room."

"Don't go starting any mess over your crazy hormonal over reactions."

Stephanie grunted again. "She better not start nothing."

"Leave it alone. Where is Corey anyway?"

Stephanie rubbed her side and laid her head back on the sofa.

"I don't know, girl. He hasn't been home since this weekend…since the shower actually."

Jada looked over at her friend.

"You okay, girl?"

"Yeah, yeah I'm fine."

Jada looked at her quizzically and went back to sorting the baby items.

"So is that normal? For him to be gone so long? Has he called at least?"

"He does that some times, but you know…what can I do about that? He's busy, so I try not to bother him."

"Busy? What is wrong with all of my friends?"

Stephanie cocked her head to the side.

"What?" she asked.

"You said he's busy like he's flying back and forth to Wall Street or something, girl. Let's face some reality shall we? Your baby daddy is the dope man."

"Jada, please don't start."

"I'm just saying. How long are you going to live this fantasy life with him? And now he just comes and goes as he pleases leaving you here in his dope house mansion."

"Stop it. There's no dope or blow or weed in this house. Corey wouldn't disrespect me like that."

"Hmm. But he'd leave his pregnant girlfriend alone frequently for days on end?"

Stephanie let out a sharp moan and bent over in a painful motion. Jada reached over and touched her arm.

"Girl, I'm sorry. I didn't mean to upset you…are you okay."

Stephanie shook her head.

"No…no. I think I'm in labor."

Jada's eyes grew wide and she began to speak slowly.

"Are you absolutely sure?"

Stephanie looked up at her and grimaced.

"No, Jada. I just wanted to scare you to death. YES, damn it! I'm sure."

Jada jumped up.

"Okay, okay…what do we do? Should I call your doctor or just take you straight to the hospital?"

Stephanie waved her hand in the air.

"Calm down…I need you to calm down. Get my purse

for me. We can call my doctor on the way to the hospital. And Corey too.

~ ~ ~

Two hours passed and Stephanie found herself laying on the delivery bed, epidural in place, preparing to push with, but the room still devoid of Corey. Jada stood by her side as the nurses busied about prepping the area for the delivery.

"Did you call him again?" Stephanie asked her friend.

Jada brushed Stephanie's hair back and smiled at her.

"I called him five times already and left two messages. Maybe he'll be here soon."

Stephanie's mind was filled with many thoughts. The stress of giving birth was escalated by the stress of worrying over Corey's whereabouts. But there was no time to focus on Corey right now. The nurses were instructing Jada to help hold her legs up so that she could attempt to push at the next contraction. She gave it all her might, a struggle against the effectiveness of the epidural. Her memory could only retain the sounds of voices urging her to push harder before she drifted off into darkness.

~ ~ ~

The room was quiet when she opened her eyes. She struggled to sit up and noticed the IV attached to her arm. Hearing her stir, a figure approached her bedside and turned on the light.

"Mom?" she could barely utter the word, her mouth was so dry.

Her mom reached over to the bed table, picked up a cartoon of cranberry juice and held it to her lips for her to sip. Absentmindedly, she drank from it and simply stared at her mother in confusion.

"You need to rest," her mom ordered. "You've been through a lot today."

"Where's my baby?" Stephanie asked softly.

"In the nursery. She's fine. You just need to rest for now."

Before she could say another word, Jada walked in and was surprised to see her up.

"You're woke! That's good. How do you feel?"

"Tired…very tired," she answered and looked back to her mother. "What are you doing here?"

"I called her," Jada blurted out. "You really needed some family here, sweetie…so I called your mother…especially after we couldn't get in contact with Corey."

Stephanie rested back against her hospital bed pillows and crossed her arms.

"I didn't think you'd care to come see about me having another one of Corey's baby."

"No matter who their father is, these are still my grandchildren," Ms. Johnson replied. "And you are still my daughter."

There was a tap at the room door and Corey strolled in nonchalantly with a big teddy bear and flowers. He sat the goodies on the guest chair and walked over to Stephanie's right side.

"What's up, mama," he said to her.

Stephanie looked at him blankly, confused on how he could be so seemingly cool after being missing for several days.

"Hi," was all she could manage to say.

"How you doing?"

"How does she look like she's doing?" Stephanie's mom retorted. "She's worn out…she had to have a blood transfusion after giving birth to your child *alone*…you would know that if you had been where you were supposed to be, tending to your family instead of out there in the streets destroying everyone else's with that stuff you push."

"Mom!" Stephanie interjected. "You're out of line."

"With all due respect Ms. Johnson, you shouldn't assume you know anything about me. I'm taking care of my family 24 - 7. You can believe that. Everything I do is for my family."

"Is that right? Well, you forgot to do one thing, son. And that's be there *with* your family."

"Mom, please. If you only came down here to argue with us then you should just leave. I can't handle this right now…I really can't."

Stephanie's mom looked from Steph to Corey in disdain. In a huff, she grabbed her purse and walked to the door. She stopped and turned back to look at Stephanie.

"This fool is going to be the death of you," she spat out before hastily leaving the room.

Jada was uncomfortable in the silence that followed Ms. Johnson's exit.

"Um…maybe I should go too. I'll come back tomorrow to check on you and the baby."

Stephanie smiled at her.

"Thanks for everything."

Jada hugged her friend tightly and whispered in her ear.

"Watch the news, girl. I love you."

Stephanie watched her friend walk out of the room with a questioning expression on her face. Why did Jada want her to watch the news? Corey sat down on the side of her bed and grabbed her hand.

"You aight?"

She nodded.

"Where were you?"

"Taking care of some business and laying low."

"What…what does that mean?"

"Don't worry bout all that," he told her. "Daddy's home now. It's all good. I'm going to go see if the nurse will bring the baby up from the nursery. You need anything?"

"Can you get me something to eat? From the cafeteria

maybe?"

Corey hopped up off of the bed.

"I'll see what I can do lil' mama."

She waited until he was out of the room for several minutes before using the bulky hospital bed remote to turn on the 6:00 news. She waited through the forecast, a special health-watch bit on the dangers of pre-packaged foods, and the story of a missing Athens college student before the story of interest hit her.

"Dekalb county officials are investigating the murder of a local man. The victim has been identified as Montae Stokes. Neighbors in the Decatur neighborhood where Stokes resided say that he was a well known guy and a small time drug dealer. Officials say that Stokes worked part time out of a local club owned by Ernest Henderson. Henderson is offering no statement at this time, except to say that he has no knowledge of Stokes dealing drugs. Stokes' body was found by a group of teenagers in a creek behind some abandoned apartment buildings on Bouldercrest Road early Sunday afternoon. He suffered two bullet wounds to the chest and one to the head. Stokes' family and some close friends have been interviewed to determine motive for this crime. At this time, officials believe that Stokes' death is the result of a struggle of power in the drug community. DeKalb's deputy director states that a full investigation will be conducted. At this time, they are not releasing the names of suspects or persons of interest."

Stephanie turned off the television and struggled to catch her breath. Her heart was telling her that Corey couldn't possibly be responsible for the man's death. But her mind was telling her that he very well could be. Apparently Jada thought so too, otherwise why would she have encouraged her to watch the news. Stephanie wasn't ready to face the reality of Corey's illegal activity. She loved him too much and desperately needed to hold on to the dream of being a real family. Sighing, she laid back against her pillows and said a quick prayer for everything to work out in her favor.

MIRANDA

Several months came and went with Miranda asking herself daily why on earth she agreed to stay married to Norris. Sure, in the beginning he tried to play the considerate husband.

But over time, he began to show his true colors, acting more and more like the man she had come to despise. It was Christmas morning and Miranda woke to find her bed empty on Norris' side. She sighed, half expecting him to be gone. She rose from the bed and went into the bathroom to wash up. When she returned to the bedroom, Norris was sitting on the bed shirtless, rolling a blunt.

"You have to do that in here?" she asked walking past him.

"Merry Christmas to you too," he responded.

She ignored him and lay down on her side of the bed. He lifted the blunt and licked it, smiling at her wickedly.

"You know you want some."

"Shut up with that."

"Look, it's Christmas. Let's just enjoy each other and stop all the damn fronting," he reasoned with her. "I'm not tripping. It might take the edge off if you smoke with ya' boy and chill the hell out. I'm just trying to chill with you, Miranda."

He lifted the weed in her direction.

"This is who I am," he told her. "Take it or leave it. I wasn't born yesterday, wifey. I *know* you light up. You gon' tell me that you can light up without me, but you can't do it with me?"

He was silent, allowing her the opportunity to consider the offer. Miranda looked at him and bit her lower lip. It was Christmas so she knew there was no way she was going to be getting anything from Corey any time soon. She took a deep breath, unbelieving herself as she reached out for the blunt being offered to her. Norris watched as she inhaled and then exhaled slowly.

"Yeah," he coaxed her as she closed her eyes and took another drag. "That's what's up. Now pass that shit, babes. Don't be greedy."

They smoked the entire joint and soon found themselves giggling and playing around like old friends.

"Where's my Christmas dinner at woman?" Norris joked, tickling her.

"I wasn't planning on cooking. I told my mom we would come over to my family's house for Christmas dinner this afternoon."

"Long as I get my smoked turkey and banana pudding…somebody needa teach you how to make that good ol' soul food."

Miranda lay back on the bed feeling her head spinning. It was a sensation she never felt before and she wasn't sure where the rush was coming from.

"You bought to knock out on me?" Norris asked, slipping his hand under her night shirt.

She fidgeted at his touch and looked up at him. She could feel her heart pounding through her chest.

"No…no…I feel weird…like woozy kinda."

He pulled his jogging pants down and began to nibble on her neck.

"Feeling like your adrenaline is pumping?" he said in her

ear. "Like you're about to spin outta control?"

She couldn't focus on his face, so she just closed her eyes and nodded.

"What the hell?"

He mounted her and entered her moist opening. Every part of her was in overdrive, she was incredibly horny, gyrating under him as he moved inside of her.

"That's that PCP baby," he told her between thrusts. "You don't know what's in ya' greens these days?"

"Hmmm?"

She couldn't focus on his words, but her body was focused on her orgasm which was fast approaching. With no foreplay and very little sensuality, Norris pumped and pumped himself into her, abusing her g-spot until she climaxed so hard she felt she was going to have a heart attack. The sensation was so powerful, Miranda screamed and grabbed his forearms so tightly that her nails dug into his skin. Her recovery seemed to never come as her heart rate felt as if it were never going to decrease. Norris came soon after her, collapsing his body onto her fidgeting one for a short time. Soon, he got off of her and hurried off into the bathroom.

Miranda continued to lie on the bed, clutching her chest trying to slow down her rapidly beating heart. Her thoughts were all a blur. Norris reentered the room at some point mentioning something about fresh air. As she focused on calming herself she heard a car peel out of the parking lot. Instantly, she sat up, trying to think clearly. She jumped off of the bed, sped through the apartment stopping only to glance at the table where her keys had been resting. She threw open the front door and stood on her porch looking out at her empty parking spot.

PCP. The memory of his words slapped her. She sauntered back into her home, curled up on her sofa and buried her head in her hands. Perhaps he would return home soon.

The sound of her phone ringing woke her up. Her body was drenched in sweat. She looked at the cellphone buzzing on the coffee table and quickly snatched it up. It was her cousin, Myra.

"Hello," she answered, voice harsh and mouth feeling cottony.

"Miranda, Merry Christmas, ma'am. Ya'll aren't coming over with the family?"

"What time is it?"

"It's 2:00. We're about to bless the food. Where are you?"

"2:00?" Miranda rose from the sofa and went into the kitchen to pour herself a glass of water.

"Yeah. Are you coming?"

"I…I don't think so…I'm not feeling well and Norris isn't here."

"Okay then. I'll let everyone know. I'll call you later."

"Uh-huh."

Miranda disconnected the call and stared at the time on her phone. 2:09 P.M. Where the hell was Norris? He'd been gone all morning and apparently all early afternoon. She dialed his cell and waited for him to answer.

"He's busy honey and don't call this phone anymore, bitch."

The phone went dead. Who the hell? Miranda called the number back again and leaned against her kitchen counter.

"What bitch? Are you slow?"

"Who is this?" Miranda demanded.

"Norris' *woman*. Something yo' ass ain't never been with ya' junky ass."

"Put my husband on the phone, trick."

"I got your trick, hoe. Norris is busy. He's playing with his daughter. It's Christmas, if you hadn't noticed."

"Daughter?"

Miranda felt herself slide to the floor, overwhelmed by this new information.

"Yes. His daughter. So, I'll tell him you called."

The line went dead. She was stunned. How could he have fathered a baby with someone else and she not know? Without much thought, she redialed his number once more. The phone went straight to voicemail.

"You sorry son-of-a-bitch. Who the fuck do you think you are leaving me in this house stranded to go play house with some hoodrat? Bring my dam car back now, Norris. I mean it. I want my damn car back, now!"

She hung up and called right back. The phone went to voicemail. She called again and the line was quickly answered.

"Yo, I'ma call you back in a minute, aight?" he said hurriedly.

"No hell it's not alright," she retorted. "I want my…"

The line was disconnected before she could finish her sentence. She screamed and called back once more.

"What man?!"

"What is going on, Norris? Who the hell was that bitch that answered your phone? Where are you?"

"I ran out for a minute. Visiting folk, man. It's Christmas. Calm all that noise down."

"Are you kidding me? Some chick just told me that you were playing with your daughter, Norris. What the hell?"

She could hear the commotion in his background. He sounded like he was struggling with someone for the phone.

"Norris?" she called out.

"Fuck that bitch," she could hear the female's voice shrieking. "Fuck her ass. If you want that bitch fuck you too."

"Norris!" Miranda called out again. "Norris! Answer me. What the hell is going on?"

His background was silent now and his breathing was heavy.

"What's up?"

Miranda banged on her cabinet door with her fist, pissed and frustrated.

"What's up? What's up, Norris? You tell me what the hell is up."

"You're tripping. You still buzzing off that shit? I'm on my way home, man."

"Who are you with, huh? Who the hell is that saying fuck me, Norris?"

Recognition set in and Miranda took a deep breath.

"That's that trick you had up in my house, isn't it?"

He didn't answer.

"You have a baby with her?"

"Man go on with all that. Look, I told you I'm on my way home."

"Answer me, damn it! Do you have a baby with that girl?" Miranda yelled into the phone. Her breathing was heavy and her eyes began to tear up.

"Miranda…"

"No. Don't try to talk circles around me! Answer the fucking question."

"Aight man, you ain't gon' talk to me like I'm some pussy nigga. You don't be coming off of any information when I ask you questions about what *you* have going on. But you wanna question me and shit? Fuck all that, Miranda. You ain't running shit around here."

"Fuck you! You lying, cheating piece of shit."

"For real? I'm a piece of shit? A nigga chillin' on Christmas and yo' geeked up ass blowing me up starting shit. Okay, you want to know? Yes. That was Tammy. And yes. I have a lil' girl with her. Now what? I'll see your ass when I get back."

He ended the call and Miranda screamed once more. She screamed long and loud, until no more sound could come from her throat. Laying on the floor she cried, her body convulsing in fits of frustration. She cried herself into an uncomfortable sleep which was interrupted an hour later by the ringing of her phone. She answered without screening the call, her voice barely audible as she said hello.

"Merry Christmas, girl," Jada said cheerfully. "What are you up to?"

Miranda rose from the floor and looked around her quiet apartment.

"Dying."

"I'm sorry, what?"

"I'm sorry…I'm just not having a very Merry Christmas."

"Why not? What's wrong?"

She walked over to the pantry and pulled out a pack of ramen noodles.

"Norris left me."

Jada sighed. "And that's not a gift to you?"

"I mean he left me stuck in the house. He took my car and is over to his baby's mama's house."

"Baby mama? When did that happen?"

She threw the noodles in a bowl and poured a little tap water into it.

"I don't know…I'm so tired of him….I'm so drained, Jada. I just can't take much more."

"He took your car, huh?"

"Yep."

"Report that shit stolen. That'll teach his ass. This isn't a community property state."

She put the bowl in the microwave.

"I can't do that."

"Why not? Miranda…that man is over there fucking that other woman, playing the family man with somebody else. Trust, he's not thinking about you or your feelings so why are you giving so much of a damn about his?"

Silence.

"Okay," Jada sighed. "Call me back later and let me know what you decided to do. I love you sweetie…but you really need to stop being a doormat for this man and leave well enough alone."

"Bye, Jada."

She pressed the end button and watched the minutes run

down on the microwave. Taking a deep breath she dialed 911 on her phone and closed her eyes.

"911. What's your emergency?"

"I'd like to report my car stolen."

ALEX

"You didn't have to get me a gift!" Alex exclaimed snatching the small box out of Clay's hand. "But I'm glad you did."

Clay plopped down on the sofa and watched as Alex opened the jewelry box. Her eyes lit up as she removed the locket from the box.

"Oh my goodness. It's beautiful, Clay. Thank you."

He motioned for her to come over to him.

"Here, let me put it on for you."

She sat next to him and he put the gold chain around her neck. She could smell the crisp clean scent of his clothes mixed with the masculine aroma of his cologne. She smiled at the familiar scent that always made her feel so comfortable.

"There you go."

She touched the locket with her finger tips and turned around to smile at her best friend.

"You're absolutely the best," she told him. "You really are. You're always there for me. I can always count on you. You're the best friend a girl could ever, ever ask for, Poopie."

He nodded and grabbed her hand.

"I really need to talk to you about something," he said softly.

Her eyebrows knitted up.

"Is something wrong?"

"No, it's just that I've been needing to tell you something for a long time and I think that now is the time for us to have this discussion."

"Okay…what's up?"

Before he could speak her cell phone rang. Alex jumped up to get the phone off of the nearby table. Looking at the caller ID she smiled at Clay.

"It's my new boyfriend."

She turned away from him to answer the phone.

"Hello," she said in her sugary sweet voice. "Tonight? Okay I guess I can go. I'll be ready. Okay, bye."

She threw the phone back on the table and winked at Clay.

"I have a date."

"On Christmas night?" he questioned. "And since when do you have a new boyfriend? Last time I checked you were just getting over the whole baby thing."

"He's not really my boyfriend, I just said that. I met him a couple of weeks ago at the mall."

Clay nodded. "So you're trying to make him your boyfriend?"

She shrugged. "I don't know. He likes me and he's not a jerk like Mario was so…we'll see. I needa get ready. I'm going with T to the studio."

"T?"

"Yes. His name is Thad, his friends call him T."

She got up to go to her room then thought about it.

"Oh yeah, what did you want to talk about, Poopie?"

Clay shook his head and waved her off.

"It's not important anymore."

She looked at him pensively.

"Are you sure? You made it seem like it was important."

He shrugged. "Thinking about it, it isn't really that big of a deal to trouble you with it. Go on and get ready for your lil' date. I'm going to bounce."

She smiled at him.

"Okay. And thanks again for my necklace. I really love it."

Clay smiled back as he rose from the couch.

"Glad to hear it. Be careful with your boy tonight, okay?"

"Always."

CANDACE

Candace drug herself from her car and up the walk to Jada's front door. Taking a deep breath she knocked on the door. Jada answered immediately, clad in her underwear and a short bath robe which was partially tied. She ushered Candace in quickly. Candace sulked her way into the dining room and plopped down at the round table.

"Well, hello to you too," Jada said jokingly. "What was the big emergency that you had to see me today girl? And take them damn glasses off, there's no sun in here."

Candace pulled off her sunglasses. Her eyes were red and puffy.

"I'm late," she said.

"Late for what? This was your idea. I know that if I don't get out of here soon I'm going to be late for Jordan's mom's birthday dinner."

Jada rummaged through her makeup bag while standing at the table. Noticing that Candace had not responded, she looked over at the smaller woman. She plopped down the makeup bag when she saw Candace's tear swollen eyes.

"What's wrong girl?" Jada asked gingerly, voice laced with concern.

"Everything. I think I'm pregnant."

"Are you kidding me?" Jada asked sitting down in the chair across from her.

Candace shook her head. "No. I would never joke about that mess. I haven't had my period in a month, Jada. I know my body. I'm telling you...I'm fuckin' pregnant."

Jada smoothed her hair down and stretched her neck.

"Okay...so have you said anything to Quincy?"

"About what?"

"About your condition...what do you mean, about what?"

Candace shook her head and Jada's eyes grew wide.

"Please tell me you haven't said anything because you don't know for sure."

Candace shook her head again then buried it in her arms on the table.

"Candace!" Jada exclaimed. "How could you be so irresponsible?"

"I know, I know," she muttered.

"Why would you be laying up with that man and not using protection? Are you crazy?"

"It was only once or twice…we were careful most of the time."

"Most of the time? You know it only takes once, right?"

Candace lifted her head, tears streaming down her face. She looked at Jada pitifully. Jada had never seen her so distraught before.

"What am I going to do?" she cried.

Jada raised her right eyebrow.

"First things first, hun. You need to take a test. There's no point in sitting up here crying about something that you're not even sure of. Stay right here."

Jada disappeared from the dining room and ran to the back. Candace tried to compose herself, wiping the tears from her eyes with her hands. Jada reentered and handed her a slender box. She reached for it.

"What do I do with this?" she asked naively.

Jada laughed. "Read the instructions, girl. It ain't rocket science. Pee on the stick and wait one to three minutes for your results. Simple."

Candace rose from the table, box in hand.

"Why do you just happen to have this?"

Jada shrugged.

"I told you we've been trying for a while. It's no big deal. I get them from the Dollar Store. Go on, girl. Don't prolong the inevitable. I've got places to go."

Candace walked the short distance up the hall to the bathroom and shut the door behind her. She read and reread the instructions before opening the package. Sighing, she eased onto the toilet and peed on the little stick. Positioning it on a piece of tissue, she laid the stick on the counter, finished her business and washed her hands. The whole time, she ignored the stick, not daring to look at it, not yet wanting to know what the answer was. She hurried out of the bathroom to find Jada standing impatiently by the door.

"Well?" Jada inquired.

"I didn't look."

"You want me to?"

Candace nodded and returned to her seat at the dining room table.

"Jehovah, please don't let this be happening to me," she prayed aloud.

Jada entered the room holding the stick and smiling.

"It's a good thing," she said.

Candace blinked, not fully understanding.

"It is?" she asked. "Oh my god…I'm not pregnant? Whooo. I am so freakin' relieved I don't know what to do with myself…I just can't…"

"Okay, okay. Pump your brakes," Jada interjected. "Maybe I should have said it's not such a bad thing."

"What?"

Jada handed her the stick and her eyes fell on the unmistakable two red lines.

"I'm going to be an auntie," Jada sing-songed.

"No," Candace said. "No. I cannot have a baby. Especially not like this. Okay…okay. Do you have another one of these things?"

"Um, yeah…but you know, it doesn't matter how many times you pee on these tests they're all going to say the same thing honey…you're gonna be a mama."

Candace threw the stick down on the table.

"My life sucks," she pouted.

"Oh please shut up," Jada said, snatching up her makeup bag. "You should be thankful that all you got was a baby. It could have been much worse. That trifling *married* man could have given you an STD or worse, AIDS. Hell, you haven't even been to a doctor yet so you don't know for sure what else he could have left you with. For your sake I pray that this is it. Some people out there are dying to have a baby, Candace. Be thankful that you're fortunate enough to be able to conceive. Stop looking at this as a punishment and get over it."

"But you don't understand," Candace whined. "My parents are going to be so disappointed in me. They're already in 'I told you so' mode about my separation from Quincy. My divorce isn't even final yet and here I am pregnant by another man…a married man."

Jada rolled her eyes.

"And whose fault is that?"

"I'll be shunned from my congregation. This type of thing is seriously frowned upon."

"And yet none of these things occurred to you while you were doing your dread-headed boo, though…right?"

"Why are you being so mean?"

"I'm sorry, girl. I'm just being real with you. You need to take some responsibility for your actions and start making some wiser decisions."

Candace stared at the glass dinette table, trying to get her thoughts together. Jada was right, but the truth definitely did hurt.

"I don't have health insurance," she thought aloud.

Jada sighed.

"I'm just in the business of rescuing everyone around here aren't I? Tell you what, first thing Monday morning I'll take you to the health department. They'll do blood work, an official pregnancy test and administer Medicaid to you all in the same day. After you get the Medicaid you can go to any ob/gyn that accepts it."

"I don't have an ob/gyn."

"Okay…I'll refer you to mine."

Jada looked at her friend and softened a little.

"It's not the end of the world, babes. Really. It'll all work out."

Candace smiled.

"Thanks, girl."

~ ~ ~

She tapped the phone, trying to decide if it was the right thing to do or not. Perhaps she should wait until Monday when she had some clearer answers. What if the number was disconnected? She had been avoiding him at work lately and he never came by the office after that incident with Sheila. Sucking it up, she dialed the number and waited for him to answer.

"Hello?" his voice sounded unsure.

"Khalil, it's me, Candace."

"Long time, no hear," he retorted. "Didn't think I'd ever hear from you again."

"Me either." She sighed. "I really need to talk to you though."

"Something wrong, pretty lady? You need to come over?"

She laughed dryly. "Are you kidding me?"

Khalil sucked his teeth.

"I'm just expressing concern, dear. Extending an open arm to you. And besides, Sheila and I are no more so you wouldn't have to worry about her."

"I'm not going down that road with you anymore, Khalil.

Fool me once…"

"Nobody's trying to fool you. I've always cared deeply for you."

"Really? And is that why you lied to me and tried to make me out to be some kind of stalker in front of your wife?"

"Let's leave the past in the past, shall we? You can't deny that we had a special bond, Candace. I'm only trying to make things right moving forward."

"I'm not coming over, Khalil. In fact, I should have never come over to begin with to avoid this whole mess."

"What are you talking about?"

"Khalil…I'm pregnant."

"Ok…"

"By you , Khalil. I'm pregnant with your child."

"Candace, I haven't touched you in nearly two months."

"That's right. And I haven't had a period in nearly two months."

"Get the hell out of here. How are you so sure it's my child? I mean, you *are* married."

"You're such a typical dude. You know good and well I had been separated from Quincy the entire time I was staying with you. Don't try to play me like I'm some skank."

"I'm supposed to just believe what you're saying?"

"Why would I lie?"

"For money."

"Fuck you, Khalil. I'm not so hard up for money that I'd scam a man into thinking I'm carrying his baby. Everyone who knows me knows that the last thing I've ever wanted was to be pregnant so I damn sure wouldn't make a joke about it just to get at you."

"Ok, ok. Calm down…calm down. Have you been to a doctor? I mean…are you sure?"

"I go to the doctor on Monday. But I took a test and it was positive…and I know my body."

"No offense, but it's been quite some time, Candace. If you knew your body so well, why are you just now determining that you're pregnant?"

"It's never been unusual for me to skip a period here and there…but skipping two is out of the norm…and I just feel different. Why am I explaining myself to you?"

"Because I should know…*if* I'm the father of this child."

"Tell you what, I'll call you on Monday after I come back from the doctor…unless you want to go with me. My friend offered to take me, but she can just as well tell me where it is and we can just go together."

"I have to work. Just call me when you're done."

"Fine. I'll talk to you then I guess."

Frustrated, she disconnected the call and threw the phone on the bed. The hard part was yet to come. Reasoning with herself, she decided it would be best to go ahead and tell her parents. They would find out soon enough, the sicker she got and the bigger she got. She was unsure as to when she would be able to move out of her parents' home, so whatever was going to happen needed to go ahead and happen so that she could get on with figuring out the rest of her life. She took a deep breath and walked out of her childhood bedroom. Candace found her parents cuddled up on the living room sofa watching a rerun of CSI.

"Mom, dad…can I talk to you?" she asked softly.

Her dad looked up at her and smiled. Her mom clicked off the television.

"What's up, pumpkin?" her dad asked.

Candace sat in the arm chair close to them, searching for the words with which to disappoint them.

"I know that you guys were not very happy with my decision to marry Quincy. And although that did not turn out the way I would have liked it, I had every intention of maintaining an honorable marriage."

"Ok…" her mom coaxed her to get to the point.

"I know that I haven't been going to the meetings like I should and I haven't kept Jehovah at the center of my life the way I should have. And I promise you that I intend to change that. I realize how important it is to have a spiritually strong foundation for your life…"

"Not that I'm not glad to hear you admit all of this dear, but I'm sensing there is something more prevalent that you wish to say to us."

"I'm pregnant."

She checked their faces for their reactions. Her mother gasped and stared at her with her hand over her mouth. Her father simply gripped the arm of the sofa and nodded.

"And how long were you going to wait to tell us this?" he asked.

"I wasn't waiting…I mean, I just found out today. I just realized earlier this week and…"

"Have you told Quincy? Not that I think a baby is a just cause to force reconciliation, but the man has an obligation to take care of his family nonetheless."

"Daddy, it's not Quincy's baby."

"Excuse me," her mother piped in. "Just what is it that you're saying?"

"Quincy and I had problems long before I asked to stay with you guys. We were separated for a minute…I was staying with a friend."

"And by friend you mean a man?"

Candace nodded.

Her mother shook her head.

"I could tell that something was up with you. Your body is changing. I was hoping that it was just my imagination. But I'm very disappointed in you young lady. Whether or not you and Quincy were having problems before is not of importance. You were still very much a married woman. You *still* are a married woman."

"Your mom is right. Stepping outside of your marriage vows like that is not favorable, Candace. And what god-fearing man would have the gall to shack up with someone else's wife? Who is this man to you? Are you running from one relationship right into another one?"

Candace grabbed a throw pillow and hugged it for support.

"No. We're not in a relationship. We just…"

"Were playing house and having sex just for the sake of it," her mom finished for her.

"Mom, please," Candace pleaded, trying to avoid the tears that threatened to fall. "Please don't judge me."

"We're not judging you, dear. Simply telling you the error of your ways."

"Do you think this young man has any respect for you, Candace?" her dad asked.

Now was definitely not the time to tell them that Khalil was much older and a married man himself. She simply shrugged her shoulders.

"You don't know? Certainly you know. If he did, he would have never laid down with you. Where is he now? Does he know?"

"He knows."

"Have you been to a doctor?" her mom asked.

She shook her head.

"A friend of mine is taking me to the health department on Monday. I think they do free testing or whatever…based on income."

"I think this young man should be covering your medical expenses. Is he going with you?"

Another shake of her head.

Her father sat straight in his seat and looked her dead in the eyes.

"You have disgraced yourself, you know that don't you?"

She blinked through the tears.

"I know that but…"

"I encourage you to ask Jehovah for forgiveness and repent immediately…But no matter what, you are still our daughter and we love you regardless. I would have liked to think that your mother and I taught you to have a little more self-respect than this…Who ever this man is, Candace, I want to meet him. If you won't do it, I will…I will make sure he understands that he has an obligation to take care of this child and that we, as your parents expect him to step up to the plate."

Candace nodded her head in understanding.

"You're going to the doctor on Monday, right," her mom said. "Invite the young man over for dinner Monday night. We can all sit down and talk about this like adults."

"Okay. I'm really sorry to spring this on you guys like this. I really am."

"We're your parents, dear. You can always come to us."

Candace rose and hugged her parents before hurrying out of the living room. It went over much better than she had anticipated. But what was going to happen when her parents came face to face with Khalil?

MIRANDA

It had been silent in the apartment since Norris left her on Christmas. It had only taken three days for the police to find her car. But, upon finding it they had also found Norris with less than an ounce of marijuana on him. Sure he had been arrested, but they had not detained him. Miranda knew that he was out, but he just had not come back home. She was on pins and needles, waiting for him to show up and retaliate for her setting him up. As she anticipated his violence, her habits progressively got worse.

Riding around looking for the trap, Miranda was feeling uneasy. Corey had made it clear that she was not to come to his home for pickups. They'd worked out a plan which generally entailed them meeting at a mutually convenient location. But today Corey was adamant that he couldn't get away and that she would have to meet him at the trap. So there she was, pulling up in front of a shabby ranch style home in the depths of Decatur. She slowly dragged herself from the car and to the front door. There was no doorbell so she had to knock. The door was answered by a big, dark man that made her think of Willie B.

"Sup, ma?" he questioned her, looking over her shoulder toward her car and down the street.

"Is Corey here?" she asked.

"He expecting you or something?"

She nodded.

The man chuckled.

"You sure you 'pose to be coming round here? You sure

this what you want?"

She rolled her eyes and sucked her teeth.

"Just tell Corey I'm here."

"Aight then, lil mama. Come in."

She stepped inside and instantly the man began to pat her back and legs.

"Excuse you!" she protested.

"Safety precautions," he said matter-of-factly. "Aight, you clean. Come on."

She followed him through the living room and into the kitchen where Corey was sitting bagging up little packets of what looked like a pile of flour. He looked up at her and raised an eyebrow.

"Mannie, you got that dime?"

A short, younger guy wearing a baseball cap down low rose from his seat on the stool at the kitchen counter where he'd been counting money. He walked over to Miranda and handed her the bag.

She took it and handed him a ten but addressed Corey.

"I was wondering if you could…I mean, if I could try something…different…harder."

Corey kept bagging.

"What I look like? A damn candy store? You wanna come up in here and taste-test shit? Get outta here, man."

"Fuck you, Corey. I've been putting money in your pocket consistently. Don't talk to me like I'm a waste of your time."

"So I'm supposed to up and let you sample what? Some blow?"

She looked at him blankly. He chuckled.

"You don't even know what that is, huh?"

"Yo, she five-oh?" the big man asked Corey.

He shook his head.

"Naw, she's a fuckin' mistake. Go on, Miranda. Get out my spot. Stick to what you know. This ain't for you. Don't make me sorry I put your ass on."

He went back to focusing on his work and the big man gently guided her by the arm towards the front door.

"Bullshit," she spat out.

The man followed her onto the porch and closed the door.

"Aye," he called to her. "I got something for you."

"Huh?"

"You grown, do what the fuck you wanna do."

He flashed a tiny baggie in his hand. Miranda's eyebrow went up and she clutched on to her purse.

"What am I supposed to do with that?" she asked him softly.

The man tapped his nose and sniffed before covering his mouth quickly to cough.

"How much?"

"For you, $25."

She took a deep breath, nodded, and reached inside her bra for the money that was resting there. Hesitantly she pulled the money out and handed it to the man. He quickly snatched it from her and replaced it with his product.

"If anything, you didn't get it from me."

He turned away and disappeared back into the house. Miranda hurried back to her car and rode off down the street before looking at the baggie clutched tightly in her fist. Sitting at a red light, she continued to clutch it in her hand, her heart racing quickly with fear and an excitement she couldn't explain. Miranda had no clue what she was getting herself into.

ALEX

Dating an industry dude was truly a thrill for Alex. Being in the studio with T and watching as he and his boys did their thing was exciting. Alex was impressed by the way he was so passionate about his rhymes. She ignored the fact that all of the other people in the studio were puffing away on one blunt after another. She coughed when the smoke got too thick for her, but continued to sit there, staring into the booth as T spat out his lyrics with conviction. She rocked to the beat, feeling it, just before he abruptly stopped.

"Yo, Ricky, this ain't working," he spoke into his mic.

Ricky, T's friend and producer, stopped the instrumental and waved T out of the booth. T joined his partner, plopping down into the chair next to him.

"It was good, money," Ricky stated. "What you feel's missing?"

"That hook, man. It doesn't feel right with me just spitting on it...It needs some softness...I need a vocalist."

"You wanna put a chick on it, shawty?"

"Yeah...yeah, man."

"Who you got in mind?"

T shrugged. "I don't know, man. I don't really have anyone in mind. You know somebody? And not that chick that be hanging around during everybody's studio time. What's her name?"

"Erica. Yeah, I heard she'd let you hit it man."

The men laughed and Ricky elbowed T as Alex rose and walked over to him.

"Baby, are you done?" she asked leaning on her new boo. "Are we about to leave?"

T fidgeted, trying to move away from Alex.

"Aye be patient, alright? I told you it was gone be a minute."

Alex bit her lip, not wanting to cause a scene in front of all of T's friends and business associates. Ricky began to play back the track T had just laid and Alex stood beside T, not knowing what to do or say next. They'd been at it for hours. Although it was fun watching them create music, Alex was ready to get on with the date that T had promised her. Dinner and a movie, her choice.

"You might as well go on and kick it with ya' girl," Ricky urged T. "Our time is up in like seven minutes so it's all good."

"Aight then," T consented. "I'ma check around to see who knows somebody that can set this shit off man. It has that whole Hustle and Flow vibe...you know that song I'm talking about, homie?"

"Yeah...Hard out here for a pimp," Ricky sung back.

"Yeah, man. Like dat there."

T rose from his seat and motioned to the others parlaying on the couches.

"Aight ya'll. We bout to be out," T announced.

A series of goodbyes, pounds, the rustle of paper and personal belongings being gathered occurred before T finally ushered Alex out of the studio. He put his arm around her and they exited the office building, walking into the crisp evening air.

"Man, I just wanna go somewhere and chill out, ma," he said, kissing her forehead. "Let's grab something and go back to your place."

Alex couldn't contain her disappointment.

"You said we were going to do dinner and a movie," she whined.

"Baby, I'm tired as hell. You can't feed your man and let him chill out? We ain't gotta always go out and spend a lot of money just to be together."

Alex bit her lip again, not wanting to argue, but also not wanting to be conned out of a date. In the short time that they had been dating, Alex noticed that T never wanted to do anything that involved him spending money. They spent most of their time either eating fast food at her apartment or sitting around the studio as he and his boys did their thing. Alex didn't want another boring date, but she also didn't want to piss him off, causing him to leave her alone for the night.

They rode in silence in T's old gray Camaro, listening to a throwback Outkast CD. Riding through downtown Decatur, getting closer to Alex's apartment, T reached over and massaged her left thigh.

"What you wanna eat baby? Chick-fil-A, huh?"

It was more of a directive than a question. Alex simply smiled and nodded.

"That's fine."

T approached the Chick-fil-A drive-thru and leaned back in his seat as they waited in line for their turn. His hand still caressing her thigh, T looked at her through slanted eyes.

"Baby, you mind spotting this?"

What the hell, she thought. *Is he for real?*

She sighed. "I guess so."

Reaching into her purse she grabbed a twenty and handed it to him. As he ordered their food and drove them home, Alex said nothing. Silently she was debating whether or not this relationship was really worth her time. The thing she liked the most about T was his passion for music. It was seemingly the only thing he took seriously and invested any real time, energy, or money in. Many times she'd watch him write his lyrics, tuning out everything and everyone around him. She admired his drive. What she detested was the fact that he still lived at home with his mother, never took her out, but was always sitting around her house, eating her food, spending her money, and expecting sex at the end of it all.

T was very rough around the edges. He was a real street dude, in Alex's opinion. His hard, thug-like demeanor was also a turn on for Alex. Although it irked her whenever he shut her down, she liked that he had such a domineering, aggressive personality. She wasn't scared of T, but she definitely found herself monitoring her words so as not to piss him off.

As they finished their Chick-fil-a sandwiches, Alex decided to entice him with conversation about that which mattered most to him.

"So you need a female singer, huh?" she asked him.

He nodded. "Yep. Bitch gotta be bad too. Need her to have that confidence in her voice like *Whoa*."

"You know, I can sing a lil bit."

T laughed.

"Oh for real? You can sing?"

Alex pouted.

"Why you laughing at me?" she asked him, playful slapping at his arm.

"Man I been kicking it with you for like a month now and you ain't never said nothing to me about being even remotely interested in being in the business."

"I mean, it's not something that I've always aspired to do, no...but I was just saying...just letting you know...making conversation, letting you know that I can sing."

"So, what? You wanna audition for me now? What is this? T's Hood Idol?"

T laughed heartily and Alex rose to clear their trash from

the living room table. As she moved to walk towards the trash can, T grabbed her arm.

"You know I'm just fucking with you, right?'

"You play too much. I was just letting you know something about me."

"Aww, don't be salty, baby. You know how many chicks, and dudes for that matter, get at me only to try to get me to put them on?"

"So what? You think I was telling you that for you to give me my big break," she asked mockingly, no longer trying to curb attitude.

"Man, go'on with that. I'm done with groupie girls trying to get their two minutes of fame or land them a balling ass rap star. That's why I was saying I don't even want my mans trying to put that leech Erica on. That girl be up in everybody's session trying to be down."

Alex laughed to herself at the thought of him calling someone else a leech. She moved to leave the room and he grabbed her by the waist, pulling her down into his lap.

"I just be messing with you, baby. I know you down for me."

He kissed her abruptly, stealing her breath from the quickness and the intensity. She let him run his hands over her breasts through her t-shirt. He squeezed her right breast like he was inspecting fruit. Pulling back, he looked into her eyes. Alex had to admit to herself that the chocolate brother was very cute.

"I can count on you, can't I?" he asked her, looking into

her eyes intently and seriously.

Alex touched his face, stroking his cheek lightly.

"You know you can," she answered, swept up in the moment of his tenderness.

"I got some studio time booked for this weekend, but I'm short $150. You know I wouldn't ask unless it's very important...and you know ain't nothing more vital to me than this music thang."

Alex was speechless. Here she was thinking that he was about to reveal something personal about himself, when all he really wanted was some money to invest in his dream.

"You haven't asked me anything," she responded, making him work for it since he had the gall to be going there anyway.

"Come on baby," he whined. "Can your boy hold $150? I'ma get it back to you as soon as possible."

She was reluctant to comply with his request, unsure of whether or not she'd ever see her money again. Optimistically, she hoped that his career took off and she'd be the dime piece on his arm. She desperately wanted to be in on all the hot parties in Atlanta, flying out to LA with other celebrities, and partaking in that fast-paced life. Helping T out and holding him down on his rise to stardom could be considered as her paying her dues. If she hung in there with him while he had nothing, surely he'd take care of her once his album dropped. T had talent and Alex believed that he would make it. She just wondered how long it was going to take because certain things about him were beginning to piss her off.

Alex sighed and kissed her boyfriend on the forehead.

"I'll go by the bank tomorrow, okay?"

His hand found its way to the buckle of her jeans.

"Thank you, baby. I'm so thankful to have met you. Let me show you how thankful I am."

Alex jumped out of his lap just as her cellphone rang.

"Why don't you go watch TV like you said you wanted to," she teased him.

Looking down at her phone she saw that it was her mother calling. She raised her eyes to the heavens and accepted the call.

"Hey, mommie," she greeted.

T raised an eyebrow, then raised his body from the couch and exited the room. He wasn't interested in hearing her girly conversation with her mother.

"How are you doing, Alex?" her mom asked

"Fine. How are you?"

"I've had better nights."

"What happened?"

"I got something very interesting in the mail. Usually, I don't open mail from the insurance people because it's normally them trying to find a way to get more money out of us."

"Uh-huh."

Alex had a sinking feeling in the pit of her stomach. She

gripped the side of her chair, waiting to see what her mother was going to say next.

"You want to tell me what kind of procedures you've been having? And why you were in the emergency room?"

Hell no I don't want to tell you about that, she thought.

"Um, mommie…I was going to tell you about it…I mean, it's been so hectic lately."

"Stop it right there, young lady," her mom interjected. "I'm not slow you know. I can read this statement of services rendered quite well. A D & C, Alex? How could you have gotten pregnant and gone through all of that without saying anything?"

"I didn't want you to be disappointed," Alex whispered.

"Disappointed? So you thought that hiding it from us and bottling up your emotions and issues was a better way to go? That we'd be less disappointed in that? You haven't even told me anything about a boyfriend let alone that you were *that* close to someone that you allowed yourself to get pregnant….Pregnant Alexandria. My goodness…"

Alex was silent as she listened to her mother's sniffles. She genuinely felt bad for causing her mother such frustration. This was exactly what she wanted to avoid.

"Do you have any idea how hurtful it is for me to know that my baby…*my baby*…was laid up in some hospital in pain, needing someone to be there for her and she chose to *not* call me?"

Alex's eyebrow rose. *Huh???*

"I am your mother, Alex. I may not like your decisions in life, but it's your life. But at the end of the day, you are my baby and I will always want to be there to support you. I can't imagine what it must have been like for you to go through that…losing a child alone."

Alex felt her own tears rolling down her cheeks as she listened to her mother's sobs. For all her good intentions, she'd still somehow managed to get it wrong.

"Mommie I'm sorry…I wasn't trying to close you out or anything," she explained. "I just didn't want you and daddy to be upset with me for getting pregnant in the first place. It was a mistake…the guy was a real jerk and I was contemplating having an abortion anyway…I never wanted to do anything to make you or daddy think less of me."

"Alex, you're our daughter. Like I said, we may not like your decisions. But, we're always going to support you and love you…we're your parents."

"Did you tell daddy?" Alex inquired.

"You think I shouldn't?" her mom countered.

"He'll be mad, mommie…"

"Yes he will be. Do you understand the seriousness of this? What if something had gone wrong during your procedure? No one wants to get an out of state call from some hospital saying our child is in critical condition."

"I know…"

Her mom sighed.

"It's between us this time, Alex. But please…don't ever

sell your parents short like that again, baby. We want to be there for you always."

"Okay, mommie. I'm sorry."

"I love you."

Alex could feel her mother's smile through the phone and wanted nothing more than to be hugged by her.

"I love you too, mommie."

STEPHANIE

Since returning home with the new baby, Stephanie found herself completely on edge. Corey spent more and more time away from home, not telling her where he was or when she should expect him back. She'd come to expect this from him, but with her uneasy feelings about the murder in Decatur, Stephanie wasn't sure if she could put up with Corey's shenanigans any longer. She respected the fact that whatever was going on, if anything, he kept it away from their home and their children. But still, she was his girl and she had the right to know what the hell he was up to.

Desperate to figure some things out, Stephanie found herself rummaging through his things one night. In the top of their closet he kept many shoe boxes. Corey had a thing for sneakers. She opened and searched through each shoe box, finding nothing but the Tims, Jays, or Air Force Ones that belonged in the boxes. She went through his bureau drawers, still finding nothing unusual. Going back to the closet, she rummaged through miscellaneous bags on the closet floor. Still nothing. Mindlessly, she began patting down the pants he had hanging up. She stopped when she felt a bulge in one pair. Quickly, she snatched the pants down and reached into the pocket. She pulled out a wallet and instinctively flipped it open. Her breath escaped her as she instantly recognized the name on the ID card staring back at her. Montae Stokes. But why was this dead man's wallet hiding in Corey's pocket? It didn't make sense to her.

Stephanie sat down on her bed, holding the wallet in her hand and trying to figure out why it was there and what she should do next. Puzzled, she reached over and grabbed her cordless phone, calling the only person she felt confident enough to confide in.

"Yes, ma'am," Jada answered the phone.

"I have a problem."

"Of course you do. Seriously…do you people only call me when something's wrong? No one ever calls me to say they missed me, see how I'm doing, tell me they love me…none of that. Ya'll suck."

Jada laughed at her own joke, but Stephanie was in no joking mood.

"This is serious, Jada."

Jada sighed. "Ok, boo. What's wrong?"

"Well, you remember the news story about the dude shot in the Dec, right?"

"Of course I do."

"I'm staring at Montae's driver's license."

"Say what?"

"I found Montae's wallet in a pair of Corey's pants…"

Silence.

Stephanie tossed the wallet on her bed and jumped up.

"Jada!" she yelled.

"What?"

"Say something, bitch. I'm panicking over here."

"Hell, I was waiting for you to tell me that you need me to come help you pack. What do you want me to say, mama?"

"Tell me what I'm supposed to do…I mean, why the hell would Corey have this man's wallet?"

"Tell you what to do? I need to get a new set of friends because ya'll chicks are wildin'. What do you mean, tell you what to do? Clearly your boyfriend is, what? *At least* an accessory to a crime…and that's at best. What do you think you should do? Ask Corey about it? Give Ernest back his wallet? Come on, girl!"

Stephanie bit her lip.

"You think Corey really killed that guy?"

"You don't? Everyone knows Corey is *THE* dope man in the Dec, Steph. You're not oblivious to this. From what I hear, Montae must have been trying to push your boy out of business and Corey had to show him who runs shit."

"But he wouldn't do that…Corey wouldn't hurt anybody like that."

"Okay, tell me again what you called me for."
"To help me, Jada. Come on. This is serious. If Corey killed that man, my children's father may go down for murder. But worse than that, if this Montae had a street team those niggas might try to come back for Corey."

"Some solid, loving advice, Stephanie…get the hell out of there. This is not the situation to rear your children in. You need to run."

Steph sighed and picked the wallet back up.

"I can't run out on him, Jada. I know you don't understand this…but I love Corey. I promised him that I was in this relationship to the end."

"I can't listen to this. Baby girl, things can only get worse."

She rose from the bed and moved to stuff the wallet back into Corey's pants pocket.

"I'll figure things out. Thanks, girl. I gotta go."

She clicked off of the phone before Jada had a chance to respond to her statement. If Corey was in deep, Stephanie was dead set on helping him pull through and convincing him to move their family the hell up out of Atlanta before shit went too far.

CANDANCE

Since she first mentioned the baby to Khalil, he became more evasive than ever. They agreed for him to come to her parents' place for dinner following her first doctor's visit. But, weeks had passed before he finally committed to a date and time. Candace was nervous about how the interaction between him and her parents would go. Never had she imagined that her lover and her parents would come face to face. It was funny to her how things worked out sometimes. Sitting in her parents' living room she fidgeted, waiting for him to show up at the door. Already he was half an hour late. Her father, who was not a very lenient man, was not very pleased that he would be so disrespectful as to stand them up.

Candace stared at her nails, lost in her own thoughts and trying to avoid apologizing to her parents for Khalil's absence. Just as her father walked into the room looking at his watch, the rhythmic sounds of hip hop forced their attention towards the window. Khalil was pulling up in their driveway to everyone's relief. Candace walked out of the door to meet him at the bottom of the sidewalk.

"You're late, you know," she said to him.

He shrugged nonchalantly. "I got held up with something. I'm here now."

He walked up to her and gave her a weak hug. She didn't return the embrace, but looked at him sternly, speaking softly.

"My parents are not very understanding people and they are already not happy with either one of us. So please, put your 'I don't give a damn' attitude in check."

"Look, I'm not going to sit up in here and be intimidated by you or your parents, so you can forget that, sweetheart."

"Don't sweetheart me. Please, just be respectful and hopefully this whole dinner will be over soon."

She turned away and he followed her up the walk to the front door where her father was awaiting them. She took a deep breath as her dad stepped back to let them enter the living room. Her mom was standing behind her father, waiting patiently with her hands clasped.

"Mom, dad, this is Khalil. Khalil, these are my parents Rebecca and Walter Lewis."

Khalil held out his hand to her father and the two men gave a firm shake.

"How are you, sir?" Khalil asked her father.

"Fine, son. Nice to meet you."

Khalil smiled at her mother.

"How you doing ma'am? You have a lovely home."

Mrs. Lewis smiled. "Thank you. Come on in and have a seat. Dinner will be on the table in about ten minutes."

"Oh, thank you for the invitation but I've already eaten. Thank you."

Mrs. Lewis looked to her husband whose lips were tightly

pursed.

"Okay…" she said. "Okay. Well come on…have a seat. Would you like something to drink? Lemonade or sweet tea?"

"Tea would be fine," Khalil answered as he sat down on the love seat.

Mr. Lewis took a seat on the sofa across from him and toyed with the remote that was resting next to him. Candace perched herself on the arm of the love seat, waiting for her father's opening remarks.

"Candace did tell you that we were expecting you for dinner, right?" Mr. Lewis asked Khalil.

Khalil nodded.

"She did. But my plans changed a little bit."

"We were waiting for you. It would have been a little more considerate if you had let us know that you wouldn't be joining us."

"My apologies. Something came up with my son and I ended up eating with him."

Candace nearly fell off of the love seat. *Son? What the hell? Was he making this shit up as he went along?*

"Oh, you have other children?"

"Yes sir. Two sons and a daughter."

"How old?"

"10,6 and 1."

"All with your wife?"

"The oldest two with my ex-wife and the 1 year-old with an ex-girlfriend."

Mr. Lewis' left eyebrow rose and Mrs. Lewis entered the living room with a glass of tea for Khalil. She sat beside her husband as Khalil nearly drained his glass. Candace assumed he needed the hydration since beads of sweat were forming on his forehead, no doubt as a result of the interrogation her father was giving him. Candace herself was in shock at everything coming out his mouth, from the kids to the ex-wife. She knew he was married to Sheila, but had no idea that he'd been married prior to her. It was hard to discern his truths from his lies.

"Do you see your children often?" her father asked.

"Oh you have other children?" her mother asked, having missed the beginning of the conversation.

"Yes ma'am…and I don't see them as often as I'd like. The older two live in a different state. They're in Virginia."

"Exactly how old are you, son?"

"41," Khalil answered.

Mrs. Lewis looked to her daughter questioningly and Candace simply looked away.

"Do you know how old Candace is?" her father asked.

Khalil nodded. "I do."

"You're six years younger than me…you're practically old enough to be her father. You couldn't find a grown woman to fool around with?"

"Dad," Candace interjected. "I am a grown woman, age is just a number."

"Is it? With age comes wisdom and you're not there yet, dear. Consider this present situation you're in."

"That has nothing to do with my age. Everyone makes mistakes."

"Okay, we're losing sight of the point here," Mrs. Lewis chimed in. "Mistake, lack of wisdom…whatever…there is a new life we are all bound by now. It's a shame that this child has to come to life in this type of situation, but we need to figure out how we're going to handle this."

"Well, with all due respect, Mr. and Mrs. Lewis, I want you to know that I have every intention of taking care of this child and being there for this child. I understand your concern for Candace and her baby. If the situation was reversed and it was my daughter, I'd be asking questions too. But don't worry. I know how difficult it is to raise a child and what all needs to be done. Trust me, Candace isn't in this alone."

"Candace and her baby," Mrs. Lewis repeated. "Do you understand that this is your baby too?"

"I understand that…"

"So don't say Candace's baby. This is y'all's baby. As in we expect the two of you to handle whatever needs to be handled to care for *your* baby."

"I understand that. In the same token, to protect myself, I will have to have a DNA test done after the baby's born."

"What?" Candace asked, unable to contain her contempt. "What are you trying to say, Khalil?"

He raised his hand at her.

"Calm down. I'm just saying it is the only reasonable thing to do. Let's be candid shall we. I mean, you *are* married. It could just as easily be your husband's baby, right?"

"It's not Quincy's baby. You know that. I haven't had sex with Quincy in a couple of months. Why would you say that?"

"I'm just trying to be responsible, sweetheart. That's all."

Mr. Lewis chuckled.

"Responsible? If either of you had been responsible we wouldn't be having this conversation. But, speaking of spouses…Have you advised your spouse of your new expectation?"

"My wife and I are separated. But no, she doesn't know."

"Since you have children and you say you know what all needs to be done to care for a child, you understand that she'll have doctor's appointments to go to frequently, bills associated with health care, and once the baby is here it'll need health insurance and things in general?"

"I do. Once the baby is born and we've done the DNA test, I insist that the baby be placed on my health insurance. I'm sure Candace will get plenty of incidentals from baby showers or what not, but I don't mind purchasing the bulk of major items like furniture, a car seat or whatever."

"Okay, but what about living situations? Candace doesn't have a home anymore…We're not exactly equipped to house a second family in our home. She and the baby will need their own space."

Khalil sighed and looked at Candace.

"I guess I could assist with a deposit on an apartment for you. Just find one and let me know what I need to do."

He looked at her parents reassuringly and softened his tone.

"Mr. and Mrs. Lewis, I know this isn't the most pleasant situation in which to introduce a new life into the world…and I know that you may not believe this, but despite what you think about the way Candace and I came to create a child together, I do care for your daughter. Candace knows that she has a place in my heart and that I'd do anything to help her and *our* child. In fact, Candace knows that she could stay with me if she wanted to versus getting a place of her own."

Candace sucked her teeth and looked away. She couldn't stand to watch the show he was putting on for her parents' benefit. Perhaps he knew that she wouldn't tell them about the scene that went down between the two of them and Sheila. But this fake, loving persona he was fronting with was making her sick.

"Out of the question," her father told him. "Even though you are both separated, you are both very much still married. Either of you could decide to return to your spouse at any time."

"Highly unlikely on my end, sir. But I understand your conviction on the matter."

"What are you going to do about child support?" Mrs. Lewis asked.

"We can figure that out before the baby gets here," Khalil responded. "We don't have to involve the courts. Give me the

DNA test for reassurance and I will gladly provide for my child. I don't need any judge to tell me to take care of what's mine."

Mrs. Lewis touched her husband's arm.

"Sounds feasible," she told him, searching his face for his thoughts on the matter.

Mr. Lewis nodded.

"Okay. As Candace's father, I'm hoping that you uphold all of your promises you made here today. As a man, I hope that you're as good of a father as you're portraying yourself to be. Children need both parents in their lives."

Khalil nodded and gave Candace a sideways glance.

"Yes, I know what a difference that makes. Candace can count on me."

Khalil looked at his Timex and smiled at Candace's parents.

"I have to be going now, I have another engagement. Thank you for the tea and the talk. It was really nice to meet the both of you. I guess we're all sort of like family now, huh?"

Khalil's attempt to make light of the situation didn't go over with Mr. Lewis very well. The older man simply ignored him and looked over to Candace.

"When's you next appointment?"

"In three weeks. They're going to do an ultrasound."

Mr. Lewis looked back to Khalil.

"I trust you'll make *that* appointment, right?"

Khalil nodded and rose from his spot on the love seat. He touched Candace lightly on the leg.

"Just let me know when it is, Candace and I'm there."

Candace moved her leg away.

"I'll call you."

"Mr. and Mrs. Lewis, it's been a pleasure," Khalil stated, walking towards the door. "Perhaps next time I'll be available to have dinner with you. Whatever you've cooked smells delicious, Mrs. Lewis. You all have a good evening."

Candace walked to the door to let him out. She stood on the porch and pulled the door up behind her. Khalil turned to look at her before he went to his car.

"You know, if you need anything else before your appointment, you can call me for that too, baby girl."

She turned her nose up at his come-on.

"That's not going to happen, dear. You can count on *that*."

Khalil chuckled and touched her face lightly.

"I can guarantee you that it'll happen. Your hormones are about to be raging out of control and I can tell you that pregnant pussy is the best… and you already know that I miss the taste of yours."

Candace was mad at herself for getting moist off of his lucid comments and his gall to make them on her parents' porch.

She shuddered at his touch and tried to keep up her hardened demeanor so that he wouldn't know she was turned on.

"You're so cocky, it's a shame," she told him. "Go home and tell Sheila I said hello…after u call and check in on your three other children."

Khalil chuckled.

"Yeah…right," he commented, walking on to his car.

She didn't wait for him to pull off before she went back inside and shut the door. Her father was sitting at the dining room table as her mother was in the kitchen fixing her husband's plate.

"You pick the most interesting characters to get involved with," her father told her.

She shrugged.

"He's not all bad, dad," she said. "It's an awkward situation for all of us."

He didn't respond. Candace sighed.

"I'm gonna go wash up and help mom."

She hurried up the stairs to the bathroom, relieved to be alone from her parents. As she washed her hands she thought of Khalil's statements and his touch against her skin. She hadn't had sex in a while and she was horny as hell.

"Damn Khalil," she cursed his memory. She looked at herself in the mirror and touched her breast. They were a little tender. Probably a combination of being horny and being pregnant. She resisted the urge to pleasure herself and hurried out to struggle through dinner with her parents.

JADA

Jada took a deep breath, said a small prayer, and walked into the bathroom. Slowly, she reached for it with her eyes closed. She was too afraid to open her eyes. Her heart raced rapidly. She wasn't ready for the answer. She wasn't prepared for the let-down. Sighing deeply, she picked it up and opened her eyes. Only one. Only fucking one. She began to heave, unable to control her breathing. She clutched her chest with the stick still buried in it, trying to pull herself together. It didn't work. She couldn't breathe past the hurt or the feeling that overcame her. Slipping to the floor, feeling the cold tile against her bare legs, she leaned against the vanity and suffered through the panic attack she couldn't avoid.

She sobbed between gasps of air, her body convulsing with her struggle to breathe normally. She never let go of the object of her distress. She was so distraught that she didn't hear Jordan come into their home, calling out her name. He walked through the house, looking for his wife.

"Jada, baby where you at?"

He walked into the bathroom and saw that the door was slightly ajar.

"Baby, you in here?"

He saw her, sobbing uncontrollably on the floor. He reached for her, confused as to what was going on.

"What's wrong, baby?" he asked her, kneeling down on the floor beside her.

"Baby what's wrong? Talk to me."

He put his arms around her, hugging her lovingly, and kissed her forehead.

"Baby, what's wrong?" he asked again rocking her, trying to soothe her back into calm breathing.

He touched her hand, still clutched to her chest. Realizing she was holding on to something, he tried to pry her hand open.

"What is it? Baby, what happened? Did something happen?"

He pried her fist open, releasing her grasp on the stick. He looked down at it, trying to figure out what had made his wife so unstable and hurt. His brain was trying to process what the hell he was looking at. He looked from the stick, to his wife, and back to the stick, and it dawned on him. He threw the stick down and rose from the floor.

"Come on baby, come on. It's okay. Lemme get you off the floor."

He reached down and cradled her up into his arms. Her breathing was relaxing and she allowed Jordan to carry her into their bedroom and lay her across their bed. He disappeared briefly to get her a glass of water.

"Sit up, baby…Try to drink this. Please."

She forced herself to sit upright. He lifted the cup to her lips and she took a few sips of the cold liquid. As she drank, she looked up into his eyes and felt a tremendous bout of guilt, shame, and helplessness. Tears rolled down her cheeks from her bloodshot eyes. Jordan shook his head, knowing immediately what it was that she was thinking.

"Don't think like that," he told her. "It's just not our time."

He sat the glass down on the nightstand and took her hand.

"I love you," he told her softly. "I love you baby."

She lowered her eyes.

"As much as I want to, as much as I've tried," she said softly. "I can't give you the one thing I know you want more than anything in the world."

"I have the one thing I want more than anything," Jordan tried to convince her. "I have you, baby."

"It's not fair," she told him. "Everyone else is getting knocked up…even the ones that don't want to be pregnant. Just with ease, it just happens for them with no effort. It's not fair, Jordan. It's not fuckin' fair."

"It's just not our time baby," he said, rubbing her hand.

"I'm sick of hearing that shit," she shouted angrily. "Stop telling me that shit. When is the time, Jordan? Huh? We've been trying for over a year. It's not rocket science. It's clearly not a hard thing to do. *I* just can't fuckin' do it."

"Why do you think it's something to do with you? Maybe it's me. Something could be wrong with me, babes. I could go to the doctor and get the shit checked out…try to see what's going on."

"It's me."

"I'm just saying, neither of us can be sure until we both get checked out so…"

"It's me, Jordan."

"Let's just both make an appointment to get checked out."

She snatched her hand away from him and balled her fists up in frustration.

"It's me, Jordan!" She screamed. "It's fuckin' me! I know that it's me."

She began to cry hard and looked at her husband with

sorrow in her eyes.

"The summer after I graduated from high school I had a boyfriend," she told him. "He loved me, he always told me he wanted to have a big family and I believed him…I believed everything he told me. So I got pregnant. It just happened so quickly. But when I told him, he acted like a typical nigga, saying he didn't believe me. He stopped taking my calls most of the time, didn't want to see me…and one day, when I was sick and in the hospital because I was having difficulty with the pregnancy he practically abandoned me. I called him, to tell him where I was and that I needed him. He told me that it was my own fault and that he wasn't coming out to the hospital…then he hung up on me. I didn't want to spend my life being someone's unwanted baby's mama. I wanted a family. I wanted to be loved…I wanted the whole package...And I wanted to hurt him, the same way he hurt me. So I had an abortion and went on with life like it never happened. They told me that one of the side effects could be that my uterine lining would be scarred…from them scraping it to terminate the pregnancy…"

Jordan sat silently, taking in her confession. His eyebrows were knitted as he came to terms with what she was saying.

"So see," she whispered. "It's me. This is my punishment for killing that baby. I can't give you a child of your own."

She covered her mouth to muffle her crying, tears seeping through her fingers. She watched Jordan massage his temples, staring at the floor. He shook his head.

"God doesn't work like that, baby. He's not a cruel God. He's a loving and forgiving God."

Jordan leaned over and kissed his wife's tear-stained

cheeks.

"What you need to do is forgive yourself, baby."

Jada threw her arms around him and held on for dear life, crying into his shoulder.

"I love you and we'll have a baby when it's time, Jada," he told her. "Let's just stop focusing on it so much and just let it happen. And in a year, if you are still worried about it, we'll see a specialist. Hell, if push comes to shove, we'll adopt. It doesn't really matter to me. We'll be parents one day, one way or the other. It's all good, boo. It's all good."

She looked up at him and kissed his lips passionately.

"Thank you," she told him.

"For what?"

"For understanding and for loving me."

He held her tightly.

"The pleasure's all mine, baby love."

MIRANDA

It had been a long day. Work was extremely exhausting and all Miranda wanted to do was go home, have a glass of wine with a cup of noodles and knock out. Walking through the grocery store down the street from her house, she searched for the wine aisle. Just past the snack aisle she saw a familiar face approaching her. She quickly racked her brain trying to figure out where she'd met this woman before. The chick stopped dead in her tracks and looked at Miranda with an intensity that caused her to stop and take a step back. Then it dawned on her. She knew exactly who this skank was.

"Not so hard out in public huh?" Tammy taunted her. "What you got to say now?"

"Why don't you just go about your business," Miranda insisted. "I'd hate to have to mop this dirty ass floor with your lily white jumpsuit."

"Oh don't hate, bitch, just because your ass lacks taste and class."

"Class? What the hell do you know about class? Trying to start shit with me in a grocery store? I mean really?"

"I don't start nada…I'm the one that finishes shit."

Passersby were starting to take notice of their confrontation. Sensing the attention from the crowd, Tammy began to really feel herself. She waved her index finger around as she hurled more insults at Miranda, raising her voice to sound hard.

"And you got about one more time to say some flip shit to me before I rip that tongue out ya' big ass mouth. You jealous, bitter ass bitch."

"I'm not gon' be too many more bitches. Now if you wanna get down, we can get down. You name the place and time, but I'm not about to get into this with you in this grocery store. That's some tacky shit you might do, but I'm not going to jail with or for you tonight."

Rounding the corner, Norris walked up to the two women and Miranda felt her heart skip a beat. Her first thought was to run, but she was rooted to the spot. Trying to regain composure, she was intent on not letting her husband and his tramp intimidate her.

"What's up, Miranda?" Norris asked sinisterly. "Didn't think I'd run into your ass did you? You know I should beat the shit out of you right here."

"Don't waste your energy on this mud duck, baby," Tammy said, stroking Norris' arm. "She ain't worth it."

"Listen to your girl, Norris," Miranda encouraged. "She must be an expert on worthlessness."

"Fuck you," Tammy spat out. "You're just mad cuz he's not stuck under your homely looking ass anymore."

"If you're done wasting my time, I'm going to go on about my business," Miranda said, clutching her purse tightly as she moved to walk past the couple.

"Watch your back," Norris warned her. "This shit ain't over."

"I'm done with you," Miranda responded.

Tammy laughed.

"Her ass is done in general," she giggled to Norris.

Miranda slightly passed the girl and quickly turned around, clocking her with her heavy faux leather purse.

"On second thought, maybe I'm not done!" Miranda snapped, swinging her purse over and over again across Tammy's face and head.

The younger girl was caught off guard by Miranda's attack and stumbled to the side twisting her ankle on her Baby Phat platform shoes. Her squeals of 'stop, stop, stop' were muffled under the blows Miranda continuously put upon her. A crowd was growing, but Miranda couldn't stop herself. In her blind rage, she swung her bag repeatedly until the strap broke from the force. Norris was pulling on her arm, effortlessly, urging her to chill the hell out. Tammy lay cuddled up on the floor, trying to protect her face from the blows. Tired of the bag, Miranda dropped her purse and grabbed Tammy up by her arm.

"Come on, bitch. Talk shit now."

Tammy's lip was busted and her left eye was beginning to swell. She struggled to her feet and spat in Miranda's face. Her blood tainted saliva slid down Miranda's cheek.

"Fuck you, you shiesty trick," Tammy retorted.

On instinct, Miranda threw a fist to punch Tammy, but Tammy was too quick. Getting her moxie back, Tammy stepped to the side and just as Miranda's energy was spent from missing her punch, Tammy grabbed Miranda's arm and landed a punch of her own against Miranda's nose. Blood dripped out on impact. Miranda struggled to free herself of Tammy's grip as the crowd hooted and hollered. A manager ran over to the scene.

"Ladies, stop!" the middle aged gentlemen pleaded. "Ladies! Ladies. You have to leave the premises with this. Call security!"

"Let her go, baby, come on," Norris said to Tammy, tugging at her arm. "Ease up man, come on. Ya'll cut this shit out in here before these folks call the damn police, man."

Tammy ignored him as she pushed Miranda into a

Koolaid display, gripping her arm with one hand and her face with the other.

"You dumb, bitch," she told Miranda. "You don't know who the fuck you're messing with. I will fuck your shit up. You think you're so smart and shit. You ain't shit. Ya' man don't want you, nobody wants your sorry ass. Put ya' hands on me again, I promise you won't put your hands on anyone else ever again."

"Fuck, Tammy. Let her go!" Norris yelled.

"Come on, ma'am," the manager continued to beg. "Please…"

Miranda gave up trying to pry Tammy's hand away from her arm, ignoring the sting of Tammy's nails digging into her skin. She reached up and grabbed roughly on Tammy's wavy track. She tugged with all her might, causing Tammy to let go of her face. A bruise was forming around her chin where Tammy's hand had been. She pulled harder and Tammy screamed, letting go of Miranda's arm. Taking this as an opportunity, Miranda tackled Tammy to the ground, choking her neck, shaking the girl, and kneeing her repeatedly in the gut. When Tammy seemed completely defeated, Miranda allowed Norris and the store manager to pry her away from the younger woman.

"Bitch," Miranda spat out.

She looked at Norris and snatched her arm away from him. Looking back to Tammy, she shook her head. Several store clerks were helping the woman to her feet. Doubled over in pain, Tammy glared up at Miranda, who gave her an equally hateful look. Norris put his arm around Tammy so that she could rest her weight against him.

"It's only a matter of time before he starts kicking your ass too," Miranda told Tammy.

An officer was by her side.

"Miss, come with me, please," he spoke authoritatively.

"You popping off at the mouth, all happy cuz you're with *my* husband. Stupid bitch. Yea, you got him…and look what getting him got *you*. Get used to getting your ass kicked, because I promise you the shit's just around the corner."

"Man gon' somewhere with that shit," Norris responded.

Miranda's vision was blurred as she was whisked through the crowd and out of the grocery store. She could vaguely remember how they got to that point. Her mind went blank as the officers spoke to her and advised her that she was going to be taken in to the county jail. She watched in what seemed like slow motion as a paramedic attended to Tammy further up the sidewalk. She felt herself be ushered into the back of a patrol car and stared at the spectators as she was carried off to a place she'd never thought she'd go. Her entire life was spiraling out of control.

~ ~ ~

"That was completely irresponsible of you…I can't believe this shit…Ya'll's asses are going to give me high blood pressure in this bitch. I mean damn…what ever happened to turn the other cheek? Or just walk away? Hell, if you wanted to kick someone's ass, why not kick Norris' ass? He's the one that has fucked you over. Tammy is just a product of Norris' bullshit."

Jada was ranting and raving nonstop as she drove Miranda home from the DeKalb County Jail. Several hours of sitting in a holding cell with hookers and other women who seemed down on their luck was more than Miranda could take. Now, listening to Jada lecture her was the perfect end to a perfectly fucked up day.

"You should be glad that girl didn't decide to press charges," Jada told her, turning down the street of her apartment complex.

"She didn't press charges because Norris probably thinks that I'd press charges against him."

"That's what any other sane person would have done a long time ago."

"I'm not asking you to understand so…"

"Good, damn it. Because I don't. Hell, I don't understand why ya'll do half the things ya'll do. No…what I really don't get is why the hell ya'll call me *after* ya'll do crazy shit and don't expect me to be real with you."

"Real or not, don't pass judgment against me, Jada. You don't know what I've been through…and this is one of those things that you'll never really understand until you've gone through it yourself."

Jada sighed and looked over at Miranda. Miranda sat with her arms crossed staring out of the window, waiting for Jada to put the car in park.

"I didn't mean to come off as being judgmental," she told Miranda. "I'm just saying, some things you just don't have to go through…you know, you put yourself in these positions and…"

Her thoughts trailed off. Miranda turned and looked at her friend. She knew the other girl only had her best interest at heart. Her body was sore, her head ached, and her feelings were hurt. She couldn't get past her own issues to see how she was putting extra baggage on the ones who cared for her the most.

"Thank you for everything," she said softly. "Thank you for being there at the hospital before. Thank you for bailing me out tonight. Thank you for always being such a great friend to me."

Jada reached over and hugged her tightly.

"I know you'd do the same for me. But Miranda, seriously…maybe you should talk to someone about how to deal with everything you've gone through…Maybe it would help you to make some healthier, wiser decisions to kinda get your life back on track."

Miranda gave a half smile. She knew that Jada meant well.

"We'll see," she told her, opening the car door and grabbing her purse.

"Call me tomorrow," Jada called out to her. "Alex is planning some kinda shindig for her birthday honey and you know she'll expect you to be there so put it on your calendar."

Miranda nodded.

"Okay. See ya' later."

She shut the door and hurried up the steps to her apartment. Once safely inside she went to the kitchen and rummaged through the pantry. She knew there'd be no alcohol there, which was why she'd gone to the store earlier to begin with. Plopping down at her kitchen table she buried her face in her hands and sighed, too exasperated and too pissed to cry. She needed something to take the edge off, something to help her through the emotions she couldn't control. She rose and went into her room where she hid her stash. Pulling out the shoe box, she reached inside and saw the little baggie she hadn't been able to bring herself to explore, until now. Turning it over and over in her hand, she debated whether or not she should try it. Once she crossed that path, there was no going back. She felt tension in her neck and moved her head from side to side. Glancing over at herself in the mirror she saw the bruises, dried blood, and the tired look in her eyes. She didn't even recognize herself anymore.

She took a deep breath and went into the living room to the coffee table. What did she have to lose? She quickly rummaged through her purse and pulled out a dollar. She'd seen this on TV. Surely it was this simple. Carefully, she rolled the dollar tightly. Opening the little baggy she stuck her finger inside the white powder and tasted it. She grimaced at the flavor. The taste made her think of biting into an aspirin. She sprinkled it out on the table, pushing it around with one edge of the rolled up dollar. She made tracks through it, separating it into two mounds.

"It must be like sucking through a straw," she said aloud, trying to brace herself.

She didn't know what to expect or even if she was going about it right. This wasn't exactly the kind of thing you could call someone up and ask about it. She took a deep breath and positioned the dollar over one of the mounds. Closing her eyes tightly she put her right nostril over the other end of the dollar and inhaled long and hard. The sensation tingled at first. After snorting half of the first pile she sat back and massaged her nose. She shook her head a little, trying to shake off the tickling inside her nose. Her heart was racing at the very thought of what she'd just done. Not yet feeling any effect and no longer scared of a horrible side effect, she picked up the dollar and finished off the first pile.

Leaning back with her head resting against the couch, she replayed the afternoon's events in her head. She couldn't believe that she'd allowed Tammy to take her to the level of cat fighting in public. But she'd whooped her ass good! She was glad that she hadn't backed down or walked away leaving Tammy or Norris to believe that she was a punk. Miranda was tired of being a victim. It was time to fight back. She had a record now, but at least she stood her ground. While feeling proud of herself, Miranda noticed that the tingling feeling in her nose had quickly been replaced with a burning sensation. She squeezed the bridge of her nose, willing the feeling to go away. Suddenly paranoid, she jumped up and hurried to the kitchen.

"What have I done?" she asked herself aloud. "What have I done?"

She went to the sink and splashed water on her face, desperate to try anything to cool off the sting. When she felt minimally satisfied with that, she poured herself a glass of water in an attempt to calm down. After a while she felt a surge of nervous energy that had her going through her closets rummaging, throwing out any remnants of Norris. This high wasn't what she was used to, but she was rolling with it. She had the nerve and the edge that she needed to start closing this chapter in her life.

"Fuck Norris," she spat out, while stuffing his clothes into a garbage bag. "I'm not taking any more of his shit. Fuck him and fuck Tammy. I'm not a fucking punching bag. I'm not a fucking victim anymore! Fuck him!"

The phone rang and she practically jumped at the sound

of it. She stared at the ringing phone, wondering if it was her abuser calling to taunt her.

"Fuck you!" she yelled at the phone as it gave its final rings.

She threw a pair of his socks at the cordless and turned away to promptly toss his game system into yet another bag.

STEPHANIE

She wasn't sure what the hell she was doing, but Stephanie knew she had to do something. She considered her options and this idea was the one that made the most sense to her. If anyone found Ernest Henderson's wallet on Corey's person or in his possession she knew her boyfriend would be tried for murder. Why he had chosen to stash it in their home was beyond her understanding. She wasn't completely sold on the idea that Corey had killed Montae, but she knew that whoever did had done so under Corey's instructions. This wasn't the man she knew that hustled hard in the streets to make life easy and lavish for her and their sons. Stephanie only knew for certain that she loved this man and wanted only to protect him and their family. Her plan was still to convince him to tie up his business dealings and move their family away from Atlanta to a place where they could have a fresh start in life. But first, she had to dispose of the evidence that could ruin that opportunity for them.

She waited until it was completely dark out so that no one would see her. The kids were sound asleep in their beds and Corey hadn't made it home, which wasn't uncommon for him. Taking the wallet out of the closet she divvied up the items in the wallet and placed them in different garbage bags. Then she divided the contents of all the waste baskets in the house into the three bags. Quietly she exited the apartment and went down to the trash receptacle. Disgusted, she tore into the bags of trash already in the receptacle and began to mix up the trash. Satisfied that the evidence was carefully concealed and its location unidentifiable she tied up her bags and took them down to her car. She prayed that Corey wouldn't come home while she was out.

Quickly, she rode down to the corner store and disposed of the trash in the store's large dumpster. Returning home she hurriedly took a shower to rid herself of the stink of trash and the twinge of guilt. She wasn't sure that she had done a good job of getting rid of it. Perhaps she should have taken it to a place that wasn't so close to their home. She convinced herself that she'd done a sufficient job. If the police wanted to pin Corey they'd go through his trash, not the trash of a corner store, right? She wondered where the gun was that had been used to kill Montae. If Corey did it, would he have kept the gun? If so, where would he have stashed it? Stephanie wanted to believe that Corey wouldn't have been stupid enough to hold on to a gun with a body on it. But then again, he had been foolish enough to bring the dead man's wallet into their home.

Nervous and scared for their family, Stephanie threw on one of Corey's white t-shirts and went into the kitchen for a drink. He kept a bottle of E & J. Stephanie wasn't too fond of brown liquor but was in desperate need of something to calm her nerves. She mixed the E & J with some cola and leaned against the counter as she let the alcohol burn down her throat. She heard the front door open and close and jumped. Turning around, glass in hand, she watched as Corey sauntered into the kitchen nonchalantly as if it was 12 in the afternoon instead of two in the morning.

"What's up, boo?" he asked her, heading straight to the refrigerator for a beer.

"You in here drinking up my shit?"

He slapped her on the ass and took a swig of his beer.

Stephanie fought back tears as she took a sip of her own drink. She lowered her head, an emotional wreck because of all the things she had been internalizing. Corey looked at her and noticed that something wasn't right.

"What's up? Why you not in bed?"

She looked up at him with tears in her eyes.

"Where were you?" she deflected, not addressing what was really bothering her.

"Working."

"This late, Corey?"

He chuckled.

"You act like I punch a time clock or some shit. My shit ain't exactly your average 9 to 5, baby."

She bit her lip.

"I know that…I just thought that you could have at least been home by 11."

"I'm home now. Are we going to have this same argument every time I don't come home when you want me to? This is my house. I should be able to come and go as I please, when I please. I'm tired as hell woman. Please don't start this shit."

He went to walk away and she reached out to talk to him.

"I need to talk to you," she spat out.

He looked at her and raised an eyebrow.

"'Bout what?"

She took a deep breath.

"I want you to get out of the game."

Silence hung in the air as Corey took in her words and she held her breath waiting to see how he would react. He studied her face and she searched his eyes for a clue at what it was that he was thinking. Unable to gage his feelings, she sat her glass down on the counter and pushed it back and forth from one hand to the other. Corey leaned against the counter beside her.

"What brought this on?"

She shrugged.

"Don't get silent now," he encouraged. "Speak on it."

"I'm tired of worrying about whether or not you're going to come home," she whispered. "When the phone rings I'm scared that it's you calling to say you're in jail or someone else calling to say something's happened to you. When you leave home, I'm sick of wondering if you'll make it back."

"This is what I do, Steph. You're not new to this shit. You've known who I am and what I am from day one."

She nodded.

"I know…but it's not just us now…we have kids we have to think about. I don't want our son seeing his dad on the news for…"

Her words trailed off and she looked up at him. His eyebrow rose as if he was daring her to say the unmentionable. She wanted him to know that she was privy to what was going on, but she didn't have the heart to utter the words and didn't want to upset him.

"You've made good money, baby," she pleaded with him. "We could take the kids somewhere quiet…away from Georgia. I could go to school and you could too if you wanted to…maybe start your own legit business doing something…I don't know…I just know that it's time to get out, baby. You can't do the same shit forever. At some point it's got to come to an end. Why not be the one to say enough is enough and let's just let it go before something bad happens…"

His expression softened as he felt the sincerity in her words and the fear in her voice.

"Do you feel unsafe, Steph? Cuz you and the kids are here with me? You wanna go back to how it was? Living separately?"

She shook her head.

"No, Corey. I don't want to be away from you. We're a family. I just want our family to be safe and stress free."

She lightly touched his arm.

"Baby, you have the potential to be so much more than this. You're a businessman…"

He snatched his arm away and took another swig of his beer.

"So much more than this expensive ass upscale condo you're in? None of your friends have half the shit we got baby. You got steaks and shit in the freezer. You ain't gotta want for nothing. Ain't no regular job out there for me, Steph, that's gon' keep us in this type of lifestyle. It just ain't happenin'."

"We have money saved…we don't need fancy food or a fancy apartment, Corey. That shit's not important."

He held his beer bottle up in her face.

"If I wasn't ballin' you wouldn't have looked twice at me back in the day. You loved this thug shit and this money, Steph. Don't front. I know what the hell it's like to be poor. Don't know where ya' next meal coming from, don't know how you gon' pay the bills, or if you even gon' have a place to stay period. I don't wanna worry about that shit for my family."

"We'll figure it out, Corey…we can figure something out…please…"

He took another swig and nodded his head.

"Lemme think about this shit, aight," he told her, turning

around to leave.

He stopped and looked back over his shoulder at her.

"You know I got you, right? I ain't gon' let nothing happen to you or my kids, Steph. I need you to believe that shit, ok?"

She nodded unable to look up at him. Corey walked out of the room and Stephanie released the tears she'd been trying hard to hold back. She turned up her glass and emptied it in one gulp. She knew his intentions were good where the family was concerned, but she also knew that nothing good could come out of this situation unless they got out immediately. She touched the chain of keys that always hung around her neck and wondered for the first time in a long time what other troubles they opened up for them. She felt defeated and didn't know what else to do or where to turn.

CANDACE

Time was steadily passing and Candace was still trying to adjust to the idea of sharing her body with a little person. Pregnancy was not fun for her. The morning sickness was getting on her nerves and she was now starting to feel a change in the way her clothes fit. Having kids was never something she planned on doing and it was definitely putting a cramp in her diva-like demeanor. She constantly felt chunky and self-conscious about her appearance. If she wasn't puking or munching on snacks, she was increasingly horny. This was a feeling that truly sucked for her because she had no one around to alleviate her frustrations. Khalil was out of the question. In fact, Khalil's ass was M.I.A. All the crap he'd told her parents about being there for her, helping to get her a place, and stepping up to his responsibility turned out to be as fictional as Sheila being his estranged girlfriend. Her parents frequently inquired about his whereabouts and whether or not she'd heard from him. Each time that she had nothing to report she could see the rage growing in her father. She knew her parents didn't want to get stuck with footing the bills for both her and a newborn. Candace wanted nothing more than to move out of her parents' place and have her own space again, free from their disappointed and disapproving glances.

She hadn't heard from Quincy at all. That was fine with her. She was ready to close that chapter of her life anyway. Horny or not, she was not about to let him touch her body ever again for any reason. She recently filed for divorce. Since their marriage was short lived and they had no shared assets, she was confident that it wouldn't take long for the papers to be ready for their signatures. The sooner, the better. Candace was ready to move on. But most importantly, she was ready to get her freak on.

Stopping by a popular rib joint in the heart of the DEC, Candace was in the mood for a greasy rib sandwich and fries. Sauntering into the small hole-in-the-wall with her black slacks and lavender blouse, she noticed a familiar face smiling at her. She turned up her nose, not wanting to give him any eye contact, and went on to the counter to place her order. As she waited for her food to be ready, she stared out of the window at the rush hour traffic crawling down Candler Road.

"What you doing 'round this way?" his southern drawl was close to her ear.

She flinched, wondering where he got the nerve to approach her like that.

"I work not too far from here," she answered reluctantly.

She looked at him, noticing for the first time ever how smooth his chocolate skin was. Her hormones were messing with her senses.

"What *you* doing 'round this way?" she mocked him. "You moved on up, remember? To ya' mansion in the sky with ya' wife and kids."

"We ain't married."

"Might as well be. You know that girl loves you with a passion."

He ran his hand over his perfectly maintained waves and shot her a knowing smile.

"Look like somebody been loving you with a passion."

Instinctively Candace pulled down on her blouse and smoothed the fabric over her belly.

"What are you talking about?" she asked defensively.

"Ma'am, your order's up," the cashier announced.

Candace grabbed her greasy bag and headed out of the soul food joint. He followed her to her car.

"Aye, man. I didn't mean to piss you off or nothing. I didn't mean it in a bad way, ya' know. I was just saying. It looks good on you."

She gave him a questioning look.

"How does being pregnant look good on somebody? Its synonymous with being fat."

He opened her car door and leaned in a little too closely for someone that was definitely off limits to her.

"Pregnancy is beautiful on chicks that take care of their bodies. Makes you phat in all the right places."

She watched as his eyes surveyed her body and felt as his hand lightly grazed her ass once she moved to get into the car. He shut the door behind her.

"You got my number?" he asked.

"Yeah," she said coyly. "Your house number."

"Aight, you got jokes. Giggle it up now. I promise you I'ma get that."

"What-the-hell-ever."

"Mark my words, baby girl. A nigga knows which chicks he can and can't pull."

"You don't think you're being a little arrogant? You

talkin' all this trash. How you know that I'm not about to get on the phone and tell your girl what type of dog you are."

"Cuz you won't. And even if you did, she wouldn't believe you."

He flashed his cocky smile, tapped her car, and turned away.

Candace pulled off and considered their conversation as she drove to her parents' place. It had been a while since she'd had some attention from a man. Her ego and her body were screaming for it. Since she knew her body wasn't going to get any of the satisfaction that his forwardness alluded to, she figured there was no harm in allowing her ego to be stroked by his come-ons. It was just friendly, flirty banter. No one was harmed. Would she call him? Of course not and not just because the only number she had for him truly was their house number, but, because it would have been completely out of line.

However, later that night as she lay in bed alone she replayed their conversation once more, taking special notice of how his lips curled when he smiled at her. How his hand lightly touched her. She worked herself up so much over the memory of such a brief, trivial moment that she began to wonder what it would be like to have his hands stroking her bare ass, her sensitive nipples, and her aching pussy. Her fingers slid down to her kitty as she envisioned him entering her with his tongue. She wasn't surprised to find it slippery down there, she stayed super wet these days. Candace let her index and middle fingers enter her body as she toyed with the erect nipple of her right breast. Her eyes shut tightly, she could see him thrusting inside of her, holding her legs tightly up in the air as he pounded away.

"Uhhhh," the moan escaped her lips as she imaged his climax. Her body began to shudder at the thought of him violently cumming in her massive wetness, his body crashing down hard against hers.

As if on cue, she felt her walls constrict against her fingers and she thrust them deeper and harder into her pussy, opening her legs wider and raising her hips slightly off the bed. She felt her body cross over the edge into ecstasy and caught herself from whispering his name into the stillness of the room during the throes of her own passion. Recuperating from her moment, she felt a twinge of guilt for masturbating at the thought of someone else's dude. But, at least she wasn't actually off somewhere creeping with him. Candace turned over on her side and cuddled her pillow. She missed having someone next to her to sex her then spoon her to sleep.

ALEX

"I can't believe this," Alex whined.

She swiped her card again. After punching the series of

buttons she was given the same result. *Insufficient funds*. The clerk looked at her, annoyance written all over her face.

"Would you like to try another form of payment?"

Alex sucked her teeth and looked over at Clay. He nonchalantly reached over her and swiped his own debit card to cover her purchase. Exiting Party City, carrying her bags for her, Clay said nothing. Alex bit her lip, embarrassed but so relieved to have had Clay chauffeuring her around that day. He opened the door for her and she slid into his black Honda Accord. As they peeled out of the parking lot she smiled at him.

"Thanks so much, Precious," she cooed. "You know you're the best right?"

Clay chuckled.

"Yeah, the best at rescuing you, you spoiled little princess. You going broke trying to give yourself the birthday bash of the year? This party can't really be all that worth it."

Alex sulked.

"No, I'm going broke supporting T's ass."

"Come again?"

"I loaned him money for a few things."

"Such as?"

"Such as studio time, a new phone, and a few clothes...but that was more like a gift because I wanted him to look fly for this showcase he did."

Clay tapped the steering wheel as he waited for the light

to change. He shook his head in disbelief of his friend's naivety.

"So when's ol' boy paying you back?"

Alex shrugged and examined her nails.

"Who knows…hopefully he'll get this deal locked and we can be on our way to seeing some real money soon."

"We?"

"Yeah…"

Alex looked at Clay questioningly, wondering where his sarcasm was coming from. Clay simply shook his head again, choosing to drop the conversation.

"What?" Alex challenged him, turning her body in her seat to face him full on. "You don't think my relationship with T is valid or something?"

"Valid? Man go 'on, Alex. I'm not trying to go there with you."

"Go where? Uh-un… come on, Clay. Let's go on wherever you're headed. What's your problem?"

"Kick rocks, Alex."

She slapped his arm.

"Kick deez. Now, what's your *problem!?*"

He made the left onto Alex's street and headed toward her apartment.

"I'm not the one with the problem." He sighed. "You

keep picking up these dudes that don't treat you right and every time the shit falls apart you have this deer-in- headlights reaction to it…like you didn't know they weren't shit to begin with."

"So what are you saying? You think T isn't really feeling me? You don't even know him, Clay."

"Hell, you don't even know him, Alex. One or two dates in and you're ready to put your name on his bank account and a marriage license. What type of intent has he shown you to make you think that you're gonna be walking down the red carpet at the Grammy's with him?"

Alex sat with her mouth opened, wanting to respond, but not quite sure what to say.

"I…I..." she stuttered. "I'm investing in him. I believe in him…and…and if any relationship is going to work you have to believe in the other person."

"That sounds like a whole lot of b.s.," he said flat out as he put the car in park.

"You're investing in being a part of the glitz and glam of the industry. You probably don't even like this cat as a person. And no doubt you're fucking him already. Giving him all your little money, your cookies, and your time in exchange for what?"

"A relationship is give and take. And while you're all up in my business, where's your better half, Clay?"

"Oh my bad, I'm a lil' more selective with who I give my all to. I don't make a habit of trying to force myself into a relationship."

"Force myself? You think I'm forcing myself on this man?"

"I think you need to exercise a little more discretion when you're dating. And you need to inquire with dude as to when you're going to get your money back."

"Unbelievable," she muttered.

"You're right. It's unbelievable that he has any intention of giving you back a dime."

Clay got out of the car, leaving Alex stewing in anger. Clay grabbed her bags from his trunk and stood beside the car waiting for her to get out. With her pouty face on, she slowly exited the car and stood in front of Clay with her arms crossed.

"I can't believe that you are talking to me like that," she whined. "What did I do to you? Why are you being so…mean to me?"

"Mean? Alex, are you kidding me? I'm just trying to hip you to some game. You keep picking these knuckle head ass dudes…this isn't what you need, I mean T and Mario…those type of dudes aren't for you."

"Who are you to tell me who I should and shouldn't be with? What gives you the right to…"

"Forget it," Clay said, handing her the myriad of shopping bags. "Forget I said anything. Go head, stick it out with your boy. I hope ya'll get married and have lots of kids."

He moved away from her and walked around to the driver's side of the car.

"Where are you going?" Alex demanded. "You're not going to stay and help me with the party?"

"You don't need me," he called over his shoulder. "Go

call up your boy. Let's see how quickly he comes to your rescue."

He slammed his car door and quickly backed out of the parking lot, leaving Alex standing speechless on the curb.

~ ~ ~

"He was tripping hard. I can't believe he left me like that, being all extra dramatic. I've never seen him act so funny like that."

Alex was venting as Candace touched up her makeup in preparation for her birthday party. Jada stood to the side, looking over her list, trying to make sure that they remembered everything that they needed to do for the evening ahead.

"He said that I force myself into relationships…he implied that I'm only dating T so that I can have some kinda celebrity by association thing going on. Like, I'm a gold digger or something."

"I don't think you're a gold digger," Candace responded, touching up the eyebrow powder she previously applied to Alex's brows. "Nothing wrong with wanting to be with someone who has something going for himself…or has potential to be going places."

"Exactly…Maybe he was having a bad day or something. If I didn't know better I'd say that he was jealous."

Candace looked over to Jada who made a smirk and turned away. She bit her lip and smiled at her clueless friend.

"Well, girl…maybe he is."

"I don't see why. Clay is always dating a new chick all the time."

"Yeah, he never is with the same girl, right? Well, maybe that's because he's keeping his eye on one special chick and waiting for the perfect time to scoop her up."

"That's his business. He ain't gotta rain on my parade in the meantime."

Candace threw down her compact in defeat.

"Ugh. Okay girl, I'm done with you."

Alex stood up and looked at herself in the full length mirror. She was stunning in her black tube dress. The fabric hugged her curves in all the right places.

"Well, I hope he gets over his attitude and gets his ass back here to my party. He knows better than to bail on me on *my* day."

"Is your boyfriend coming?"

"Girl, yes! What kind of question is that?"

Candace shrugged.

"Just asking. It would have been nice if he came and helped us get ready."

Alex didn't respond. She'd been thinking the same thing herself but didn't want to voice her concern to the girls. After Clay's blow up about her relationship, Alex really didn't want to hear what anyone else had to say about T. It bothered her that she hadn't heard from him. All the things that Clay had said bothered her too. But she desperately wanted to believe that things would work out with this guy. Alex just wanted to be loved and adored by someone.

"Okay, girl," Jada was saying. "I'm going to run home to shower and change. I'll see ya'll back at the club house in a little bit."

Alex smiled and hugged her friend.

"Okay, friend. Thanks for everything."

"No problem."

Jada rubbed Candace's tummy and left the room. Alex turned to Candace and smiled.

"Never thought I'd see you pregnant," she giggled.

"Never thought I'd see me pregnant either," Candace responded, sitting down on Alex's bed. "Girl, it's a major adjustment. Stay on your birth control, Alex. You don't ever want to be in this boat."

Alex gave a half smile and looked away from her friend. She went back to looking in the mirror and fooling with her hair, marveling over her beauty.

"So what's the deal with your baby's daddy?" Alex asked Candace.

"No deal. His ass hasn't called or come by the house. My parents are too through with his ass. I'm not worried about him. Trust and believe that I will be at the child support office as soon as this kid is out of me."

The girls shared a laugh and Alex's phone began to sing. She picked it up and looked at the caller ID. It was T.

"Hey," she answered, giving Candace a love-sick grin.

Candace rolled her eyes and excused herself from the room.

"Where are you?" Alex asked, hearing the sound of commotion in T's background.

"With my boy, Tony. We down here about to hook up with this producer he know that wanna talk about that track we did last month…you know, that one 'Tribute to the A'. He might wanna put us on, babes."

"That's so good, T…But, do you have to meet him tonight? You know tonight's my party."

"I know but, the biz don't stop just cuz you have a birthday, yo."

"But, T…"

"Baby don't start all that whining and carrying on, man. I called you to let you know I'ma be late. I'ma still try to make it, but I gotta handle this business. You understand that?"

"Yes, but…"

"I'm making history out here, baby. I'm doing this for us."

Alex was silent. She wanted to believe him, but her instincts told her that he was just running game. Clay had placed a lot of doubt in her mind that she didn't want to give in to. She sighed and bit her lip.

"Okay," she caved in. "Call me when you're on your way."

"Bet. Later, baby."

He hung up before she could say anything else. She was disappointed and hoped that he made an effort to show up in support of her. Throwing the phone on the bed, she looked herself over in the mirror once more. *He'd be crazy not to come to this,* she thought to herself with a smile.

THE GIRLS

The party was jumping and the club house of Alex's apartment complex was filled with lively party-goers. Wings, chips and dip, and mixed drinks floated everywhere as the sounds of the hottest music blasted through the room. Stephanie leaned against the wall next to Jada who was watching the activity around them and nursing a vodka and cranberry juice. Her head bobbed to the music as she was enjoying being out of the house, away from the children and a little bit free of her concerns over Corey's business dealings. In all, she was enjoying herself. But, the sight of Miranda approaching Corey across the room rubbed her the wrong way. She tried to gauge their facial expressions, but couldn't tell what their exchange was about. She nudged Jada.

"Have you talked to Miranda much lately?"

"Somewhat," Jada answered shrugging. "I mean, she had an altercation with Norris and his lil' girlfriend a couple of weeks ago. But I haven't really talked to her since that whole thing went down."

"Yeah, she hasn't been calling or getting up with me either. But she's looking real cozy and friendly with someone."

Jada followed her friend's glare and shook her head.

"Naw now, don't start that. Miranda wouldn't go there and you know it. Stop tripping."

Stephanie took a sip of her drink and cocked her head to the side in disagreement.

"I don't know...there was that time that she just showed up at our place out of the blue. I don't think she knew I was there, but she played it off like she was coming over to talk to me."

"Don't start being paranoid about something that's *not* going on. You have other real Corey issues that you should be concerned with. Trust me, nobody wants your little thug."

Stephanie cut her eyes at Jada and returned her attention to her boyfriend and her friend.

~ ~ ~

"Why you avoiding me?" Miranda asked Corey. "I've been paging you nonstop."

"Yeah and I wish you would stop," he responded as he helped himself to a plate of hot wings.

"What did I do to you? I keep money in your pocket, so why you acting like that?"

Corey looked around, trying to keep his cool. He caught Stephanie glaring at him across the room but wasn't about to feed into her insecurity.

"I'm not having this conversation with you in here, man."

Miranda looked around herself and moved in closer to Corey so only he could hear her, which was a challenge over the music.

"Look, I just need you to hit me up with a little something…just this once."

"What you talkin' bout, just this once?"

Corey looked at her and took in her antsy disposition and the look of desperation in her eyes. There was a sullen hardness in her face that he never noticed there before, but had seen in his business often enough.

"I don't know who got you on, but that's who you need to go holler at. Steph ain't gon' kick my ass cuz you playing in a big man's game. Fuck that shit."

Miranda sucked her teeth.

"This ain't about Stephanie. This is business, right? You're a business man, right? This is your business. This is my business. This ain't none of Steph's business."

Corey's attention trailed off as he slyly watched Candace enter the kitchen area to grab herself a bottle of water. She walked away and began to head past the dance floor when a tall dude in a black tee stopped her. He noticed her body language and assumed that ol' boy was kicking some game to her as she giggled in response. Corey whipped out his cell, barely listening to Miranda's mantra.

"I could go anywhere, Corey," she tried to convince him. "But I come to you because I trust you."

"You say that shit like you're doing me a favor. Like this is some ordinary, loan you a few bucks, baby sit ya' kid type situation."

He quickly sent a text and returned his phone to its holster.

"No…but it's about money. That's what you're in it for, right? The money?"

He looked at Miranda as she gave him a serious look. He could understand a junkie's need for the product because he himself had an addiction: money.

"$25 a hit. Get me busted with my ol' lady, I'm fucking your shit up."

"You're trying to play me, Corey. That shit's $20 anywhere else."

He raised his eyebrow.

"For you its $25 so hopefully you'll change your fuckin' mind. But if you don't like it, you can go somewhere else and risk a mutherfucker lacing yo' shit with something that'll kill you. Your choice. This conversation is over."

He grabbed his plate and moved to walk past her. He stopped and whispered in her ear.

"And if you gon' play junkie, you gon' play it out all the way. Cop yo' shit from the trap. Don't hit me up anymore."

He walked off and Miranda surveyed the room to make sure no one was paying them any attention. She folded and unfolded her arms, unsure of what to do next. She looked around and decided to mix herself a drink and head outside for some air.

~ ~ ~

Candace was feeling the music at Alex's party. She danced until her feet hurt and her forehead began to sweat. Taking a time out, she went into the kitchen area to grab a bottle of water. As she walked away, a tall dark skinned brother approached her and touched her lightly on the arm. She looked down at her arm and back at the cutie.

"Sorry, miss lady, but can I holla at you for a minute?" he

yelled over the music.

Her brow frowned and she cocked her head to the side, having not heard what he'd said.

"What?"

"I said can I holla at you for a minute?"

She shrugged.

"What's up?"

"What's your name?"

"Candace."

"Candace, you're looking pretty fine tonight. You here with your man?"

Candace giggled as she watched the dark brother lick his lips as he spoke.

"I don't have a man."

"Well my name is Kevin and I'd like to see how I can be your man."

She giggled again at his forwardness, repositioning her body to a sexy stance to maximize his view of her figure in her jeans. It was nice to know that she still had it, pregnant or not.

"You don't even know me to know that you wanna be with me like that."

He lightly touched her face.

"With a smile like that, pretty mama, I don't need to know anything else."

She felt her cellphone vibrate as he spoke. She reached for it and he grabbed her hand.

"Go' head and put my number in your phone cuz I'ma be calling you later."

She smiled at him and quickly clicked off of the message indicator on her screen. She handed him the phone.

"Here. Put your number in."

He coded his number into her cell then called himself so that he'd have her number locked in too. Handing her back the phone, he gave her a once over.

"Aight, stay cute 'til you hear from me."

She sucked her teeth.

"That shouldn't be too hard," she teased in response to his corny line.

He smiled.

"Aight, lil' mama."

She walked away from the cutie being sure to put on her sexy walk knowing that he was watching her retreating profile. Candace headed over to Jada and Stephanie who were huddled up across the room in the middle of a discussion of their own.

"Having fun?" she teased them. "Ya'll so lame over here in the cut gossiping instead of out there on the floor shaking your asses."

She bumped Jada, trying to liven her up.

"Yeah, you shake your ass enough for the both of us so I'm good."

Stephanie laughed.

"Ha, ha," Candace retorted. "Don't hate."

"Keep it up girl, the next time you drop it like it's hot you're gon' drop that baby right out on the floor," Stephanie joked.

"Shut up. Where's Alex?"

Jada took a final swig of her drink and shrugged her shoulders.

"Last time I saw her she was talking to some of her coworkers."

"I was wondering if her new boo made it here yet. Has anyone even met him yet?"

Both girls shook their heads no. Candace sucked her teeth.

"His sorry ass."

She thought about her statement and shook her head, dismayed at herself.

"Hell, I'm one to talk. My husband *and* my baby's daddy are some sorry ass jokers."

"Hmmm," Jada remarked.

Candace felt her phone vibrate again. She pulled it out and saw that she had two text messages. She read the first one that had come in while she was flirting with Kevin.

You know that lame nigga ain't what you want.

She couldn't help but laugh. She went on to the next message.

You looking phat in 'dem jeans. Feel like being tasted?

"Are you for real?" she said out loud, in shock.

"I'm just saying, she's been acting real funny lately, not like herself," Stephanie said.

"Who?"

"*Miranda!*"

"Huh? What are ya'll talking about?" Candace was confused.

"Who got you all open in your text messages that you can't pay attention?" Jada joked. "Stephanie's tripping about Miranda's attitude…she's over here trying to convince herself that Miranda is doing something that she's not."

Jada shot Stephanie an 'I'm trying to tell you' look and Stephanie waved her off.

"Something like what?" Candace asked.

Jada looked at Candace and laughed.

"Nothing girl, go back to your texts. It's not even important."

Jada turned to Stephanie.

"Really, boo. It's nothing. So let that go, okay?"

Jada walked off in pursuit of Alex and Stephanie looked over to Candace who was still lost.

"A woman's intuition tells her when shit ain't right. Mark my words, Candace. Some shit ain't right."

Candace bit her lip, feeling some kind of way about Stephanie's statement as the other girl left her alone with her thoughts. She looked back down at her phone, knowing that she should just delete the messages and go on with her evening.

How did you get my number? she texted back, just out of curiosity. Several seconds later, she got her response.

I have my ways. Meet me tomorrow at that bbq place. I wanna get up with you.

It wasn't a good idea, but she was starving for the attention. Most importantly, her body was dying to be touched by hands other than her own.

~ ~ ~

Two and a half hours into her party and T still wasn't there. Alex managed to still have a great time without him, but every time someone new walked in she glanced over to see if it was him. He hadn't called or texted and on the inside she was livid with herself for allowing him to disregard her the way he frequently did. Clay was right. She seemed to gravitate to these men who did nothing but treat her badly. But never would she admit to him or her girls that this relationship, like all the others, was going nowhere.

As she was talking to a group of her coworkers, Jada approached her and gave her a friendly hug.

"Having fun, friend?"

She gave her a big smile and nodded.

"Yep. Nothing better than being a real princess for a day."

Jada looked over Alex's shoulder to the door and gave a smile of her own.

"Well you're about to be even happier, cuz look who's here."

Alex's heart skipped a beat, hoping that her mystery guest would turn out to be T. She turned around and was mildly disappointed to see that it was only Clay. She should have known better. Jada had never met T to be able to say it was him. Clay approached them with a small black bag in his hand and a bouquet of pink and white roses. He gave her a tight squeeze and a kiss on the cheek.

"Alexandria, is this your boo you're always talking about?" one of her coworkers asked playfully.

Alex gave a polite smile and shook her head.

"This is my best friend Clay," she said.

Clay waved to the group of women then motioned to the kitchen area.

"Let me talk to you for a minute."

She nodded her consent and followed him to the kitchen. Jada walked beside her.

"Everything okay?" Jada asked.

"I guess. He probably wants to apologize for being such a meanie."

Jada raised an eyebrow and fell back, allowing the two of them their privacy.

No one else was in the kitchen. Clay handed her the flowers and smiled at his friend.

"You look nice," he complimented her.

She sniffed the flowers and cradled them in her arms.

"Thank you," she replied. "For the flowers and the compliment."

He sighed. "Look, I'm sorry if I hurt your feelings earlier, especially being that today was a special day for you. For that I'm sorry."

"Yeah, poopie. You're supposed to always be on my side," she pouted. "That's what best friends are for."

"I am on your side," he assured her. "Always. But, that doesn't mean that I'm not going to tell you the truth, Alex. I just want the best for you."

Silence. Alex looked down at her flowers, swaying back and forth not wanting to tell Clay that he really had nothing to be sorry for because he was completely right. In her heart, she knew that he would never intentionally hurt her. She knew that she could always depend on Clay to be there for her when she needed him and to have her back always.

"I know," she muttered. "I know you're just looking out for me."

She looked up at him and tried to keep a straight face to make her next statement convincing.

"But I've got this, Clay. I'm a big girl now, and I've got this."

Clay looked at her knowingly. Alex could never fool him. But he didn't want to argue with her about it anymore. He only wanted her to enjoy her evening and to know that he was always there for her, no matter what.

"I got you a gift," he told her, holding out the little black bag. "It's no Tiffany diamond, but I worked mad hard to save up for it so I hope you like it."

Alex reached out for the bag.

"You know I *love* me some jewelry," she said.

Before her fingertips could touch the handle of the bag, Alex's eyes were drawn to the figure heading in their direction. Her eyes squinted through the crowd, but she would have noticed that physique anywhere. As he hurried into the kitchen, Alex dropped her hand and carelessly tossed the flowers onto the counter. T threw his arms around her, disregarding Clay standing there.

"It's going down, ma!" T yelled as he embraced her tightly and wildly. "Whoooohooo, its going *down* baby!"

Alex was overwhelmed and stunned. She just allowed him to bear hug her until he finally let go. In one hand he had a bottle of Hypnotic, in the other hand a little gold box.

"I'm glad you came," Alex said excitedly.

"Yeah, baby! Fo 'sho. I know this your night. But, baby…I got the deal. Ya' man got the deal!"

"You signed with a label?" she was baffled.

Clay stood to the side, listening and watching their exchange, holding his gift in his hand. He didn't like the sight of T. Maybe it was the chains around his neck and his sagging jeans. Maybe it was his boastfulness. Or maybe he was just plain jealous that the dude burst in at a time when he was trying to get his nerve up to come clean with Alex.

T held the bottle up in the air and nodded his head repeatedly as he bounced around.

"That's right, that's right. Ya' boy is about to fuckin' blow up. I'm in baby! I'm fuckin' in!"

He grabbed Alex up again and kissed her ferociously. She barely had time to pucker her lips and kiss him back as his mouth crushed hers. Withdrawing from the embrace, he handed her the little gold box.

"Happy birthday, baby," he told her. "Nothing but the best for you."

She opened the box and pulled out a thin gold chain with a pendant of her name dangling from it. Clay surveyed her smile, thinking that she looked like she'd just won the lottery or something. He recognized the standard gold jewelry box and the cheap gold plated chain she held on to lovingly. It was a typical item from a typical jewelry kiosk at North DeKalb Mall. The dude probably spent a total of $20 for the gift.

Alex threw her arms around T and kissed him passionately.

"Thank you, baby. And congratulations on your deal. I knew you could do it."

T grinned like a Cheshire cat and held the Hypnotic bottle up once more.

"That's right! Now let's celebrate off in this thang-thang. Yo, where the cups at?"

T turned away and busied himself with pouring up a drink, never once acknowledging Clay. Alex didn't even bother to introduce her best friend to her new beau. The rest of her girls sauntered into the room and circled around her.

"T's here," she motioned over to her boyfriend. "But look what he gave me."

She showed them the necklace and they all gave polite responses as she hurriedly put the jewelry around her neck. Clay, leaning against the counter, said nothing.

"Come on lemme, introduce ya'll to my boo. He's so crunk cuz he finally signed with a label tonight. I knew it would work out for him."

The girls walked over with her to T and Alex began the introductions. Fed up with the scene, Clay nodded his head in defeat and sat the black bag on the counter. He was done playing second best to all the other dudes Alex encountered over the years. Without a good bye or a gesture, he briskly walked out of the party and out of Alex's life without her knowledge.

ALEX

It took a lot for Alex to clean her apartment after the party. All the gifts, leftover food, and knick knacks that were left at the club house once the party was over all ended up haphazardly in Alex's living room. She and Kacey took their time going through each bag and each container until everything was perfectly in place. A small pile of gifts sat in the corner of the living room untouched, but Alex was too pooped to go through them. She plopped herself down on the couch and watched Kacey enter the living room with a glass of lemonade in one hand and a wad of plastic bags in the other.

"Here girl," she offered Alex the glass. "I'm telling you, you had the jam of the century, girl."

Alex giggled.

"It was so fun. And did you see T? He was so crunk, right?"

Krystal gave a phony smile and cocked her head slightly to the side.

"A lil drunk, don't you mean?"

"He was excited," she defended her boyfriend. "He's been working hard to get a deal. He deserved to wild out a little bit."

"A lil bit? Girl him and his boys were getting straight toasted up in there. Almost didn't know if it was your party or his."

Alex fingered the necklace dangling from around her neck and shrugged. She had just been glad that he showed up.

"It wasn't that big of a deal," she said. "I had fun."

Sensing that she was striking a nerve Kacey let it go and balled up the already wadded plastic bag.

"Hmmm," she said scrambling to unwad the bags. "Something's in here."

Alex drained her glass and watched as Kacey pulled out a tiny jewelry box.

"This must be a gift you overlooked girl," she said, opening the box.

Her eyes widened and intrigued, Alex jumped up and grabbed the box from her. She peered inside and saw a beautiful solitaire diamond ring. A gift card was stuck to the inside of the box. She snatched it out and read the imprint.

A promise of everlasting friendship and whatever else is to follow.

She looked at Kacey who was looking right back at her.

"Who the hell is that from?" Kacey asked. "And please don't tell me your broke ass rapper boyfriend girl 'cuz we all know what his idea of fine jewelry is."

Alex ignored the jab at T and returned her eyes to the beautiful ring in the box. The memory hit her instantly. Clay was trying to give her the gift just as T waltzed in and commanded her attention that night. She read the card again and felt chills tingling up her spine. What did he mean by whatever else is to follow? Where had he gone that night? She didn't remember seeing him at the end of the party. Quickly she pulled out her cell and dialed his number. She was stunned to hear an automated recording telling her that the number she had dialed had been disconnected. Thinking it was a mistake, she dialed the number again. She received the same message.

Sitting down on the sofa she held the ring box in her hand and stared at the ring inside of it. She had ignored Clay when T came in. Perhaps that had hurt his feelings. Was that when he left? What was he going to say? What was he trying to say by giving her such a sentimental piece of jewelry? For the first time, Alex realized that Clay was truly digging her. For years she'd seen him as just a friend and was sure that he felt he same way. Sure, he was always there to rescue her. Sure she felt extremely comfortable with him. But she never really entertained the idea that he was in love with her…or maybe she did know all along and just chose to ignore the signs.

She looked at her phone and then back to the ring. There was one thing she was now sure of. Whatever chance they stood was long gone. Clearly, Clay was tired of standing in the shadows and had decided to be done with her. His phone had never been disconnected before for any reason. It was no coincidence or mistake. He was gone. Alex snapped the ring box closed and covered her mouth with her hand to muffle the sound of her cry. Not only had she missed out on knowing what kind of future they could have had, she had also lost her best friend.

Candace

Her body was aching in ways she'd never experienced before. As time went on, her belly expanded, her mood altered, and her parents became increasingly annoyed with having her around. The feeling was mutual. She was tired of not having a place of her own as well. Her entire situation was stressful and unbelievable. At times, Candace felt like she was watching a Lifetime movie instead of living her own life.

Her divorce from Quincy was completely final now. She was glad to be rid of him and his antics. She hadn't seen him in months prior to their court appearance for the divorce. When he saw the swell of her belly, he sneered at her knowingly. She expected him to tell the judge that she had obviously been unfaithful to him during their marriage, but he didn't. When the judge asked if she'd be seeking child support for their unborn, she'd just shamefully shaken her head no. Quincy laughed and the judge commented on how irresponsible and naïve young people were today. Although it was an uncomfortable situation, Candace was glad in the end to finally be done with Quincy's sorry ass.

Shaking Khalil's sorry ass was another story. Her parents had given up asking about his whereabouts and intent because it was clear to everyone that he had no desire to play an active role in their child's life. Secretly, for the child's sake, Candace hoped that he'd come around once the baby was born. She understood the importance of having a father in your life and didn't want her child to be cheated out of that necessity. Still, she couldn't force the trifling dude to do anything. At this point, she didn't care whether he called, came by, or what. She wasn't feeling like dealing with his nonsense and she definitely wasn't trying to go back to sleeping with him. Khalil swore that he had her open but these days Candace had her eye on someone totally different and totally wrong for her.

She knew going into the situation that it was a complete no-no. But, sometimes the danger of a situation was what made it so hot and tempting. On this day, she managed to escape her parents' shameful glances and comments and was out of the house for the evening. Much like they needed a break from her, she needed a break from them. Pulling into a small, yet cozy apartment complex she scoped the buildings looking for building number 12. Finding it, she parked, exited the car, and sashayed her pregnant body up the walkway to apartment 12b. It felt a little secluded to her, the way she had to walk around to the back of the building to reach the unit. Totally private and no one could see her comings and goings. She understood why he'd picked this place. Before she knocked on the door she quickly applied some shimmering lip gloss and shook out her newly done kinky twists. She was ready for whatever was about to go down.

He opened the door wearing nothing but a pair of black basketball shorts and socks. His killer smile was enough to make her melt right there in the door way.

"What's up?" he greeted her.

She gave a tiny smile. "What's up with you?"

He stepped to the side to allow her entrance and she walked by taking in the scent of his cologne. Yummy. He closed the door and walked up on her from the back.

"Was it easy to find?" he asked seductively in her ear.

She nodded, turning her head a little, playing as if she didn't want him that close to her. She walked away and dropped her purse down on the single couch in the living room. She turned and looked at him as he walked over to her. He slapped her on the ass and sunk down onto the sofa.

"Sit down, mama," he told her.

She took a seat beside him and looked around the scantly decorated apartment. Nearly nothing but essentials adorned the place, but it was clean and had the perfect homey touch given to it by the scented candles and incense he had throughout.

"So what is this? Your home away from home?" she asked him.

He threw his head back.

"Something like that. So what's good with you? What you got going today?"

"Nothing. Just really needed to get out of the house."

She found herself rubbing her belly. He placed his hand on top of hers and she quickly snatched it away. Not missing a beat, he began to rub her belly. Noticing her comfort with this, he pulled her shirt up and moved over to kiss her protruding stomach. The touch of his lips against her skin felt so soft. It had been a few months since she'd had someone touch any part of her body other than her ob/gyn.

"Take your shoes off," he ordered her.

His demanding tone sent a chill up her spine that turned her on. Following his instructions, she kicked her flats off quickly. She watched as he knelt down on the floor and began to massage her feet.

"Do your feet get swollen?" he asked her. "Do they hurt?"

She shrugged.

"They're not really swollen, but they do get sore. I definitely can't wear my heels anymore and that sucks because my heels are a part of my sexy swag, ya' know?"

He nodded.

"You got some cute little fat feet," he joked.

"My feet aren't fat," she playfully pouted.

He massaged her heels then each individual toe. She watched as he worked his magic, enjoying being pampered even if the situation was completely foul. As she felt her body relax she was further amazed when he slowly wrapped his lips around her big toe. The sensation shot up through her body and she could feel herself instantly getting wet. *DAMN*, she thought to herself. He suckled each toe on her left foot and then promptly paid the same special attention to each toe on her right foot. She leaned her head back on the sofa and gave herself over to the feeling he was giving her.

She didn't protest when he reached up to pull down her leggings along with her underwear. She opened her legs for him when she felt him push them apart. He kissed the inside of each of her thighs as he ran his finger back and forth across her clit. Her juices were running down onto the sofa as she became more and more turned on by his touch. She moaned slightly when he entered two fingers inside her. Her body arched as fingers continuously hit against her G-spot. She couldn't control her orgasm. As quickly as the penetration began, she felt her pussy muscles contracting around his fingers. Just as she settled from the climax, he rose from the floor and dropped his shorts. She knew exactly what was about to come next.

"Turn around," he ordered. "Here, put the pillows under you if you need to."

He was so matter-of-fact about it, but Candace went with the flow. She was eager to feel him deep inside of her. She didn't comment on the fact that he neglected to put on a rubber. She just bit her bottom lip as she felt all nine inches of him sink into her body. She clutched onto a pillow, overtaken by his girth. He thrust into her wetness hard and forceful, lifting her butt cheeks up and apart for greater depth. It was a sensation like none other she ever felt. And his shit talking drove her crazy.

"Oh shit," he moaned, pumping in and out of her. "This shit is wet. Throw it back baby…throw it back."

She moved her body to meet each of his powerful thrusts. He slapped her ass hard.

"Yeah, baby. Just like that. Throw that shit back."

She was into it, caught up in how good her pussy was feeling as he assaulted it and how dirty she was feeling with each word he spat out.

"Damn," he groaned. "Mmmm.. yeah…yeah…wait, hold up, hold up. I can't do that, can't do that"

He grabbed her ass to cease her movements and he stood still. She referred back to her Kegel exercises and began to squeeze his dick with her muscles.

"Shit!" he spat out. "Fuck it."

With all his might and vigor, he pounded into her, holding her lower back with his large hands. Candace couldn't contain her own moans of pleasure as his speed increased and he finally pushed himself to the point of no return. He climaxed hard inside of her, reaching around to tickle her clit as he ejaculated. So turned on by his touch and the force of his thrusts, Candace found herself cum right behind him. The two of them quickly tried to regain composure as he pulled out of her and she flipped herself over to a more comfortable position. He sat on the couch beside her and threw his head back.

"Damn," he commented. "I swear ain't *nooo* pussy better than pregnant pussy. I swear."

Candace focused on his hard, chiseled features as he closed his eyes and regulated his breathing. Now that the deed was done, she felt a twinge of guilt creep into her heart. She didn't like him, but she was sexually attracted to him. She knew that she could have found any other dude to just fuck or even date. She knew that taking things to this level with him was something she would never be able to take back. But she also knew that this was a secret she would definitely take to her grave. With all her wrongness lately, she knew that Jehovah would not be proud of her. She knew she was dead wrong. But for the moment, she just wanted to live a little bit free of the pressures of being presumably good and right in everyone else's eyes. Right now, as crazy as it was, she was enjoying being of the world.

Stephanie

It was really bothering her thinking about Corey's legal problems and her suspicions. Corey wasn't exactly the type of guy she could just flat out accuse of something and it blow over well. So, she kept her mouth shut much like she had done about finding the man's wallet in their bedroom closet. Sitting on the couch folding clothes, she watched and listened as Corey walked around complaining about any and everything. For whatever the reason, he was in a foul mood. The baby slept nearby in a playpen and Damien sat on the floor by the sofa playing with his cars, oblivious to his dad's antics.

"What the fuck do you do all day, man?" he bitched. "All these damn clothes should have been washed and put away. You're at home all the damn time…"

"Someone has to be," she muttered.

He knocked over a stack of towels.

"Aye watch ya' mouth aight," he ordered. "I'm for real. When a man comes home he expects his shit to be in order."

"I'm doing my best, Corey…the baby requires a lot of attention. It would be nice if you could help me more with her. Or with any of this."

"I'm doing what I'm supposed to be doing. Out there making that money so we can be living up in here like Wheezy and George."

Corey laughed at his own joke and went into the kitchen. She could hear him slamming around in the fridge and cabinets and simply tried to ignore him. She looked over at Damien as he rammed his cars into one another.

"When are you going to cook dinner?" Corey called out to her.

"I ordered a pizza," she called back.

He stormed back into the room, beer in hand, and stood next to her.

"Pizza ain't no damn dinner. You too lazy to get yo' ass in there and cook? All that food that's in there spoiling and you want to go order a pizza?"

"It's something quick. What's wrong with that?"

"You feed his ass junk too much," he said, pointing his beer at their son. "He needs some damn vegetables and shit. Not greasy ass pizza and hamburgers and shit. Spending money on that bullshit all the time."

"It's not all the time. You act like I never cook."

"You rarely cook," he corrected her. "I'm not saying you never cook. Yo ass rarely cooks these days."

"Because I'm tired, Corey. Dang."

"From sitting at home with your kids all day? What kind of shit is that?"

They both heard the buzz of his text message indicator and Stephanie watched as he pulled out the phone and read the message. He gave a quick reply and replaced the phone in its holster.

"If I could just get some help so I can rest…"

"Call ya' girls over here to help you. I ain't never heard anyone say they need help being a parent."

"That's not what I said. Why are you jumping on me?"

"'Cuz laziness ain't sexy, man. You act like you don't wanna cook, don't wanna clean, damn near don't wanna fuck. Don't wanna keep yourself up…man, we was better off living in separate places. This ain't the type of shit I had in mind."

Stephanie fought back her tears. He was really starting to hurt her feelings and she pursed her lips together to remain silent in hopes that he would catch on and shut up too. But he didn't.

"A nigga wants a bitch that's down for him. Someone

that makes him feel like a king in this damn castle. A chick that's gon' nurture his seeds, take care of him, and keep her shit tight. Don't nobody wanna come home to clothes all over the damn place and some greasy ass pizza."

She arranged the children's clothes into an empty basket to take to their room. She kept her head low so that he couldn't see the tears that managed to escape her eyes despite her efforts to hold them back.

"Do you hear me talking to you?" he asked.

She didn't respond.

"You ignoring me now? What kinda shit is that? Huh?"

Still nothing.

He began to shake the contents of his bottle out at her, drops of beer landing in her hair and on her shoulder.

"Stop it!" she demanded, jumping up and facing him. "What the hell is wrong with you?"

"You're the one sitting up here acting like a damn baby, pouting and ignoring me. And what the fuck are you crying for?"

She grabbed a towel and wiped her face.

"You're being mean to me for no reason. You haven't said one nice thing to me all day…"

"I'm just telling your ass the truth."

"You think I'm lazy. You think I'm a bad mom. You think I'm not a good woman. Fuck you, Corey. I put up with too much of your shit and I take care of your damn home when any other bitch would have left you by now."

"Be any other bitch then, Steph," he shouted. "Fuck, you wanna leave, get the fuck on."

The baby began to cry and Stephanie hurried over to soothe her and place the pacifier back into her mouth.

"Stop yelling, you're scaring the baby."

"Be her damn mama and pick her up then," he retorted. "You're not going to shut me up in my own house that I pay the fuckin' bills for. If you don't like it here, take your ass on somewhere. Trust me, there are plenty of bad ass dimes that would love to be up in here."

She shot him a look mixed with hurt and fury.

"I bet some already have been up in here."

"What?"

Corey walked up on her like he was about to swing and Damien quickly ran to his mother's aid.

"Don't hit my mommy," his tiny voice shrilled.

Corey looked down at his son and balled up his fist.

"Nobody's gon' hit your mama," he said through clenched teeth. "A real man won't hit a female."

He took a final swig from his beer and stared hard at Stephanie. He plopped the bottle down on the coffee table and leered at her.

"I'm fucking leaving," he announced.

He turned away and headed towards the door. Stephanie was fast on his heels.

"So what? You're just going to disappear for two, four, six days and leave us here alone? Where do you go, Corey? Laying up with someone? Are you fucking around with someone else? Trying to guilt me into feeling like I'm not shit and not worthy of you, your money, and your house."

"Get the hell on, Steph, with all that bullshit."

"It's your bullshit, Corey! All your drama, your lies…I've been good to you, I have continued to be there for you through all the bullshit and you treat me like shit whenever you fuckin' want to."

"I love your ass, girl. Nobody treating you like shit. I'm fuckin' tired of you walking around here acting like you don't want to be with a nigga. Like some shit is bothering your ass. Go tend to your kids, Steph. I'm gone."

She grabbed his arm.

"Don't you walk out on me! Don't leave me, Corey."

She was crying pathetically. But, she didn't want him to leave the house because she didn't know what to expect of him once he was gone. Corey shook her off.

"Go on, man," he said.

"Where are you going?" she questioned. "Where are you going? Are you going to see some bitch? Huh? Are you fucking Miranda?"

Corey looked at her with a raised eyebrow, shook his

head, and chuckled.

"You don't know what you're talking about, man. You wanna know what the deal is with your homegirl…ask her."

He opened the door and left quickly. Stephanie threw herself against the heavy oak door and screamed at Corey.

"You bastard," she pounded on the door. "I hate you. I fucking hate you. I hope they catch your ass and you fuckin' rot in jail. Go fuck her. Go fuck her, you bastard."

She buried her face against the door and sobbed loudly with Damien at her side, hugging her legs.

"Don't cry mama," he pleaded sweetly. "Daddy didn't mean it."

Her body shook as she tried to collect herself. She could hear the baby crying once more and knew that she had to get it together. With tears in her eyes, she reached down and hugged her son.

"I love you, Damien," she told him, holding him tightly. "I love you more than anything. You're mommy's big boy."

She released him from her embrace and hurried over to pick up the crying baby. Cradling her in her arms, she looked at Damien and was ashamed of herself for being so emotional in front of her children. She looked around the living room at the mounds of clothes in disarray and sucked her teeth. She wasn't a bad mother, like Corey insinuated. But, she definitely needed to get some things in order. Stephanie went to the kitchen and warmed a bottle for Mariah. Back in the living room, she changed baby's diaper, and began to feed her while Damien nuzzled up on the sofa beside her. She kissed the top of his head and sighed deeply. She wondered if and when Corey would return home.

A brisk knock at the door interrupted her thoughts. Damien jumped but Stephanie kissed him again and gave a reassuring smile.

"It's just the pizza man," she told him, rising from the couch.

She placed the baby inside of the play pen and headed for the door. Without taking a look through the peep hole, she carelessly opened up the front door and was quickly bomb rushed by a small group of men in dark suits.

"Stephanie Johnson?" one of them asked.

She was shocked and confused.

"Yea…Yes??"

"I'm Agent Weber and these are my team members. We're with the GBI. We're investigating a homicide."

Damien was scared.

"Mommy, are we going to jail?" he cried out.

"I…I don't understand," Stephanie muttered, trying to get her thoughts together and afraid of what was about to happen next.

"No son," one of the agents answered Damien. "We just want to have a talk with your father and take a look around your house."

"My house?" Stephanie repeated, turning to the consoling

agent. "What are you talking about? Why do you need to look around our house?"

"Is your boyfriend, Corey Polk, home, Ms. Johnson?"

Stephanie shook her head no.

The kind agent turned back to Damien in askance.

"Daddy's gone," Damien cosigned. "Him and mommy had a fight and daddy said he was gonna leave us…then my mommy was crying and…"

Stephanie waved him off.

"Damien, baby, go to your room okay."

"The police are our friends mommy. Maybe they can make daddy come back."

"Go to your room," her voice was elevated.

The baby was agitated by Stephanie's tone and began to cry again. Nervously, she lifted the infant from the play pen and rocked her with nervous energy. She turned her attention back to Agent Wilbur.

"Corey is not here. Why do you have to look around our home? I'm telling you he isn't here."

"Then you won't mind if we have a look?" the agent countered.

"But why?" she asked puzzled. "Why? What is it that you're looking for? Corey isn't here."

"As I stated, we're investigating a homicide and your

boyfriend is a person of interest. We're looking specifically for anything that may tie him to the crime. So, do you mind?"

"Yes I do mind," she answered defiantly. "This is my home…my children are here. You can't just come up in someone's home and rip it to shreds…Don't you have to have some paper or something from the courts giving you permission to do that?"

Agent Wilbur held up what looked to Stephanie to be a brochure.

"What you're referring to would be called a Search Warrant," he told her. "Yeah, we have one of those."

He handed it to her and she took it absentmindedly, still half-heartedly rocking the baby back and forth. Her heart was racing and she was half wishing that Corey's ass would walk back through the door at any moment and save her from having to deal with this humiliation.

"You take the back rooms, we'll look up front," Agent Wilbur ordered two of his colleagues.

He looked to the nicer agent and motioned towards the kitchen. They proceeded and Stephanie was right behind them, crying baby in tow and search warrant clutched in her hand.

"Please, don't tear my house up…please."

The friendly agent turned to her and smiled.

"This would go a lot smoother and quicker if you would just wait in the living room with your daughter, ma'am. I promise, we'll try our best not to leave things in disarray."

Stephanie was speechless and helpless. With no recourse,

she returned Mariah to her playpen and settled her down with her pacifier once more. She was tempted to pull out her cell and inform Corey of what was going down. But, she thought better of it knowing that they would just seize her phone and fearing that they would have a tap on it and find Corey's whereabouts. Even though she was pissed with him for being so mean to her and having an affair with one of her best friends, she still felt protective of him. The sad truth was that she simply loved the man and never wanted any harm to come his way.

Agent Wilbur reentered the living room and engaged her in interrogative conversation as his colleague searched the room.

"Do you know where Corey is, Ms. Johnson?"

She shook her head no.

He took and deep breath and nodded knowingly.

"You know, if you're hiding information you could go down with him as an accessory."

"To what?" she challenged. "I didn't do anything and I don't know anything."

"So you have no idea where your boyfriend has gone off to? Is there any usual place he goes when he leaves the house? Do you know where his stash house is located?"

"Excuse me?"

"Don't play coy, Ms. Johnson. A man is dead and I'm almost positive that your boyfriend can tip us off as to exactly how that happened. If you're aiding and abetting him I'll have no remorse in taking you in too…that would leave your children in the custody of the state and I'm sure you don't want that, do you?"

Stephanie looked down into the play pen at Mariah, who'd finally fallen asleep despite the ruckus around her.

"Please don't threaten me, Mr. Wilbur," she said, masking her fear. "I've told you that I don't know what you're talking about and I have no clue where Corey went. Like my son told you, we had a fight and Corey decided that he'd rather not be with us. He's gone and I don't expect him to come back."

The two men returned from the back of the apartment and shook their heads at Mr. Wilbur.

"Nothing," one of them reported.

The friendly agent joined the crowd.

"Zilch," he chimed in.

Agent Wilbur took a deep breath. He nodded to the men and the trio headed out of the front door. Wilbur reached into his pocket, pulled out a couple of business cards, and handed them to Stephanie with a half smile.

"If you can think of any place we may want to look for your boyfriend or if you recollect any information about Mr. Stokes 'death, please call me," he encouraged her.

Stephanie looked down at the cards, moving them from one hand to the other. Wilbur noticed her nervous behavior and smiled.

"Oops," he said reaching for one of the cards back. "Gave you one too many, huh?"

She gave over one of the cards and cocked her head to the side.

"Have a good evening, Mr. Wilbur," she said flatly.

He shook the card at her and smiled once more.

"Same to you."

He headed for the door and stopped short at the threshold.

"Take care of those beautiful children and we're sorry for any inconvenience."

She watched as he slowly closed her front door behind him. Quickly, she ran over to lock and bolt the door. Turning around she saw a timid Damien lurking around the corner, looking at her with questioning eyes. She released a breath that she didn't realize she had been holding. Going into her bedroom she surveyed the damage done to her property. Clothes thrown about, papers out of order, and miscellaneous items were all over the place. She sat on her bed and just stared at the mess. Looking into the closet she looked at the clothes left dangling from lone hangers, including a couple of pairs of Corey's jeans. Stephanie wasn't worried about their search. She knew they'd come up with nothing because the one thing that could have nailed them was long gone.

~ ~ ~

She'd swallowed her pride and begged her mother to watch the children for a couple of hours. She made up some story about how Jada was sick and Jordan was out of town so she desperately needed to go to the hospital with her best friend. Her mom had always liked Jada and the type of friend she had been to Stephanie over the years, so she agreed to watch the children for just a couple of hours.

With no intention of going to Jada's whatsoever, Stephanie mustered up her courage and drove deep into the Dec to where she assumed that she would find her children's father. Although she willingly turned a blind eye to his shenanigans and illegal activity, Stephanie wasn't as naïve and clueless as others thought she was. She knew the hood-secret of where the neighborhood trap was really located and she knew that her boyfriend was THE dope man in the DEC. Watching cars behind her and around her, she drove cautiously hoping to catch him there tonight.

The GBI paying them a visit was very real to her. It was a clear sign that it was time for them to take the money and run. She desperately wanted to start over and give their children a life devoid of the game and the risks that Corey took constantly. Sure, he was a pain in the ass and wasn't very nice to her at times. But, he was her pain in the ass and she wanted to save him, and them, from this world before it was too late.

Pulling up to the house she surveyed the block. It was still and quiet. No cars in sight, but that didn't mean that Corey couldn't still be hiding out in the house. She said a quick prayer and quickly got out of the car. Scurrying up the stairs she tapped on the door and kept her eyes glued to the streets watching for and suspicious or sudden movement. A big man came to the door, took one look at her, and stepped back allowing her entrance. She silently passed him and walked into the house. The big man closed the door and she looked to him for direction.

"Wait here," he ordered.

She assumed that he was going to go get Corey for her, but was surprised to see his homeboy Antonio emerge from the back instead.

"Yo what up, Stephanie," he greeted her. "You know you

really shouldn't be up in here man."

She ignored his warning.

"Where's Corey?"

"Aye I'on know, but check it. I do know that dude wouldn't be too thrilled for his girl to be up in here. The block been hot for a minute so this really ain't where you wanna be. If he comes through or hits me, I'll tell him to get at you…but, you gotta leave, Ms. Lady. On everything I love, you gots to leave."

She studied his eyes looking for some hint of foul play. But Antonio's expression indicated that he was dead serious. Before she could speak or make a move, there was a weak knock at the door. Antonio motioned for the big man to check it out. He looked through the peep hole then turned to report to Antonio.

"It's ol' girl, the quiet chick."

It was as if they were speaking in code. Antonio shook his head.

"Tell her ass to get on. We on ice around here man."

The big man opened the door and his frame prevented Stephanie from seeing who he was addressing.

"Hey, is he here?" the woman asked.

"Nobody's here," the big man answered. "We just coolin' it 'round here. We'll holla at you when we got that."

"Look, he's not answering my calls. If you could just hook me up, I've got the money."

"Man, go'on, girl. I'm telling your ass we straight in here. Aight. We'll let you know something."

"Why do ya'll keep tripping like that?" the woman whined. "You get more money than a little bit from me so what is the problem?"

Stephanie was uneasy listening to the conversation. Hearing someone beg for some crack was sickening to her. But what was worse was that she recognized the voice.

"Yo, bye man."

"Tell Corey I said fuck him, I'm sick of this shit," the female shrilled. "I'm fuckin' sick of this!"

Stephanie gasped and hurriedly brushed past the big man to come face to face with one of her closet friends.

"Miranda!" she exclaimed, wanting to throw up immediately at the realization.

Miranda was stunned and nervously went about brushing back her hair and tugging at her clothes. She bit her lip, not sure what to say to Stephanie. She looked around, avoiding eye contact with her friend. Stephanie stepped out onto the porch and touched her friend's face, forcing her to look her in the eye.

"What's going on with you?" Stephanie asked her softly.

She could hear the sound of the door close behind her, the two men inside wanting nothing to do with this accidental intervention.

"It all makes sense to me now," Stephanie said, brushing back her friend's hair.

She studied Miranda's physique and body language. Her face looked harder than she ever remembered and she constantly kept pinching her nose although Stephanie could tell she was trying hard to appear her normal self.

"All this time I thought that you were fucking around with Corey. But all this time you've been fucking up yourself with Corey's shit. I don't know whether to be mad at you for being so stupid or to pity you for being so obviously lost that you turned to this."

"Don't judge me," Miranda said curtly. "Like you're perfect or something. Don't judge me. You don't know what my life is like, what I'm going through, or how I feel."

"All you've ever had to do is pick up the phone, girl."

"And call you, Steph? You're always too busy worrying about who Corey is under to be concerned with anyone else's problems."

Miranda looked down at the ground and sucked her teeth.

"You're probably gonna go run and get on your phone to tell the other girls what you think you know…tell them then, Stephanie. I'm dying on the inside anyway, so nothing else really matters."

She looked back up and stared deep into Stephanie's eyes. Stephanie felt her skin crawl and shivers ran up her spine.

"Then again, you practically said it yourself," Miranda stated. "You're really just glad to know that Corey isn't fucking around on you…well at least not with me."

Before Stephanie could respond, Miranda descended the steps and disappeared down the block to where her car was parked in the distance. Stephanie took a quick look around and retreated to her own car. As she drove off towards her mom's house, her mind was fixated on the memory of Miranda's thin body and her pitiful voice nearly pleading to cop a hit. Their circle had once been so close. But, clearly they were becoming distant for all of them to miss the fact that something was seriously wrong with Miranda. She felt herself crying as sheer memory led her back to her mom's house. Her focus was shot to hell. She sat in front of the house crying onto the steering wheel feeling helpless for the second time that day.

It had been a long, rough day for her. She felt sorry for Miranda for feeling so alone that she had nowhere else to turn but to drugs. She also felt a since of responsibility because it was her boyfriend that had undoubtedly turned her out. How he could have done such a thing and not mention anything at all about it was beyond her. How could he willingly allow something like this to happen to someone that she was so close to? Corey was clearly unscrupulous. Anything to make a dollar. Stephanie felt sick with disgust, pity and shame. The very money he made off of Miranda was the very money that contributed to her lifestyle. In turn, they'd all become monsters associated with the game. She prayed that Corey would call soon. It was definitely time for them to make a grand exit. The signs were so clear to her. Miranda was already lost to her, she didn't want to risk losing anyone or anything else to this life.

Jada

She wasn't sure if it had been a good idea to invite all of the girls over for dinner, but Jada felt it would be an opportunity for everyone to have some release from all the things that they were going through. That and she really wanted to unload all of the stress her friendships were putting on her. She and Jordan were still having problems conceiving and her doctor seemed to believe that she was just under a lot of stress. Dr. Gregory told them that once they both relaxed and stopped worrying about making a baby that it would happen for them eventually. The thought of not being able to give Jordan a child scared her. Before they got married they use to talk about the type of life they wanted to live. Both agreed that they wanted to have a large family. Now it was time for her to make good on the agreement and she was coming up short.

All the girls were experiencing some type of hardship and neither of them had seen much of each other since Alex's party. Dinner was ready and she was waiting on the girls to show up, unsure of how the night would end. Candace was getting along in her pregnancy and Jada wasn't sure that she could stomach watching her and her swollen belly all evening or listening to her complain about the circumstances of her pregnancy. Life was just totally unfair. As she spooned seafood pasta into a decorative serving dish she heard the chiming of her doorbell. Jordan had decided to meet some of his boys at the neighborhood Dugan's while she and her girls had the run of the house. She wiped her hands on a dish towel and quickly went to greet the first of her dinner guests.

Standing at the door was Stephanie and Alex. The trio hugged and Jada allowed them entry into the living room.

"You got it smelling good up in here, friend," Alex complimented her.

"Thanks, boo. You know how I do."

Stephanie looked towards the kitchen as she sat her purse down on the coffee table.

"Where are the other two?"

Jada shrugged.

"Oh the way I guess. Ya'll want some wine?"

"You already know the answer to that," Stephanie said jokingly.

Jada headed to the kitchen and again heard the chiming of the doorbell.

"I'll get it," Alex offered, and sashayed over to the door.

From the kitchen she could hear the giggles and oohs and ahhs and knew instantly that Candace had arrived. She hoped that Miranda was with her so that they could go ahead and start dinner. She walked back into the living room and put a smile on her face.

"Hey girl," she greeted Candace.

"Hey, hun. How are you?"

"I'm good…I was hoping Miranda would be with you."

Candace's facial expression signaled trouble as she shook her head.

"I called her to see if she wanted to ride with me, but I didn't get an answer. I assumed that she either she didn't want to talk to me or she was here already."

"Did she tell you she was coming?" Stephanie asked.

Jada now shook her head.

"I texted her just like I texted ya'll, but she didn't respond."

Alex clapped her hands together.

"I say let's go ahead and eat. And if she shows up, great. If she doesn't, more for us."

"I'm with that," Steph chimed in.

"Shoot me too," Candace giggled.

The women filed into Jada's dining room and Jada busied herself with setting out the food. There was seafood pasta, veggie lasagna, Caesar salad, and garlic bread sticks. The open bottle of white wine also rested on the table. Jada returned to the kitchen and came back with a newly opened bottle of sparkling cider. She placed it in front of Candace.

"I got that for you," she told her as she slid into her own spot at the table.

Everyone was helping themselves to the pasta dinner. Candace gave her a sincere smile and poured herself up a glass.

"Thanks. You're so considerate."

"I try."

There was clanking, shuffling, and the sound of chewing as the girls munched on their meal. Candace was the first to break the silence.

"So…has anyone talked to Miranda at all lately?"

A series of head shakes. Stephanie cleared her throat, unsure of whether she should respond or not.

"I've seen her…"

Jada raised an eyebrow.

"Oh yeah? When?"

"Last week," she treaded lightly.

The other girls looked at her, waiting for her to say more but she just continued to eat her lasagna, avoiding eye contact.

"Okay, sweetie," Candace spoke up. "Can you be a little specific for us? Last week when? Where? How was she? And what did she say?"

"I saw her at this place I went to…I was out handling some business…and you know, we just ran into one another."

"Un-uh," Jada said, chewing and pointing her fork at Stephanie. "You're lying. What is it that you're not telling us? Don't sit up here feeding us no bullshit, Stephanie. What's the deal with Miranda?"

Stephanie pushed her food around on her plate, unsure of how to say what it was that she knew. A part of her didn't want to put Miranda out there. But another part of her was dying to share this secret. Besides, they were all girls and it was apparent that Miranda needed an intervention or something at this point in her life.

"Ok fine," she said, giving in and throwing her fork down on her plate. "I saw her at the trap."

"The what?" Alex asked.

"The trap, heifer. You heard me."

"The 'trap' trap?" Candace asked, using air quotes.

Stephanie nodded.

"Wait, what were you doing there?" Alex asked.

"Undoubtedly something stupid," Jada interjected, raising an eyebrow at Stephanie.

Stephanie sighed.

"Corey and I are going through some things and I was trying to find him."

Candace diverted her eyes and took a gulp from her drink as the other girls gave Stephanie their full attention.

"I was desperate to find him and I figured he would be over there, so I went to the spot looking for him."

"That was stupid," Jada commented. "Girl, what were you thinking? What if it had been a bust or something while you were there?"

"I don't know," Stephanie said. "All I knew was that I had to talk to Corey ASAP and I was sure that that's where he would be. But he wasn't. So, before I left this chick came to the door right. I could hear her voice, but I was standing behind this big dude, one of Corey's runners or somebody, so I couldn't see her…but the voice was so familiar to me and after a minute I realized that it was Miranda."

"Okay, cut to the point now, girl," Jada said impatiently. "What are you trying to tell us."

Candace poured herself up another glass of cider and continued sipping. Alex was eating and listening, intrigued as if she were watching a movie play out right before her eyes.

"The writing's on the wall, hun," she paused. "Miranda is a crackhead."

Candace spat out her cider. Alex choked on her mouth full of pasta and bread. Jada's fist hit the table.

"That's some bullshit, Steph," she shouted. "You're taking this shit a little bit too far."

"I'm just calling it like I see it," Stephanie responded.

"Calling it like you see it, my ass. You have been gunning for that chick for a minute now. And now, the second she's not around you're trying to paint some picture like the girl, *our friend*, is a fucking junkie. That's low…even for you."

"What you mean, gunning for her?" Alex asked between coughs as she tried to regain some composure.

"Stephanie has been assuming for a minute now that Miranda is fucking Corey's sorry ass."

Stephanie's right eyebrow rose.

"So you think I'd make some shit up just to throw salt in another bitch's game?"

"I think that you're delusional. Seeing shit differently from how it really is. The same way you're totally wrong about Miranda messing around with Corey."

"Why would you think they were messing around anyway?" Alex asked. "We may not make the best decisions as a group when it comes to men, but I'm pretty sure none of us would go after any one of the other's man. That's just breaking the code, Steph. And we respect the code around here. Right ladies?"

"That's what I've been trying to tell Sherlock Holmes over there," Jada commented.

Alex and Jada looked to Candace for confirmation. She bit her lip and nodded, then tried hard to sell it.

"Yeah, girl. That's just crazy. Besides, Miranda has her own issues with Norris. Why would she want a whole 'nother set of man problems?"

"I know she's not fucking around with Corey," Stephanie spat out to shut up the group. "I mean, I admit that I was a little curious about their interactions…some shit just didn't sit right with me. But all the time that I was thinking they were getting up with each other, she was really just hitting up her dealer."

"I don't want to hear any more of this," Jada said pulling out her cellphone. "I'm calling Miranda to see where the hell she is and what the hell is going on."

"I heard her ask the man for the shit with my own two ears, Jada," Stephanie told her. "And when I stepped out to confront her she basically told me not to judge her and that she knew I was going to run back and tell ya'll."

Jada had already dialed Miranda's number but the line just rang and rang until finally going to voicemail. As she looked into Stephanie's eyes, the truth she didn't want to face sunk in. She knew Stephanie wasn't lying by the way she stared at her intently, unwilling to back down or take it back. Jada hung up the phone and focused on Stephanie's eyes.

"How did she look?" Jada whispered.

Stephanie's voice softened now that she could sense that Jada had finally come to terms with the news she had shared.

"Like she's living a hard life."

The room was silent. No one knew how to take this or what to say about it. Jada tried to picture in her mind how Miranda had gotten so far under her radar. Sure, she was sick of rescuing the girls and sick of all their unnecessary drama, but had she given her friend the impression that she couldn't come to her when she was feeling desperate and troubled? She just couldn't understand how any person could one day just say, 'hey, let me try some crack'.

"So how does that feel for you?" Alex asked, pulling Jada away from her own thoughts.

Alex was addressing Stephanie who in turn gave her a questioning look.

"What do you mean?"

"How does that feel for you? You thought she was screwing your man, but come to find out she wasn't. However your man was in fact screwing her...or at least helping her screw herself. How does it feel to know that the very poison running through your friend's veins, which could possibly kill her, was placed in her hands by *your* boyfriend?"

Jada could sense the tension growing. She held her hand out, trying to run an early interference.

"Wait, hold up now...Let's not do this."

"Corey didn't put a gun to her head and make her take a hit, Alex!" Stephanie spat out. "That was a personal decision of Miranda's."

"How do you know that when you barely know where the hell he is or what the hell he's doing?" Alex retorted. "Until a week ago you're assumption was that he was doing her."

"He wouldn't force anyone to do anything, no matter who it is."

"You talk about him like he's some saint or something. You kill me with that. Stephanie, your man is the neighborhood dope man. His job relies on your neighbors' and their neighbors' and, hey even your friends', vulnerability, desperation, and naivety."

"Alex stop it," Jada begged. "Stop it, please."

"They're not my neighbors," Stephanie remarked as she took a long sip of her wine.

"Oh yeah," Alex said sarcastically. "That's right. Because your neighbors are the white people your boo has moved you next to to get your family out of the hood while he continues to poison the hood."

Jada jumped up and went over to Alex and grabbed her arm.

"You need to take a walk now," she urged her. "This is going too far."

"Corey was right. You're jealous because you don't live the lifestyle we live. I'm not worried about ya' petty lil' comments. Go on, keep being a hater. Trust, your little rapper wannabe boyfriend ain't gon' ever have the kinda paper we have."

"Yeah? I won't have the guilty conscious your ass has either," Alex spat out, snatching her arm away from Jada.

Alex leaned close to Stephanie's face, invading her

personal space. Jada was afraid that Alex was going to slap her. She had never seen Alex so riled up before.

"Your boyfriend's killing one of your best friends, Stephanie. And the money he makes off of each of her hits is the same money you put towards the steak you eat alone while your man's out dealing and whoring."

Impulsively Stephanie threw the remnants of her wine in Alex's face taking everyone by surprise, especially Alex.

"Fuck you, Alex," she said, slamming the glass on the table.

She rose and walked out of the room as Alex wiped wine droplets from her eyes.

"I don't need this shit!"

Everyone followed Stephanie into the living room, unsure of what to do or what would happen next. Jada ran back to the kitchen to get a dry dish towel for Alex to wipe her face and hair with.

"If you're waiting for me to take some responsibility for what's going on with Miranda, I'm not doing it," Stephanie spat out. "That was her choice. HERS. And she has to live with that. Not me."

"Well then why are you so defensive," Candace asked, rubbing her belly.

Stephanie wanted to slap her, but turned away instead to focus her attention on back on Alex.

"Because she's sitting up here making me out to be the bad guy," she said pointing at Alex who was steadily blotting her head.

"No, your boo is the bad guy, honey," she retorted. "The problem is that you're so stuck on him that you don't see him for who and what he really is."

"Is that right? And you have such a great perspective on the men in your life, Alex? Where's Clay, Alex? You're so stupid and such a gold digging opportunist that you don't realize that the only true man you've ever had in your life was Clay…but no, you'd rather attach yourself to someone that you perceive to have status and will upgrade your underprivileged background ass."

"Wow," Candace reacted without meaning to. Alex stared at Stephanie blankly not having the words to respond. Instead, she turned away and went to Jada's bathroom. Jada stood with her hand over her mouth surprised at the low blows being passed out at her dinner party. She looked at Stephanie and shook her head.

"Don't give me that look," Stephanie responded. "She had it coming. Acting like she's without fault."

"She was shocked, Steph…just like the rest of us."

"Be shocked…don't be spiteful."

Candace sat down on the couch, exhausted and exasperated by the turn of events. She propped her feet up on the nearby ottoman.

"As much as I would love to stay to be further insulted, I gotta go," Stephanie announced. She grabbed her purse from the coffee table and headed for the door.

Jada followed her.

"Wait, Steph. Wait…don't leave like this. You guys need to patch things up. Everyone is upset and not thinking clearly…don't go."

Stephanie shook her head.

"I have my own problems to deal with. I really don't wanna sit up here and be berated over someone else's issues. Later."

Quickly, Stephanie exited the apartment. Jada touched the door wanting to go after her, but not sure of what to say to her. Everything had happened so quickly she hadn't had time to truly process the information that had been shared with them. Taking a deep breath she turned around and noticed that Candace had quickly fallen asleep. She sighed and returned to the dining room to clean up the partially eaten dinner resting on the table. Alex entered the room with the towel around her neck.

"Need help?" she asked softly.

Jada shook her head.

"I got it."

"You sure?"

Jada threw forks onto a plate and turned to look at Alex with her hands on her hip.

"Yeah, you can help me with something. Tell me why you had to go and insult the damn girl and ruin my damn dinner?"

Alex looked hurt.

"That wasn't my intention," she offered. "I was just

mad…you know she acted like Corey was such a saint in this situation…I mean Miranda is our friend…and Steph's man is basically pushing her over the cliff."

"Everyone's dealing with something," Jada said. "None of us have the right to throw stones at each other."

Alex sucked her teeth.

"Really? You were pissed for a minute too, friend. Don't put it all on me. When you thought she was dragging Miranda through the mud, you were hot."

Jada nodded.

"Yeah…I was…but you were trying to pick a fight with her. Getting all up in the girl's face. You asked for that drink in the face."

Alex sighed.

"Okay…okay…maybe you're right. We're all going through something and I'm not exempt from that. And Steph was right…I was too stupid to realize how much Clay cares for me…but I'm not a gold digger…I'm not…"

Jada rolled her eyes and went back to cleaning up the dining room.

"He gave me the most beautiful ring for my birthday, Jada. Only I didn't even notice it until two days after the party. He left the sweetest note in the lil' ring box. Now he's changed his number and I can't contact him…I may have lost out on my shot at true love, Jada."

"Shut up," Jada told her. "Shut up. Ya'll are fucking killing me."

She turned and looked at Alex once more.

"Ya'll are so caught up in yourselves and your drama that I really think you've all become detached from reality. Seriously, Alex…it's hard to believe that you are really just now getting that Clay wanted you. A blind man could have seen that from ten feet away girl."

Alex looked down at the floor like a child being chastised.

"And even if you are just tuning in, so what? He's pissed at you. And? It's not the end of the world honey. Surely he hasn't moved to another city or state since your party. You know where he lives. Stop waiting for some fairy tale situation and carry your spoiled ass to his crib and apologize for being so freaking slow. End of story. There's your fuckin' happily ever after."

Alex scrunched her face up, offended by her friend's tone.

"Why are you being so harsh?"

Jada sighed and picked up the stack of dishes off the table.

"I'm tired, Alex. I'm tired of not being able to deal with my own problems because I'm too busy dealing with everyone else's."

She left Alex in the dining room and went to the kitchen to load the dish washer. She felt her breathing quicken and placed her hands firmly on the counter with her head down in an attempt to gain some composure. She could hear herself heaving and she shook her head, warding off the panic attack that was steadily building. Jada was lost in her episode and didn't hear the front door open and shut as Alex left. She didn't hear Candace enter the kitchen and was barely able to answer her when the other woman called out her name.

"Jada, girl I guess I'm going to get on out of here too and get out of your hair."

Jada tried to be silent as her body swayed.

"Jada…you okay girl?"

She nodded.

"Mmhmmm."

But no sooner than the sound left her lips, her body went limp to the floor and she began to struggle for breath as her body convulsed. Candace's eyes grew wide from shock. Instinctively she ran to Jada and tried to sit her upward against the counter.

"Don't touch me, don't…don't touch…don't touch me," Jada stuttered nearly indecipherably.

She curled her body up on the floor near the dishwasher and rocked as her chest heaved and her cry was hysterical. Candace was unsure of how to proceed. She whipped out her cell phone and started to dial 911. She wasn't sure if this was a seizure or what. Before she could press send she heard the front door shut. Within seconds Jordan found them in the kitchen, both women on the floor and he knew something was wrong.

"Come on baby," he coaxed Jada who was now shaking uncontrollably. "Come on, let me get you up."

He moved slowly so as not to startle or upset her. Gently, he lifted her from the floor and carried her off into their bedroom. Lying her down on the bed, he covered her up with a blanket as she balled herself up once more. Returning to the kitchen, he found a stunned Candace still sitting uncomfortably on the tiled floor. He reached out to her and helped her up.

"What the hell was that?" Candace asked.

Jordan busied himself with getting Jada a glass of ice water.

"She has panic disorder," he stated flatly.

"When did this start? I never heard her mention it."

"When did she have a chance to mention it? Every time ya'll ring her phone it's to get help with your problems. What? You thought she didn't have problems of her own?"

Candace was taken aback by the briskness of his tone as well as the message he was conveying. She stared at him as if waiting for him to say more.

"You can let yourself out," Jordan told her. "I needa go tend to my wife."

Without another word, the man disappeared to the back of the house.

Stephanie

Still pissed at Alex for what she'd said earlier, Stephanie drove home in silence replaying the scene in her mind. How dare Alex try to pin Miranda's situation on her? She was tired of being looked down on because of Corey's business dealings. Besides, none of them had perfect men so who were any of them to be judging her's? Of course she knew that what Corey did was wrong, but if there weren't people out there wanting to get high on their own free will Corey wouldn't have a business to begin with. She wanted Corey out of the game so that he wouldn't get caught up, or even worse, get hurt. She wasn't worried about his negative effects on the neighborhood. Like she'd told the girls, it wasn't as if he put a gun to Miranda's head and forced her to use the shit.

Sitting in her living room now downing a glass of Corey's liquor, Stephanie was filled with mixed emotions. Although she was pissed for being blamed for Miranda's decisions, she also felt sad for her friend. She hoped that Miranda would show up for Jada's dinner. She was really hoping to see her doing well and looking better than before. Her not showing up at all only led Stephanie to believe that she was somewhere coked out of her mind or was simply hiding out from the shameful looks and judgment of the girls.

She threw back the drink and pursed her lips as the liquor stung her throat. She massaged her temples and felt like she was about to scream from frustration. Faintly, she heard the muffled sounds of her phone ringing. Scrambling she reached across to the loveseat to grab her purse. Buried deep inside among papers, her wallet, lip gloss, and other items she finally found her phone. She rushed to answer before the caller hung up, prayerful that it would be Corey.

"Hello," she said breathlessly.

"Where've you been?" his voice was angry.

"At…at…at Jada's," she answered caught off guard.

Then she realized that he had been the one to previously run out on her.

"Where have *you* been?" she asked sarcastically.

"Locked the fuck up because of your stupid ass."

Her heart skipped a beat and she sat up straight, trying to shake off the effects of the alcohol.

"What the hell are you talking about?"

"What? You haven't seen the news, Steph? Shit's all over the fuckin' news tonight. What the fuck made you take the wallet out, Steph?"

The question was a bit muffled but she heard it all the same and the feeling of doom fell all over her.

"Where are you?"

"Home," she said softly.

"Pack some stuff and leave the house. I need you to do a real solid. You got those keys?"

"Yes…"

"Check your text messages. My dude texted you an address earlier when I was first trying to reach you. Go there. In the closet are two garbage bags. Take the bags and you and the boys go to North Carolina or somewhere for a while until I call you again."

"What?" she was having difficulty keeping up and understanding his directions.

"Why are you sending us away? Do you think they know that I threw the wallet out?"

"This shit is bigger than the damn police and GBI, Steph. Just do what the fuck I'm telling you to do."

"I don't want to leave without you," she cried into the phone, frantically hurrying to the children's room to throw some things in a duffel bag.

"Don't worry 'bout all that. Where the kids?"

"At my mom's."

"Aight, I gotta get off this phone. Some dude in here got a cellie. I'll call you back when I can tomorrow. Be out of town by then, Steph."

"But, I don't…"

"Just do what I'm saying. Don't ask questions you don't want the answers to, aight?"

Before she could respond the line was disconnected. Tears blinding her, she threw clothes into a bag for herself. As she hurried into the living room to slip on her shoes and grab her purse she looked at her phone. Four missed calls and two text messages. The entire time she'd been at Jada's her phone had been left in the purse. She read the first text, which was an address in Roswell. The second text was from Miranda's cell, much to Stephanie's surprise.

Watch the news…only 'cuz I think you should know.

She touched the chain around her neck and felt for the keys. Without giving it a second thought, she grabbed her things and quickly exited her apartment just as Corey had instructed. In the car, she used the navigation function on her cell to direct her to the Roswell address. Her mind was racing with a million thoughts and she was more fearful than ever. She wondered how the hell anyone had come across that damn wallet and how it had gotten tied back to Corey. If the police had figured out that

Corey was responsible, she feared that they also knew that it was she that had disposed of it. Perhaps she was just being paranoid, but she knew that Corey wasn't sending her and the kids away for no good reason.

This entire night had gone horribly wrong. She was unsure of what to expect once she reached the Roswell address. She prayed that it wasn't another trap house that he was sending her to at night. As frantic as she was, Stephanie tried to keep herself calm and maintain the speed limit so as not to cause unwanted attention. She had so many questions in her head and she wondered if and when she would ever get to receive the answers from Corey. How had she managed to get herself into this predicament? She desperately wanted to call Jada for comfort but thought better of it. After the blow up at her house she got the feeling that Jada would not have welcomed anymore of her drama as it pertained to Corey. Plus, she found herself to be a little pissed with Jada too for not being more supportive of her when Alex was being such an ass.

Within thirty minutes she arrived at the address. The quaint apartment complex was quiet and still. There were few cars in the parking lot. Chills ran up her spine as she parked and exited her car. The scene just didn't feel right to her. But, as instructed she walked around the appropriate unit which seemed to her to be discreetly tucked away. Using the keys, she let herself into the apartment and quickly closed the door. Flipping on the light, she looked around the room at the scanty decorated apartment. Instinctively she knew that this was Corey's second home. A pair of his sneakers sat neatly near the couch, an ashtray next to it. The room had the faint aroma of incense, a Corey trademark. Slowly she walked into the kitchen. The only thing sitting on the counter was a half drunken bottle of E & J.

She turned and went into the apartment's only bedroom. In the closet, just as he stated there were two bags. She grabbed them, afraid to look inside, and turned to walk out of the room. But, she quickly hesitated when she heard the sound of the front door close. Someone was in the house with her. Her heart began to race and she felt rooted to the spot. She looked behind her as if searching for an exit, but there was only a narrow window. She considered using it to escape, but just as she moved to go toward it, she heard the voice call out.

"Corey, are you here? You left your door unlocked, hun."

Her nostrils flared, eyebrows rose, and eyes grew cold. She knew that voice all too well. Dropping the bags to the floor she burst out of the room and into the living room to face the backstabber.

"No bitch, but I'm here," she spat out.

Candace

She nearly jumped out of her skin. Mentally, she could have kicked herself for not listening to her little voice earlier and not taking her ass home. But here she was stuck in this unavoidable, unforgivable moment of truth. The two women stood staring at one another, each waiting for the other to speak. Candace couldn't begin to find words that she thought would smooth this situation over. She stood there, protruding belly and all, gripping her purse with her eyes wide with fear. Stephanie's fists were clenched, anger radiating off of her like heat. She stepped to Candace and Candace placed her hand on her stomach as if to brace her belly for the blow she was sure she was about to receive.

"You backstabbing bitch," Stephanie spat out. "You trashy ass hoe! All this time you sat around listening to me complain about how I thought Miranda was fucking around with my man…and all the time it was your skank ass that was fucking him."

"It's…it's not what you think," Candace stuttered. "Please…"

"Oh no? What? You gonna tell me that you've been buying shit from Corey too? And that you drive your sadity ass all the way over here to get it instead of to the trap like any other average crackhead? Fuck you, Candace. Fuck you if you think I'm stupid enough to buy that shit."

Candace shook her head, trying to convince Stephanie to believe her.

"I'm telling you, it's not like that. It's not."

"How long?" Stephanie asked cutting her off.

"Nothing happened," Candace told her. "Nothing happened, Steph."

Stephanie saw an extension cord plugged into the wall nearby. Partially thinking, she snatched the cord out of the wall, quickly wrapped some of the length around her hand, then turned and swung the loose end whipping Candace across the face.

"Oooouuuuuuu," Candace screamed, moving backward and grabbing her face with her hand.

Blood dripped onto her fingertips.

"How fuckin' long!" Stephanie screamed.

Candace cried hysterically, cradling her face still.

"Just a little while," she spat out. "Damn it, Steph. I'm sorry... I'm so sorry. I never meant to hurt you. I never wanted to hurt you."

Stephanie raised her hand to swing the cord again and Candace flinched. Steph's eyes fell to the girl's stomach.

"A little while," she repeated.

Candace looked up at her with sorrowful eyes and followed her stare. She shook her head, tears falling nonstop.

"It's not his, Steph. I swear to Jehovah, it's not his. I was pregnant long before we ever hooked up, I swear it."

Stephanie dropped the cord and shook her head. She looked at Candace in disgust and frowned.

"You're a sorry ass excuse for a woman. You'll fuck anybody, won't you? You got married to a dude you barely liked, got pregnant by a nigga that barely liked you while you were still married...now you're fucking your friend's man..."

Candace looked away ashamed.

"I'm sorry," she whispered.

"Damn right, you're sorry," Stephanie concurred.

Stephanie turned away and walked back to the bedroom to get the bags. Returning to the living room she walked up to Candace so closely she could feel the girl's breath on her face.

"The only reason I'm not whooping your ass is because of that baby in your stomach. We're fucking through bitch. I hope the next chick's nigga you fuck gives you AIDS."

She walked away from Candace and headed towards the front door. Candace turned to watch her and shouted out to Stephanie's retreating figure.

"He came on to me, Stephanie! He came on to me more times than one way before I ever gave in. If he tried me I'm sure he tried other chicks too."

Stephanie stopped walking and turned to face her former friend.

"What the fuck is that supposed to mean?" she asked. "You want to hurt me, Candace? Well, you've hurt me."

"No," Candace interjected. "No damn it! I told you I never intended to hurt you…it wasn't about hurting you."

"I don't give a fuck what it was about. Maybe Corey was fucking other chicks. Oh fuckin' well. But you know what the difference is between any of those bitches and your ass? *You* were supposed to be my girl. *You* were supposed to have my back. *You* should have fuckin' said no!"

Stephanie turned away and proceeded to the door. Candace trailed after her.

"Steph, let me explain," she called after her. "Please, Stephanie. Please."

Stephanie ignored Candace's pleas as she opened the door to exit the apartment. Candace approached the door way as she stepped out and moved to round the corner.

"Stephanie! I'm sorry. I'm so sorry," she cried, following her friend into the darkness.

Stephanie continued to ignore her as she walked through the stillness of the dark, stepping out of the cut of the apartment building. Without warning, shots sounded blaringly and sounds of Stephanie's cries interrupted the silence of the parking lot. Candace saw Stephanie's small body fall to the ground as she was gunned down by assailants in two dark vehicles. It was as if she witnessed the incident in slow motion. Her own screams of anguish, fear, and helplessness were drowned by the noise of the shells being emptied into Steph's body.

Candace fell to the ground, sickened and petrified, as she was unable to help her friend. The offenders never even looked in her direction. She could hear herself crying aloud and screaming Stephanie's name in vain. No amount of screaming was going to raise her friend's body from the pavement. Candace watched on in horror as one car sped away. Sirens could be heard faintly in the distance. Quickly, a figure jumped out of the remaining car and snatched up the bags that Stephanie had been carrying to her car.

"Hope your nigga gets this message loud and fuckin' clear," Candace heard the man shout at Stephanie's lifeless body.

To add insult to injury, he spat on her body. As quickly as he hopped out, the man hopped back in still paying no attention to Candace's body crouched on the ground in the bush silently frightened. The car sped off and Candace continued to cry as she stared at her friend's body lying just a few feet away from her. From nowhere, a neighbor appeared by Candace's side.

"Honey, are you okay?" the woman asked.

Candace jumped.

"My friend," she said hysterically. "My friend! My friend! They shot my friend."

The sirens were closer. Candace struggled to pick herself up off of the ground. She waddled over to Stephanie with the nosy neighbor trailing behind her.

"The police are here, honey," the neighbor told her. "You can come inside my apartment to get yourself together dear…oh my, are you bleeding?"

Candace lowered herself to the ground and threw herself over Stephanie's body.

"Stephanie," she cried. "I didn't mean it, Steph. I didn't mean it. Please…please hold on, please hold on."

"Ma'am, we need you to step away from the body."

She was unaware of the growing commotion around her. The police were trying to pry her from Stephanie's bleeding body and a paramedic was off to the side waiting. A few neighbors from the small community had begun to gather, curious to know what was going on in their quiet little complex.

"Stephanie…please get up…Get up, Steph! Get up! Get up!"

Her cries turned into screams just as a male officer was able to pull her away from Stephanie. She could barely stand upright. The pain of the shock and horror was cutting into her abdomen. She felt sick to her stomach.

"Ma'am are you bleeding?" the officer asked her.

She pointed to Stephanie.

"They shot my friend…they just shot her…they just shot her."

"Ma'am, ma'am…we need you to focus…are you experiencing any pain?"

A paramedic was now questioning her. Candace simply shook her head no, yet her body swayed. She was finding it increasingly difficult to remain standing. The paramedic caught her as she wavered.

"How far along are you ma'am?"

"I tried to tell her I was sorry," Candace rambled. "I tried to tell her."

"She's delusional," the medic stated. "Get the gurney. I think this lady's having a miscarriage."

Alex

The day after Jada's failed dinner party, Alex found herself sulking with anger in her living room. She hadn't seen T in days, but today he finally called to say that he was coming by. His disappearing act was annoying all by itself, but it was the letter in her hand that was the true cause of her frustration. She tapped the pink envelope on her leg as she waited for T to pour himself a glass of juice, without asking first, and finally plop himself down on the couch next to her. He acted as if nothing was wrong and they were on great terms. Boy was he mistaken.

"What's good, ma?" he asked her, taking in the attitude bouncing off of her.

She handed him the envelope. He didn't reach for it, but looked at her quizzically instead.

"What's that?" he asked. "A love letter?"

"It's a bill."

He pushed her hand away and finished off his drink.

"Baby girl, I'm not in any position to pay off one of ya' bills right now. A deal don't mean instant dough boo boo."

She threw the envelope at him and lost control.

"You can't pay a bill for me? Let me be a little clearer…*that* is a collection notice for a purchase *you* made…"

"I made?" he questioned, pulling the letter out of the envelope.

"Uh-huh…seems that you bought some music equipment using my credit card and didn't bother to tell me, T! Then you had the audacity to *not* pay the bill."

"Oh shit," he said, rubbing his head. "Man, I meant to tell you about that, baby. It was an emergency. I had to get some shit to hook up a lil' studio area at my spot. But you never check your statements? You should have been known about those purchases."

She was stunned that he would have the gall to turn the situation around on her. She stared at him in amazement, wanting nothing more than to ring his thick ass neck.

"You're trying to make this out to be my fault? Negro you basically stole from me."

"Stole from you? Man watch out. You act like I took some money out ya' pocket or something."

"Uh….yeah! Basically, you did! You've jacked my credit up and now I'm responsible for paying back this bill."

T said nothing. Alex was done. She rose from the sofa and held her hand out.

"I'm gonna need some money on this," she told him.

He looked her up and down like she was out of her mind. Seeing that she wasn't budging, he simply waved her off.

"I ain't got it right now. I'll hit you up with some bread later."

"Later my ass, T!" she screamed. "I'm sick of this shit. I have helped you, splurged on you, and let you straight up use me…this is over. I want every penny back for this bill or…"

"Or what?" he said, standing up in front of her with an edge to his voice. "What? You not gon' give me none? You barely do that now. What? You not gon' help a nigga anymore? That's cool. That just let me know what type of chick you are or aren't. A real chick holds her man down."

"A real man wouldn't put his chick in a position to always have to make the sacrifice in order to hold his ass down. A real man doesn't steal from his woman. A real man does what he has to do to take care of himself and his woman instead of the other way around."

Without warning, T hit her in the mouth with enough force to bust her lip and cause her to stumble backwards. Instinctively, she covered her mouth with her left hand and looked up at him in fear. Thoughts of Miranda's words months ago when the girls were all together at Candace's came back to her. She was not so desperate for love that she would let some dude beat on her.

"Another thing a real chick knows to do is shut the fuck up sometimes," T told her.

She spoke slowly, the tone of her voice even and deeper than usual.

"I am giving you all of three minutes to get the hell out of my house before I call the police."

T chuckled and moved to sit back down on the couch.

Alex pulled out her cell phone and dialed the three digits.

"Don't test me, T," she threatened. "This shit is over."

He paused and tried to gage her sincerity. Thinking better of it, he stood upright and walked past the tall, dark skinned beauty. He turned back and whispered in her ear.

"You're going to realize how big of a mistake this is when you see me on the Grammy's."

She snatched the gold-plated necklace he'd given her from her neck and turned to throw it at him.

"No, you were the mistake, with your sorry ass."

T shrugged off her comment and pocketed the necklace.

"Fuck you then," he told her, and exited the apartment.

Alex quickly ran to the door to lock and bolt it. She touched her face, still in shock that the bum had the nerve to hit her. Her phone was still in her hand and it startled her as it rung. Thinking it was T, she pressed ignore without looking at the screen to check the caller id. Tears began to slowly fall down her cheeks as she contemplated how her personal life had taken a horrible turn. She desperately needed to be comforted and consoled, but was in no mood to hear the I-told-you-sos or answer any questions from her girlfriends.

Alex grabbed her purse, jacket, and keys and headed out of the apartment. Taking the train and bus she decided to try her hand at the one person that she knew always gave her great comfort and understanding no matter what. She just hoped that he was in a forgiving mood.

~ ~ ~

It took nearly two hours on MARTA to reach Clay's apartment. By the time she arrived, her face was stained with tears, eyes were red and puffy, and she was completely exhausted. Taking a deep breath, she knocked on his door and prayed to the heavens that he wouldn't leave her standing out in the cold. When he opened the door, she could tell that he was shocked to see her standing at his threshold.

"Alex?" he said, turning to look behind him. "What are you doing here?"

He didn't move to let her in and Alex looked at him pleadingly.

"I know you're mad at me, Clay," she whined. "I get it. I really do…but I need you."

His eyes were sympathetic. He stepped back to allow her room to walk in.

"I know it's got to be hard," he said softly, closing the door behind her.

Alex's phone began to ring again and once more she silenced it. Her eyebrows knitted as she considered Clay's statement. How would he know what had happened with T? Before she could ask, a short blond girl came down the hall and into the living room looking at her questioningly.

"What's going on, Clay? You're not ready to watch the movie?"

"I didn't know you had company," Alex said softly.

The girl snuggled up to Clay and smiled nastily to Alex.

"I'm Amanda," she announced.

Clay ran interference.

"Amanda, this is Alexandra. An old friend. Alex, this is Amanda. We're dating."

"An old friend?" Alex repeated. "More like his best friend. In fact, there probably isn't even a word to describe what we are to each other."

Her tone was laced with anger and Amanda looked to Clay for an explanation.

"What's going on?" the blond asked him again.

"Um, perhaps today's not a good time."

Amanda stepped away from him and cut her eyes at Alex.

"What…what are you saying? You want me to leave?"

Clay ran his hands over his head and looked over at Alex with compassion. He shrugged and gave Amanda a weak smile.

"She's really going through a tough time and needs to talk," he explained. "I'm really sorry. We'll do dinner tomorrow night. Your choice, okay?"

Amanda was hesitant, but hopeful.

"Ok," she told him.

She grabbed up her belongings and placed a kiss on his cheek before heading to the door. Looking back at Alex she gave her the same nice-nasty smile.

"I hope things get better for you," she told her.

Clay and Alex watched as Amanda exited the apartment. For a few moments they were silent, each looking at one another and searching for the words to say.

"Nobody knows me like you do," Alex told him. "Nobody knows how I feel, what I think, why I behave like I do sometimes…nobody understands me but you."

Clay moved forward and took Alex's coat and purse. Quickly, she melted into his embrace and cried. He held her tightly.

"I'm sorry," she cried. "I'm so sorry."

"It's not your fault, Alex. You shouldn't beat yourself up about it."

"It is my fault. I should have paid closer attention…I should have never been with T."

Clay pulled back and looked into her face. For the first time, he noticed her lip.

"What the hell," he spat out.

Alex lowered her head in shame.

"He hit me. That bastard. He ran up my credit card bill and hit me when I was asking for the money back."

Clay shook his head. Alex's phone rang again. She silenced it again.

"You came all the way over here to complain to me about T?" Clay asked in astonishment.

"Yes…I mean no…I came to say I was sorry," she cried. "I came to tell you that you were right…that I don't belong with any of those other guys. That it's always been you who's been there for me…I came to tell you that I love you."

"Then you don't know," Clay asked her confusedly.

She grabbed his hands and stared into his eyes with her own puffy, tear blinded eyes.

"I *do* know, Clay," she insisted. "I found the ring you bought. I read the card and I get it…I know how you feel and I'm sorry I didn't get it sooner. I…"

"Alex, I have to tell you something," he cut her off.

"No, you've been telling me all this time in your own way, but I get it, Clay…Really. You have to believe me."

He dropped her hands and firmly grabbed her by the shoulders.

"Alex, shut up, please. I need to tell you something."

She shook her head no, not wanting to face the reality that the opportunity had passed. She didn't want to hear him tell her that she was too late and that there was no happily ever after for them.

"No," she told him. "No. Don't say it…you don't mean it, Clay. You don't mean it. I love you…I really love you. Please don't say it."

Clay grabbed her hand and led her into his bedroom. Quickly he changed the channel on his television to the early evening news. They'd been running the same story all day and he knew that it would be covered now if not in a few moments. Alex was still crying and protesting, not understanding what was going on or what Clay was trying to do. He listened to her rambling and crying until the story popped up again. Turning up the sound on the television he positioned her right in front of it.

"Shut up," he ordered. "Shut up and listen."

Alex tried to focus on the newscaster, but each word that was spoken knocked the wind out of her and Alex felt as if her spirit was floating above her body and watching as she fell apart.

"Officials are calling last night's homicide a message to the neighborhood drug lord Corey Polk. Polk's long term girlfriend and the mother of his two children, Stephanie Johnson, was gunned down in a small Roswell apartment community in the middle of the night. Johnson was leaving one of several of Polk's homes when witnesses say two cars arrived out of nowhere and proceeded to empty their guns into the woman's small body. Johnson was determined D.O.A. and officials have no leads as to exactly who her assailants were. But, members from Johnson's neighborhood in Decatur are telling authorities that they believe cohorts of Montae Stokes are retaliating. Earlier on Friday the GBA announced that Polk had been picked up for questioning for the murder of Montae Stokes which occurred earlier this year. A spokesman for the GBA told us that new evidence of Polk's involvement had been found, including his fingerprints on the wallet and identification of the slayed man. No further information has been released regarding whether or not Polk has yet been formally charged with the murder."

Alex swayed, but Corey was right there to catch her. He eased her onto the bed and cradled her body in his arms as she wailed and screamed. He kissed her forehead and continued to hold her tightly until she had no more tears left to expel. Sitting in silence, she laid her head in his lap, her body tingling with grief and an emotional pain she'd never known before. Memories of T hitting her, her anger from earlier, and her fear over losing Clay were all replaced with the terrifying knowledge that she would never see one of her best friends again in life. Her phone rang again, but this time Clay reached for it.

"It's Jada," he told her.

Alex shook her head, realizing that it must have been Jada all along calling to tell her the news. She wasn't ready to grieve with the girls yet. She wasn't ready to listen to Jada pull it all together and try to get them all composed. She was perfectly content for now with lying in Clay's lap and being allowed to be a bundle of nerves and emotions. She'd call the girls later, when she found a way to come to terms with the loss of Stephanie.

THE GIRLS

A couple of weeks after the funeral they all agreed that it was time. They had each been there to watch their friend be placed into the ground. Several of them had gone back to Steph's mom's house to help with the children. But they hadn't had the opportunity or the strength to come together and grieve for their girl by themselves, in their way. Today, it was time. They met at Alex's place for a change, for wine and cheesecake. Jada and Candace arrived together. The three of them were surprised when Miranda showed up at the door. Although she texted saying that she would be there, they still hadn't been too sure. During Stephanie's funeral, they spotted her in the very back. Why she had decided not to sit with the rest of the girls was unbeknownst to them, but they were definitely glad to see her with them on this night.

There hadn't been much dialogue between any of them since their last meeting at Jada's and especially since the funeral. There was an uncomfortable, unusual silence between them as the women sipped their wine and savored their dessert. Really, what does a group say when they've lost one of their members?

"This cake is really good," Alex said.

Leave it to her to mention something about food. Candace giggled.

"You know I love my New York Style cheesecakes from the Publix," she replied.

Jada laughed this time, the feeling therapeutic to her soul.

"Something is seriously wrong with the two of you," she commented, sipping from her lone glass of water.

"What? I'm just saying," Candace giggled.

A sigh fell over the room as each remembered what brought them there tonight.

"It doesn't feel the same, does it?" Jada asked the group.

A series of head shakes ensued.

"I feel so horrible still," Alex confessed. "For the rest of my life I'll have to deal with the fact that my last interaction with her was an argument…I didn't really mean to come at her the way I did…"

"I know," Jada consoled her. "I know."

She looked at Alex, hoping to get her to end it there versus continuing and embarrassing Miranda.

"I was just shocked, you know. And mad…mad at Corey really…but I was pissed that she couldn't see how poisonous he is."

Miranda looked up at Alex.

"What were you arguing about?"

Alex looked at her tenderly.

"You," she said softly.

All eyes focused on Miranda to see how she would react

to this. She simply nodded her head in understanding. Surprisingly to the rest of them, she didn't appear ashamed or embarrassed.

"So Stephanie told you, huh?" she asked. "I figured that she would. I knew she would. And it's okay."

She looked at her friends and smiled.

"You don't have to look at me with pity, you guys. I'm good."

"Can I ask a question?" Alex asked. "And please, excuse me if it's a little bit abrasive but I just have to know."

"Shoot."

"What made you do it? Crack I mean…I mean, I can't understand what would make any sane person *want* to shoot some shit in their veins or up their nose…I just don't get it."

"And I don't expect you to," Miranda told her. "You're right. No *sane* person wakes up and says 'hey let me try some crack'. It's a progression. I didn't just start off with that shit."

"You were on some other shit too?" Candace asked.

Miranda shrugged. "I was smoking weed consistently, every day. After a while, I needed it to get through the day and all the shit I was going through with Norris. After a minute it started to not be enough…I felt like I had to go harder."

Alex shuddered, not wanting to hear anymore and not wanting to picture her friend laid up somewhere coked out of her mind.

"Do you still do it?" Candace asked softly, looking at her

friend for signs that she was coming down from a high.

Miranda shook her head.

"I decided I'm going to go to a rehab center. Voluntarily. Do I think about it? Yes. But, since Steph…"

Her thoughts trailed off but the others understood.

"I'm not a junkie," Miranda told them. "I'm not. I just have to make better decisions. This clinic, they're teaching me new ways to cope with my feelings and stress. So that I won't get high, you know?"

They all nodded, ready to put this uneasy discussion behind them.

"The day Stephanie saw me at that house I knew she was ashamed of me…I knew she was going to go back and tell ya'll and that you all would be ashamed of me too. That's why I stopped calling and coming around. I didn't want to look at the shame and pity in your eyes."

Jada toyed with her water glass.

"Are we really judgmental like that?" she asked

"You're human," Miranda answered her.

They sat in silence considering this thought. Again, forks clanked against porcelain as the girls devoured their cheesecake.

"Did ya'll know that Stephanie thought Corey was cheating on her with me?"

The question stunned them all. To tell Miranda the truth that they'd all been discussing her behind her back was hard to do, but today was a day for honesty. Jada nodded and Alex followed her lead. Candace took a sip of her wine and looked at the group.

"So I guess it's my turn to confess," she said.

Alex raised her eyebrow.

"Well, when I found out that you were there the night Stephanie was shot a few questions came to my mind…"

"I'm sure…so I'll just say it. I was fucking around with Corey, briefly. When I left your house that night Jada, I went to that apartment in Roswell where I'd met him before to…you know…I didn't realize that Steph was there and Corey wasn't…you know, until I actually went inside."

"That's so foul," Jada commented. "So foul. Why would you even go there, Candace? To mess with your girl's dude like that?"

"I don't know," Candace offered weakly. "I was feeling so rejected and disappointed in myself from messing with my series of losers…I just got caught up in the attention he kept throwing my way. He was the one always coming on to me."

"That still doesn't make it right," Alex interjected.

"You're right, it doesn't. And if I could take it all back, I would…but I can't. Alex, you feel bad that when you last saw her ya'll had a petty argument…"

"Which you could have helped subside by admitting that you were the one screwing her baby's daddy, I'm just saying…"

"Well…I have to live with the fact that she died hating me…and that I had to watch her die so horribly."

They were silent again, considering Candace's mixed emotions. As a group, they had all been through so much, hurting one another in ways they had never imagined.

"I know that wasn't an easy thing for you to deal with," Alex said softly, reaching over and offering her hand for support.

Candace squeezed Alex's hand and fought back her tears.

"It was like watching a movie, I swear. And there was nothing I could do. Nothing…I didn't even realize I was losing the baby because I was so…so fixated on losing her."

Alex hugged Candace and Jada patted her leg

"But the saving grace is that there is a God, Candace," Jada offered. "A God that knows your heart and gives you just what you need when you need it. Zoe may be fighting for life, but at least she is still here to fight."

Candace hadn't lost the baby. At just six months, the doctors had informed Candace that she was going to have to birth the child prematurely. There was no way that they could keep the baby from coming. The trauma she endured had caused her to go into labor and she was hemorrhaging from the blow she'd taken when she'd fallen to the ground in fright as the guns had begun to blare.

Her daughter, Zoe, weighed 2 ½ pounds now and was being cared for in the newborn intensive care unit at Crawford Long Hospital. The entire ordeal was tiring and stressful for Candace, but she was ever so thankful that Jehovah had pulled her and the baby through and had brought them thus far. Khalil still hadn't been to the hospital to visit his daughter, but Candace wasn't going to press the issue. She wasn't about to school the older man on how to be a good parent. Instead, she decided to let child support enforcement deal with getting her the money she would need to care for Zoe.

Miranda joined the girls and they all embraced in a group hug. So many emotions flowed through them and so many memories shared between them. Shaking off the moment of nostalgia, Miranda poured herself another glass of wine and exhaled.

"We are one fucked up group of chicks," she joked. "I don't know about ya'll but I desperately need to hear some good news."

Alex beamed and put on her best princess voice.

"I've got some good news," she announced.

Candace and Jada shared a look and laughed.

"Everybody knows your good news, Alex," Candace replied. "It's written all over ya' face."

"Yeah, girl," Miranda chimed in, her smile extending past her lips to her eyes. "I saw Clay escorting you around at the funeral."

Alex beamed and threw her head back against her chair.

"He loves me," she gushed.

Jada threw a pillow at her love-sick friend.

"And it only took you forever to realize it," she joked.

Alex reached for her glass.

"Hey!" she exclaimed. "Don't shit on my happily ever

after."

The girls laughed.

"We are definitely not," Jada told her. "We're glad you've finally got a good man so you can cut down on your drama, boo. Kudos to you."

"Ha ha."

Miranda went around refilling their glasses with the bottle of Riesling. She reached for Jada's glass and Jada put her hand over the top.

"None for me, thanks."

"What's up with you, Jada?" Candace asked. "You giving up alcohol, girl? Isn't it a little early for you to be starting your little New Year's resolutions."

The others chuckled but Jada smiled nervously.

"No," she said softly. "It's just that I peed on a stick the other day and I don't want to mess anything up."

Miranda looked at her quizzically and Alex scratched her head. But, Candace got it immediately and sat up straight in her chair.

"Are you saying what I think you're saying?" she asked.

Jada smiled. "Jordan and I are going to be parents."

The girls enveloped her in hugs and kisses, each equally and sincerely excited for their patient and deserving friend.

"I was wondering when ya'll were gonna put a bun in that

oven," Miranda commented.

"I'm so happy for you girl," Candace told her. "I really am. You truly deserve it…and you're doing it the right way. I'm so proud of you."

Jada smiled, wanting to tell them how much of an accomplishment this truly was for her and Jordan given everything they'd been through. But, she didn't want to harshen the moment. Instead she just relished in the joy of being with child and having her friends be happy for her. She looked around at the girls as things seemed to be reaching some level of normalcy for them. But she felt the void of Stephanie in the room, they all did. It was a feeling she was sure would take time for them to overcome, if ever.

Their group had been through so much in the last year. They had happy times and sad times. They had gone through births and death. They had seen each other through break ups and new unions. They also discovered that each of them had areas to work on in order to be better friends to one another. But one thing was definite, one thing that none of them ever wanted to change. They were girls and that was a bond they intended to keep for life.

4894345R00256

Made in the USA
San Bernardino, CA
13 October 2013